MENDED HEARTS

The Hearts of Emerald Bay
Book 2

SYDNE BARNETT

ISBN:

eBook: 979-8-9903198-5-1

Paperback: 979-8-9903198-9-9

Cover Art: Shanoff Designs

This book contains mature themes and is only suitable for readers 18+

For every neurospicy lost girl…
For the ones who preferred to cuddle the pup in the corner rather than engage in the party—although you appreciated the invite…
For the 'old souls' that didn't 'cause trouble'…
Who cared more about earning that stamp of approval than standing up for yourself…

We never should've needed a diagnosis to be loved as loudly as Leigh and Ollie love Tillie.

Welcome home, Sunshine. We have hearts to mend.

$$\rule{6cm}{0.5pt}$$

Rhodes Family Appendix

RHODES FAMILY APPENDIX

The Rhodes family is made up of twelve rowdy siblings, many many cousins and a handful of 'pseudo-siblings'. And before you say what everyone is thinking, yes, families that big do exist. I married into one ;)

*For simplicity's sake, I've **only** listed those mentioned in **this** book.*

MILO RHODES
Dad, retired captain of the *Rhodes Away*

JUNIPER RHODES
Mom, keeper of the chaos, deliverer of epic hugs and warm food.

I. JEANNE
Eldest sister, world-traveling surgeon, divorced, location unknown. Spontaneously appears on family text thread, usually around the holidays.

II. RHYETT
Eldest brother, entrepreneur, current location Sarasota, Florida. Adorably—some would say obnoxiously—optimistic. He has a daughter—Quinn, or 'Quinny'—with his wife, Brexley.

III. JAMESON
Captain of the family fishing boat, located in Mistyvale, AK. Engaged to Noel McShane. Bestower of sardonic witticisms and tough love.

IV. Elora

New York City-based life & business coach, author, public speaker, and soon to be reality television host. Newly married to Broderick Allen, with a baby on the way. Designated family know-it-all and planner of events.

V. Axel

Fisherman, single, currently in Mistyvale, AK, but travels for the winter. Equal parts sunshine and sarcasm.

VI. Paxton

Pro quarterback for the *Emerald Bay Bombers*, single. Gazelle-like focus on his career, hates the cold.

VII. Hadlee

Travel blogger and influencer, single, location unknown. Aka, Hurricane Hadlee due to a propensity for chaos.

VIII. Alessandra

Aka. "Alice" Hart, married to Greyson Hart.
Emerald Bay, CA.

IX. Finnegan

Aka. "Finn", digital nomad, we think he's in New York? That could change tomorrow though. Quietest of the twelve.

X. Leighton

"The Feral One", obsessed with good music, classic films, and Marvel comics. Twins with Kaia, waitress. Currently in Emerald Bay.

XI. Kaia

Twins with Leighton, hair and makeup artist, currently in Mistyvale, AK but comes to Emerald Bay for the winter. Lover of all things beautiful.

XII. Maverick

Attending college in Washington, receiver for their football team. Bogarts the good tunes, sympathy crier.

"Pseudo-siblings"

Max—Best friends with Elora, Hadlee and Alice, right hand to the CEO of Jorogumo defense. Travels as much as an authentic

Rhodes, single, impeccable taste in both clothes and booze, currently in Mistyvale, AK.

<u>Cousins</u>

Charlie - Mistyvale Sheriff, widower, single dad.

Jake - Single. Charlie's brother.

Author's Note and Content Disclosure

Hello there, dahhling, thank you for joining me for Leighton and Ollie's story!

While *Mended Hearts* can be read independently, I **highly** recommend reading the first book in the series, *Salvaged Hearts*, as it adds so much context. You can read it on Amazon HERE. If you prefer to shop small, you can save by shopping directly from the author HERE.

If you get to the end and are just dying for more of the Rhodes, check out their lighthearted parent series, *The Nomadic Rhodes*, for Rhyett, Jameson and Elora's stories.

Happy Reading!

As always, your mental health matters, so here are the content disclosures for this book.

The following trigger list *_does_* contain spoilers, so if you're not worried about something specific, please keep that in mind before proceeding.

This story contains but is not limited to:

Off-page violence, mention of (no on-page 1st person content) human trafficking, murder.

On-page foul language, explicit sexual content, abusive parent(s), narcissistic ex-wife/mother, discussions of infertility, discussions around health/cardiac trauma, panic attacks, and anxiety.

Ollie's daughter, Matilda, has many neurodivergent traits and tendencies. She's a culmination of experiences gathered between me, my daughter, sisters, and friends. If your experience with neurospicy kids doesn't mirror the way I've portrayed her, please remember that no one character can represent an entire group of people, and neurodiversity is gauged on a 'spectrum' for a reason. I hope someone feels seen in her sweet little voice.

Professionals were consulted for medical and police scenarios, however, it is important to keep in mind that this is a work of fiction, and some artistic liberties are taken, while working to handle these topics with the care they deserve.

The team works to keep these as comprehensive as possible, but if we missed anything distressing, please feel free to email us at flame andfiction@gmail.com.

Revenge of The Uterus
LEIGHTON

August

Hefting my seven-million-pound tote higher on my shoulder, I raised my hand to knock on the imposing solid wood door of Oliver Hart's monstrosity of a house. If I had a superpower, it would be making fast friends—and my sister's new brother-in-law and his kids had been no exception.

What can I say? I'm delightful like that.

Our lives had only collided three months ago, but this ten-thousand-square-foot testament to modern architecture had already become a home away from home for me.

Before I could so much as knock, the door flew open. I staggered back a step, eyes widening as I took in a rather haggard-looking version of the sexiest single dad in the city. It took all my self-control not to laugh at the man who occupied most of my brain space these days.

"Thank you," he exhaled like I'd just plucked him from a burning building instead of showing up to babysit.

Ollie looked like he'd fallen through an irrigation canal before being hauled out and hung off the back of a truck bed to dry. His normally coiffed black hair was disheveled, his button-up shirt hung open, revealing that spectacular, tattooed chest he liked to parade around at family functions like a walking thirst trap. Only... I was fairly certain there was jam on his hair-dusted six-pack. And what on earth was smeared over the hem of his sleeve?

"Um. Good morning?" I hedged as I stepped into the foyer.

Ollie shoved his luscious, shampoo-commercial-worthy hair away from his face, and I tried not to wince at the dark circles under his eyes.

"Another one bites the dust, huh?"

"She's trying to kill me, I swear to God."

"*Cruella?*" I asked, snickering when he glanced around in irritation.

The 'she' in question was his terrible, gold-digging, narcissistic ex-wife. But being the chivalrous goodie-goodie he was, Ollie hated when we disparaged her in the kids' vicinity. I grimaced, wishing my mouth would sometimes let my brain catch up before opening. Wincing, I muttered, "Sorry."

"Meh," he grunted, which I took as resigned agreement. Now certain the kids were out of earshot, he shook his head. "I swear, does Carly think this is some kind of game? This is the eleventh nanny in the last twelve months she's run off. It's like she enjoys reducing sweet, college-aged girls to tears. Grey is helping me find a permanent solution, but you're saving my skin."

Greyson—Grey to his inner circle—Hart was the formidable Titan of Emerald Bay, i.e., my new brother-in-law. He knew everyone, and for God knows what reason, everyone else seemed to fear the asshole. Maybe it was his penchant for taking over companies with the ease of making a sandwich. Maybe it was the whole ex-Navy SEAL thing.

Neither stopped me from frequently reminding him I'd feed him to the nearest pig farm if he hurt my sister.

If I wasn't one of a litter of siblings, I'd find it peculiar how the two of them shared DNA. Okay—yeah, they had the same olive skin and dark features, but man oh man, I certainly wasn't about to show up unannounced with pizza and a new vinyl at Greyson's. Something Ollie seemed to love.

"Y'all will find somebody great. You always land on your feet."

"Yeah," he breathed, shoulders slumping in defeat. I was about to ask where the kids were when the pitter-patter of little feet thundered through the living room toward us, and my face split in a grin as Ollie's four-year-old son, Beau, came sprinting in.

"Did you b'wing it?" he squeaked excitedly.

Swinging my personal *Mary Poppins* bag off my shoulder, I snagged my camera and dropped it to the floor as he squealed in victory.

Diving in, pudgy arms first, he fished out the superhero masks he always tried to squirrel away. The moment he jammed one on his face, I snapped a photo before he bolted, clutching them in his little hands.

"You're a saint," Ollie sighed.

"And don't you forget it."

Later that morning, as our Minecraft game reloaded, I asked, "Why does everybody call you Mattie?"

Ollie had sounded so damn stressed when he called last night for last-minute coverage. His uncertainty was a testament to his idiocy, because *of course* I'd hang out with the kids while he was at work today.

I was the tenth of twelve siblings, though that label was generous—seeing as the eleventh slid into the doctor's hands precisely ninety seconds after I did.

Being at the tail end of a dirty dozen meant the house was always full. These days, I found my empty Emerald Bay condo unbearably boring. Little Beau's declarations of war over his toy soldiers and Matilda's ongoing yammering were infinitely more familiar—and significantly more appealing—than the silence waiting for me at home.

The 'duh' in my response last night had been obvious enough that I hoped he still felt like a moron fourteen hours later. I'd be eating the last of his Girl Scout cookies today as retribution for the absurd hesitation in his tone. Which reminded me—

"Cookie?" I offered, peeling open a box of those orgasmic caramel coconut ones.

She glared at me—clearly, I was breaking our unspoken mid-video game buffer rules.

"Yeah."

Or maybe she was insulted I'd even *asked.*

I smirked, grabbed a short stack, handed her the box, and prompted, "And what about my other question?"

She snapped off a bite before shrugging a little shoulder and tightening her dirty-blonde ponytail. "I dunno. They just always have."

I scanned over her black Converse, black denim pants, and faded charcoal Guns N' Roses crop top. Hair bands and monochromatic palettes, save for holiday attire, were the norm for our adorable little grunge girl.

My brothers would nominate her for president the instant they met her.

"I just mean... do you like it?"

"What's not to like?"

"That wasn't an answer," I observed.

She scowled at the loading circle on the screen, obviously willing it to work faster, before glaring down at her remote.

Matilda Hart, heiress to the Hart empire, was ten going on thirty, and I found her absolutely fascinating. Like a baby girl-*Sheldon* from *The Big Bang Theory.*

But in my experience, 'Matties' came with bleach-blonde hair, more glitter than coding skills, and inevitable homecoming queen titles after leading the cheer squad.

They weren't hyper-intelligent ten-year-olds kicking ass in seventh-grade science.

A theory I'd affirmed when I realized she rolled her eyes anytime her family called her 'Mattie.'

"Nobody has ever asked me that before," she said.

"Still not an answer," I sing-songed, prying open the box of mint cookies.

With a little huff, she stared contemplatively out the window for a solid four breaths before answering, "I mean. It's better than Matilda."

She wrinkled her nose, and I snickered into my hand as I broke off a bite of mint-chocolate wafer.

"I can't argue with you there. I have no idea what your dad was thinking."

"He wasn't."

"Obviously."

"No," she shook her head, ponytail flipping. "*He* wasn't. Carly picked my name. Daddy got Beau's."

It wasn't lost on me that her mother was always 'Carly,' while Ollie got the affectionate 'Daddy.' Couldn't blame the poor girl.

"So?" I prompted when her little shoulders curled in.

"I mean, not really. But what other nicknames come out of Matilda?"

"May?" I suggested, cackling when her eye roll hit catastrophic proportions. "Milla?"

"Those are as bad as Tilda."

"I heard Grey call you 'Mads' the other day."

"Not really better, is it?" she said, pursing her little lips.

I studied her for a moment and popped another cookie in my mouth.

I took my time chewing it over—the name and the cookie—before suggesting, "What about Tillie? Way more rock and roll."

She was silent, eyes on the loading screen as she savored a bite.

I might not know her that well yet, but the last few months had blessed me with enough time around these incredible kids to recognize when her brain was working overtime.

Finally, she smiled, a bit bewildered, and said, "I kinda like it."

"We could just try it out for a few days? See what you think?"

"'Kay. But just us?"

There was so much hope—so much trust—in those three words that my chest swelled.

"Our secret," I promised, zipping my lips shut.

"Just until I'm sure I like it."

"You got it... *Tillie*," I said, grinning when she beamed.

I kicked my bare feet up on the coffee table, and at precisely that moment, four-year-old Beau came running over, mad as a hornet, holding out two Lego pieces he couldn't jam together.

I chuckled, reaching out to show him how to connect them.

THE FAMILIAR PANGS of impending female devastation worked their way up my spine and around my hips throughout the day. By the time Ollie texted to let me know he was heading home, I was already bracing for a shitty couple of days. No time left to gloat about his pillaged retribution cookies.

It was for that reason alone that when my sister, Alice, showed up to take the kids across the street to her and Greyson's to swim, I chomped at her offer.

On a scale of pantyliner to crime scene, my periods—when they actually decided to show up—landed firmly in the massacre-of-the-Jedi camp. Except instead of a Sith wreaking havoc, it was my uterus on the warpath.

The sporadic demonic ritual sacrifice was topped off by excruciating cramps—when I was super lucky, migraine headaches—and an ongoing sense of seasickness. It was four or five days of feeling like I'd been drop-kicked off a balcony onto my skull, beaten, and then locked in the wheelhouse in the middle of a tempest.

By the time Preston, one of the Hart's assistants, dropped me off at home, my farewell smile was more of a grimace. It was getting hard to breathe because the cramps were so intense.

Gathering my sweatpants, I scurried into the bathroom to clean up and prepare for an imminent battle with my defective baby box.

Only once my raspberry leaf tea was brewed, my gallon of water was set on the table, the Ibuprofen located, my ice cream dished, and *Gilmore Girls* queued on the television, did I finally collapse onto my leather couch, wrap my body in hot pads like a human burrito, and tuck a fuzzy black blanket up to my shoulders.

The familiar theme song had me blowing out a breath as I scooped a tiny gold heart spoon into my chocolate-walnut-fudge dessert.

Everything tastes better on tiny spoons. Don't ask me why—it's just a fact.

Two episodes and an entire quart of chocolate later, I jackknifed upright when the front door banged open, hitting pause on my television.

Technically, this place belonged to Alice, and she still had her key despite moving into Greyson's ridiculous beach estate. I couldn't complain. Her titan of a suit daddy had paid it off and laughed himself stupid when I demanded to pay rent.

But it wasn't my sister barging into my space.

Oliver stood there, looking like he'd run his hands through his dark, luscious curls one too many times today. His navy suit was open, a gold tie hanging limply around his neck as he scowled at my pile of shoes before kicking his off to add them to the small mountain.

"There are racks for those," he grunted.

I rolled my eyes and burrowed deeper into my hot pad burrito.

"Ever heard of knocking?" I demanded. There was no bite to it. I liked Ollie. Probably more than I should, given that our lives were tied together so long as Alice and Greyson were. And if they ever split—yikes—that'd probably be worse. It was for that reason alone that I hadn't already climbed the man like a tree.

"Ever heard of locking?" he countered, glaring at me this time before hoisting takeout bags up like a flag of surrender.

I was so excited by the Chinese food that I almost didn't hear what he said. Almost.

Scowling, I said, "I always lock up." After all, I wasn't in Mistyvale anymore. Emerald Bay was nestled in SoCal, and I'd witnessed more police presence in my first month here than my entire life back in Alaska.

"Well, then call your landlord, because the thing was open. *Oh wait,*" he added pointedly, arching his brows until my face returned to an accusatory glower.

Technically, Hart Investments owned this place, making it as much Ollie's as Grey and Alice's.

"What are you doing here, anyway?" I asked, lifting my nose like that would somehow help me assess exactly what he'd smuggled over.

Was that beef and broccoli? Definitely some chow mein. My stomach gave a humiliating snarl of approval.

"Well, it's nice to see you too, Trouble."

"Very nice to see you—how was work? Good? Good. Kids? Oh, the kids were great. Now, what did you bring me?"

I freed one grabby hand and motioned for him to pass over the goods, unwilling to abandon my hot pads.

"I'm here because I bought you that extra spicy Moo Shu Pork shit nobody with taste buds actually likes as a thank you for saving my ass today, and you were gone before I got home."

Had befriending Emerald Bay's most notorious playboy been on my bingo card this year?

Certainly not.

But as he fished boxes out of the flimsy plastic, arranging an impressive display of all our collective favorites over my coffee table, I firmly decided it was worth it.

"Sorry, evidently it's shark week."

Confusion furrowed those dark brows as he set the last container on the table.

Oliver Hart was like a living, breathing embodiment of Dionysus—his dark hair always coiffed from the office, except for one stubborn curl that hung down over his expertly exfoliated olive skin, just begging a girl to play with it.

Soulful brown eyes betrayed his happy-go-lucky demeanor and convinced me from day one that he wasn't the shallow, self-indulgent womanizer the media made him out to be.

The concern pinching his forehead together said as much.

"Shark week?"

"*You know.* Aunt Flo. Mother Nature's blessings have been bestowed. The endless sentence. Hell week. Pick a phrase, it sucks however you slice it."

"I'm lost."

I choked on a laugh.

Not every guy grew up with six sisters like mine did, and this was the moment I remembered he wasn't one of them. "My period hit, rather…unexpectedly."

"Oof," he blew out a breath, shifting his weight while trying to look at ease. Which was endlessly entertaining for me. Ollie shirked out of his suit jacket and rolled his sleeves up to his elbows, putting his gorgeous vascular forearms on display, before yanking impatiently at his collar until his shirt popped open—just enough for his chest hair to peek out.

Why the fuck did that do something to me?

Maybe it was the memories of the tattoos just one button away —or hormones' cruel sense of humor that I was easy to rile on my miserable cycle.

Hot and reminiscent of butterflies in my belly, my blood seemed to boil.

Instant karma. This was my punishment for making him squirm discussing menses, wasn't it?

My mouth dried out as he loaded a plate with all my favorites. For Pete's sake. Someone explain to me why working tendons are a turn-on.

I'd just forced a swallow, diverting my eyes from Oliver Hart arm porn to the television, when he spoke.

"I never understand why girls say that."

"Hmm?" I hummed stupidly.

"Unexpected? Isn't it monthly?"

"You'll notice that wasn't an option in my previous vernacular."

"Twenty-eight days, right? That's what Carly's was like."

Her name hung like a curse word in the air between us.

I rushed to take the offered plate for something to do with my hands other than miming a felony.

"Yeah, not for me."

"What do you mean?"

"I have PCOS, so that bitch kinda just shows up whenever the hell she feels like it."

"What?"

"Poly—you know what, never mind. It's a hormone disorder. Makes my cycles a form of torture and completely irregular. Some are twenty-eight days, the next will be ninety. No point tracking. I even had ovarian cysts burst when I was in college. That was hell."

"Ovarian... I'm so glad I'm male."

I snorted, snatching the chopsticks he held out.

He had no idea.

The incident with the cysts bursting resulted in an emergency surgery due to internal bleeding—they flew me from Mistyvale to Anchorage in the only medical helicopter on the island.

I was a junior in college for that fiasco.

Combined with my extensive medical history, it came with a horrid prognosis.

Permanent birth control, my little brother had said, like it was a perk, when the doctors told me I wouldn't ever conceive.

He didn't mean to be a dick—he was just a dopey teenager in the fuck-anything-that-moved stage, and didn't think about what that prognosis meant to a twenty-year-old woman who'd always wanted a house full of kids.

Not willing to open that can of worms, I just said, "You can say that again."

"I'm terrified of all this stuff for Mattie."

"She'll figure it out. Mine are extra shitty, but I've got a protocol now."

"Can you work?"

"I usually call in sick."

"And they allow it?"

"*Allow it?*" I scoffed, glaring his way as I hit play on the television. "Not much of a choice when I'm curled in a ball puking from the pain."

"Well, shit."

"Yeah."

I used my chopsticks to spear a spectacularly slippery hunk of mandarin chicken. "Thanks for this."

"Thanks for saving my ass today," he countered, twisting a cap off a bottle of beer and handing it to me.

I grinned as he did the same to his own.

As far as brothers-in-law go, Alice could've done a hell of a lot worse than Oliver Hart.

"For those two?" I smiled, flashing him a quick wink.

"Anything, anytime."

With an uncharacteristically sheepish smile, Ollie held out his beer, and we clinked bottles before wordlessly watching at least three more episodes together.

When I woke up, he'd tucked me in before locking up when he left.

2

Yeeted Off A Bridge
LEIGHTON

October

"I got *yeeted* off a *bridge* and you're *firing* me?!"

Just to emphasize my point, I wielded my sling-bound arm at my pissed-off manager.

Four weeks ago, Alice, Tillie, and I were on our way home from my brother's first game quarterbacking for the *Emerald Bay Bombers*, when our vehicle was *shot at* by gun-toting psychopaths.

All because—allegedly—my sister was worth a pretty penny on the ransom market, and they trusted the wrong guy: a sweaty ball goblin by the name of Royce. But that was a whole other story.

According to the detective I'd been annoying on a weekly basis, law enforcement still hadn't made any new arrests—gotta love Southern California—and I'd done my best to forget the whole thing in the weeks since. Which wasn't hard, because nobody seemed to want to talk about it except story-starved reporters.

But that wasn't the important thing.

The important thing was *Chad*—a six-foot dickweasel with the beginnings of a beer belly, either the world's worst hairpiece or a terrible combover, and a smile that fought to compensate for it— standing in front of me when I walked in for my shift Friday night.

"You've been out for four weeks, Leighton," he supplied conde-scendingly.

Like I hadn't fought off death itself in a mad scramble to escape that sinking SUV, after breaking three ribs and my collarbone in the impact.

But Chad wasn't done.

"And you show up for your first shift back with a horde of reporters as an entourage."

"You have *got* to be kidding me," I drawled. "Like I invited the stalkarazzi?!"

"Apron," was his grunted response, waving me forward. "And your order book, please."

If I cracked a molar because my boss was a sniveling idiot, would that be covered by workers' comp?

I certainly hoped so as Chad jerked his chin toward the window behind me.

I didn't have to look to know he was right.

The problem with my beautiful, brainy sister falling in love with her equally beautiful bulldog of a boss, was that the Hart name came with a colossal mountain of baggage. The least of which was America's obsession with everything that came in contact with their lives.

Their newest fascination? The no-name 'stripper' that hauled the empire's heiress to shore.

I.e., *me*.

I.e., *not a stripper*.

Never in my life had I stripped off clothing in my place of employment... Well, except for right now, as I unlaced my apron with gritted teeth. *Fuck*.

Chad took a nice, long glance at my cleavage as I did.

Not going to lie, I have good cleavage, but it wasn't proudly on display for *this* aspiring jerk-off.

It was for the cutie in a *Bombers* jersey sitting at table six, smiling at me the instant I walked in the door.

He had 'tips well' written all over his eager face.

And I was wearing my brother Paxton's number thirteen tank. *Kismet*.

Or it would've been, if Chad wasn't a limp-dick shitwaffle.

"May both sides of your pillow be eternally warm," I gritted under my breath, slamming the wadded-up apron into his waiting hand.

"What?" Chad mumbled, blinking pointedly.

Pulling my cash out of the order booklet, I slapped the branded black folder into his hand next, scowling when I found his gaze still firmly planted in my chestal region.

"Eyes are up here, asshole."

He furrowed his brow, setting my apron on the bar counter beside us.

It appeared to take great effort to drag his gaze to my face as he said, "Look, it's nothing personal. We just don't need this heat on the restaurant. Wrong kind of attention. Our patrons value discretion."

"It's a *sports bar*, Chad," I deadpanned, bypassing him.

"The only thing you're discreet about is how much MSG is on the menu."

He puffed up his chest, cheeks reddening like a petty little beet as his beady eyes darted around.

I just wished it wasn't an opening shift and there were more people around to witness my five seconds of glory.

"What a ridiculous thing to say."

"What's *ridiculous* is that toupee," I countered with a wink before shouldering him aside with my good arm.

Didn't stop the twinge of pain on the opposite side, but it was worth it as I stormed outside, holding back the scream of frustration boiling in my chest.

Fuck. My. Life.

I SPENT the drive home thinking through my options.

My arm and ribs would heal, and serving burgers and booze to lusty middle-aged men was never the long game.

It just fell into my lap—an easy gig since chaos was my second language. Nobody could serve a big top of rowdy bikers like one of twelve, let me tell you. And they tipped exceptionally well when I flipped them shit as quickly as they dished it out.

My older sisters were all firmly established in the careers of their dreams.

Alice found her calling crafting PR stories, and my twin sister Kaia was a goddess behind a cosmetics table.

Everyone expected me to follow suit when she started making money with her makeup brush.

That's the thing about being pretty.

People assume beautiful people all somehow work *in* beauty.

They never ask what your interests are, or what sport earned you a scholarship, or what kind of obsolete diploma you have framed and hanging on your office wall—*business and journalism, by the way*.

They just assume you're destined to make other people feel pretty, or *be* pretty for the satisfaction of those around you.

From the first creep that tells you what a *beautiful woman* you are before your tits even bud, to the guidance counselor at your high school, there's an unspoken rule about career potential that eventually sounds a lot like: congratulations about your *face*.

Me?

With motherhood off the table and my soccer career unceremoniously amputated by the cruel hand of fate, I'd always wanted to write.

To get my hands dirty digging for truth in the stories that set my soul on fire.

But with papers all but extinct, and every Jenny with a semi-functional laptop running a blog these days, it seemed like a lost art.

The Harts had newspapers, but writing for one felt too much like a handout I wasn't willing to ask for—and working for a competitor felt sleazy, since I spent at least three days a week in one of their living rooms.

If I had an ounce of experience, I'd love to help small businesses refine their processes. But that felt like something that would take decades of experience to justify.

Which left me...sitting in my parking garage, tears in my eyes, with absolutely no idea what I wanted to be when I grew up.

I had less than a grand in the bank, plus a few hundred in my pocket from the last of my on-hand cash.

Alice's condo was paid off—no rent, thank God.

My new Jeep was a different—very expensive—story.

Shit, I loved that car.

I barely had enough to cover this month's payment and a week of groceries.

Maybe I could donate plasma or sell some stuff from the loft and cover my phone bill next Monday.

Oh God, what if my Jeep got repo'd and—

No.

It was fine.

I was fine.

I always landed on my feet, and this would be no different.

I wouldn't let it be.

But that didn't mean I wasn't gonna freak out a little first. This was a full pot of coffee on the back porch with my mom kind of conversation.

Maybe a phone call would do.

Problem being, Tampa was three hours ahead of us, and my early-bird mother was likely snoozing.

Still, I snatched my phone and fired off a message.

LEIGHTON

Mama, you awake?

LONG MINUTES PASSED WITHOUT A 'READ' notification.

The longer I stared at the screen like a pot refusing to boil, the harder my heartbeat drummed in my ears.

Juniper Rhodes might've been certifiable for having *twelve* kids, but the woman bent over backward to be there for us.

If she was awake, she would've gotten back to me already.

Before I'd really thought it through, I palmed at my cheeks and backed out of my parking spot, instinctively heading toward the boujee part of the city where Alice and Greyson lived across from Ollie and his kids.

The brilliant nepotistic real estate hoarders had bought up the whole neighborhood—their Nona, uncle, and cousins all owned plots in one ridiculously ostentatious subdivision that *Home and Garden* would drool over.

But it was the row of meticulously manicured drives that somehow soothed my heart when I finally pulled onto their ocean-front road.

One glance at Greyson and Alice's dark windows, and I winced internally.

It was eight o'clock, and Alice had been passing out early ever since the event-that-shall-not-be-discussed.

She'd sustained a concussion in addition to broken bones, and needed her rest.

Greyson would scold me if I accidentally woke her.

If you still think mama bears are terrifying, you clearly haven't seen Greyson fuss over my sister.

With a sigh, I turned into Ollie's driveway and parked in front of his massive garage.

The kids fought bedtime like Americans fought the last draft.

But it was a school night.

And I was... I was *spiraling*.

The lights finally automatically turned off by the time I lifted my head to look at the house.

Dimly lit. A soft blue flicker made me think someone was watching TV in the living room past the foyer.

I'd been here every day for the last two weeks.

At some point, before school or after, I'd managed to sneak in a visit to check on Tillie, and give Ollie shit.

But if I told him what happened, he'd scramble to fix it.

He'd try to offer me cash or some equally insulting billionaire gesture, and I was a bad bitch who absolutely did not need saving.

I'd figure it out.

I always figured it out.

Even if I had no idea what that looked like this time.

Even if that was utterly terrifying.

It could be worse.

I could still be in a hospital bed.

It was the vibration of my cell in the cup holder that finally snapped me out of my shell-shocked state.

OLIVER HART

You coming in, Trouble?

WHEN TEARS BURNED MY EYES, I blinked them away.

Stupid.

His little nickname was not a reason to be emotional, but it was oddly comforting.

Like I had someone in this damn city who actually gave a shit.

My phone buzzed again.

OLIVER HART

I'm past my daily caloric allowance and have a large deep dish, Chicago-style pepperoni pizza with your name on it. Stop casing the joint and come inside, you weirdo.

WITH A WATERY LAUGH, I glanced in the mirror, wiped the mascara from beneath my eyes, pinched my cheeks so I would resemble a zombie slightly less, and opened the door.

OLIVER

NORMALLY, I'd leave Leighton to let herself in, watching her approach the doorbell camera on my phone.

Normally, I'd keep scrolling through Halloween costumes with Mattie and Beau as they argued over what they wanted to be in a few weeks.

We always picked themed outfits. Cheesy, I know. But if I only got eighteen of these with my kids in the best-case scenario, I was damn sure gonna make them count.

But... she'd sat out in her Jeep for nearly forty minutes.

Just... *parked,* in my driveway.

No kicked-open door with armfuls of food.

No new vinyl dropped from one of Mattie's favorite artists.

No pissed-off declarations vowing to end a reporter's career over the bullshit they spewed in a gossip magazine.

I might not have known a whole lot in this life, but I knew this: 'silence' did not belong in the same sentence as 'Leighton Rhodes.'

The woman was hell on wheels. Or *heels*, occasionally, though she was more prone to Converse.

Powerful curves packed on a compact little frame gave her the air of an athlete, but fuck me if that muscled body wasn't exactly what I looked for in any crowd.

There were beautiful women, and then there were the Rhodes sisters.

While I'd always thought my brother's wife was stunning, Leighton was... out-of-this-world beautiful. With a temper to match, much to my amusement.

Temptation, personified.

Even if lusting after Greyson's new sister-in-law wasn't just poor form to begin with, being nine years her senior drove a nail through the coffin of that thought the moment I'd had it.

But, friend? That I could do.

And my *friend* looked nothing if not downtrodden.

So I told the kids to keep looking, handed the iPad to Mattie—who wasn't phased for a second—and headed for the front door.

It should be a crime to make a woman's shoulders slump like that.

Leighton was futilely trying to lift her chin, curling in on herself in an oversized *Bombers* hoodie.

Those gray-blue eyes were red-rimmed like she'd been crying, and my heart sank.

Suddenly, I was back on the bank of the bay they'd miraculously made it out of after hurdling off the bridge—holding her and Mattie in my arms as we all fucking cried in relief and terror and grief.

Nothing prepares you for that kind of horror.

Before I'd even processed closing the gap, I had, and she crumpled into my open arms.

"Hey, Trouble," I breathed against her hair, trying very hard not to catalog every note of citrus, or the way her warmth collapsed against my body in a kind of surrender. "What's going on?"

"Shitty day," she squeaked into my shirt.

"I see that," I said, snorting when she jabbed a finger between my ribs.

That was about as long as I could hang onto her before my dick would demand to make his feelings known, so rather than risking being *that* creep, I unspooled us and motioned her toward the house.

Twenty-three.

She was *twenty-three* and fucking *crying*.

There was no universe where this woman wanted to be saluted by an erection right now. Certainly not mine.

"Come eat."

"I'm past my calorie count, too."

"Bullshit," I scoffed. "Get your ass inside and eat some pizza. Mattie and Beau are picking Halloween costumes."

"Halloween," she repeated vacantly.

"Ghosts, goblins, and ghouls. Trick-or-treat. Devil's Night. *You know.*"

Finally, she snapped her eyes to mine in an accusatory glare.

"Yes, I know what Halloween is, thank you very much," she said before marching inside, leaving me to follow.

There she is.

I smiled to myself.

This clearly wasn't 'I damaged my spinal column in the accident' bad.

It was just regular bad.

Everyday issues I could work with.

Hell, spinning them was kind of my thing.

I pretended I didn't hear her work to clear her throat as she kicked off her shoes, then hollered, *"I hear there are two ghouls in this house?"*

Smirking as she hustled around the corner to the thunderous rumble of two pairs of tiny feet, I bent down and snatched her shoes off the ground, placing them neatly beside mine on the shoe rack by the door.

My ears strained but could only catch snippets of the kids' elated chatter as they filled her in on what I was sure was every single moment of their day.

Whether or not she knew it, Leighton filled a hole in their lives.

A gaping chasm left behind by their narcissistic mother.

And while nothing could replace an actual mother raising them, at least Alice, Leighton, and my cousin Emmaline showed them what it was to be nurtured.

I probably didn't thank any of them enough for that.

For being that for them.

For us.

"No way. Halloween is my favorite too," Leighton proclaimed as Beau did a little dance in his *Mickey Mouse* pajamas.

My little man was the spitting image of my late brother—ironically, his namesake—with his dark, tousled curls over light blue eyes.

His chubby little hands were just at that stage where I knew he'd stop looking like my baby soon.

Before long, he'd trade that tubby toddler tummy for a lanky, never-still Hart frame, and stop needing interpretation on every third sentence.

I wasn't fucking ready.

"Mine as well," I said from the entryway, not entirely sure why I was interjecting myself into her moment.

"Really?!" she squeaked, danger flashing in her eyes.

Oh boy.

"Always liked the masks."

Before I could explain, she waggled her eyebrows, and I glared skyward.

This woman would be the death of me.

Clearing my throat, I continued, "All the anonymity—nobody's better than anybody else. Just a bunch of kids running around like hellions getting free candy from strangers."

"Wholesome," she teased, following the kids toward the sectional.

"But it is," I laughed.

At least compared to what Beaumont and I used to get into. Greyson was too busy pleasing—or pissing off—our father to keep his focus away from us. Not that he thought I knew.

But we knew.

Or at least, suspected.

Not sure when he stopped prioritizing protecting family in favor of throwing us all on the chopping block.

"Look, look, look!" Beau squeaked animatedly as he clambered onto his sister's lap, pointing at the screen.

Mattie was holding the iPad in her cast arm—covered in band stickers and signatures from the 'non-douchey' kids at school—and while she'd made the most of it, I couldn't wait to get the damn thing off my baby girl.

He was already too big to sit with her, but she didn't shove him off this time.

Small mercies.

She'd been uncharacteristically affectionate the last few weeks, and while that was sweet, it also had me concerned about what she wasn't saying.

Curious, I wandered into our expansive living room and around the back of the leather couch they were piled on.

"*I'm looking, I'm looking!* Ooooooh, very nice. Your Aunt Alice would approve, little man," Leighton said.

I bent over the couch to see the *Captain America* costume he was excitedly showing her. He tapped on the image to swipe through the carousel.

Quirking a brow, I asked, "But Auntie Leighton doesn't?"

She wrinkled her nose before her voice came out rapid-fire, "My sailor's-daughter vocabulary alone would make me and *Steve* incompatible. I was always more of a *Bucky* girl."

"*Winter Soldier?!*" Mattie gasped in disbelief.

Poor kids had watched the entire Marvel catalog on a loop.

Side effect of having a single dad who wasn't sure what the hell else to do with them.

"I have a feeling Leigh read the comics, baby," I speculated, watching her for a reaction.

Sure enough, she shot me a playful smirk-glare combination that made me burst out laughing.

"Bucky was a lot cooler in the comics."

"*Yeah,*" Leighton emphasized. "And he and *Black Widow* were in love."

"What?!" Mattie barked at the same time Beau said, "*Eww!*"

A comic book girl.

That was deeply satisfying.

Why didn't comic book girls look like *that* when I was in high school?

Not that I should fucking care.

Not that I *did*.

Because that would be wildly inappropriate.

Only once Leighton had gone on to explain the *Black Widow* relationship did Mattie finally sigh and say, "Okay, so a Marvel theme would let the whole family join in. Uncle Grey and Aunt Alice and Auntie Emmaline."

I ground my teeth, finding my feet.

Over my dead body was this about to become a whole family affair.

Not after... well... everything.

"We'll order tomorrow," I said, forcing a smile as I held out my hand for the iPad.

With an irritated huff, Mattie flipped the tablet into my palm and slid Beau off her lap.

"But I think that was a good start."

Like a backpack full of stones, I shouldered the weight of Leighton's eyes on me as I turned to leave the room.

She didn't know everything about that damn 'car accident.'

Just what Greyson had decided they could tell her.

Her mind had filled in the gaps, and nobody had corrected her.

The reality was, it was *my brother*—who had always been my go-to, my ride-or-die, the one person I could trust—who placed that bullseye on our family.

3

A Little Liquid Courage, and One of Many Bad Decisions
OLIVER

"Trick or treat!" a half-dozen kids chorused on my front porch a few weeks later. "Cool costumes, guys! We've got *Thor, Elsa,* and do I spy a *Bluey?*"

Said blue doggo rejected my fist bump and hid behind her big brother, whose face was caked in an impressive layer of black-and-white skull paint.

I deposited a king-size candy bar in each of their buckets and bags, grinning as the little one squealed with excitement.

As they ran off, I shouted, "Happy Halloween!"

Waving to their parents as they departed down the sidewalk, I was about to close the door when a smokeshow in a short red wig sauntered around the corner, clad head-to-toe in skin-tight faux leather.

Father forgive me, for I am about to sin.

Leighton dressed up as *Black Widow?*

Shit, she was hotter than the original, and as she spun in a circle, the sight of that perfect ass in spandex had me thinking very not-familial things.

Grinning, she threw her arms out wide, her camera dangling from her wrist, twisting those perfect hips from side to side.

"Did I bring it? *I think I brought it.*"

Did she have any clue how fucking sexy her confidence was?

I'd never realized how hot that quality was in a woman until Leighton sauntered into my life.

Shaking my head, I didn't bother to hide my smile, gesturing down at my own *Captain America* costume.

She shrugged airily.

"Yeah, yeah, Bucky is better," I bit out, rolling my eyes as that bright smile grew. "But Cap is the OG. The big *dawg*."

Leighton wrinkled her nose, and I flicked it.

"I mean, technically, *Iron Man* came out first."

"But *Captain America* is literally *The First Avenger*. Did you just conveniently forget that part?"

Her eyes brightened, and she dropped to her knees with a squeal.

"My *Winter Soldier!*"

My kid—who liked literally no one—launched himself out the front door and into her arms like a projectile.

I shook my head, grinning as she crushed his tiny body against her chest.

The kids always loved Leighton.

But after the car accident, she'd been around even more than usual—always checking in on Mattie, helping her with her hair, bridging the gaps in ways I hadn't even realized needed bridging.

In the process, even my chunky little guy had fallen in love with her.

"Auntie Lay! Auntie Lay! Look!" Beau wrenched out of her grasp to show her how shiny his fake metal arm was.

"*Sick, dude!* But where's your hair?" Running an affectionate palm over his short dark buzz cut, she grinned as he hopped away from her.

"He's got shor' hair in da' new ones. We take a picker?"

Needing no translation, she grinned back at him.

"Heck yeah, big guy!"

Without hesitation, she whisked her camera into her palm, held it out selfie-style, and snapped a photo.

And with that, Beau bolted back inside, screeching for Matilda.

Sighing dreamily, Leighton said, "*God*, he's *cute*."

"Yeah," I agreed, rubbing the back of my neck as we both wandered inside after him. "But he knows it. That's the problem."

A body nearly slammed into her, and I lunged forward, snaking an arm around her waist to haul her back as the new nanny, Oaklyn, skidded to a halt.

Every time I touched Leighton, I had to remind myself the ensuing spark could mean nothing.

We were adults. We could master chemistry.

"Where's the fire?" Leighton quipped.

"Fire?" the little blonde repeated, blinking dazedly.

"You know, like, where's the rush?"

"I don't understand. Is something on fire?"

Leighton pursed her lips, turning to look at me pointedly.

It took all my self-control not to burst out laughing.

"Never mind," I said, shaking my head. "Everything alright?"

"Yeah, just hunting for Matilda's boots. She's in a bit of a panic, and—"

"Piano room beside the bench," I supplied quickly. With a little girl who was particular about everything, I'd gotten very good at remembering where all of it lived.

"Piano room," Oaklyn parroted, looking no less dazed.

"Beside the dining room in the back," I prompted again, as Leighton bit her lip to keep from laughing.

"Right. Dining room. On it." And she practically ran away.

Not looking at Leighton as we walked toward the kitchen, I muttered, "Don't say it."

"What?" she balked, too-innocently. "She's cute. She just skedaddled off like a tiny river dancer."

When I chuckled, she rocked her shoulder into me.

"Although it does seem like she's afraid of your daughter."

"Who isn't?"

She shrugged. "I'm not."

"Yes, but *you* had eleven siblings to beat the fear out of you," I pointed out.

"And I give that little sunspot two weeks max before those kids chew her up and spit her out."

"I'm running out of options. I swear we've gone through half the female population of Emerald Bay."

"Drama king."

"You interview a handful of these nineteen-year-old, one-named bimbos and tell me I'm wrong."

"*One-named bimbos?*" she laughed as we rounded the corner into my favorite room in the house.

The kitchen glowed with warm evening light pouring through the wall of windows overlooking the pool. Rich mahogany cabinetry, wide counters—my sanctuary, tucked away from the prying eyes of the world.

"*Stacy, Kimmi, Tasha,*" I mocked, Leighton's laughter growing with every complaint. "None of them have last fucking names."

Every syllable dripping in her radiant smile, she muttered, "You've lost it."

"I'm not denying it. Parenthood is the toughest hood."

"Oh, I know it's bad if you're pulling out dad jokes," she scoffed.

"Trust me, you'll get it someday, when some tiny you is terrorizing your household and you have to trust them to a stranger."

Her expression pinched—but just like always, it vanished before I could fully analyze it.

Though her smile wasn't quite as jubilant when it returned.

What the hell did I just stick my fat mouth into?

Clearing my throat, I hoisted up her newly cast-free right hand and asked, "How's the arm?"

"Fine. And I no longer have to jam a pencil into my skin to scratch an itch, thank God."

"A little weak?"

"Yeah," she shrugged. "Nothing I can't rebuild."

"You like that physical therapist?"

Leighton groaned. "So obnoxious. Honestly, it feels like a waste of time for an arm."

"Leighton," I scolded, bursting out laughing as she screwed up her face.

"*Ollie*," she mocked in the same tone. "I'm fine, okay? I've got eleven siblings and two overbearing parents hovering like helicopters. I'm well acquainted with rehab protocol. I promise, I'm *fine*."

My gaze fell to that thin silver scar playing peekaboo with her v-cut costume. I'd always wanted to ask her about it—but judging by Alice's glower when I brought it up once, it was a sore subject.

Not my story to tell, she'd snapped before walking off.

With that dismissal in mind, I stuck to safer territory and chuckled, "I'm not beyond demanding reports."

"Don't I know it," she muttered. Stepping into a golden wall of light, her sass vanished for a second. She tilted her face into the sunshine and sighed dreamily, her blue-gray eyes sparkling, her smile punching me directly in the ribs.

Get it together, asshole.

Luckily, a teenage grumble saved me.

"Oh thank God." Mattie slid out of the breakfast nook, glaring at Oaklyn with the enthusiasm of a scorned sixteen-year-old.

"Leigh, this is wrong." Mattie wasn't opposed to physical affection, but she rarely initiated it.

A fact made even more glaring when she walked straight into Leighton's arms.

Right. Good reminder why you can't think about Leigh like that.

"Looking good, *Wanda*!" Leigh wrapped her up, careful not to squeeze too tightly.

Mattie, dressed head-to-toe as the *Scarlet Witch*, rolled her eyes massively.

Oaklyn had tried. But her attempt at a smoky eye was muddying the whole vibe.

"Oaklyn did her best, but this is wrong," Mattie muttered in a poor attempt at graciousness.

Points for trying.

"Don't worry, I've got you, baby," Leighton said easily.

The endearment bottomed out my stomach. I cleared my throat

and turned to the fridge, fetching water bottles before we ventured out to conquer the neighborhood.

By the time I turned back, the girls were settled in at the table. Leighton was wiping away the black eyeshadow, much to Mattie's relief.

Because the universe has a spectacularly cruel sense of humor, the front door chirped open.

"Are you guys ready?" came Alice's voice.

I loved Alice.

I did.

But with her came the ever-present storm cloud of my brother, and I just wasn't ready for that particular shitstorm.

The problem was—

"Auntie Alice!! Unca' Grey!!"

That.

That was the problem.

The rapid patter of Beau's little feet as he bolted across the house—and inevitably into his uncle's arms—set my heart racing.

I needed a shot of whiskey to get through tonight.

Greyson and I might not see eye to eye on his involvement in questionable after-hours activities, but he had always been a solid presence for my kids. I didn't want them in the spotlight. But keeping them away from him these past weeks had been grueling, to say the least.

There were only so many times I could break their hearts with lame excuses for his absence before their heartbreak fractured my resolve.

"Hey bud," my brother said, a smile creeping into his voice before they even made it back into the kitchen.

"Looking good, big guy."

"I thought that title was exclusively yours," Alice chirped, never missing a beat.

"I can share it with my Beau man."

"Well, that's just confusing."

"Are you likening him to a dog, princess?"

"No," she bit out—and judging by the ensuing giggles, Beau was being tickled.

My attention dragged back to Leighton as she *growled*, "If you don't hold still, I cannot help you."

"But Uncle Grey!"

"Can wait," Leighton grumbled, pinching Mattie's chin between her fingers, angling her this way and that as she drew sharp lines away from her eyes.

With a final flourish of her brush, she leaned back to examine her handiwork, nodded in satisfaction, and waved Matilda away.

Leighton was still shaking her head in amusement as she scooted off the bench, her eyes locking on mine a beat before she canted her head curiously.

I need to get control of the subtitles on my face if we have any hope of making it through tonight without a family implosion.

Greyson was *my* problem.

I didn't need to make him my kids' concern. Or Leighton's.

The last thing any of us needed was a pissed-off Leighton Rhodes, digging around in business she had no right to expose. Because if anybody could get to the bottom of it through sheer stubborn willpower, it would be Leigh.

Her sister had figured it out in less than a day once she started looking—and that was saying something, considering Greyson's 'side business' had been hidden behind government-approved firewalls.

But the Rhodes girls were nothing if not startlingly intelligent.

I handed her a water bottle before all but ripping the cap off my own and taking a long swig—just for an excuse to keep my mouth closed.

We rounded the corner right as Grey and Alice appeared in the living room. The girls' older brother, Paxton, was tight on their heels. Much to my amusement, America's favorite quarterback was dressed up as a Wookie, the enormous furry mask hanging from his hand.

Oh, the press would have a field day with that.

"Nice Wookie suit," I muttered, bypassing my brother in favor of our prize acquisition of the season.

We'd traded Paxton to our *Emerald Bay Bombers* over the summer, and so far, he'd rallied our rag-tag team of washed-up talent into a somewhat formidable offensive line.

Another season or two, and we might actually be contenders for the first time in decades.

"Thanks. Nice spandex," he said, smirking in a way that was pure Rhodes DNA, making me smile despite myself.

"No interest in the family theme?"

"Going for full anonymity, if you know what I mean."

"Smart," I muttered, pulling my own mask off the end table as the group made a beeline for the front door. "Gonna stay a fur beast for the team party after?"

"To be determined," he said, flashing a broad smile before plunking the Wookie head onto his own. "It smells like a glue factory in here."

I chuckled, shaking my head as we made for the front door. "Who's ready for some trick-or-treating?!" I called out, sounding more boisterous than I felt.

The kids rallied, of course, rushing to grab their bags and following me into the crisp evening air.

But I didn't miss it.

Greyson wasn't the only one watching me.

Leighton was too.

Her expression was puzzled, her fingers absentmindedly brushing that curious scar, her slate eyes flicking between me and Grey before settling back on my face.

I offered what I hoped was a convincing smile, snatched Beau's little hand in mine, and led them out into the chaos.

One big, happy fucking family.

LEIGHTON

PAXTON MIGHT NOT HAVE BEEN a stranger to the spotlight, but with seven years between us, I'd been too young to really absorb what his fame entailed before now.

That was likely amplified by the miles between us—me finishing my degree back home in Alaska, him playing for Chicago.

I might've come as the Wookie's wing-woman, but he certainly didn't need me.

If anything, the blush climbing up his neck like wisteria told me he still wasn't a fan of the spotlight.

All I could do was snicker and shake my head from where I watched the chaos from across the rooftop bar.

The Harts were nothing if not generous with their entertainment.

Maybe that was just a league thing, but my God—no expense had been spared.

Fog rolled across the entire floor, illuminated emerald green by hidden lights.

Some celebrity DJ had the dance floor bustling, and I'd thoroughly enjoyed every moment of grinding against one player or another until my legs demanded a break.

A break I found sitting in a sleek high-top chair, waiting for my Dracula-inspired blood-red cocktail and fanning my sweaty face with a folded napkin.

The players and coaches were great, honestly. It was the socialites that made me scowl permanently. A feeling that only burrowed deeper when a pack of vapid women in slinky couture sauntered up to the bar.

Hell, the jewels hanging off the leggy blonde beside me probably cost more than I made in a good month. And that might not have bugged me... if my bank account wasn't currently sitting in the double digits, and I hadn't just squeezed my ass into a costume I'd had since high school.

"Oliver Hart is such a waste of a beautiful face."

I nearly flailed at the disembodied snark before catching myself, poorly concealing the flinch by turning to face the bartenders.

Excuse me?

My ears perked as a second voice scoffed, "Honestly, babe, I don't know why you bother. The man's married to his calendar. No time for distractions."

"Unless you count his kids," a third voice said bitterly.

If hearing Ollie's name had made me bristle, that tone—*tossing* aside Tillie and Beau *like distractions*—made my muscles bunch with rage.

Vapid idiots.

"Come on though, he's the hottest single dad in Emerald Bay. Can you imagine the tabloids if he bothered to open his eyes to what's right in front of him? Power couple in the making."

I choked down my laugh as the male model of a bartender set my drink down with a smile.

Golden-skinned, golden-haired—he looked straight off a cologne ad.

Typical Hart hospitality: models tending bar.

"Pffft," the third viper snickered.

"He doesn't date. He just... finds other ways to *relieve stress.*" There was so much innuendo packed into that last line it practically needed its own velvet rope.

And sure, I'd assumed tabloids were right about Ollie sowing his wild oats... but I'd spent enough time dropping by unannounced to know better.

I'd never seen a car in his driveway that wasn't family.

If I'd learned anything, it was how expertly people twisted truth to fit their narrative. Hell, I'd watched Alice craft stories that were entirely fictional.

"I'd happily relieve his stress," the first voice said, dropping sultry enough to cloud a mirror.

The three of them collapsed into titters fit for a high school gymnasium.

Staring down at the fog rolling off my drink, I threaded my fingers around the stem of the martini glass.

Slowly turned halfway toward the party.

Zeroed in on the huddle slobbering over one of my best friends.

Perfect, polished, poised.

Everything I was not.

"And maybe poke some holes in the condom box and pray for the best," the second one snickered.

My spine straightened involuntarily.

I smiled blandly at the bar, wondering what dry ice would do to eyeballs if I poured my Dracula cocktail down her face.

"Gah, no kidding. Did you see what his ex-wife got in the divorce settlement?"

"Insane!" the redhead exclaimed.

"I'd have his babies if it meant I got to live like that."

"Well, you better hurry," Mermaid Barbie said, tilting her drink toward the corner where Ollie held court for the evening.

"He's been watching her all night."

I followed their gaze—and there he was. Shock of black hair. Polite smile aimed at a bleach-blonde bombshell leaning provocatively over his table.

I recognized her vaguely—maybe a sports reporter? Pretty, polished, professionally blonde. I was almost positive I'd seen her cover one of Paxton's games.

My stomach churned as he chuckled, her shiny hair cascading over her shoulder.

"Can you imagine playing truth or dare with *that*?" the redhead asked pointedly.

"Dare, dare, dare!" one of them squealed.

I lost track of their conversation. All I could see was the maybe-reporter's manicured hand on Ollie's costumed arm.

Truth or dare, huh?

Maybe it was the alcohol.

Maybe it was the California warmth.

Maybe it was the territorial monster roaring to life inside me.

Whatever the reason, I tossed back my drink—which tasted like the bartender mixed *all* the alcohols and dumped in a jar of maraschino cherries—coughed in protest of the vile concoction, and slid off my stool in a fit of very, very bad decision-making.

With determination, I weaved between chattering partygoers, slid between Ollie and Blondie McBimbo with a muttered, "Pardon me," threw my arms around his neck, and crushed my lips to his like I'd come to stake my claim.

Ollie's body went rigid for a beat before I pulled back. The moment our eyes locked, his lips twisted into a smile, and he brought his mouth to mine as his hands found my waist.

There was a high probability that sound from my periphery was a disgusted scoff of outrage from Blondie McBimbo, but I couldn't find it in myself to care.

Because Oliver Hart was kissing me. His hands tightened, pulling me flush against him, deepening the kiss. His sweet cinnamon scent wrapped around me, heat bloomed against my skin. Gentle but demanding, warm and pliant, he took my kiss and made it better.

When we finally peeled apart, a little breathless, he tucked a strand of my wig behind my ear with maddening affection.

Arching a disbelieving brow, he drawled, "Well, hello, Trouble."

"Hello," I chirped dumbly, grinning so hard the world tilted sideways.

"What was that for?"

"You *lookedlike* you needed savin'," I blurted, the blush burning hotter than the rooftop lights.

His brows winged up, mischief dancing in his eyes. "You're drunk."

"There's a slight probability I have achieved the perfect buzz," I admitted solemnly, "but I promise I'm nowhere near sloshed."

"Have you eaten anything?" he asked, steering me gently into a bar stool at his table.

"Mmmm—tiny portions, *weirdfood*, looked like fish eggs."

Chuckling, Ollie shook his head. "So, *no*."

"Very astute."

"Jesus, Trouble."

His eyes flicked over my shoulder like he was checking for witnesses. I *tried* not to be insulted by that.

Hell, part of me hoped the hags at the bar got a good look. Over my dead body was he going home with the condom-stabber.

"You wanna get outta here?" I said brightly. "Those bitches were obj-objec-*tifying* you like their next meal."

Ahh, shit. My words were starting to slur.

Nice way to leave an impression, Leighton.

But when his smile fell over me, it was better than the last kiss of summer sun.

He nodded, standing and motioning for me to lead the way.

"Can I tell you a secret?" I said, weaving slightly.

"Oh, this is gonna be good," he muttered good-naturedly.

"I've always wanted to know what it would be like to kiss Oliver Hart."

———————————

4

Tacos, Temptation, and
Terrible Life Choices
OLIVER

———————————

"Ahhhh, that's better," Leighton sighed contentedly, flopping onto the couch beside me in her oversized *Bombers* hoodie and a pair of cheeky shorts I was adamantly trying *not* to look at.

I'd known when she asked me to come inside for a movie that it was a terrible idea. But she flashed that magazine-worthy smile that brought those damn dimples to life—and I caved like a dollar store lawn chair under a linebacker.

Had anyone ever been strong enough to tell this girl no?

Stupid.

This was so stupid.

All that tan skin on display, and now her eight-seat sectional felt way too small without her siblings or my feral children running interference.

The instant we got inside, Leighton scrubbed off her makeup and traded her red wig for a pile of chaos on top of her head.

What does it say about me that her sloppy messy bun is somehow even more appealing?

A dark, wavy strand fell loose across her forehead.

The fantasy was nice.

The real thing was infinitely better.

And what the fuck was wrong with me?

"What'cha in the mood for?" I asked, jerking my gaze to the mounted flatscreen and leaning forward to grab her chaotic plate of mix-and-match tacos.

"And who the hell likes fish with their Picadillo?"

"I didn't stick 'em in a blender," she complained. "Variety is the spice of life, Hart."

"*Spice* is the spice of life," I countered, carefully lining the perfect

31

trail of hot sauce across my carne asada tacos, keeping my eyes *firmly* glued where they belonged.

She snickered.

"You look like you're solving a calculus equation. Need help there?"

She elbowed me between the ribs.

Of course, I needed help.

It was taking every ounce of self-control not to touch her. Not to take that kiss and raise it to NC-17. Not to act on every crazy thought pounding through my head.

Clearly, I'd overcorrected when I stopped working through the model circuit, because celibacy was making me a lunatic. That *had* to explain my obsession with the one woman most definitely *off-limits.*

Hell, Greyson would kill me if I added any more complications to his life. If he didn't get the chance, her five older brothers sure as hell would.

But that kiss...

Hottest goddamn moment of my life.

And the crowd had been too sloshed to notice us duck out.

Well—except Jax, Greyson and Alice's bodyguard.

Him, I'd owe an explanation to.

When her nudge didn't get a response, she opted for jamming a finger into my ribs.

"You having a stroke, Hart?"

"Listen," I said, wincing, "you don't grow up this close to the border and not learn a thing or two about salsa to cilantro ratio."

She snorted.

I, however, jammed my eyes closed as my brain caught up to my mouth.

Salsa. To *cilantro.* Ratio.

Jesus Christ, I was off my game.

"Just pick a movie, Trouble."

"I'm feeling nostalgic."

"Half your body weight in vodka will do that."

"Just making sure I get my veggie intake."

"What?"

"You say potatoes, I say vodka. Tomatooo, tomahhhhto," she sang.

Smirking, I shook my head, finally forcing myself to look at her, and wishing I hadn't. Beautiful. So fucking beautiful when she smiled like that.

Hell, I'd waited my whole life for Carly to look at me like that —light and overjoyed, just living in the moment—and looking at me like my ability to deliver tacos ranked me as king of the hunter-gatherers, rather than a pre-punched ticket to the upper echelon.

"So what's nostalgia mean to Leighton Rhodes?"

Yes. Good. Say her full name. Fully grasp who you're talking to.

Twenty-three.

Permanently entangled in your life.

"Mmmmm," she hummed around a mouthful of fish and pico.

The woman even swallowed sexy.

God, she *would* swallow sexy, the idea of her on her knees—

Pull yourself together, man.

Jerking my gaze to the TV, I watched as she navigated through apps.

"I'm thinking *The Mummy*."

"No way," I laughed, pouring a mountain of spicy sauce over my skirt steak, shoveling down an entire taco just to create a five-alarm fire in my mouth. Maybe then my brain would stay where it belonged. "I hear nostalgic, and I think *Casablanca* or *When Harry Met Sally*."

She nearly choked, slapping a hand over her full mouth to contain it.

"*What?* Didn't peg you for a closet romantic."

"Rude," I muttered as my eyes watered, nose burning in protest.

"Please. What guy suggests a Meg Ryan movie?"

"She was—" I gasped, "—America's sweetheart when I was a kid."

Leighton cackled, passing me her cherry cola.

Gratefully, I chugged it down even though it failed to extinguish the fire burning my tongue.

"Did you know spice isn't a flavor?" she chirped. "It's literally just pain."

"Delicious."

"Masochistic."

"Maybe," I allowed, blinking through the burn.

When I finally caught my breath, she pointed at me with her taco.

"I was mocking you for your taste in cinema."

"Mock away. I have no shame." That much was evident. "Mom loved her," I said without thinking.

"Aww," Leighton crooned. "Well, fuck me, that's cute."

Smirking, I jerked my chin at the TV. "Pick a movie, Leigh."

"Okay, so you like Meg. Not *Courage Under Fire* or *Proof of Life*? You went full chick flick?"

Another shrug. "Carly liked it. And after we had Mattie... She had colic, and I spent a lot of nights rocking her to sleep—went faster with some background noise." I tried to ignore the weight of her watching me, focusing on my plate until finally meeting her curious gaze.

"What?"

"She's an idiot," Leighton said flatly.

"Maybe. Maybe not."

"No, *she is*, Ollie. Do you know how few men could even *say* what you just did? You're a great dad."

"Maybe that was the problem."

I love that you're a devoted father, Ollie, but God, I just don't know where I fit in your life these days.

The memory twisted my chest.

"I let them consume me, you know? Everything became about the kids. Workload is heavy. It got easier when Grey came home, but man..." I shook my head. "It's easy to fall into being a stage parent. Especially with a kid as demanding as Mattie. That little girl became my whole world."

"You say that like that's a bad thing, rather than a natural rite of passage."

"It is a bad thing if you neglect their mother."

"I highly doubt you neglected her," she scoffed.

"You weren't there."

"No. But Greyson was. And if he nicknamed her after a Disney villain, I'm inclined to think you're being too hard on yourself."

I snatched the remote from her limp hand, earning a squeaked protest.

"You snooze, you lose," I said, aiming for playful, but missing the mark. I didn't talk about this shit. Harts didn't dwell on our emotions, and we certainly didn't air our dirty laundry for somebody else to exploit. Clicking through tiles until I found that familiar front cover, I started the film and returned to my tacos.

"Was she always... you know..."

"*Cruella?*"

Leighton nodded.

"No," I said honestly. "At least, not to me. We were young. Stupid. Hormone-fueled. Had a little too much fun—and then along came Mattie."

"You got married."

"Yep."

"What then?" she asked, with no regard for the intro happening on screen.

I set my plate down on her coffee table.

Another resigned shrug. "People don't always grow in the same direction. I wanted a family. She didn't. I wanted to pursue the legacy. Preserve it so Matilda had something worth holding onto."

"She didn't?"

"Eh," I sighed, wishing we could talk about literally anything else. Famine in third-world countries would have been more warm and fuzzy. At least I was no longer sporting an erection. "She said she was supportive."

"But?"

"Jesus, you're like a detective on a trail."

"Just trying to understand. My bad."

"No," I sighed, palming my face. "You're just... persistent."

"Chalk it up to eleven brothers and sisters. If you don't pry information out of them, it's all too easy to lose touch."

Grinning, I nodded, setting my hand on her knee where she sat crisscrossed beside me, giving her a reassuring squeeze. "I'm just not used to anybody giving a shit."

"You and Grey holding your life close to the vest does not equate to nobody giving a shit."

I cleared my throat uneasily. "Point taken."

"*So?*"

I shook my head, staring at the screen without a single image registering. "The late nights add up. Empires aren't built—or maintained—on standard hours. The demand takes a toll."

"So she said she'd support you, but couldn't actually deal?"

"We didn't last six months after Mattie before it got rocky."

"Hmm," she hummed thoughtfully, shaking her head. "Her loss, Ollie. You're like... pretty decent. Most of the time." Her dripping sarcasm took a hammer to my anxiety.

There wasn't pity churning behind those gunmetal-blue eyes. None. Just understanding. Empathy. Somehow, that was validating in a way nothing else ever was.

"No point in dwelling on the past," she said cheerily, tucking her back against my arm. I opened for her, wrapping my arm around her shoulders, tugging her closer—and wondering how on earth she could feel so perfect against my side.

"Know a lot about that?" I mumbled, settling my cheek against the top of her head.

"It would be pathetically easy to live in what-ifs. *What if* my body didn't betray me? *What if* I'd made it through college into pro ball?"

"Volley?"

"Foot."

"Like powderpuff?"

She snorted, laughing as she shook her head, her frizzy hair tickling my nose.

"Soccer."

"Hmm. You get hurt?"

"Something like that."

Before I could press further, she added lightly: "But there's no point in living there. You know? It happened. I'm okay. The path changed, and frankly, I don't have a single clue where it's leading now." She shrugged. "I was only going to college to play, but ended up staying because I didn't know what else to do. And I didn't want my family mother-henning me more than they already were—when there are a million of them, it's super overwhelming."

"I can imagine."

"So," she continued, "we forge ahead. You have two incredible kids, Ollie. They love you to the moon and back. And a brother who would do anything for the three of you."

"Yeah," I muttered, trying not to sound bitter. The truth was—seeing him tonight had reopened that wound. I fucking missed the asshole. He'd dragged our family into the sights of monsters with his need for control—his god-like alter ego—and I couldn't even stay mad.

"You loved it?" I asked, desperate to shift the focus back to her.

"Lived and breathed it."

Nodding, I thought about that scar, always peeking out of her shirt. I was about to ask about it when she added: "But it's in my past. It'll stay there, too."

"Still. Sucks though."

She gave a little huff of a laugh. "Yeah. But here we are."

"Here we are," I agreed.

After a long moment, she sighed contentedly, relaxing against me.

Voice uncharacteristically soft, she said: "'Here' is not so bad."

"No," I whispered against her coconut-scented hair, notching up the volume to an even number. "No, it's not."

We watched the movie in silence.

Not the weighted silence of burdens shared—but the ease I'd come to expect from Leighton.

Because Leighton existed in a bubble *without* expectations. She was just... easy to breathe around. Easy to *be* around. I didn't have to have my game face on. Didn't have to mind my p's and q's. Didn't have to worry about what the press would say about me, or my status, or my family. Leighton couldn't have cared less if she tried.

And for the first time since the accident, I felt myself truly relax.

Right up until Leighton's laughing fit about halfway through the film, when Meg Ryan faked an orgasm in a crowded restaurant.

"You enjoyed that far too much," I observed, grateful she couldn't see how broadly I smiled at the sound of her unashamed cackling.

There was nothing refined about Leighton. She laughed with

her whole body. She sang and danced and loved and fought with everything she had.

She was the polar opposite of my doormat of a mother, or my image-obsessed ex-wife.

Not once had I seen her make herself smaller to fit into someone else's box, or quiet herself for fear of waking the neighbors at half past midnight because she was laughing so hard she might piss herself.

I was a tremendous fan of her shamelessness. If I were honest, I envied her too.

A sentiment that only amplified with her next statement.

"The perk of only ever sharing my bed with a trusty silicone vibrator is I've never had to do *that*," she giggled, sighing as she caught her breath.

Every muscle in my body went on high alert, like I'd misinterpreted what she just said.

"Been a while?" I hedged, squeezing her shoulders.

"Pffft," she scoffed. "Throbby Wand Kenobi serves me well whenever I please."

"Throbby—"

"You heard me."

"Is that—"

"My vibrator? Yes."

"Jesus Christ, Trouble."

"I'm gonna start taking shots every time I make you say that."

"You'll never walk straight again at this point."

"Good thing I'm stone-cold sober."

"Pretty sure you'd go into immediate liver failure."

"At least the ending would be swift."

"Are you saying what I think you're saying?"

"That I've never bothered with a man when silicone can do the job?"

"Not Anakin VibeWalker?"

She burst out laughing, hands flying up to cover her mouth. Of everything that just came out of it, that was the thing that embarrassed her?

Fuck, I needed to see what shade of pink painted her skin when she was *really* riled.

"Hold on," I said, nudging her out of my arms and pausing the movie. I just couldn't move past this.

Hell, I didn't know girls that made it through high school with their virginity intact.

And here she was—twenty-three, drop-dead gorgeous, a mouth like a sailor—and somehow...

"Leighton, what are you saying right now?"

"That between fighting for my life and getting Tillie out of the water after the accident, I had the terrifying realization that I might die a virgin? Yes. Yes, I did."

Fuck. Me.

"You're joshing me."

"*Rude.*"

"You're telling me the woman who marched up to me at a crowded party and gave me the hottest kiss of my life is——"

"A little Virginia. Yep." She blinked, as if challenging me. As if every snap of those lashes said: what of it?

"Jesus Christ, Trouble."

"That's two."

I couldn't come up with a single damn thing to say.

I just sat there, staring at her. Studying her. All tan skin, dark features, and those gunmetal-blue eyes that drove me fucking crazy. Gradually, her amusement carved deep dimples into her sun-kissed cheeks.

"You gotta stop looking at me like that, Ollie."

"Like what?"

"Like you're about to say something life-altering. Frankly, it's terrifying."

I cleared my throat. Still, no words would form. "*You* kissed *me.*"

"Yep."

No regret. No hesitation. No second-guessing.

"Why?"

"I wanted to."

"That simple?"

For the first time, she looked almost...perplexed. "Do you not kiss the people you want to kiss?"

"Valid point. But..."

"*But?*" she prompted when I trailed off. "You're even cuter when you panic."

"You're..."

"I never said I hadn't locked lips, Ollie."

"Yeah. But..."

"Breathe."

"Did you—did it—are you—we—"

"Good job. That was sentence-adjacent."

I finally managed, "Did it mean anything? Your—um—the kiss?"

"Do you want it to?"

"Not the question I asked."

"Nope. It's the one *I* did."

"Yes."

Her eyes rounded. "Yes?"

"What would you say if I did? What would you say if I told you I've wanted to do that since the moment you confronted Greyson?"

"I'd probably tell you I've wanted to do that since you took me out for sushi to conspire together after we left."

"This whole time?" Equal parts elation and terror clogged my windpipe.

She felt like skydiving. Like BASE jumping without knowing if you packed the right chute.

"I told you," she said coyly, her smile twisting into something devastating. "I've always wanted to know what it was like to kiss Oliver Hart."

"That wasn't an accurate representation," I protested. "You blindsided me."

"*Kissing* Oliver Hart," she clarified. "Not *being kissed* by you."

"Oh, so the plan was always to shock the shit out of me?"

"Maybe," she said playfully.

"And what if I've always wanted to know what it was like to kiss Leighton Rhodes?"

"I'd say you're painfully slow off the mark."

"Ouch."

Only once I was done miming being shot—earning a trill of nervous laughter—did I smirk back at her.

On one last steadying breath, I scooted forward. Raised my hands to her cheeks. Relished in the slide of our skin as I shifted to hold her neck. In the breathy little sigh that poured from her, as her lashes fluttered closed and her full lips parted.

I held steady, just a hair's breadth away from her mouth. Not out of hesitation. But just to draw it out. Just to savor the dream-state I was clearly trapped in.

She moved first. Of course, she wouldn't wait for me.

But I smiled, shifting back, grinning when her eyes flew open in surprise.

Slowly, I grazed the tip of her nose with mine. Traced the peak of her mouth with my lower lip. Smiled against her skin as her breath caught in her chest.

And then—with all the tension of the last five months burning through my veins—I finally claimed her mouth.

There was no slow start.

No tentative tiptoe into the shallow end.

The moment my lips touched hers, Leighton unleashed herself.

Her hands slid under my hoodie, heat flooding every cell in my body. Mine found their way into her hair, the other pinning her jaw up so she couldn't take over completely.

It was a power struggle. A battle of wills. I licked into her mouth, and she chased my retreat, tasting me just as hungrily. This woman didn't have the word *submit* in her vocabulary. It was half kiss, half war. And I wanted every last second of it.

Gingerly, I worked my palm down over her breast, drinking in the sharp gasp she gave in return.

Meaningless sex, I knew. But touching Leighton could never—*would never*—be meaningless.

Slipping beneath her oversized hoodie, I found smooth, heaven-wrapped skin. I eased her onto her back, peeling our mouths apart only when her hands fisted my hoodie up over my head.

I let her work it off, eyes snapping to the strip of skin above her shorts.

Fuck, she's mouthwatering.

But I wanted to take my time.

It was supposed to be *just* a kiss.

Just a kiss.

Her hands scraped over my skin as our mouths collided in desperate, coiled up anticipation. This whole time. This whole time I could've said something—*done* something—and we'd both held back. Her hand found my throbbing cock through my jeans, and I groaned, clamping her lower lip between my teeth.

Easing away, I shook my head. Even as my instincts screamed to take more, feel more, *serve* more.

"You gonna remedy that for me, Ollie?"

Fuck. I could show her pleasure so consuming she'd toss that damn toy in the trash.

"We shouldn't," I breathed.

She laughed and leaned up to kiss me again. I turned her head aside with my nose, trailing kisses along her jawline instead.

"You were drinking."

"Hours ago."

"Still. I should go."

"I'd blow into a breathalyzer for you," she teased, "but that's not the kind of blowing I had in mind."

"Jesus, Trouble."

"That's three."

I snickered—but my mind was warring with my body.

"Why me?" I whispered.

"Stop over thinking. Do I seem like a woman who is uncertain?"

"No," I admitted.

"Then don't tell me what I want."

"Leighton."

"It was a lack of time. Not some virtue signal."

Panic warred with the scrape of her fingers over my skin, the buck of her hips, the feel of my cock painfully pressed against the zipper of my pants. I needed her more than my next fucking breath. And that feeling wasn't new. It had been there. For months.

"At least you give a shit about me. I trust you, Ollie. More than anyone I've ever known."

"You want *me*?" Washed -up single dad. *Married* to his desk.

She snatched my hand in irritation, and slid it down her soft stomach. Dipped it below her waistband and guided me straight into heaven. I groaned as my fingers slid through her soaking wet folds.

Soft.

Perfect.

"You tell me."

5

Nothing Says 'Casual' Like Family Breakfast
LEIGHTON

The Fam Damily:

KAIA

T-minus three weeks to Emerald Bay!!

PAXTON

Hell yeah!

MAVERICK

I don't get in until Thanksgiving morning. Save me some pie.

BREX

We'll miss you guys! Can't wait to see you all this Christmas!

ELORA

Same. *pouting GIF*.

FOMO activated.

MAV

Try keeping your legs closed next spring, and you won't miss Thanksgiving next year, sis.

PAXTON

Seriously, Mav?

You had to go there.

MAV

I joke, I joke.

Kind of.

You know I will love all of your crotch goblins.

Keep that baby dust away from me, though.

JAMESON

Keep your dick in your pants and that won't be an
issue.

MAV

Middle finger emojis

ALICE

It is NINE in the morning.

MAV

And some of us have class.

ALICE

Yes, you seem very invested in your lecture, atm.

BREX

No more babies for us.

I enjoy keeping my food down, thank you very much.
Who's up next?

MAV

Rhy getting snipped after baby girl is earth side?

JAMESON

Can we not talk about genital mutilation before
breakfast?

MAV

I'm just saying.

Gotta do something, and Brex has done her part.

My man doesn't miss.

HADLEE

Barfing emojis

I'm out. *peace sign emojis*

HADLEE RHODES HAS LEFT THE CONVERSATION

RHYETT

Jesus Christ, can we not run off the sisters please,
jackass?

RHYETT RHODES HAS ADDED HADLEE RHODES TO THE
CONVERSATION

GREYSON HART

Menaces. All of you.

KAIA

Yoo-hoo!

Leighton! Get your ass out of bed, sleepy head!

PAXTON

I'm headed that way with coffee and danishes. I'll drag her ass out.

ALICE

Approach with caution. Jax says she was drunk enough that Ollie had to take her home last night.

PAXTON

Raised eyebrow emoji She looked fine to me.

KAIA

You know how she is whilst hungover.

PAXTON

Valid argument. What if I bring a sludge cup and an extra danish?

GREYSON

Guard your face.

THE INCESSANT BUZZ of my cell had me peeling open my eyes into the warm autumn light of mid-morning. Only the Rhodes could vibrate a phone right off a bedside table—the big, lovable lunatics. Glaring at my cell on the floor, I decided I was keeping my liquid body right where it was, tucked snugly into my duvet, drifting back to sleep with the sun on my skin.

This was my favorite time of day in the loft—the golden blanket of sunshine pouring through the windows lit up the entire space, and I soaked up every single ounce of it. I felt... rested. And oh-so-content. Hell, even the ache between my legs was welcome.

My eyes flew open.

I rolled over like an alligator, tangling myself in the sheets—only to come face to face with none other than a sleeping Oliver Hart.

Breathtaking. Sun-drenched. Dark curls fell across his forehead, and miles of gorgeous olive skin stretched against my white bedding. My mouth went dry. I had to physically restrain myself from tracing that stunning shoulder tattoo.

My hands flew to cover my mouth as the night before flooded back.

So much alcohol.

Laughing the entire drive home.

Tacos, coffee, and half of some nineties chick-flick.

Oh, sweet baby Jesus. His lips grazing over my scars in a silent benediction—like he didn't need the story to pay homage to their existence. The delicious lash of his tongue against my clit as he ate me out like his life depended on it. Every touch came with a tenderness that screamed of something far beyond a hookup.

Not that I had any real frame of reference.

Oh, holy hell. I thought I'd dreamed all of it.

Fuck, fantasizing about Ollie had already cut Throbby Wand-Kenobi's time-to mission success in half this year.

I...

We...

Oh my god.

Ohmygod.

Oh. My. *God!*

A frenetic peek beneath the sheets confirmed we were gloriously, stupendously naked. And that anaconda he'd had hidden in his pants? Definitely aware it was morning. Was that rug burn stinging the shit out of my back?

And I... *we...*

Like he could sense my heart slamming against my ribs, Ollie's eyes opened. The sunlight turned them more gold than brown, and when he smiled—damn.

Just... *damn.*

Still in a daze, I barely managed to engage my facial muscles as he reached for me, those broad fingers warm against my cheek before gliding down to cup my jaw.

"Good morning, Trouble," he rasped.

Three simple words. And my heart liquefied like a cartoon character melting into a puddle.

"Morning," I breathed dreamily.

"You good?"

I nodded gingerly. His thumb grazed over my cheekbone, expression softening. I looked then—really looked—at the gold saturating his beautiful skin. I couldn't stop myself from reaching out and touching him.

Oliver Hart was in my bed, looking at me like I was the sunrise. And my body felt suspiciously like goo.

"You look happy," he observed, voice still rough with sleep. Satisfaction sparked in his eyes—golden-brown and soft and full of something dangerous.

It was a struggle to remember how to swallow, nodding as my fingers skimmed the expanse of his glorious shoulders, and his eyes fluttered shut in contentment.

"Yeah. You?"

"Never fucking better," he breathed, tugging my wrist up to pepper kisses along it. "Kinda thought I was dreaming."

"Same."

"You feel convincingly real."

I chuckled. Pinched him. Grinned when he scowled. "Sorry. Just checking."

"*Trouble*," he murmured, amusement coloring the word. "Want some breakfast? I make a mean eggs Benedict."

"You won't find anything but cornflakes and instant coffee out there," I warned, then added—way too quickly—"grocery day." Which was code for: I'm walking down the street and attempting to donate plasma today just to keep food on the table.

"Fuck that. I'll have someone deliver. What do you want?"

I hesitated. Pride screamed at me to decline, but I was too warm and too wrapped in Oliver Hart to leave this bed. He tucked me against him, nose nuzzling into my hair.

Absolute, ecstatic, bone-deep bliss.

His touch made my body sing. If heaven existed, I was pretty sure it felt like *this*.

"Bacon? Eggs? Maybe some fruit?"

"Easy. Give me thirty minutes."

I let my hand trail down his torso, grazing his thick morning wood. "I can think of something to do while we wait."

"Not sore?"

Smirking, I shook my head. When he arched a brow, I admitted, "A little. But it's worth it."

The man pressed his lips to my forehead, humming contentedly, and *I swooned*. Somehow, I melted deeper into the mattress. Apparently, it was noticeable, because his hum transformed into a chuckle. I was just thinking I'd bottle that sound to play on rainy days when the alarm system chirped.

Then came the familiar baritone that popped our blissful bubble.

"Leighton Alexandra! Get your ass up. I come bearing espresso!"

Our eyes snapped open at the same time. "Is that—"

"*Paxton!*" I hissed, springing upright, my brain flashing every single check-engine light as I rushed to find my clothes. Ollie followed at a slightly more dignified speed.

I loved my big brother. So, so much. But I could've punched him in his smug, gorgeous face.

"Where are my pants?" Ollie hissed, grabbing his hoodie from where it was crumpled on the floor. I blushed, remembering that I'd worn nothing but that sweatshirt into the kitchen at some point last night.

Oh fuck me. "Living room."

"Leighton!" the wank biscuit sang. "*Oh, Leiiiighton!*"

His obnoxious, high-pitched sing-song was getting closer. I snatched a pair of oversized sweats off the armchair and hocked them at Ollie.

Just perfect. My brother was about to see us tumble out of my bedroom looking disheveled, me with freshly-fucked hair in a spider's nest of a bun—and Ollie, pants-less.

His *boss.*

I'd just handed my virginity to my brother's future-sculptor like an Amex card.

My stomach flipped. I pressed my palm to the slight ridge of my scar.

Oh god—*Tillie.* Matilda and Beau. Alice. Greyson.

What the hell was wrong with me?

"Leighton! Family breakfast!" A triple-knock rattled the door, and about sent my stomach right out my ass.

"Keep your pants on!" I barked, eyeing Ollie where he stared down at my sweats clinging to his legs, barely covering the goods. He looked ridiculous. Ridiculous enough I had to swallow a laugh.

"Sheesh. Good morning to you too, Punky." Smirking, Oliver mouthed, Punky? I narrowed my eyes.

"Fuck off, it's early!" I hollered.

"It's ten a.m.!" Paxton shot back.

"And I gave my pajamas the night off, so don't open that door unless you want me to have another thing to bitch to my therapist about."

"Five minutes or I eat your danish."

"I'll take my sweet damn time, and if you like your balls on the outside of your body, you'll do no such thing."

Ollie chuckled. That glow in his eyes—pure affection.

"Jesus, I'll wait on the balcony!"

"Thank yooouuu," I sang, locking eyes with Ollie a beat before his lips crashed onto mine. Forcing myself to peel apart, I breathed, "Perfect. Let me get him outside. Keep him facing the city. You get outta here."

"I hate this," he whispered.

"Same." I forced an unconvincing smile.

There was no way I was throwing Ollie to the wolf in *my* fucking sweats. Paxton might be a teddy bear at heart, but he was six-foot-four, and two hundred and thirty-five pounds of pure muscle, with a protective streak a mile wide. He'd made my college boyfriend look ready to piss himself just by *getting out of the truck.*

"Got a better plan than your star QB finding out his boss boned his baby sister?"

He grimaced. "I'd prefer a face-to-face. Ideally wearing my own pants."

We both glanced at the very impressive tent in his lap.

"Still?" I chirped.

"It's. Morning," he grumped.

"Got another idea?"

With a sigh, he kissed me again—this one harder, more desperate. "Come by the house later?"

I nodded, but the crab of guilt was pinching at my belly.

What the fuck did I just do?

A single lapse in control and I could've rewritten my entire life. I'd never meant to be a one-night stand kind of girl, but dating Oliver? That could never be casual.

We were too intertwined. And dating a single dad skipped steps one through twenty in favor of mach-five, because the moment kids were involved… everything accelerated.

Especially kids I loved with my whole damn heart.

What if Tillie thought I'd been hanging out with her just to get close to her dad?

What if this blew up and I couldn't even be in the same room as the people I loved most?

My heart sank at the very real possibility that I finally took what I wanted and could lose three of my favorite people as a result.

As I turned to leave, Ollie caught my wrist and drew me back to him.

"Leighton." His voice was hoarse, urgent. This kiss was molten—desperate, as he teased his tongue along the seam of my mouth.

"I can practically see you overthinking in that beautiful head of yours," he whispered. "And I need you to know that you could *never* be a mistake, Trouble."

OLIVER

MUSIC—BLASTING.

Sun—shining.

Panoramic sunroof—wide open.

The rumble of my Bentayga through the floorboards had me itching for open roads to let her run.

Traffic—terrible, but I was too goddamn happy to care.

The aftertaste of Leighton Rhodes was a heady concoction on my tongue, and every inch of me buzzed with the echo of her touch.

Holy shit. She kissed *me*. Wanted *me*. Welcomed me into her home—and then her bed—and looked like a damn angel beneath those lust-drunk lids this morning. If the last thing I saw in this life was her face when that first orgasm hit, I'd die a very happy man.

She was a dream. And I had no intention of waking up.

Still grinning like a teenager, I waited for the gate to open and pulled into the driveway. I was back in my own gym set, her folded sweats resting in the passenger seat, the glorious sun warm against my face as I stepped from the car.

Men talked about walking on top of the world with the right woman by their side. I used to think they were suckers. But now? I damn near floated through my front door, breathing in the scent of bacon and coffee and the delighted laughter of my kids. I was one step from levitating when I rounded the corner into the kitchen to find Beau and Mattie bopping along to some kiddie tune with the nanny.

"Good night, boss?" Oaklyn chirped, already reaching for the coffee pot.

I just grinned and leaned down to kiss both my kids' cheeks. Happy. I'd forgotten what that felt like. "Morning, sunshines."

"Morning, Daddy," they chorused.

Coffee in hand, I strolled toward my office, planning to clear a few emails before brunch. That plan ground to a halt the moment I stepped inside and saw Greyson sitting in the chair across from my desk, looking far too serious for a Saturday.

What was it with brothers shitting on the perfect day?

He cleared his throat. "Where you been, Ollie?"

"Out," I clipped, circling him and ignoring the jackass perched in my chair like he paid the mortgage.

"Care to expand?"

"Not particularly." I crossed to my espresso bar, setting down the black coffee and reaching for a sugar packet. "What do you want, Greyson?"

I could feel him watching me for a long beat, analyzing, strategizing. Even as I fetched a carton of plant-based creamer from the mini fridge and stirred it into my mug before returning it.

The man dominated the conference room only in part because of his strategy. What the opposition never realized was how much power he held in his ability to stay silent. Waiting. Eventually, they would crack under the weight of his stony, expectant glare. He'd always had it, but fuck if it wasn't worse after his time in the Navy.

But this wasn't some executive takeover.

This was my house. *My* office. And I might answer to my brother on the board, but not here.

"You're in my chair."

"I am."

"It's Saturday. I blocked this morning off."

"You did."

"So, what are you doing here? Is Alice okay?"

"She's fine. Thank you for asking."

I turned and finally faced him.

"Take a seat," he instructed.

"I don't think I will." Just to be petty, I leaned against the espresso table and took a slow sip. The first cup of the day was sacred, and he was fucking with my ritual.

We'd fought before. But not like this. Not for this long.

"I've got plans," I said. "Get to the point or get out."

He clasped his hands, elbows on *my* desk, and held my gaze. "You know I love you."

"Thought you did."

His eyes narrowed. "My love for this family has never been in question."

"You've got a funny way of showing it."

"I didn't come here to rehash what we both know needs to be done."

"What you do after hours is none of my business. But keep it away from my family."

"I'm working on it."

"You could walk away. Then there'd be a hell of a lot less to work on."

"There are bigger things at play, Ollie. What my team is doing goes way beyond us."

"And what happens if your monsters come after my kids again?"

"They have you. And a small army of security. Me. Alice. Emmaline. Nona. Hell, even Reggie would take a bullet for them."

"Reggie's a dick."

"Yeah. But he still gives a damn. What about the kids with no one? Who protects them? The whole point of the organization is to *be the someone* coming for the ones the world forgot."

I bristled but kept my mouth shut. Took another sip of coffee, trying to drown the unease. Something like jealousy collided with my irritation. Because while my brother risked his neck to protect strangers, I signed off on marketing plans behind an iron gate. And I had the audacity to be mad at him for it.

"I never meant for this to blow back on you or the kids. Don't forget, my wife was in that car too."

"And Leighton," I snapped. "You owe her an honest fucking explanation."

"The less she knows, the better."

Ten points for the default answer. Classic.

"It's been six weeks. You think Riviera can hold her off forever? She's a Rhodes. We both saw how fast that house of cards fell under one set of their eyes."

His mouth twitched before he locked it down again. "Alice says we're good. Unless you've got new intel…"

I shook my head. No, Leighton hadn't said anything. But I was tired of biting my tongue. And if last night meant half as much to her as it did to me, I wouldn't be holding back much longer.

"Tell her. Or I will."

He smirked like the smug bastard he was. "Why's that?" His eyes narrowed as his grin sharpened. Like a cat scenting blood. "*What are you doing*, Ollie?"

"Drinking coffee with a jackass."

He snorted, a smile turning his cheeks up even as he shook his head. "I've never given you shit for making the rounds, but Leighton isn't some random lay. She's part of the package now. My *wife*. Your kids. Our family. You screw this up, and you don't just lose her. You shake the whole damn tree."

"What the fuck are you talking about?"

"You went home with her. And the Bentley was still gone when I left for my run."

I took another drink to buy time. The coffee burned down my throat, but it gave me something to focus on while we held the staring contest of the century.

"You spent over a year building this team. You've finally got a shot at a Super Bowl. Don't fuck with Paxton's head now that things are working."

"Now we're talking football?"

"He already gets shit for me and Alice. The last thing he needs is more rumors that he's a nepotism pick. He earned his place on that field."

"And he shows it every Sunday."

"The kids love her, Ollie."

"I know."

"Can you really risk her being another person they lose?"

My mouth opened. Nothing came out.

Because he wasn't wrong.

And fuck him for that.

He stood, adjusted his jacket, and headed for the door—but not before pausing to squeeze my shoulder.

"I love you, little brother. But think long and hard before you lose more than you bargained for."

6

The One Where It All Goes To Shit

OLIVER

Paxton Rhodes' bright blue Ford Raptor pulled into Greyson and Alice's driveway about twenty minutes after my brother left me standing like a statue in my office. I eventually gave up on my coffee in favor of a shower. Like if I scrubbed the scent of her off my skin, I might actually be man enough to make the right goddamn decision. Because her scent alone was enough to make me fold.

Asshole.

The irony was, *I'd* confronted *him* after he wrestled Alice into agreeing to marry him. But it wasn't the same. Alice was his direct employee—and she'd fucking hated him.

That wasn't us. Had never been us. Leighton clicked into my life like she'd always been there, a piece I hadn't realized was missing. She became one of my best damn friends. And she was, hands down, the most radiant woman I'd ever seen.

Coming from a guy who grew up around the Emerald Bay model circuit, that was saying something.

But she wasn't like them. No hate to the women who kept our city's cosmetic surgeons busy, but Leighton was their polar opposite —soft in all the right places, with an expressive forehead and a smile that could blind a man. She was just as likely to post a video of her Jeep kicking up desert dust as she was to snap a sun-drenched beach selfie. And I fucking loved it. She breathed life into this house without even trying.

But...

A great deal of that life was the joy she brought my kids. Especially Mattie.

I sat watching my little girl piece together a three-D magnetic puzzle that made my brain hurt just looking at it. I wasn't sure if she'd build rockets or run a company someday, but I knew she'd be brilliant at either. Mostly, I just wanted her to be happy. Healthy. Ideally *now*, not ten years from now when she was unraveling all the damage we'd done through years of bullshit with Carly.

A day that had started on cloud nine had abruptly dropped off a cliff. I felt like Wile E. Coyote in a Roadrunner cartoon—only instead of an anvil, it was my older brother and his ruthless logic.

Leighton didn't strike me as the type who would just walk away from us.

Them.

From *them*, I corrected internally.

But she also did everything at full volume. No halfway. No hedging. It was all or nothing. Which made her addictive as hell. But if I messed this up—if sex was what broke us—would she pull out with the same intensity she'd come in with?

Fuck.

What the hell had I been thinking? *Wrong head, idiot.*

I palmed my face and glanced between Mattie and the Raptor parked across the street.

Clearing my throat, I asked, "Who's in the mood for pancakes?"

"We just ate, Daddy," Mattie replied, not looking up from her puzzle.

"Yeah, but Auntie Alice makes the best syrup—with the butter already melted in. I can make room for one more if you guys wanna crash Saturday brunch."

Her eyes flicked up, narrowing suspiciously. Beau, however, let out a cheerful *yippee* and made a beeline for the front door.

"To Uncle Grey's?"

I nodded. Mattie slowly set down her tiles with surgical precision. Thankfully, her hesitation melted in the foyer. The moment her Converse were tied, she was out the door, racing after her little brother.

"BEAUTIFUL DAY," I noted as I approached Leighton, where she stood on the beach watching the waves behind Greyson's place. After a round of hellos and making sure the kids were happily situated with Alice, I wandered outside to find her. Maybe it was the fisherman's kid in her, but when she was thinking, she was always by the water. Then again, maybe it was just a coast-baby thing. I was the same.

"The best," she agreed, but when she turned to face me, it wasn't joy I saw. It was worry. Fuck, I wanted to kiss it right off her face.

"Not hungry?"

"A little nauseous."

"Yes, well—a gallon of vodka will do that."

She snorted, a genuine smile lighting up her face. "Come on, I wasn't *that* bad."

"No," I said, scoffing as I bumped her elbow with mine. "But I was hoping that look on your face was just a hangover, and not my doing."

"Ollie," she chided, looping her arm through mine. "You're not the cause of my premature grays."

"Grays?" I echoed, eyeing her messy bun, frizz-curls falling over her lightly freckled nose. The breeze tossed one across her cheek, and it took every ounce of restraint not to tuck it behind her ear. I followed her gaze out to the ocean, searching the horizon like maybe some sign would appear to tell me I hadn't just broken everything. Again.

I let the silence stretch too long before finally asking, "Whatcha thinking, Trouble?"

She swallowed. Kept her eyes on the water a beat longer before turning toward me. "I'm thinking you seem...*troubled.*"

"Punny."

"I try." She smiled, then tugged gently on my arm. "Did I mess up? Did I ruin this?"

Fear. That was fear in her eyes.

Without thinking, I cupped her face, bending just enough to meet her gaze. "God, no, Leigh. Takes two to tango, beautiful." I wasn't sure where to start, so I just hedged, "It's not—"

"But it is," she interrupted, easing my hands from her face with practiced grace. Like she already knew what I was going to say. Like she'd seen the wheels turning and was sparing me the burden of voicing it.

"It's fine, Ollie. Really. I didn't expect anything from you. Thanks for...showing me a good time. I had fun."

Knife. Heart.

"Fun?" I scoffed. "You say that like I took you to Disneyland, not—"

"Do me a favor," she said, arching a perfectly skeptical brow, "and save the post-game analysis for Coach Sartori."

"Probably a good plan," I muttered.

If there had ever been a metaphorical elephant in a room, it had never sat so squarely on my chest.

She pursed her lips, rocked on her heels, and then turned to me with a smile I hated—too polished to be real.

"Leigh, you're—"

"Still me," she said quickly. "Are we still...us?"

"Always," I said, ignoring the way the word scraped my throat raw.

One time? I finally got to kiss the girl of my dreams and it was going to be a one-time thing? Fuck. Me.

"We have to be, right?"

"Maybe it'll be easier, now that we got it out of our system?"

I laughed. I couldn't help it. There was no getting Leighton Rhodes out of my system. She lived under my skin. Every breathy laugh and moan burned into my memory.

"Me, you, pizza, tunes with Tillie. Little Beau. Staggering sexual charisma aside, it works, right?"

I laughed harder, even as something inside me cracked. "That aside, yeah. I guess so. Only fools mess with what works."

"Exactly!" she chirped, but I wasn't the only one swallowing around that lump in my throat.

"I meant what I said earlier."

"That only you could give me better orgasms than Obi? You know, I believe that." She elbowed me and I grinned despite myself.

"No. That you were incredible. It wasn't a mistake. I don't regret it. Couldn't."

She nodded, her voice softer now. "But it can't happen again?"

"Right."

"Because the family dynamics would just be..."

"Weird," I supplied.

"Can't have that." She rocked on her heels and held out her pinky. "Zero weirdness."

"*You're* the weirdo. Don't look at *me*."

"Rude."

I laughed and linked my pinky with hers, locking her in. "Is that legally binding, Rhodes?"

"You know it," she said with a huff, letting me wrap an arm around her shoulders as the wind picked up.

"Leigh!" Alice's voice cut across the yard. She and Grey stood side by side in their matching Lululemon, Jax behind them, Beau bouncing on his toes beside Alice. Mattie stood still, hands in her pockets. "You coming?"

"Be right up!" Leighton called, then turned to me with a soft smile. "Wanna take a walk? Alice finally feels good enough to move."

"You want me to hang back?"

"I'd prefer you came."

Maybe. Probably not. But I smiled anyway. "Lead the way, Trouble."

And just like that, I watched the woman I'd dreamed about for months slip through my fingers like sand.

I spent the whole day regretting every word we'd said, bracing myself for her absence.

But I shouldn't have bothered.

Because Monday night, the security system chirped—and before I could mope my way to the front door, Leighton Rhodes had kicked her shoes off and was bouncing barefoot across my foyer, holding two pizzas over her head like a goddamn champion.

"Hi, Ollie," she muttered like an afterthought, already yelling, "Tillie!! Move your cute little ass!"

"*Leighton!*" I scolded.

"Oops. Sorry. Tillie!! Skedaddle your keister! Neon Purgatory's new album dropped and I've waited all damn day to listen with you!"

"Leigh," I warned, even as my grin split wide.

"Right, fuck—darn. I've waited all darn-tootin' day to play it together!"

She hoisted her phone like a boombox, shoved the pizzas into my arms—and Jesus, were her hands made of iron? Those were scalding hot—and marched up the stairs like nothing had changed at all. Like we were still just...us.

Q-FOUR IS ALWAYS A SHIT SHOW, but this year was worse than most. Leighton had, in fact, stopped dropping by for the bulk of November. That—or I'd just been gone too much to see her. Since I hadn't had a face-to-face with my kids in two weeks, the latter felt more likely.

Between holiday campaigns rolling out and final sign-offs on Black Friday launches, end-of-year meetings, charity galas, and next-year goal setting, I'd basically been drinking my calories since Halloween.

Add in our cousin Ellington—acting GM for the *Bombers*—and Coach Sartori waiting on my final okay for mid-season performance reviews, trades, and contracts, and I was cooked. Ellington handled most of it these days, but he still wanted me visible. Which was why I'd been guilted into appearing at this year's Turkey Trot, our annual five-k fundraiser for youth sports.

Come Thanksgiving, I felt about as good as the dead bird Greyson's chef was about to roast.

But I wasn't the only one who looked like death warmed over.

When Leighton opened her door after my third knock, she gave a half-hearted smile before turning and slogging through the loft.

I peeled a scrap of paper off her shirt where it clung with static—some crumpled receipt. "Uh... Hey, Trouble. You okay?"

"Yeah," she yawned, dragging herself toward the coffee machine. "Kaia, Alice, and I were up too late. Didn't get home until two."

"Oh shoot, I didn't realize she was in town already."

"Yep," she said through another yawn. "Maverick gets in this morning."

"Excited to see him. I, uh... figured you'd be ready to go, but you're looking a little—"

The glare she leveled at me shut my mouth on impact. She looked exhausted.

"Nothing a carafe of coffee can't fix," she mumbled, grabbing the carafe and filling it with filtered water, yawning as she did.

"You get *any* sleep?"

"Maybe? Some? I don't know. I just can't seem to feel rested lately."

"You sick?"

"I don't think so. Just... stressed."

"Well. Splash some water on your face and pull yourself together—we have a race to win."

"We?" she asked skeptically, arching a brow.

"Well, *you*. But you get the picture." I, unfortunately, would be manning the registration booth with a few of our more charismatic players. As I watched her nearly fumble the carafe, I stepped forward, bracing a hand against her lower back and swiping the glass from her hand.

"Here. Let me help."

"Mmkay. Thanks, Ols."

"*Ols?*" I chuckled, watching as she rubbed her face with both palms, then gave her cheeks a slap like she could force herself awake. She pulled the coffee canister from the cabinet, but once she returned to the machine, her scowl deepened and she started flinging open drawers.

"Leigh." *Slam.* "Leigh?"

"What?" she snapped, before catching herself. Her eyes shut tightly as she exhaled, then softened. "I'm sorry. I'm... anxious. Stressed. It's fine. You're fine." Gentler this time: "What?"

"What are you looking for?"

"Out of filters."

"Oh," I said, deflating a little as I glanced at the now-full reservoir. "That's alright. Get cleaned up, I'll buy you a sludge cup on the way. My treat."

"It's fine," she muttered, ripping paper towels off the roll and cramming them into a makeshift bowl before pouring the grounds directly on top. All I could think was... bleach. And extra fiber?

"Stop looking at me like that. Why is everyone giving me pity-eyes lately?"

"You just seem a little..." The daggers in her glare had me adjusting course. "...burnt out."

"Not all of us can be Ollie the jolly billionaire," she muttered, and something about the bitterness in her voice made my spine straighten. Leighton had never—not once—thrown my money in my face.

"Hey," I said, stepping in closer, lowering my voice as I met her tired eyes. "What's going on?"

"Nothing. I'm sorry." She pressed her fingers to her sternum, rubbing lightly over that scar I'd kissed like a prayer only a month ago. When her eyes opened again, they were softer. "It's not you. Terrible night. Let me wash it off and we'll start over?"

I wanted to say we didn't need to start over. That I was here if she needed me. But the little nod she gave me was so Alice-coded it shut me up. And just like that, she disappeared down the hall, and I heard the shower turn on.

Yikes.

What the hell happened at work last night?

I turned for the fridge to find her something warm before dragging her downtown—and stopped short.

Empty.

Like, truly empty. An expired tub of vegan yogurt. Half a bottle of creamer. Peanut butter.

I moved to the pantry. Same story. A few slices of plain sourdough, a couple cans of vegetables, an oversized bag of rice, and another of russet potatoes.

Shit.

I toasted the bread and spread some peanut butter across it before grabbing the honey and cinnamon from her spice rack. Then I sprinted out to the Bentley, snagged a couple bananas from my backseat snack stash, and sliced one up to layer on top. I poured her a cup of coffee and set both on the counter.

Trying to play it cool, I poured my own cup and wandered into the living room.

Which was a mistake.

That damn sectional. The same one where I'd first kissed her. Where I'd stripped her bare. Where I'd...

I was so caught up in the memory that I didn't even see what I knocked off the armrest. Bending over, I picked up a small stack of envelopes—and froze.

I'm not usually a nosy fucker, but when the top envelope had a red **FINAL NOTICE** stamp, I tensed.

A credit union. Power bill. Her Visa.

Two of them had red slips inside. Past due.

Confusion buzzed down my spine, followed by something a hell of a lot sharper.

If she was struggling for money... why the hell wouldn't she say anything?

When Leighton reappeared, skin dewy from the shower, hair braided back in two perfect rows, and wrapped in a track suit that would've had me drooling if I weren't so preoccupied wondering what the fuck I'd missed in the last three weeks.

Her eyes flicked from her toast to me, then down to the stack of envelopes in my hand.

Her face paled.

"What the hell are these?"

7

Turkey Trots and Dizzy Thoughts

OLIVER

"What do you mean, what the hell are these?" she snapped as I got to my feet. "You forget how to read, Hart?"

"Right, but they're all overdue." I held the stack out. "What's going on, Leigh? What aren't you telling me?"

"I lost my job after the accident," she said flatly, shrugging like it meant nothing. "I was out for a month, and when I came back, paparazzi followed me to work, trying to get a story. Didn't go over well with the crotch stain that was my manager." Rather than sitting down to eat, she plopped onto the marble floor and tugged on her tennis shoes. "Not sure if you've noticed, but the job market sucks right now. I'm about a day away from selling feet pics. But I'll figure it out."

"You have nice feet," I deadpanned.

"Exactly."

"But, Leigh, why didn't you say something?" I didn't even bother hiding the hurt in my voice. I couldn't.

"I'm not looking for a white knight, Ollie. I got myself this far—I'll get myself out."

Frustration eclipsed my worry, and I closed the distance between us. Greyson caused this. And now he wasn't even keeping tabs? I could kill him for it.

Dropping to one knee in front of her, I shook my head. "You didn't choose to get in that accident. You didn't choose to have a psychopath ransom your sister, pull that trigger, or drive off a goddamn bridge. None of this is your fault."

"No," she agreed softly, tightening her laces as red crept up her throat. "But it's not anyone else's fault, either. Evil people do evil things. Bad things happen to good people." It sounded rehearsed—

like something she'd said a hundred times just to survive it. "It's fine, Ollie. I'll figure it out."

I held up the stack again. "This is figuring it out, Leighton?"

"Ollie, I love you, so I'm not gonna say what I want to say right now. But I am gonna beg you to drop it."

"Yeah, *no*. That won't be happening."

"*Ollie*," she warned as we stood. Hands on hips. Eyes flaring.

"Don't 'Ollie' me, *Trouble*. Why didn't you say anything?"

"Because I don't want your fucking money, Oliver! *That's* why!" Her voice cracked with the emotion I could see she was trying to shove down. "You're beautiful, and you've got a gorgeous heart, and of course you'd wanna swoop in and save the day—but I don't want a fucking dime from you." She huffed, expression twisted somewhere between grief and fury as she tossed a braid over her shoulder. "*And* I knew you'd look at me like *that*."

"Like I'm worried about you?"

"I don't need your pity, Hart."

"And you don't have it, *Rhodes*. You've got my anger. My disappointment. You think between me and Greyson, we don't have enough connections to land you somewhere solid? That we couldn't help you rise above a shitty market?"

"I don't need to cheat my way into a job."

"Cheat?" I choked on the word. "You think I'm offering you some backdoor shortcut? Jesus." I followed her to the door and shut it before she could slip out like we weren't mid-argument. "Listen to me." She turned, glaring. I dropped my hand from the doorknob. "Nobody gets anywhere without help. A hand up. The right meeting at the right time. I'm not trying to be your knight in shining armor —I just want to help. But you have to let me."

"Not all of us are cut out for corporate ladders."

"Fine. You like hospitality? We own a dozen restaurants in the city."

"That feels an awful lot like a handout."

"I've worked in kitchens, Leighton. Dad made us all get jobs in high school to understand what work actually meant. The people in food service are some of the hardest-working people I know."

"Still—"

"Don't want to work for us? *Fine*. I know half the restaurant owners in this city. I can make a call, see who's hiring. But you've got to tell me you're looking. I had no idea. Did you even tell Alice? Paxton?"

Her nose wrinkled. Eyes hardened.

"Jesus Christ. You're so fucking stubborn."

"And this is, frankly, none of your business."

"*You're* my business." The words came out before I could stop them. "Harts take care of their own."

"I'm not a fucking Hart."

"You're *family*." My voice lowered. "If it matters to you, it matters to us."

Her mouth parted slightly, eyes widening like I'd slapped her. But before either of us could speak again, there were footsteps—and the door flew open.

In one panicked motion, I yanked Leighton away from the frame, catching the door with my opposite hand just before it cracked her shoulder.

"Oh fuck—I'm so sorry! You okay?"

My eyes snapped shut at the sound of her brother's voice.

And in walked... a giant inflatable turkey.

Leighton burst out laughing, full-blown jovial now, like our argument hadn't just happened. She wiped every trace of tension from her face in a heartbeat as I stepped aside to let the walking mascot in.

"Oh. Hey, Ollie. Didn't expect to bump into you here," Paxton said from behind the stupid little mesh face window.

"Hey, Rhodes. Just came to drag Leighton's ass to the fundraiser."

"Beat me to it," he laughed, ducking under the threshold. The more I got to know the guy off the field, the more I liked him. He had the same flair for chaos I did. Or used to.

"If it's all the same, I think I'll ride with Pax." She looped her arm through the turkey's and shot me a glare that dared me to challenge her. "We haven't had a lot of time to chat about his season."

"That's fine," I said through a tight smile, trying not to take the bait. "We'll catch up later."

"I'm sure." She squeezed her brother's arm as his face dimmed behind the costume.

"Did I interrupt something?" he asked, voice sharpening with concern.

"Nope. Just our brother-in-law behaving very... brotherly," Leighton chirped.

Brotherly? Oh, absolutely not.

"We're not in-laws," I said, narrowing my eyes.

"Yes, but 'our sister's brother-in-law' is just too wordy, isn't it?" She grinned, twisting the knife. "After all. We're all *family*. Right?"

Should've known that line would bite me in the ass.

Swallowing my irritation, I forced a tight smile. "Right."

"Okay, what did I miss?" Paxton asked, his inflatable head bobbing as he looked between us.

"Nothing, Pax. Let's get out of here." She glared at his tail. "How the fuck did you drive here in that?"

"Dally drove. I rode in the back."

"Dallas is here?" she gasped, whirling for the hallway.

Of course.

My jaw tensed.

Dallas Miller was one of our best receivers and a local media darling. And maybe—*maybe*—if he weren't plastered across every billboard in a twenty-mile radius, I wouldn't want to punt his ass to another city.

Note to self: if there's a trade option for Dallas, make it happen.

As Leighton dragged the oversized turkey through the door, I threw up my hands and barked, "At least take your breakfast with you!"

I WASN'T SO self-absorbed that I took for granted how blessed my life was. There had never been a time I couldn't put food on my table or keep the lights on. I'd never felt that kind of stress. But with a life of privilege came a bit of a god complex—something that sure as hell wasn't helped by the paparazzi following my every move, gossip columns foaming at the mouth for an inside scoop, or the ability to auction off photos with my kids in the name of charity.

The allure of the spotlight wore off sometime during adolescence, before dad started scandalizing our name in the media, but after I'd had my heart broken one too many times by girls who wanted the bank account, not the boyfriend.

So, in some bizarre way, I could admire what Leighton was doing—if only for the selfish reason that she was so determined not to make this about money. Not about my resources. Not about the name.

I wasn't used to that. And if I'm being honest, it irritated the absolute shit out of me.

She'd made her point. So why the hell wouldn't she take the help?

Much to my disappointment, I didn't see her for the entire fundraiser. She and the giant turkey had vanished back into Pax's truck, and I watched her peel out of the parking lot with the windows down, Dallas Miller riding shotgun and AC/DC blaring loud enough to wake the neighbors.

I wasn't particularly accustomed to problems I couldn't fix. Not with time. Not with effort. Not with money. And certainly not with the resources at my disposal.

Problems like my brother endangering our family by bankrolling mercenaries to fight monsters most people didn't even know existed.

Problems like the woman who held my heart in her hands refusing to let me help—even when she so clearly needed it.

Or problems like my goddamn ex-wife stepping into her red Porsche just as I pulled into the driveway, tossing her black-and-white hair over her shoulder with a flirtatious finger wave like she hadn't just declared emotional war by showing up uninvited on Thanksgiving morning.

Fuck. My. Life.

That smug little smile of hers could only mean one thing: I was in for a world of pain when I went inside.

Sure enough, I opened the front door to find Oaklyn—our nanny—standing in the entryway with her duffel in one hand, eyes red, and makeup smudged.

She was wiping at her face as she made for the door.

"I'm so sorry, Mr. Hart. I quit."

"What? *Why?*" It came out as more of a growl. All anger. No confusion. I already knew the answer. But still—I asked. I had to.

As she tried to sidestep me, I gently caught her elbow, lowering my voice. "Oaklyn, you've been doing a great job. What did she say to you?"

"N-*nothing*," she stammered, voice cracking on the word. "I'm just not a good fit for this. Thank you."

"You can't just leave us hanging—at least give me time to find someone else."

"I'm sorry, Mr. Hart." And with that, she slipped out of my grasp and marched straight to her sedan without another word.

The door shut behind her like a period at the end of a brutal sentence.

And the hits just keep on coming.

LEIGHTON

"YOU SURE YOU'RE OKAY, PUNKY?" Paxton asked as we rode the elevator up to my floor. "You're still looking a bit peaky."

Despite waking up on the wrong side of the bed to another "friendly reminder" email about my past-due car payment, I'd thrown on my game face and made the most of the morning. We'd had a great time. I'd had Paxton's back through the entire event, and —if I'm honest—it was pretty damn surreal to stand beside him, snapping photos for eager kids who just wanted a signed print with their favorite quarterback. Who also happened to be *my* favorite big brother.

I'd told Pax and Dallas I was too exhausted to run, but still wanted to help. He'd parked me at the photo op tent at the halfway mark. A win-win—stay out of the sun, and out of range of my nosy not-a-brother-in-law, while still helping the cause.

But around eleven, the ground started tilting under me. My heart fluttered, once, then again. It hadn't acted up in a while, and I took it as a sign to get the hell off my feet.

"Yeah," I finally answered as we reached my floor. "I swear I'm alright."

"Did you get enough water in?" Pax pressed, one hand hovering protectively near my shoulder, like he was ready to catch me.

I batted the big, beautiful, overbearing ass away. "Yes, *Dad*. I drank plenty. It was probably just the heat."

"I'll still feel better once I know you've seen a cardiologist."

Right. *Because those* are just lining up for me right now. With my referral stuck in Anchorage's backlog, it would be months before I got an appointment. Might be faster to fly home and wait another four to six weeks.

"My annual is in February," I hedged. "I promise I'm diligent."

"I know," he muttered as we reached my door. "But aren't you supposed to check in if there are any changes or symptoms?"

"Geez Louise, what is it with the men in my life today?" I muttered under my breath.

Having a major cardiac event as a teenager was traumatic enough. Add eleven siblings, and that trauma came with a never-ending rotation of protectors. The whole family had put their lives on hold during my surgery and rehab. Even now, years later, if I so much as jogged too fast, I got scolded from thirteen directions.

It hadn't helped that we lived in a town small enough for the sheriff to personally swing by and tattle to my parents. It wasn't until I moved to Emerald Bay that I could so much as take a hike without someone catching up "just to check in." I knew it all came from love —but my god, it was suffocating.

"What?" Pax asked.

"Nothing," I sighed as he keyed in the door code and held it open for me. "If any red flags pop up, I promise I'll make a call. It was probably just the sun, and I feel fine now."

Which was only kind of a lie. The sun hadn't been that hot, maybe low eighties. And I'd been wiped all week. The guilt scraped at my insides. Fatigue. Lightheadedness. The same symptoms I'd ignored before the first time.

But cardiology care wasn't cheap—even with insurance—and I didn't have money sitting in the couch cushions. Every job I'd applied to in the last six weeks had ghosted or rejected me outright. Degree or no, experience trumped ambition, and nobody wanted to train someone "just eager to learn."

I knew Pax would help me out if I asked. Hell, he'd cover all my bills and drag me to the damn hospital himself. But I didn't want to turn to him. Didn't want to call my parents or beg someone to bail me out. And I especially didn't want to be another leech in Oliver Hart's life. He deserved someone who didn't look at him and see dollar signs.

At twenty-three, I should be able to pay my own goddamn bills —and that included managing my defective ticker.

I must've been too wrapped up in my own head, because I didn't hear what Paxton said next until he stepped in front of me, blocking my path with his brows furrowed.

"If you need something, you know you can tell me, right?"

"I know," I chirped, turning on the cheer. Everything was fine. My heart was fine. The perfect job was coming any day now, and I'd be right as rain in a matter of a few weeks. At least, that's what I was telling myself as Paxton lowered those concerned Rhodes gray-blues on me.

"I mean it, punky."

"I know you mean it, bubba."

His expression softened immediately at the old nickname. When we were kids, Kaia and I couldn't pronounce "brother" properly, and somehow all six of them became bubba-*something*.

I squished his face between my sweaty palms. "Now let me pass the fuck out for a few hours before dinner and I promise, all will be peachy keen."

"Honestly, a nap sounds great," he muttered, already pulling out his phone. "First time in years I'm not playing today."

Which was code for: *I'm* nervous, so *I'm texting the group chat for backup.* I smirked, watching him type. Probably just tattled to the sibling hivemind.

HART HOUSE WAS absolute chaos by the time we stepped inside that evening, after an hour-long video chat with my mom and the siblings who made it to Florida. The decadent aroma of roasting turkey, stuffing, and cinnamon-spiced *something* embraced me like the warmest hug. Combined with the symphony of laughter and mingling voices, it created the homiest vibe I'd ever felt in this gargantuan museum of a house. Maybe ol' Suit Daddy did have a heart after all.

A broad grin stretched across my face as Kaia's exuberant laughter rang off the walls. People can say whatever they want about twins, but having a built-in best friend—and rival—was the highlight of my childhood. Nobody, and I mean *nobody*, has your back like your literal other half. Something about sharing a womb really cements that sibling loyalty.

I'd just slipped out of my peacoat when the heavy thuds of familiar footfalls had me turning just in time to see my six-foot-four brother bounding toward me like an overenthusiastic Great Dane. Maverick might be the baby of the family, but at two-hundred-and-lord-knows-how-many pounds, I couldn't help but panic as he barreled forward, looking far too eager for my liking.

"There she is!" he boomed in that bass voice that still startled the shit out of me every time he opened his mouth. From the bowels of the house, Chip, Alice's Maltese, began yipping frantically, gradually getting closer.

"Mav, don't you dare!" I screeched, throwing my hands up. Too little, too late. He snatched me off the ground, crushing my arms into useless T-rex limbs between us, and spun us in a full circle, my feet dangling at least eighteen inches off the floor.

"Put me down, you overgrown Labrador! *Jesus Christ.*"

"Not a chance," he growled, squeezing me tighter as he buried his face against my shoulder. "I fucking missed you, beautiful!"

"Can't...breathe," I croaked, wriggling uselessly against his absurd biceps. The yipping grew louder, accompanied by the begrudging chuff that announced their German Shepherd's arrival.

"Mav," Pax drawled from somewhere behind him, dry as ever. "If you break her before dinner, Alice will demand your head."

"He has a point!" came a familiar but delightfully unexpected male baritone, right as I reached to pinch the ever-living shit out of the arm I could get ahold of.

"*Ouch,*" Mav complained, finally setting me down as more footsteps signaled the arrival of another branch of our chaos tree. "Haven't seen you in months and that's the greeting I get?"

Chip was now a furry pogo stick between us—promptly piddling all over the floor.

"Ah man, *gross,*" I groaned, scrambling back as a maid magically materialized with paper towels and disinfectant. I scooped up the overly excitable rescue to prevent another panic pee and burst out laughing when I finally looked up at my "little" brother.

Like Pax, Mav was all Rhodes—towering, warm brown hair, tan skin, and telltale blue eyes. But where Pax was all thoughtful consideration and furrowed focus, Mav was a living dimple with a megawatt smile and boundless energy.

"I see you got properly boa-constrictored," Kaia noted, beaming over her glass of white wine as she closed the distance and threw an arm around my neck with an actually-acceptable level of enthusiasm. "'Bout damn time you got here," she muttered, smacking a sloppy kiss to my cheek before passing me off to Alice.

"Don't listen to her," Alice insisted. "You're right on time."

"Thanks for hosting, sissy."

"Of course."

"And you!" I squeaked, dropping the dog into her waiting arms and whirling to meet the expectant, sparkling brown eyes of her best friend.

Max might've had a decade on me, but that bright smile and open arms felt like a sliver of home—a little piece of Mistyvale, personified. I threw myself into his hug, burying my face in his chest.

"You came!" I squeaked.

"I did, and you look nearly as fabulous as I do tonight, darling."

Max was always—always, without fail, even on rainy days—dressed to the nines. Tonight was no exception.

"Aww, thanks, Maxi."

Before I could say more, Mav demanded, "And what am I, chopped liver?"

"Max just has good taste," I jabbed.

"And *I* would like some credit," Mav said, straightening his tie. Emerald Bay green.

I snorted. "Brown-noser."

"Come on now, I thought it was a nice gesture."

"For Pax, or our hosts?"

"Mmmmm, both," he decided. "But mostly whoever is currently feeding me."

"That would be me," Alice said with a rare full-scale grin.

"Or at least your fancy chef," Mav teased.

"I'll have you know I baked every pie myself."

"And the turkey?" I challenged, narrowing my eyes with a smirk.

"Seasoned via my nose... after Greyson's chef cleaned out all the nasty inside stuff."

"There it is," Max said with a victorious laugh, tugging me along beside him.

"You'll eat it and enjoy it," Alice sniffed.

"Speaking of things we eat and enjoy," Mav cut in, "who the fuck ever decided to eat an egg?"

"What?" Pax balked.

"Come on. It's weird, right? Just plops out their ass with no warning and some Johnny looks at it and goes, 'Looks like breakfast'? Make it make sense."

"How are you still alive?" Paxton jabbed.

Kaia snickered. "Did Mama drop you on your head, and I've just forgotten or…?"

"Oh, piss off," Mav scoffed, exploiting that ridiculous reach to ruffle her hair, sending me into a laughing fit as she swatted him away.

Home. This felt like home.

No wonder I'd been so downtrodden. These were my people. I was never built to fly solo. I wondered, for just a moment, if I could convince Pax to stay with me and Kaia for the winter.

"What the hell are you even on, kid?"

"It's like pineapples," Mav shrugged.

"*Pineapples?*" Alice coughed.

"Well *yeah*—who the hell looked at that spiky little motherfucker and thought—" Maverick's words cut off like a record scratch as the front door opened.

Emmaline.

She slipped inside, shedding her trench to reveal a gorgeous, curve-hugging gold dress that somehow made her blonde hair even blonder. Curls half-pinned, tied with an emerald bow, she looked like a goddamn storybook.

But her bright smile dimmed the instant her eyes landed on the huddle of Rhodes in the foyer.

Maverick went statue-still.

An uncomfortable silence settled between us, as one by one, we all looked between the two of them.

"Evening, everyone," Emmaline said, clearing her throat.

"Happy Thanksgiving!" Alice chirped, clearly trying to cut through the what-the-fuck-was-that still hanging in the air.

"Happy Thanksgiving," Emma echoed woodenly. She'd just come back from college over the summer, and based on the palpable tension between her and Mav…

"Do you two know each other?" I blurted.

"Oh. We're *acquainted*," Emma replied in a tone that said it all. "Met at school."

Before I could demand context, Ollie rounded the corner, looking so unfairly handsome in his perfectly tailored black suit—ridiculous turkey tie and all.

"Hey, Trouble," he said with that crooked smile. "You got a sec?"

8

Fresh Outta Nannies

OLIVER

"Before you go getting all stubborn and digging in your heels, just hear me out." Not my smoothest opening line to a negotiation. In my defense, the day had been long, the house was loud—even behind the study's closed door—and my kids had barely re-composed themselves after Carly 'came to visit them' for Thanksgiving. I needed a goddamn restraining order at this point. As it was, security would no longer be permitting her onto the property. I was so far past sick of her shit, it wasn't funny.

"Thirty seconds," Leigh said with a devilish smile.

Well, someone looked like she was feeling better. Fuck, she looked incredible. Not that I could say that.

"Deal. No interruptions."

"I do believe we've managed an abundance of conversations without arguing."

"Can you just agree to let me get this out?"

"Christ, Ollie," she muttered—but there wasn't any bite in it. Her smile grew as she shook her head. "I can't stay mad at you, jackass. You meant well." She held out an expectant pinky. "I solemnly swear I will hear you out."

Relief whooshed through me. At least for now, our mountain-goat-worthy head-butting seemed resolved. I wrapped my pinky around hers and we shook.

The instant I let her hand go, her brows arched expectantly. I took a breath, trying to figure out how to frame this. What angle gave me the best shot?

"You love my kids. And they love you."

She snorted, leveling me with a playful glare. "That's not news."

"What did I say about interrupting?"

"That stipulation was agreed to when I thought you had a point."

"You're at my house all the time."

"Again—that's not—"

I darted my hand up, pressing my fingers lightly to her lips. Her breath hitched, those steel-blue eyes widened, and her lips parted beneath my touch. My blood roared. I pulled back like I'd been burned, and we both swallowed.

I cleared my throat. "Listen, Trouble, I'm in a pinch. And frankly, I trust you more than anybody else in my life. I mean, my life's a fucking dumpster fire right now. Honestly, I'm just kinda sick of everything and—"

"Ollie," she cut in, softer this time. "*What do you need?* Say the word."

I exhaled. "I'm fresh outta nannies."

"What!?" She practically choked.

"Carly scared off Oaklyn."

She scowled. "What a useless fucking cuntcake. What is her fucking problem, anyway?"

My laugh caught in my throat. "Yeah, well, it's gonna take a bulldog to deal with her shit," I said, dipping my chin in her direction. If Leighton could handle Greyson fucking Hart, Carly didn't stand a chance.

"I mean, she lasted longer than I thought she would and—oh. Oh." Leigh stepped back, brain catching up. "Ollie, I…"

"Need a job," I finished. "One that doesn't make you work twice as hard to barely scrape by. And *I* need someone I won't have to replace in three months. Someone who can handle overnights when I travel, unpredictable hours, who won't drive me up a wall on family trips. Someone I trust to get the kids to practices, therapy, classes—without me picking my cuticles bloody from anxiety. Honestly, you'd be doing me a colossal favor."

"Ollie, I don't have any childcare experience."

I huffed a humorless laugh. "Leighton, I'm not looking for a degree—I'm looking for someone who will love my kids the way they deserve. And it certainly helps that they're both head over heels for you. Plus, you're the only one who can keep Carly from running off the next poor soul I hire. Between the two of you, my money's on you every time."

She bit her lip, brows drawn. "Ollie—"

"The pay's decent. But honestly, name your price. I'd sign the check, even if it was highway robbery."

"Okay, hold up." She hiked a thumb over her shoulder, cocking a hip. "This morning, I tell you I don't want your money. That I'll figure it out. And now you're going all *Prince Phillip* charging the gates? I'm not in a coma, Ollie—I meant what I said."

Shit. Treading dangerously close to disaster here.

I shook my head. "We're not talking about a handout. You made your point—perfectly. But you'd be amazed what you could accomplish if you just accepted a little help."

"'You' and 'help' in the same sentence is a natural oxymoron."

"So is 'self-made man,' but that's not the point."

"Then what is the point? Because you're threatening my appetite and that's dangerous business when Alice has spent all day—"

"I'm offering you an honest-to-god nine-to-five—well, seven-thirty to seven. Plus some weekends. And travel. And you're pretty much always on call, but... same difference."

"You're fucking serious?"

"As a heart attack."

Her eyes narrowed. Whoops. Poor word choice.

"Listen, Trouble. I just need them with someone I trust. And the list is short."

"How short?" she asked, her voice uncharacteristically soft.

I flashed her a crooked smile. The one that got me invited back into more houses than I cared to admit. "*One candidate* short."

"I don't know what to say."

"Yes. 'Yes' would make my life infinitely better."

She chewed on her lower lip. I stuffed my hands in my pockets to keep from reaching out and freeing it. "Didn't Oaklyn live with you?"

"You can have her old room. I don't need help cleaning or anything. I won't bug you during off hours—"

She shook her head, and my stomach sank.

"Ollie, I'm sorry. But I can't work for you. Let alone *live* with you."

My shoulders sagged. "Why the hell not?"

She arched a brow. "I think you're perfectly capable of answering that question."

"I swear to be a perfect gentleman."

"It's not you I'm worried about." She sighed. "Seeing you every day, being under the same roof, taking care of sick kids, bumping into each other at events... It's a terrible, horrible, very bad, no good idea."

"Name one person better suited to care for them."

Leighton scowled, like the concept insulted her.

"*See?* I rest my case. You're the logical answer. You need a steady job, and I need—well *Mary Poppins*. But shy of a magical bag and flying umbrella, you're the closest embodiment. Hell, even your objections come in the form of children's stories."

"Hazards of a big family." She bobbed her head, and I resisted the need to laugh.

"Regardless."

"Okay, I—"

"What? Wait, are you saying yes?"

"*No*. Not yet," she cut me off, narrowing her eyes in suspicion.

"*Yet* is good. I can work with yet. Now, what's your concern?"

"Ollie…" she chastised, like I should already understand. "Even if I felt qualified—*which I don't*—I cannot in good conscience live with you."

"I don't follow."

She laughed—the sound light and glittering like an entirely different person than the woman digging in her heels this morning. She felt like *my* Leighton. I couldn't help the smile that pulled at my lips.

"Look, this whole 'friend' thing is a stretch for me on my best days. A girl can only show so much restraint."

I was suddenly incredibly relieved that I'd lucked out being born into a featherless species, because if I had, I would absolutely be preening.

"Don't look at me like that," she demanded, shoving a hand against my chest. Yep. Definitely preening.

"Like what?"

"Like you wanna jump my bones."

"Leigh, just because our circumstances aren't conducive to continuing where we left off… don't kid yourself into thinking I don't dream about it on a daily basis."

"*Daily?*" Her eyes sparkled.

"Daily."

"See? This—I—you—*we*—"

"Very good," I teased. "That was almost sentence-adjacent."

She narrowed her eyes as I parroted her words from Halloween. With a flustered huff that painted her cheeks pink, she snapped, "It's not conducive to the whole 'come work for me' debacle, and it's entirely reinforcing that under absolutely no circumstances can I sleep under the same roof as the man with my v-card in his wallet and a smile like *that*." She gestured violently toward my face. "Do you have any idea what ovulation does to a woman's common sense?"

I just grinned wider. "Okay. So. What if you keep your condo?"

"What do you mean? How the hell would that work?"

"It'd make for longer days. I leave for work around seven-thirty —eight at the latest. If you can be there by seven-fifteen, I don't see a problem. I'll increase your salary to account for rent."

"First of all, that's wildly unnecessary. And… purely hypothetical here, what would that—again, *entirely hypothetical*—salary be?"

"I had Oaklyn at a hundred and sixty thousand a year, paid monthly, plus benefits."

"Are you fucking kidding me?" she squeaked, her eyes practically bugging out.

Glowering, I shook my head. "I am not kidding you. I'll adjust to account for housing, of course, but if you need more—"

She slapped a palm over my mouth, eyes wild. I stared at her in surprise. The woman had brass most men couldn't even fathom. It was fucking adorable.

"Ollie, are you high?" she hissed, looking more terrified than thrilled—not exactly the reaction you expect when offering someone a six-figure salary. "You're offering to pay me *six fucking figures* to take care of two of the coolest kids on the planet?! Have you lost your mind?"

I peeled her hand off, tracing my thumb over her knuckles as I asked, "Is that a yes?"

"That's way too much! I already told you I don't want your money, and this feels an awful lot like you trying to fix my problems."

I scowled. "On the contrary, that's the going rate in this neighborhood."

"*Seriously?*"

"Ellington pays his nanny more. Granted, his kids are feral."

"Holy *Hawkeye*." She stared at me, like she was waiting for a punchline. "Shit. What the hell does Carly do to these nannies?"

"Steadily destroys their self-esteem. Paints them as the villains to the kids."

"Good luck," she muttered. "Carly could kick me in the shins daily and, for thirteen grand a month, I'd smile while she did it."

"Jesus, Trouble—*wait*. Are you saying yes?"

"I don't know. I've never—but this is—*you are*—the *kids* are amazing and—umm." She jammed her eyes closed and sucked in a deep breath, releasing it slow and steady. I kept thumbing soft circles across the back of her hand, relishing the stolen contact. Finally, she whispered, "This isn't charity?"

"Fuck no, Leighton. You're the only person I thought of when Oaklyn walked out. The only woman I'd trust to handle not just my kids, but their psychotic mother."

"I make no promises to leave her face intact."

"I have attorneys on retainer."

"No need. My brothers taught me how to get someone to swing first."

I shrugged. "Self-defense is a viable argument."

She laughed but dropped her gaze, chewing her lip. I stayed quiet. Greyson's strategy. Sometimes silence did more than words. And sure enough, when she looked up again, her walls were down.

She blew out a breath. "I keep my condo."

"Done."

"You're *not* paying me extra for housing. That concept makes me vomit in my mouth, and Greyson already paid off Alice's mortgage, so..."

"Valid point."

"We keep things perfectly professional."

Rule number one of sales: clarifying questions are a good sign. Means the pitch is working. She could hit me with as many as she wanted. I'd take 'em all.

"Find me a Bible and I'll put my hand on it."

"And you treat me like any other employee. No weird strings." She waggled her fingers in my direction.

"I'll henceforth pretend you've never seen me naked."

"Ollie!" she barked, glancing at the doors.

Chuckling, I held up a hand. "Sorry. One last joke. For old times' sake."

"You're a menace."

"Yes, I am. But I'll behave—if you agree."

"And the sky is green."

"I mean it. I'll follow your lead. Your rules."

"No more naked jokes?"

"Fine."

"No tattling to my siblings about my prior predicament. Or any future hypothetical personal things you learn from being around me."

"I'm no fink."

"No giving me special treatment just because I'm—well, because I'm me. If I suck at this, you call me out. If I cross a line—"

"You won't."

"But if I do."

"I'll be the first to tell you. Well, or Mattie will."

I wasn't even sure she realized she was still holding my hand. But then she squeezed it, and said—abruptly, like ripping off a Band-Aid—"Okay."

My heart stuttered. "Is that... Was that a yes?"

She pressed her fingers to her mouth and turned toward the window—presumably facing my house across the street. From the other side of the doors, the sounds of kids running and laughter filtered in.

I waited.

Finally, she turned back to me with a grin that could have lit the whole block. She nodded once. "Yeah. Yeah, I think it was."

9

In Mint Condition
LEIGHTON

The Fam Damily:

KAIA

Today's the day gif

ALICE

Go Bombers!

LEIGHTON

Go Pax! We'll be cheering for you!

MAVERICK

So bummed I had to leave. Kick some ass, Pax Man.

RHYETT

Look who's talking. Congrats on the win yesterday, Mav. Your final catch of the game was fucking phenomenal.

BREXLEY

Agreed. My friend Josie says you've got crazy potential.

JAMESON

Talent scout?

BREXLEY

Literary agent.

JAMESON

thinking face emoji

BREXLEY

Squint all you want, but she won a pretty penny betting
Pax would be a first-round draft pick when he was a
FRESHMAN. She's got the eye.

AXEL

All this excellence is making me nauseous.

LEIGHTON

LMAO I love you, too, Axe.

AXEL

Good. Somebody has to.

KAIA

Finally figure out there's no long-term gratification in
one-night stands, man-whore?

MAVERICK

Ohhhh! Shots fired.

HADLEE

eyeball emojis

AXEL

Charge your batteries, Kai. Your sexual frustration is
showing.

JAMESON

Play nice, kids.

NOEL

Eating popcorn gif

KAIA

My frustration is due to the need to wear a hazmat suit
to your house.

AXEL

You're not even on the island anymore, wtf do you
care?

KAIA

The knowledge of the bleach required to sanitize when
I come back is plenty distressing. I'm worried I'll get an
STD by proxy.

AXEL

Mama raised gentlemen. I wrap it up every single time.

JAMESON

What is it with you people and using the family thread
for this shit?

AXEL

Not all of us go to therapy, Jameson.

KAIA

And it shows.

JAMESON

Stop making your problems all of our problems.

AXEL

Kaia started it.

FINN

I never know wtf I'm gonna open this thread to.

SNICKERING, I tucked my cell into my pocket and straightened to check my reflection in the mirror, tightening my half-ponytail before clipping in an Emerald Bay bow. In the week since Ollie and I officially signed on the dotted line, we'd broken the news to two—mercifully elated—kids, and I'd gotten the full rundown on the house, security protocols, the panic room, and a long-ass list of routines and classes.

And honestly? It was fucking awesome.

I'd been more than a little hesitant when Ollie pitched the idea at Thanksgiving—so much so, I'd called Mom to hash out the pros and cons. Maybe her advice would've differed if she'd known about Halloween, but the truth was, this job was a goddamn miracle. I loved Mattie and Beau to the depth of my soul, and Ollie wasn't half bad either, when he wasn't sticking his perfect nose into my fuckups. In the seven weeks since Chad—the human-shaped yeast infection—canned me, I'd depleted the last of my savings, maxed out a credit card, and found out I was medically disqualified from donating plasma for grocery money. As if being rejected from the few interviews I'd actually landed wasn't humiliating enough, now not even my bodily fluids were deemed 'qualified.'

'Stressed' didn't even begin to cover it.

But Ollie handed me a check for my first month the moment I poured my coffee in his kitchen Monday morning.

Twenty minutes after I got home that evening, a knock at the door revealed a man with very little hair, many, many freckles, and the too-confident smile of someone in on a secret. He held out a sleek black box wrapped in a red satin ribbon, and a jaw-droppingly gorgeous bouquet of asters and morning glories.

Scowling, I asked, "What's this?"

"Couldn't tell ya," he replied with a shrug that screamed bull-shit. "Mr. Hart said to personally see that it was delivered."

Nothing about him radiated innocence, but the glint in his eye had me glowering between the outstretched offering and his sparkly face. I arched a speculative brow.

"Can you hang onto those?" I asked, nodding to the flowers as I slid the box off his palm.

"You got it," he said, craning his neck slightly as I peeled open the lid.

My mouth popped open.

"Holy shit." It came out as a breath, a prayer, a reverent sigh of a decade-long obsession.

Hard plastic CGC slab. Legit Marvel logo.

"Holy shit."

Nine-point-eight grade.

"Oh my fuck."

The delivery man might've chuckled, but I was too busy drooling over the contents. *Winter Soldier #1.* Vivid colors. My man front and center, rifle in hand, that iconic silver arm gleaming.

Oh, fuck me sideways in a cast-iron skillet—that was a first edition.

Eyes wide as saucers, I whispered, "Holy shit, this is the Dell'Otto Variant."

"Yeah, it is," Freckles replied smugly. "Oliver had us all in a tizzy over the weekend."

"That bastard."

"There's a note…"

But I was already grabbing the card tucked between the bright purple and blue bouquet.

To my favorite superhero,
Thank you for saving my skin.
Enjoy yourself.
OO
—Ollie

"UNLESS YOU'RE PULLING a *Meg Ryan, it seems like you enjoyed yourself," Ollie had muttered, that lazy, self-satisfied grin slung across his face like sin. Like some love-drunk idiot, I'd just thanked him when he expertly deliv-ered my first-ever second orgasm—with his mouth. For the love of all things holy, I wasn't sure what the hell I'd waited so long for, because sweet baby Jesus, I was in heaven. Skin buzzing, mind spinning, I felt high. Like 'accidentally stumbled onto Alice's special brownies' high.*

"You're really fucking good at that," I panted into the crook of my arm, still sprawled across the couch where he'd pinned me. Didn't even care. That man was a goddamn gift to womankind.

"Oh, beautiful girl, you haven't seen anything yet."

"Madam?" The freckled tall guy was still standing there, watching me expectantly.

Blinking the memory away, I looked down at the card still in my hand. "I'm sorry?"

"Are you alright, ma'am?"

"Um," I croaked, clearing my throat. "Yes. Fine. Thank you."

But I wasn't fine.

He'd sent me a bouquet of my birth flowers and a collector's edition of my favorite comic book. All in the name of doting on his two amazing kids.

My "are you kidding me" text had gotten a saluting *Captain America* gif in return. No explanation.

How the hell was I supposed to look at him after *that?*

Luckily, I didn't have to. Ollie barely had time for a hello and a wink Tuesday morning. Same on Wednesday. And Thursday.

By Friday, the kids and I had found a rhythm. Every morning started with giggles from Beau, and every afternoon ended with Tillie dishing tea fresh out of junior high like it was a sacred duty.

Saturday passed in a fatigued blur—I became one with my couch and read a full Madison Bellevue novel in a single sitting.

And today? Today was the big day. Game day. And—lucky bitch that I was—I would be sitting in the owner's suite, beside a certain bloom-bestowing billionaire.

Naturally, I'd exfoliated, scrubbed, polished, and painted every square inch of applicable skin. My curls had been creamed, plopped, scrunched, and diffused until they poured over my shoulders like a lion's mane. I felt... *hot*. Beautiful, even.

All for *appearances*, obviously. The Harts had a reputation to uphold.

I repeated that lie the entire drive to the stadium, through security, up the elevator, and down the hall to the Hart family suite.

I was still repeating it when I walked through the door—until I saw *that* smile.

It aimed right at me from across the room where Ollie was mid-conversation with some guy in a suit, and I swear to God, I forgot how to breathe.

He turned fully, said something to the man, then crossed the suite with that lazy, cocksure stride and *those* fucking hands buried in his pockets.

"Hey, Trouble. You look beautiful."

I shrugged, like I hadn't spent four hours getting ready to hear those three little words. "Thanks. Not so bad yourself."

"How was your Saturday?"

"Mellow. Full hermit. You?"

"A hermit day sounds fucking perfect. I can't wait to get through the holidays. The kids are good. We hit the tree lighting last night. Beau loved it."

"But Tillie didn't," I deduced.

"She likes the lights, but the crowd is…"

"A lot," we finished in unison.

He smiled wider. I didn't stand a fucking chance.

"So. We need to talk."

He deadpanned. "If you quit right now, I might fling myself off the balcony."

"Jesus Christ," I laughed. "About the comic book, Oliver."

"Oh." That grin of his tightened, smug and satisfied. "Pretty cool, right?"

"Are you kidding me? It's a first printing, in mint condition. Do you have any idea how rare those are? How the hell did you even find it?"

His grin broadened. "So you liked it."

"Liked it?" I scoffed. "It's amazing. It's also way too much."

"My first pick was *Tales of Suspense #52*."

"Oliver!" I smacked his shoulder, eyes wide. Two servers actually startled. "That's a 1964. You can buy a car for less!"

He laughed. "You can thank Alice for vetoing."

I tongued a molar, trying to collect myself. "You're insane."

"Maybe," he agreed, that slow, creeping smile returning—and taking my self-control with it. "You, uh… you look beautiful today."

I rolled my lower lip between my teeth and replied, "You said that already."

"Yeah, I did," he agreed quickly, oozing that confidence every socialite knew him for. "But you look damn good in Bomber green."

"How fortunate for me."

"Fortunate for *you*? Try for me. My eyes should pay you royalties."

"Royalties? For what?" I laughed, brushing my hair back over my shoulder.

"For every time I'll think of you when—" A thunderous clang sliced through whatever salacious declaration Ollie was in the middle of. My heart slammed against my ribs as glass shattered behind us.

I instinctively clutched his arm for balance as every head turned toward the source of the noise. A grimacing server stood frozen, a silver tray at her feet, drinks soaking into the plush carpet and shards of glass scattered like confetti.

Kaia and Alice were by her side in seconds, helping to mop up the spill and sweep away the debris with napkins and composure. Greyson arrived a breath later, tugging Alice gently away and waving in more staff to assist. I was fairly convinced the man would carry my sister everywhere if he had his way—her feet never permitted to touch the ground again.

But my pulse was a roar in my ears, the whoosh of blood sounding far too much like the lapping water from that night.

"You okay?" Ollie breathed, suddenly so close I could feel his words skate along my cheekbone.

Blinking, I nodded, trying to center myself as I scanned the room.

Then I saw her—Tillie. Statue-still. Wide-eyed. Staring at the floor like she was reliving something in real-time.

"Ollie," I whispered, jerking my chin toward her.

Tillie didn't talk about the car wreck. At least not with me. I knew Ollie had her in therapy once a week, but as we moved toward her, I wondered if it was enough.

"Hey, sweetie," I murmured, placing myself between her and the room. "You okay?"

Those shrink-wrapped blue eyes—flecked with gold—lifted to mine. Her mouth parted, but no sound came. Then her little hand jerked out to grab mine, and I swore my heart cracked right down the middle.

"*Sweet baby*," I whispered, lowering my head to kiss the top of hers. She melted into my chest, her little arms locking around my waist. I held onto her as she stiffly did the same, my gaze landing on Ollie, where his features were carved in concern.

Tillie's little chest shifted at hummingbird speed, and I grimaced. Fuck, I knew that feeling.

"She's okay," I told him—told both of us—as I ran my hand over her back. Her tears soaked into my shirt, each drop a blade to the heart.

Ollie mouthed, *Is she crying?* When I nodded, he shifted to shield her from view, one steady hand rubbing slow circles down her spine. "Babygirl, you're okay," he murmured.

Tillie shook her head against me, her little fingers curling tighter in my sweater. "She's okay," I repeated, pressing my cheek to her curls. "I know it doesn't always feel like it, but you are."

"I... think I'm dying," she squeaked.

"Look at me, punkin," I said gently, but firmly. Her fists only gripped harder. "Tillie. Look at me." When she finally lifted her gaze, tears streaming, I tugged my sleeve over my palm and used it to dab her cheeks. "Did the glass startle you?" A tiny nod. "Did it make you think about the accident?" Another nod. More tears.

Fuck. The stadium. The crowd. The sound. It was too *much.* Too soon. We'd been on our way home from one of Paxton's games when it happened. The lapping of water, the crunch of glass...

"I've got you, okay? I'm right here. And your daddy's right here, too. He's not going anywhere, isn't that right?"

"You got it, sweet pea," Ollie added softly. "Anything you need."

Another jerky nod.

"Okay," I said. "Now let's breathe together. Hand on my chest. Can you feel that?" She nodded again. "In for four, out for four, okay?" I waited until she gave the smallest dip of her chin.

But when I started the breath, her lip wobbled and she whimpered, "I can't."

"You *can.* Just focus on me. Just me. Ready?" She nodded. "In, two, three, four. Hold. Out, two, three, four."

We did it together. Twice. Then again.

And by the fifth breath, something in her began to settle. The storm behind her eyes started to calm.

"You're..." she sniffled, then blew out a breath like we'd practiced. "You're really good at that."

I chuckled, brushing a thumb under her eye. "Had some practice." I met Ollie's gaze. "Can your daddy hold you now, sweetie?"

"Don't leave," she blurted, eyes wide with panic.

I shook my head. "I'm like glitter, baby. You're stuck with me. But he looks like he needs a hug, too."

A tiny smile flickered across her mouth as she turned and let Ollie pull her against his chest. His eyes found mine again, raw and grateful. "Thank you," he mouthed.

I nodded.

He looked down at his daughter—safe but shaken in his arms—and then back at me. Helpless. He couldn't fix this. Couldn't magic it away. And it was killing him.

"I want to go home," Tillie whispered.

"Baby, kickoff is in a few minutes," Ollie said gently, but his voice caught.

"I want to go home," she repeated, her eyes lifting to mine this time.

"Okay," I said immediately, nodding. Ollie's gaze darted between me and the man he'd been talking to earlier. Panic, guilt, frustration—it was all there.

The media might glorify and romanticize the Hart name, but they never saw this. They never saw a father stuck between duty and the daughter who needed him more than anything.

"We'll go," I told him, watching Matilda press herself into my side. "I've got her."

"Leigh…" His voice broke. "The game."

"It's just a game. I love my brother, but I've been watching him and his stinky socks play since I could walk." I rocked Tillie gently. "We've got a blanket fort waiting for us at home."

"Really?" she whispered, eyes shining.

"With twinkle lights," I promised. "And *Lord of the Rings*. And chocolate ice cream."

"You're just appeasing me."

I grinned. Sometimes she sounded like a seventy-five-year-old retiree who'd lived through five wars. "What if I told you this noise totally blows and I'd rather hang out with you anyway?"

She studied me for a long beat, then nodded. "Really?"

"Really, really. Want me to scoop up Beau?" I asked Ollie, who glanced toward where his son sat happily on Kaia's shoulders.

"Nah, he looks content. Take Reynolds with you, and text me when you're home."

"Of course."

"Can we…" Tillie's voice dropped to a whisper. "Can we take the long way home?"

Translation: *Don't drive over that fucking bridge.*

"You got it."

Just as we turned to leave, Ollie's hand closed around mine. That familiar zing raced up my arm. I turned back, and his eyes locked on mine—tortured, conflicted, soft.

"Thank you."

10

Mean Brains and Viggo Mortensen

LEIGHTON

MOM

Awe, poor thing. I'm proud of you, baby. You're doing great. I'll record the game for you, and you can watch it when you come home for Christmas.

LEIGHTON

What do I tell her?

MOM

I think you said all the right things. Let her open up on her terms, and you'll know what to say.

LEIGHTON

Thanks Mama.

MOM

Text me when you're safe at Ollie's please.

LEIGHTON

You got it.

One exhaustingly long, precariously quiet drive home, an extensive text exchange with my mom, and a rather elaborate fort later, I found myself lying on a floor bed made entirely of pillows and Mattie's favorite blankets, looking up at Viggo Mortensen and his luscious hair and general ass-kickery. I passed the popcorn to my feisty little companion and found her staring up at the enormous television with a little smirk on her face.

"What?" I asked, curiosity getting the better of me.

"Did you know he broke his toes kicking a helmet?"

"What?" I nearly choked—thank God I didn't have a mouthful of popcorn, or I would've died.

"Yep," she said matter-of-factly. "In *The Two Towers*, Aragorn's scream after kicking the orc helmet wasn't acting. He broke his toes, and Peter Jackson kept the take because it felt authentic."

I blinked, smirking down at her before glancing back up at the man in question. "So… he method acted his way right into a hospital?"

"*That's* commitment," she said sagely, hearts basically pulsing in her eyes as she dreamily stared at the screen. *Same, girlfriend. Same.*

"Leighton?" I popped my head out of the tent to see a looming Jax Reynolds leaning in the archway to the foyer. The man was easily six-three, broad-shouldered, and had that whole blond bad boy vibe going. One of Greyson's Navy buddies, and seemingly allergic to tying his motorcycle boots. He wore a leather jacket, hair still damp from walking the perimeter in the rain—paranoid, as always. Jax had been behind the wheel when those psychos opened fire. He'd needed surgery and a terrifying number of transfusions. The fact that he was standing there, casually checking in, was a freaking miracle.

"You good?" he asked.

"Yeah, thanks, Jax."

"Of course. The guys are briefed. Everything looks good on my end. Need anything before I head back to the stadium?"

"I think we're good." I shook my head and glanced at Tillie… who was now pink in the cheeks and definitely struggling to hold still.

I elbowed her. "Hey. What was that? You got all squirrelly."

"Uhhhhhg," she groaned dramatically, burying her face in her hands.

"What?" I smirked.

"I just like them when they're wet and angry."

"What!?" I barked, bursting out laughing.

"Captain Reynolds. His shaggy hair, all wet like that. It makes me… *mmmmm.*"

"Did you just purr?"

"Humans don't purr," she condescended.

"Sounded like a purr."

"I didn't purr. I'm not a cat. I just… like looking at him."

"Well… sure, but he's got nothing on Viggo."

"No man does," she declared, like it was gospel.

Oh, Ollie was so fucking hosed with this one. I couldn't be sure, but I was pretty certain I didn't even notice boys until I was fifteen—

and even then, I definitely didn't have opinions about their hair or moisture levels.

"Did you know Sean Bean was afraid of helicopters?" she asked suddenly, switching topics with the whiplash speed of a ten-year-old. I shook my head. She nodded, dead serious. "Yeah. He hiked up the mountains in full costume while everyone else flew."

"What?"

"Yep."

"Wait a damn second. Like… in his armor? All that chainmail?"

I stared at her profile to check if she was messing with me, which is how I caught the eye roll as she flicked her gaze toward me. "He had to leave two hours earlier than everyone else."

I snorted, glancing back at the screen to process that little nugget. "That is absolutely the most Boromir shit I've ever heard."

"I know, right?"

After learning that Orlando Bloom broke a rib falling off a horse and nearly drowned in his armor, I finally went for the elephant in the room. "You feeling better, sweetie?"

"Yeah. I'm okay."

"Good. You know you can talk to me about anything, right?"

"Yeah. Daddy takes me to Dr. Christner, though."

"I know," I said, shrugging, but turning back to the film when she squirmed uncomfortably. "But sometimes it's nice to talk to someone just because they love us."

"You love me."

"Very much, yes."

"Hmm." She sat in contemplative silence for a beat. "Sometimes finding the right words is hard for me."

"That, I understand. Believe me."

"Yeah. Like tonight. That wasn't fun."

"No," I agreed. "It didn't seem very fun."

"My brain acted like I wasn't safe. Even though we were."

"Sometimes, when traumatic things happen, our brains can be mean, and hang onto it—even after it's over. They don't always know how to let go." Talking to Tillie was like balancing on a tightrope. One minute, she was thirty. The next, she was a snuggly little sweet potato. I never knew which version I'd get.

"Yeah," she said quietly. "You and Daddy made sure nobody could see me cry. I liked that."

"We've got your back, sweet pea."

"Sometimes, I wish you were my mom instead of Carly."

If my heart could've grown wings, it would've launched itself off a cliff right then. As it was, it lodged squarely in my throat.

Oh, sweet baby.

"We make pretty good friends though, right?"

"Right." She nodded and grabbed a handful of popcorn, stuffing it in her mouth like that settled the matter.

"Sooo… I have an idea for tomorrow and I want to run it by you."

"Okay," she mumbled around her snack.

"Have you ever had a worry jar?"

"A wha'?" she asked, then rushed to swallow.

"A worry jar. You decorate it to match your room, and when you're feeling something big—like tonight—you write it down, put it in the jar, and seal the lid."

"What does that do?" she asked, skeptical.

"I think writing our fears out helps us process them. And then sealing them in the jar is like… giving them to God. They're not your problem anymore."

"I'm not certain I believe in God."

"Well. The Universe, then."

"I give my fear to the universe?" she asked flatly.

"Yep," I said with a sage nod. "You can't worry about it anymore—it's the universe's problem now."

"Hmm…"

"Wanna try it? It might help, you never know."

She paused the movie and raised a skeptical brow. "*You* want me to try it?"

Grinning at her emphasis, I nodded. When she harrumphed, I had to bite my cheek.

"Fine."

"You're appeasing me," I accused.

"Yes," she agreed, then looked at me like I was a circus act when I burst out laughing.

"It just doesn't seem scientifically—"

I ruffled her hair and gave her a light shove, laughing harder when she broke into giggles. "Oh, cut it out and hit play so we can get to the door scene."

Still giggling, she breathed, "Legendary."

"Agreed."

"But that's in the next movie."

"Damn."

I WOKE UP, dazed and confused, still in the blanket fort, my hand automatically drifting to Ollie's cheek, where he was illuminated by the twinkle lights and looking at me like I'd hung the freaking moon.

"Hey, Trouble."

Blinking, I pulled away from his neatly stubbled face as I realized what I was doing. "Sorry."

"Don't be," he said, that gentle smile growing. "Not gonna lie, I'm just glad that's your reaction to waking up to my ugly mug."

"*Ugly mug*," I scoffed, sitting up and blinking as the world tilted around me, stars glittering in my vision. Whoops. Must've moved faster than I realized. I blinked again to clear them, catching the way Ollie canted his head.

"You okay?"

"Yeah," I said, yawning. "Just sleepy. Where's Tillie?"

"I tucked her into her bed. Debated letting you sleep, but figured you'd lose circulation in your arm if I left you there."

"Mmm," I hummed, slowly stretching my arms and neck. He was right, of course—I'd had it propped under my head like a pillow, and the joint was annoyingly tight.

"You two were pretty cute, all cuddled up in there. Didn't wanna disturb either of you, but I figured you'd kick my ass if I left you on the floor."

"Eh." I shrugged. "I don't mind. She did great, by the way. We're going to decorate a worry jar after school tomorrow—today?"

"Today," he confirmed with a grimace.

"Thank you, Leigh. I don't know what I would've done without you tonight."

"Figured it out, like you always do."

"Maybe. But I don't think so. She would've had to sit through three hours of that chaos feeling that low, and… yikes."

"You would've figured it out."

"Maybe."

"You know," I said with a pointed look as he extended a hand to help me up, "she's gonna be trouble."

"What?" he asked, pulling me to my feet. I accepted the steadying grip and absolutely did not get butterflies at the simple contact.

"She's already got a thing for Viggo."

"Oh." He chuckled, smirk growing as he shook his head. "And Orlando, the boy wonder. I knew I was screwed when she swooned over Zac Efron at age eight. Tried to marry a boy in kindergarten."

That made me laugh, a hand covering my mouth as I yawned. "*And* Captain Reynolds."

"What?" he asked in disbelief, eyes going wide.

"Oh yes. He walked the perimeter in the rain tonight, came back drenched—pretty sure they'll have to slice that leather jacket off him—and she was beside herself."

"Awe, man. I liked him, too."

"Yep. Said she likes when 'they're wet and angry.'"

He threw his head back, one hand flying to cover his heart like I'd mortally wounded him. "Dammit. I thought I had years before this shit."

"Maybe she'll lose interest between now and high school." I straightened my skirt and snatched my discarded bow off the coffee table as Ollie wandered toward the foyer.

"God, a man can only hope," he muttered. "How do we get her into the cootie phase? I thought I got one of those."

"Nope. Straight to noticing long hair, sharp jaws, and strong hands."

"God has a cruel sense of humor."

"Apparently."

"And you?"

"What about me?" I laughed as we rounded the corner, and he handed me a combat boot to yank on. "I'm a little past the cooties, Ollie."

He snickered. "Did you like Jax bulging out of his jacket too?"

"The man certainly knows how to occupy a space," I said earnestly, accepting my second shoe. "A little hairy, a little too macho for my taste. Besides, he's blond."

"Prefer gingers?"

I smirked at the bait, shaking my head. "Always been a brunette girl, myself."

Ollie hummed thoughtfully. He tried to keep his face impassive, but I could swear his shoulders sagged in relief. My cue to leave. This balance beam between 'professionally platonic' and 'whatever-we-almost-were' was precarious at best.

"Have you considered self-defense for Tillie?" I asked, pivoting in the most awkward segue since the girl in question. "It might empower her—give her back some sense of control."

But when I straightened, the world tilted, stars swirling, and—sweet baby Jesus—maybe Pax was right and I should call my doctor back home. Feeling a little nauseous, I set my hand on the front door and sucked down a slow breath.

"Leigh?" Ollie stepped into my space, brows pinched. "You sure you're okay?"

"Yeah. Just… lightheaded, apparently."

"Still?"

"What do you mean?" I breathed, my hand reflexively latching onto his forearm—and cursing myself when I met bare skin where his sleeves were rolled. His palms found my waist, fingers tightening as he stooped to study me, concern etched deep between his brows.

"Pax said that's why you didn't run last week."

"Dirty, rotten fink," I growled, wrinkling my nose.

He snorted. "In his defense, he'd had a scotch at dinner."

"One mid-season drink and he crumples like a house of cards. *Weak.*"

Ollie chuckled, shaking his head. "So?"

"Yeah. I think the stress of the last few months just exacerbated things. A few weeks of good sleep, good food—" I smiled, letting my eyes wander over him, "—and even better company should do it."

He nodded, but didn't let go, his jaw ticking like that answer wasn't good enough. "You're welcome to crash in the guest room tonight. I don't want you driving home if you're not up to it."

That… actually didn't sound half bad. But that didn't mean I could justify doing something stupid. "I don't really wanna sleep in this," I motioned to my stiff Bomber's cheer shirt and cute-ass mini skirt. "It's trying to strangle the girls."

He huffed a laugh, his fingers flexing at my waist. I should step back. *Should.* But I didn't. Couldn't remember how.

"I've got some pajamas that might fit, and I can order clothes in for tomorrow."

"You're too nice, Ollie. Has anyone ever told you that?"

"Never, not once," he quipped, lifting a hand to tuck my hair behind my ear. My God, the man could suck the oxygen out of a room. I'd tried hard not to get this close for a reason—he made me stupid. Staying here would be colossally dumb. Staying here in a big-ass shirt that smelled like heaven and the promise of orgasms? Colossally bad idea.

"Thank you for the offer, but Kaia's expecting me. We're doing breakfast before I head this way."

Okay, so we ate together every morning in a half-lucid, bean-juice-dependent stupor, but it was the only excuse I could come up with while his Adam's apple bobbed like it, too, was hot. I wanted to press my lips to his throat. Jesus.

"I should hit the road."

Reluctantly, he nodded. But his eyes dropped to my mouth, his tongue darting out to wet his own. He leaned in, and my chin lifted of its own accord, logic frantically trying—and failing—to slam the brakes. His breath brushed my face and heat roared to life in my veins.

A mistake.

This would be a mistake.

This would mess everything up.

This was why I was *leaving.*

Danger, Leighton Rhodes. Danger.

And yet—even as every logical neuron fired neon warning signs —his eyes, his mouth, the magnetic pull of *him* had falling—

"Daddy??" Beau's panicked voice had *nightmare* written all over it. We both froze as the thud of tiny feet hit the floor.

"Daddy!"

Saved by the toddler.

I slapped on a smile and peeled away from Ollie's gravity. Smirking, heart hammering, I whispered, "Goodnight, Ollie."

He gave me a tight smile. But the war in his body was gone. What stared back was disappointment. Pure, quiet, devastating disappointment.

"Night, Trouble."

THE GIRLS:

ELORA

You feeling any better, Punky?

LEIGHTON

Maybe last weekend put me in a sleep deficit or something because I am *wiped*.

ALICE

I mean, Emmaline picked up some bug from Eli's kids. Maybe you're fighting something off?

NOEL

My nieces and nephews are in school, and it's basically one oversized Petri dish. I swear my sister is always sick.

BREXLEY

Facts.

LEIGHTON

Nothing sunshine won't help.

ELORA

Good, yes, soak in that vitamin D.

KAIA

Does Tillie have ballet tonight?

LEIGHTON

Yep. She's dancing two roles in this years' Nutcracker, so we're at rehearsal daily.

ELORA

Awe, I remember those days. You two were the cutest damn angels there ever were.

KAIA

Until that snot tugged on my wig.

LEIGHTON

That bitch deserved it.

I have no regrets.

ALICE

deadpan GIF You punched a ten-year-old.

KAIA

In her defense, we were eight.

ELORA

Play stupid games, win stupid prizes.

NOEL

LMAO

ALICE

How is our little snowflake/angel?

LEIGHTON

Doing better today, or at least she was when I dropped her off.

ALICE

Good. Poor pumpkin.

ELORA

I can't imagine what she's feeling. That's a lot for such a little body.

LEIGHTON

Yeah. I think the glass breaking triggered her. We'll have to let her come watch a game with an empty suite, or something. Make it just us.

ELORA

I think that's a great idea.

ALICE

Agreed. We can't let those bastards ruin a family tradition. Her daddy worked so hard for that team. She deserves to enjoy it.

ELORA

What'd Ollie think of your self-defense suggestion?

LEIGHTON

I've compiled the best dojos in town, but he seems hesitant. I was debating asking Jax if he could work with her one-on-one and proposing that instead.

ALICE

That's a great idea!

ELORA

It might help her to see that he's still working at it.

KAIA

Or be triggering because he was there?

LEIGHTON

She has no qualms with Captain Reynolds.

SMIRKING at the joke none of them would get, I set my phone in my lap. Glancing up between texts to track Beau as he conquered the playground on Wednesday morning was more than a little challenging, but God, the kid was freaking cute. I was convinced he'd grown in the last two weeks. I chuckled as he superhero-leapt off one platform onto another, and dramatically landed like Spiderman, then glanced back to my buzzing cell.

BREXLEY

Uh. Guys?

NOEL

eyeball emojis

BREXLEY

My water just broke.

LEIGHTON

OMG BABY TIME!!!

BREXLEY

Of course, you're excited, you're not about to have an entire human being demolish your vagina.

LEIGHTON

Facts. *crying laughing emojis*

But TOMORROW you'll be snuggled up with your sweet little peanut.

BREXLEY

Vaginal tears.

Hemorrhoids.

Abs that feel like jelly, but hurt no matter how careful you are.

Pee that might as well be lighter fluid.

LEIGHTON

"What is… a 24-hour marathon with no prize money and a wailing mandrake at the finish line?" for 500, Alex?

ELORA

Thanks, guys. I wasn't already freaking out.

BREXLEY

Grimacing emoji, laughing emojis You'll do fine!

They're totally worth it, but for fuck's sake, I wish someone warned me the first go around.

NOEL

I distinctly remember Juniper warning you.

Repeatedly.

In graphic detail.

And bringing you Tucks pads.

BREXLEY

And nipple cream and about a million witchy little remedies I now swear by.

Your mother is an angel, ladies. Thanks for letting me borrow her.

LEIGHTON

You say that, but you've clearly never pissed her off.

ELORA

I would warn against it.

ALICE

Under no circumstances can you steal her perfume whilst wearing her high heels.

LEIGHTON

One time. It happened one time.

KAIA

Hold up. How in the hell are you texting right now?

BREXLEY

Meh. Contractions are basically period cramps atm.

Plus, your brother all but carried me to the passenger seat of the car, and now I'm watching him sprint into the house and back like he's on fire.

It's highly entertaining.

Quinn and I are just watching him go back and forth and giggling our asses off.

ELORA

Awe, I'm glad we raised that one right.

BREXLEY

He really is the best.

I HAD to give it to my brothers. Of the two who'd found their people, they both loved them so loudly that nobody could miss it.

I loved that for Brex and Noel.

Wasn't at all jealous.

Okay—maybe a little.

Mostly because Ollie had me on high alert, and I must've finally been ovulating because I needed an orgasm or a strong drink so badly I could cry. Maybe both? Hell, a stiff breeze might get the job done at this point.

Ollie—the cocky bastard—had, in fact, rendered Obi Wand entirely unappealing.

It wasn't the same. Which, I mean, *duh*. But I hadn't realized how delectable a man's bodyweight was. What whispered words could do to me.

There was something sacred about keeping our one night between us—just our little secret—but somehow not telling the girls he almost kissed me last night was harder. Maybe because it would mean something entirely different. But how the hell was I supposed to explain that my boss probably almost kissed me, and that it was somehow worse because I'd already had him in my bed?

Scanning the park, I quickly spotted Beau in his neon green t-shirt on the far side.

Note to self: always dress the kid like a traffic cone. So smart. So helpful. I deserved a pat on the back for that this morning. He moved too fast for neutrals—hell, if I could attach an LED head-lamp, I would.

I raised my hand to my mouth and let out a sharp whistle with my thumb and middle finger. His head popped up immediately, eyes locking on mine.

Little devil just grinned and sprinted up a tube slide, like I couldn't round him up if he didn't come when called.

Adorable little shithead.

Laughing, I jogged to the other side of the playground, climbed a ladder, and crouched to waddle-slide down a ramp, popping out just in time to catch him bursting from an adjoining tunnel.

Roaring like a monster, I scooped him up and tickled his tubby little belly. He shrieked and kicked, cackling like a maniac.

I would never understand how Carly just walked away from these babies.

In the years since, it was like she went out of her way to make their lives worse—and the more time I spent soaking up these giggles, the more I hated her for it.

"Okay, *okay!*" he screeched in surrender…

I threw my head back and let out a full belly villain laugh. "Muwa-ha-ha-ha!!"

"*You win, you win!*"

"Bet your bottom I win, Skippy. You think you're *so* sneaky."

"Am sneaky," he argued, giggling as I flipped him right side up and trapped him on my hip.

Poking his belly, I grinned. "Not sneaky enough, Bucko!"

"You win, you win, you win," he whined, still squirming.

I hugged him tight as we made our way to the parking lot. "You have fun?"

"So much! Dat one red kid, he was suuuper funny and had awesome Spiderman sooz. An' he like to play hide and seek. But he's not as good as you or Mattie."

"No?"

"No. But maybe jus' cause he's red."

I laughed, ruffling his hair. "You mean his hoodie was red?"

"Yeah."

"Not the best color to disappear in."

"No. He needs cammo."

"Cammo, huh?"

"Yeah. Makes us extra sneaky."

"Excellent, excellent. What'd you guys play after hide and seek?"

"Mmmm, tag. But he didn't like the funny guy."

"Funny guy?" I asked, quirking a brow as I unlocked my Jeep and plopped him into his seat.

"Yeah. Real funny. His face was all fuzzy."

A chill ghosted down my spine. Straightening, I scanned the parking lot. Empty. Still. Too quiet.

"Like… bearded? Like Uncle Maverick?"

"Fuzzier," he said matter-of-factly, still totally oblivious to the way my stomach just bottomed out.

What grown-ass man had been talking to Beau?

And how the hell hadn't I seen him? I hadn't taken my eyes off him for more than thirty seconds at a time.

Keeping my tone even, I asked, "What didn't the red kid like about him?"

"He jus' kept talkin' to us."

"Talking to you?"

"Yeah."

"What about?" I asked, tightening his seatbelt.

"Askin' about my sister. Then he said somethin' about crazy uncles, and I tol' him my Unca Grey is a hero. He had lots of questions 'bout that. Red kid got bored, I think."

"What kind of questions, sweet potato?" I asked as I climbed into the driver's seat, quickly locking the doors.

"I dunno."

"What was he wearing?"

"White shirt. Like what Daddy wears to work."

"Was he scary?"

"Not really. Just a lil' funny."

Funny. Then why was my stomach in knots?

11

Hold My Earrings
LEIGHTON

"Merde!" I swore when I spotted that familiar tiny dancer beside her too-handsome daddy Friday night.

Bemused hazel-blues snapped to my face, excitement glittering under the fluorescent lights. I was pretty sure it was some kind of unspoken law that auditorium buildings had to be lit with the worst possible lighting everywhere except the stage.

"You know *merde*?" she chirped, and if I wasn't kidding myself, I'd just won a brownie point or two.

"I was a sassy ballerina not that long ago," I said, fishing my camera out of my bag. "Okay, maybe a lifetime ago for you, but it doesn't feel very long to *me*." Plus, Ollie was the quintessential young, rich girl-dad, so naturally, if they were gonna swear, they'd do it in French.

"Were you ever a snowflake?"

"Nope," I said, smirking as she immediately posed for a photo. "Never mastered the footwork for that one. Made a pretty decent mouse and a very enthusiastic angel—right up until they kicked me out of school."

Those big blue eyes widened. "You got *kicked out?*" she asked, scandalized.

I nodded solemnly. "Don't ever punch a fellow ballerina. That's what crazy friends are for." I winked, and Ollie cleared his throat—an amused attempt at reproach that made me grin wider.

"Oh! Ollie! Didn't see you there," I said, earning a belly laugh from Beau and a little giggle from Tillie. "I was too swept up looking at the prettiest snowflake there's ever been!"

"I'm not the prettiest," she argued.

"Psh, yes you are."

"It's true. And I've seen them all," Ollie said, jutting his chin forward in a way that made me turn—and, yep, there were Grey and Alice strolling into the lobby.

"Remember, you have fifteen minutes between sets, so catch your breath and hurry to change—"

"But don't rush, because I've got time," she recited before bumping my fist.

I pointed behind her, and she squealed, flinging herself into her uncle's arms. The man was supposedly heartless—a spectacular irony Alice had exploited as his assistant—but fuck me, if he didn't turn to mush around these kids.

They were so damn cute I couldn't help it—I snapped a photo, earning an irritated flick of Greyson's hazel eyes when the flash fired.

"Uncle Grey! You came!"

"Wouldn't miss it, kiddo."

"Still," she said with a little shrug. "There are more nights. I didn't know *if* you'd make it. I know you're busy."

Alice and I exchanged a knowing look, both of us shaking our heads. What ten-year-old accounted for business obligations? One raised inside an empire, apparently. Ollie positioned himself between me and Tillie, casually enough to be subtle, but not enough that I didn't notice. He and Greyson had been weird ever since the accident—an observation that did not help with my increasing paranoia.

"Mattie, I am so stinking proud of you. You know you earned this, right?" Alice said, already halfway to emotional putty.

I snorted. "It's true," I agreed. "You earned your place on that stage, sweet girl. I'm so freaking proud of how hard you've been working."

She nodded excitedly, leaning into her dad, totally ignoring Beau, who was practically breakdancing as he swayed from one side to the other, hanging off Ollie's arm.

"Is Carly coming?" she asked, blinking up at Ollie—and oof, my heart didn't stand a chance.

"I'm not sure, sport, but I'll video it either way."

Tillie nodded, but I swear I felt her little belly sink from where I stood.

"You look so beautiful, sweet pea!" I crooned. Alice nodded enthusiastically beside me.

"Do you feel good about your routine?"

Smile back in place, she bobbed her head. "Yep! I had them both memorized weeks ago. I even helped Lizzy at rehearsal last week."

"Thatta' girl!" Greyson held out his hand for a high five, and she was quick to jump for it, her enthusiasm contagious.

A garbled announcement came over the speakers—sounded like Charlie Brown's teacher on a loudspeaker—and I didn't catch a word of it. Meanwhile, the lobby began to clear, families filtering into the auditorium or walking their dancers toward what I assumed were the staging rooms.

"You look breathtaking, Trouble."

Ollie's voice was low, too close to my ear, and just like that, my skin erupted in goosebumps.

Beaming, I gave a ridiculous little curtsey. "Thanks, handsome. You're looking quite dapper."

Of course, he was. Gorgeous, as always. Navy suit, crisp white shirt, and a kitschy silver snowflake tie that made me grin. Only Ollie would match his daughter for a ballet recital. I had an amazing dad, but not even Milo rocked anything 'feminine' like that.

"I like your snowflakes."

"Thanks, me too. Tillie picked it—*ouch*." His sentence broke off as a tiny fist nailed his stomach.

"Daddy! That's *Leighton's* nickname."

He rubbed his abs dramatically. "It's catchy."

"*Stop*," she groaned, rolling her eyes like she was personally burdened by all of us.

"My bad," he said, smirking. "We better get you backstage, *Matilda*."

"Ugh. You're the worst sometimes."

"Oh, I know," he said, his eyes landing on me in a way that made my blood heat. He stoked the flames when his hand landed on my bare shoulder blades. This dress did me so many favors, it was mind boggling.

It was a goddamn masterpiece. Christmas red, lacy, classy as hell —with a delicate button at my nape and a sexy open back that dipped just to mid-spine. It fit like it had been cut for me.

I loved it. Loved it more, now that I knew what it felt like to have Ollie's hands on me while I wore it.

I was still internally spiraling when a square of sunlight flashed across the far wall as someone threw open one of the glass doors with dramatic flair.

I turned, spotting a woman in a shimmering silver bodycon dress —the expensive kind that somehow screamed both taste and money. Great body. Red Birkin bag. Manicured coffin nails. Gorgeous.

And then I saw the dyed black hair with a halo of white framing her face.

Ollie went stiff beside me, his hand sliding instinctively into Mattie's.

Fuck me. Of course she was stunning.

"Wow, the whole family is here," she cooed, tossing her hair over her shoulder like she was on stage, wearing chintzy bug-eyed glasses that absolutely did not belong indoors. "How wonderful to see everyone," she purred, sliding the glasses down with a dramatic flick and reaching into her bag for the case.

"It's giving Gloria Swanson," I muttered under my breath, only for Ollie to hear.

His lips twitched, eyes glinting sideways. *"Sunset Boulevard?"*

"Precisely." But my snarky evaluation cut off the second she closed the distance.

"Mommy!" Beau squealed, wriggling like a happy little worm. Ollie's hand locked around him tighter, knuckles whitening like he was keeping his son from walking straight into a predator's jaws. My eyes landed on Tillie, who straightened her tutu with meticulous care—like she was bracing for an evaluation.

"Hello, babies," Carly trilled—but didn't bother to look at either of them. Nope. *Cruella's* eyes zeroed in on me first, then scraped over Ollie like he was something she owned. Her nostrils flared when she caught sight of his hand slipping from my back.

And just like that, she snapped her full attention to my face like she'd just ID'd a threat.

No wonder she'd terrified so many nannies straight out of a paycheck.

Goddammit, she had Tillie's eyes. Same shape, same ocean-blue hue—but Carly's were cold, dissecting. Tillie's held wonder. Hers held ice.

With a too-white smile stretching across her surgically flawless face, she leaned forward and offered her hand like we were brunching in the Hamptons. "You must be Leighton!"

"In the flesh," I said, giving her a firm shake and resisting the urge to shatter something in her palm.

"Pleasure."

"I'm sure." I retracted my hand like it was radioactive, catching Greyson rolling his lips against his teeth beside me. Carly blinked, clearly unprepared for anyone not falling for her charm offensive.

"Well," she began again, voice syrupy. "I have to say, it's just so sweet of you to be so involved in Matilda's life after hours. I imagine you must miss having a life of your own."

I curled an arm protectively around Tillie's tiny shoulders, flashing her a grin. "This girl brings more joy than she could possibly know. Honestly? I thank Ollie all the time for bringing such a beautiful blessing into the world."

"Yes, well," Carly sniffed, "it's miraculous what we'll do for a paycheck, isn't it?"

My jaw clenched so tight it crackled. I pictured how satisfying it would be to backhand that smug little smirk right off her face.

"Actually," I said tightly, "her performances were the highlight of my year. Built-in ballet chauffeur, remember? Part of the gig."

"How… quaint," she drawled, like the word offended her sensibilities. "Must be a small town thing."

"Nice of you to make an appearance," Greyson cut in, all venom, no camouflage.

"Well, *of course*. I never miss an opportunity to visit the theater."

Not 'to see my children,' I noted silently. Was she abducted by aliens before the last three performances?

I looked down at Tillie, giving her shoulders a gentle squeeze. "You ready? I can walk you back."

"How kind of you to offer, Leighton. I loathe how many people they pack into these places, and the dancers' rooms are always awful. It's like stepping into a middle school gym during an assembly."

"I think it's exciting," I said, watching Tillie's eyes drop to the floor like the comment had doused her light.

"It is nice to be young."

"You're awfully spiffed up for an event in a *gymnasium*," Greyson observed, voice flat as stone as he took a step back.

I slipped my camera into my bag, hands itching to be free.

"Oh, I'll take any excuse to wear couture, Grey, darling." Carly gave him a little twirl. "Isn't this dress just gorgeous? I thought it fit the Nutcracker theme beautifully. Don't you?"

She batted her lashes at Greyson. Bold of her. Stupid, too. Alice looked one word away from knocking her out.

"It sparkles like my costume," Tillie said shyly, cheeks flushing as she looked up.

"Almost!" Carly chirped, crouching in front of her. "Someday I'll take you to Jeremy. He'll get you into something that hides that tubby tummy. Good designers work miracles."

My mouth fell open. I actually gasped.

What. The actual. Fuck.

And then she had the audacity—*the gall*—to run a hand over Tillie's bright red face. "My, how I've missed those sweet chubby cheeks. What role did you land this year? Another little mouse?"

Tillie looked down at her silver leotard and ornate tutu, smoothing the fabric with trembling fingers, chewing her bottom lip like it was the only thing holding her together.

"Oh, she's always struggled to articulate herself," Carly tossed over her shoulder to Alice like they were girlfriends at lunch. Alice straightened so fast it was a miracle her spine didn't crack. She glared at Ollie like he could magic this viper out of the building.

I slid my hand into Tillie's and pulled her gently a step behind me.

"Carly, *enough*," Ollie snapped. His voice was tight, controlled—but barely.

"She's perfectly articulate when she's comfortable with someone," I bit out.

"Mattie was selected for two performances this year," Ollie continued proudly, nudging her shoulder with his elbow. "She's dancing as a snowflake and as an angel in 'Sugarplum.'"

The little one smiled up at him like he'd hung the moon.

"My, an angel *and* a snowflake!" Carly announced, loud enough to draw eyes. "Are they just handing out participation trophies this year?"

Ollie tensed. I could see him fighting to stay grounded. Meanwhile, I was praying for one last straggler to clear the lobby so I could unleash myself like the avenging angel this kid deserved.

What in the fuck had Ollie ever seen in this woman?

"She's worked her ass off this year," I snapped before he could speak.

"Sure." Carly waved me off like I was an annoying puff of air. "But let's be honest—she's never been a natural. Everyone has their strengths. Grace just isn't hers. Must get that from her father."

Tillie's hand tightened around mine, and Ollie and I both stepped forward at the same time.

"Carly," he growled, voice like smoke and ruin, "*enough.*"

But I wasn't finished. "Please tell me I'm being *Punk'd* and you're not actually standing here in your disco-ball fabric with the audacity to belittle your own daughter minutes before she steps on stage."

Carly blinked at me, scandalized. Her hand fluttered to her chest like I'd just accused her of murder. "Oh, sweetie, I'm just being honest. Critique is part of being a performer. Matilda understands that." Then, lower—like she thought whispering made it less venomous—she added, "Not all of us are meant to be soloists. But if we get her into a more prestigious school, I'm sure she'll make a lovely ensamble dancer."

I dropped Tillie's clammy hand, ready to knock her veneers into the next tax bracket—except Ollie caught my wrist.

I turned, seething, but one look at his pleading eyes—and then at Tillie's glassy ones—and I knew I couldn't swing.

Not yet.

Instead, I slapped on a smile so bright it hurt. "Let's get you backstage," I said softly, already moving. She nodded without speaking, hand sliding into mine as I led her away.

Alice appeared beside me like a vengeful storm cloud with Beau on her hip, red creeping up her neck.

Behind us, Ollie's voice cut through the air like a whip. "What the hell is wrong with you? That little girl has poured everything into this. Embarrassing yourself I can tolerate. But who says that shit to a ten-year-old?"

Oh. So he'd reached his limit. *Finally*.

"Keep your voice down," Carly snapped, like he was the one who'd lost the plot.

But I wasn't listening anymore. My mind was spinning. How could anyone be so fucking cruel to their own kid?

How had nobody put that bitch in concrete yet?

Honestly, this was why duels should still be legal. Fastest draw wins, justice served.

But I didn't need revenge. Not now. I needed to help this little girl feel strong, loved, and *seen*—before she stepped into that spotlight.

She didn't need to know Carly was a dumpster fire in haute couture.

She just needed to believe that we believed in her more than Carly ever could.

I was shaking, so I skipped a few steps ahead and flung open the door to her designated suite, stepping into pure chaos and a familiar cloud of glitter and hairspray. The backstage room was packed— kids on tiptoe, stretching, giggling, pirouetting into each other. Chaos. Beautiful, jittery chaos.

Like we'd choreographed it, Alice marched ahead, clearing a path to the corner where the other snowflakes were warming up. A few blushed, others beamed. Some were definitely one wrong twirl from vomiting in a satin slipper. The energy in the room buzzed under my skin, matching the tremble still working through my hands.

Alice turned sharply, blocking Tillie's view of the rest of the room as I crouched down beside her.

"Okay, my badass ballerina."

That earned me a tiny, wobbly giggle. Good. Still reachable.

"Look at me," I said gently, tilting her chin up with two fingers. "Can I tell you the truth? Like, real truth?"

Her lashes fluttered, and for a second I thought she might shut down again. But then she nodded, soft and shy.

I grinned, aware that Alice was doing the same behind me.

"You, Matilda freaking Hart, are a legend. That stage out there? It belongs to you. I have five sisters, so I don't say this lightly—but you were made for this. That floor, those lights, the glitter rain? They're lucky to have you stomping your sparkly little feet all over them."

I tapped her nose. Her throat bobbed, but she was still with me. Still listening.

"No wonder your heart hides sometimes. You've been trying to grow in the shadow of a woman who couldn't spot gold if it slapped her across the face. But you? You're gold. Pure and bright and strong."

I swallowed, forcing my rage into something useful.

"You've earned this, Mattie. Every practice, every blister, every night you dragged your little self home and *did it again* the next day. You didn't get here because your last name is Hart. You got here because you worked your cute little ass—"

"*Leighton*," Alice hissed behind me.

"—*behind*," I corrected, because I was nothing if not respectful of the peanut gallery. "You worked your *behind* off. So when you walk on that stage tonight, you hold your chin high and remind them exactly why they picked you."

Her lip wobbled, and I swear to God, I was gonna rip Carly's extensions out by the root and donate them to a charity that deserved them.

"What if I mess up?" she whispered.

"Then you keep on dancing," Alice said, joining me in the crouch.

"You know why?" I leaned in, conspiratorial, my voice low and fierce.

"Why?" Her smile flickered at the edges.

"Confidence makes *everything* look intentional."

"What?"

"No, seriously," Alice added. "I faked my way through my entire first year working for your daddy and Uncle Grey."

"You could freestyle the Macarena mid-snowflake number and as long as you owned it? The audience would *lose* their minds."

"Only the other ballerinas would know, and even the very best of them would be so stinking proud of you for staying in the moment and catching up once you could."

"We are all rooting for you," I promised. "They're not watching for mistakes, sweet pea. They're watching to be dazzled."

"They're watching *you*," Alice added, booping her nose.

"They want magic," I said. "And lucky for them, you're *made* of it."

She exhaled, eyes brighter now, the pink high on her cheeks finally something *earned*, not something *shamed*.

I stood, my legs thanking me for returning the circulation as I leaned in and kissed her forehead. "You can do this dance blindfolded, sweet pea. Go show them what you got."

"Go, Mattie!" Beau hollered from Alice's hip.

And just like that, she smiled.

OLIVER

"YOU KEEP TRYING to spin this like you're somehow a victim, but the only person hurting right now is Matilda. As far as I'm concerned, my brother should've filed a protection order years ago."

I might've spent the last three months mad at the man, but goddamn, did Greyson keep a poker face well. From a distance, you'd have no idea he was plotting how to destroy the nightmare I'd saddled us with because a grieving twenty-one-year-old me couldn't keep his dick in his pants once the alcohol came out.

"What was the point in coming tonight, huh?" I pressed. "Did you literally just show up to shit on her parade?"

"How dare you," she gasped, like I'd slapped her.

Admittedly, I wanted to. Didn't. If for no other reason than the legal repercussions.

"I have every right to be here to support my daughter."

"You have no right to tear down *our* daughter like she's your competition."

"You're being absurd," she snapped. "She was fine! She knows I was just joking around."

"She's *ten!*" Leighton's razor-edged voice rang down the hallway, and we all turned as she stormed toward us—more warrior than model, even in three-inch heels.

"It's funny you think you get to weigh in as the help," Carly purred, saccharine sweet, when Leighton stepped directly into our huddle. Carly batted her lashes, still putting on a show for any lingering stragglers. Leighton, however, didn't give a shit about pretense. She stepped right into Carly's space, chin high, shoulders back, glaring down her nose at her.

"You know what's *funny?* You act like some prize—like your kids should be grateful for the scraps you bother to throw their way. But let's be real, Mattie has been carrying your dead fucking weight her entire life. You show up here and play prima donna mama hoping she'll love you anyway, or to win favor from the guys, but the moment you feel threatened, you crush her. And for what? To punish Ollie for a mistake he made when he was twenty-fucking-two?"

"Excuse me?" Carly straightened, composure cracking.

"You don't get to play stupid, you dumb bitch." Leighton's vulgarity had both Greyson and me laughing into our hands, but I couldn't take my eyes off the woman in red as she stalked forward, looking more likely to swing on Carly than keep talking. "Not after that performance. Not after planting insecurity in a little girl who does everything we ask of her just to make everyone happy. Girls *die* over body image bullshit—and who the hell are you to talk, *Cruella?* Matilda is ten. And somehow, she's already *ten times the woman* you will *ever* be."

Carly's eyes darted around before landing back on the one person in the room who didn't care about appearances. Her throat bobbed.

"Spare the lecture, Leighton. You're just the nanny—*for now.* You're not her mother. Now, let the grown-ups talk."

"No, I'm not her mother. But if I could step into that role, I would in a heartbeat," Leighton said, her smile sharp and cold as Carly's face went pale. "Because I'd make damn sure she never had to wonder if she was good enough. That's what a mother does. She builds her children up. She makes sure they know they can conquer anything."

I could feel the eyes on us. Was I a little terrified this would end up on a blog or in a tabloid? Sure. But as Carly's face flushed and she shrank in on herself, I decided the time for propriety had ended. Alice might have to clean this up, calling in favors with the media outlets who owed her—or owed us—but I had a feeling she'd understand.

Should it have been arousing?

Absolutely not.

Was it satisfying? Watching the woman who'd terrorized my life look small for once?

Absolutely.

Carly looked at me like I should step in, but I just chuckled and raised my hands in the universal sign for "you're on your own."

"Awe, look at you. Reaching for the big Hart men because, just like everything else in your life, you don't even have the dignity to stand your own ground." Leighton shot me a glance before returning her daggers to my ex. When she opened her mouth, the mocking tone had saturated into a baby voice, her lips sticking out as she pouted, "And he just leaves you hanging, after you orchestrated your plans so perfectly."

"You don't know anything about me," Carly hissed, her natural tenor replacing the performative bullshit she'd waltzed in here with.

"Don't I?" Leighton growled. "Got yourself a baby to lock him down? A ring on your finger? The only thing you were too dense to consider was that Harts don't settle for *bullshit.*"

"Were you raised in a barn? For pity's sake, lower your voice."

I was fairly sure I'd never seen her face that particular shade of mottled lobster—but it suited her.

"Why?" Leighton barked, raising her voice instead, flinging an arm toward the people filing in. "Afraid someone might see you? Judge you? Afraid they'll realize if you put half this much effort into being a mother, you wouldn't have to work so hard to *look like* one?"

"If you don't shut your mouth, I'll—"

"*What?*" Leighton snarled, fists clenched at her sides.

That was my cue. I looped my arm around her waist and hauled her back to me.

"Finish the sentence. I fucking dare you."

Huffing dramatically, Carly straightened her tacky dress. "Well. *I never*—and in civilized society—this is what you've lowered our family to, Oliver? This is pathetic." She waved a hand at Leighton. "I don't have time for this."

"Of course you don't," Leighton spat as I pulled her back. Carly turned to leave, but Leigh wasn't finished. "I've met single-celled organisms with more integrity. We'd all be better off if your mother knew how to swallow."

Greyson chuckled, a genuine smile directed at the woman clinging to my arm like she was going to rip it off her waist. "That'll do, Leigh. That'll do."

Leighton laughed, watching Carly's rapid retreat before she finally relaxed into my chest, her hand fluttering over her sternum. "I thought you were exaggerating."

"I never exaggerate when dealing with the devil," Greyson muttered.

"Oooh, how is she breathing?"

"Unfortunate societal expectations," he drawled.

"She's not worth the prison time," I promised.

"If I knew I could get away with it, I'd put her six feet under. How dare she plant that kind of insecurity in Tillie? That little girl is so fucking beautiful, and *smart*, and *kind*, and generous. And even if she did have a belly, who gives a flying fuck. What a cunt."

"Knew I liked you," Grey muttered as I turned Leighton in my arms.

"You okay?"

"If by 'okay' you mean 'trying to plan a homicide,' then yeah. I'm okay."

I laughed, pressing my lips to her forehead—and when she sucked down a breath, it was like she stole it straight from my lungs. "That was quite possibly the hottest thing I've ever seen."

"You're full of shit."

"No way. I like when you bring out your claws."

"Why do you let her anywhere near them?"

"Court order. Holidays and visitation. Grey and I filed for a revision and a restraining order after Thanksgiving. If you're willing to write a letter to the judge, it might help to add this incident to the record."

"How could she possibly say something like that to her own daughter?"

"Jealousy?" I offered. But even I wasn't sure.

I cradled her face. She closed her eyes, hands landing on my wrists—and when I glanced at Greyson, he gave us a beat of privacy.

"Told you my money was on you," I murmured.

She huffed a laugh.

"Leigh!" Alice's voice rang from the stairwell. We both turned to see her and Grey with Beau, who was still blissfully unaware. God, I loved her for keeping him oblivious.

Someday, he'd know the truth. But not today.

"The battle with the mouse king started."

Leighton nodded. "Yeah. Be right up."

Alice didn't push. Just nodded and tugged Grey with her.

I turned to follow, wrapping my arm around Leighton's shoulders, tucking her against my ribs.

"Get me in a ring with her and I'll make it look like an accident, I swear."

"I know, Trouble," I said, pressing a kiss to her temple as we hit the marble stairs. Her heels clicked softly beside me. "But tonight, what matters is Mattie. That she knows how loved she is."

"I know," she murmured.

We didn't speak again as we climbed the stairs and slipped into the Hart family box. She stayed quiet through the applause, her gaze far away—until the orchestra shifted into snowfall. Then her eyes snapped to the stage, landing on Mattie, radiant in the spotlight.

I should've been watching the performance.

But I looked at the woman beside me instead, tears shimmering in her eyes.

And I knew I felt more loyalty—more kinship, more *everything*—for Leighton Rhodes than I ever had for the woman she'd just eviscerated.

As my hand settled on the back of her neck, and hers drifted to my knee, I wondered if maybe, just maybe, this aching, bruising heat in my chest… was what love felt like.

12

Does This Make Me An Objectophile?

LEIGHTON

MOM

There's no such thing as too much garlic.

LEIGHTON

Tell that to my very Italian boss.

MOM

Just never snap spaghetti noodles. Ask me how I know that.

If I was going to imbue any aspect of myself onto these children, Lord, let it be my taste in music—and not my uncertainty in the kitchen.

Growing up, the family favorites were all oldies, and if I could pass down the greatness that was Pink Floyd to the next generation, I'd die a very happy woman. That holy mission had Tillie singing *Another Brick in the Wall* under her breath as she worked on her homework at the dining room table Monday night.

Gotta start with the classics and work our way up, obviously. Beau had played until he dropped—literally—and was now passed the hell out on the couch.

What I didn't expect, as the music swapped to instrumentals, was the way my whole body went on alert. I turned from the pot on the stove to find Ollie leaning against the kitchen archway.

Jumping, my hand flew to my heart, elbow knocking the wooden spoon perched on the pot, sending it—and a ladleful of red sauce— flying. I shrieked as Ollie muttered an apologetic, "Oh shit!"

"Jesus Christ, *announce yourself!*"

"I thought you heard me."

"Make a noise or something! You're like Michael Myers just *looming* in the fucking doorway."

He snickered, shaking his head as I snatched paper towels from the counter. "Jumpy tonight, Leigh?"

"Before *you* tried to jumpstart my heart? No, I was not. Thank you very much."

"What the hell are you doing in here, anyway?" He knelt beside me, helping wipe up the marinara splattered everywhere.

"Indoctrinating your children to restore the next generation's musical taste. What does it look like?" Our hands collided as we both went to mop up the same puddle of sauce. I would not be acknowledging that the Event-That-Shall-Not-Be-Discussed had not, in fact, purged Ollie from my system.

Apparently, it did the opposite. Because something as simple as a finger graze shouldn't have the power to send heat flashing through me, but the pulse between my thighs begged to differ. One fucking night, and he had me trained like a Pavlovian dog.

Bad Leighton. This man did not—and could not—equate to the promise of pleasure in my brain.

We'd agreed—everything was simpler if we kept things the way they were.

But as I really looked at him tonight, my body didn't care. He was fucking breathtaking. His jacket was gone, dark hair perfectly disheveled, tie loosened to expose the base of his throat, sleeves rolled up to the elbow in a way that made me salivate. It was bad enough he had a heart big enough to cast a protective umbrella over the city—he just had to look like that too?

"It looks like you're cooking," he observed, snapping me out of my panic-induced micro-sleep as I stared at his hand, tendons shifting over the now-red towels.

"Is this a trick question?"

Chuckling, he straightened and offered me a hand. "I told you. You don't have to worry about that."

"Who says I'm worrying?"

"You know what I meant. Cooking dinner's not on your shoulders."

"Sure, sure, but Beau wanted to make his own pizza, and I thought it was a great idea."

"And where is *Beau?*" he asked with a knowing smirk.

"Passed the hell out in the living room."

"Fitting."

"Very."

"It smells like Nona's in here."

"As it should. Tillie insisted it was sacrilege to use store-bought sauce." I dumped the tomato-soaked towels in the trash, sliding it back under the sink in his fancy retractable cabinet. After the shit-show Friday night, I'd decided to do whatever I could to make that little girl happy.

"As she should," he said proudly.

"So I swiped the recipe from Alice, who swiped it from Emma-line, who made her vow it wouldn't leave the family. Think she'll kill me when she finds out I know?"

"You are family."

"But not technically, right?" I flashed him my best doe eyes. Because contrary to our little spat on Thanksgiving, no, I did not want to categorize Oliver Hart as "family." That made Halloween seem... icky. And it was anything but that.

Ollie turned to the fridge, grabbed some fizzy juice thing, and held one up in offering, smirking when I shook my head. "Eh. More likely she tries to marry you off to one of her innumerable grand-children."

"Forced marriage was always on my bucket list."

"Of course it was."

"I assumed it would be some mafia prince who whisked me away from my life as an indentured stepchild and then slayed all my enemies."

"Naturally."

"You got any appealing second cousins?"

Ollie made a noise like he was clearing his throat, but it sounded more like a growl.

"Don't like that idea?"

"Not even a little bit."

Chuckling, I grinned at him, shaking my head when he flashed that blinding smile. He just had to be stupidly beautiful. Couldn't have looked like a bulldog or had one of those punchable faces. No, Ollie had to be the kind of man who made every woman in a hundred-yard radius salivate. *Damn it, Pavlov.*

Peeling my eyes off the masterpiece in question, I snatched a new wooden spoon from the drawer and turned back to the stove as Ollie ducked into the dining room to press a kiss to Tillie's very focused forehead. It didn't seem to bother him that she didn't acknowledge him. And why in the hell did that sight make my ovaries weep?

I snuck a taste and grimaced as nerves twisted in my belly. I wasn't a terrible cook, but I definitely wasn't a professional, and I most certainly didn't grow up with an Italian grandmother to teach me her ways. Sure, it was hard to screw up pizza—but if anyone could manage, it'd be me. And for some reason, the idea of failing in front of Ollie made me want to crawl into the cabinet under the sink and die quietly.

"Bad?" he asked from directly behind me, startling me for the second time in as many minutes. "Jesus, Trouble, try one less coffee tomorrow. You're coming out of your skin."

Yeah. I had been—ever since Beau told me about the grown-ass man talking to him at the park. *Stupid*. Probably nothing. But it had me on edge, and I couldn't shake the feeling. I'd sent another email to Detective Riviera, but my hopes for a response weren't high.

Then that witch rode her broom into the recital Friday night, and I'd felt one shot of espresso away from a breakdown ever since.

"I don't know, honestly. I'm nervous," I admitted—right as he caged me against the counter with his body, peering over my shoulder at the simmering pot. My breath hitched.

"It needs something," I muttered.

"What?"

"I don't know yet."

"Looks good," he murmured, and the warmth of his voice ghosted over the back of my neck like a promise. "Smells good."

Yes. Yes, he did. Like spiced aftershave and *man*. God, he had a natural musk that made my toes curl. This was not good. Not good at all.

"Try some?"

"Please," he agreed. Out of the corner of my eye, I caught the slight tilt of his chin toward the spoon.

Clearing my throat, I scooped a taste and turned. My back brushed his chest, and my mouth went dry as I looked up—straight into that maddening Adam's apple. With no words to offer and a lower lip demanding I stop gnawing it, I lifted the spoon to his lips. My stomach flipped as he accepted the bite, chewing thoughtfully.

"Salt," he said, nodding. "And another pinch of oregano."

With his hand between my shoulder blades, Ollie leaned past me, grabbed the salt, and gave it a liberal dusting. Then he tossed in a dash of oregano with confident precision. I loved that the man could cook. Loved that he had more money than God but still got his hands messy and treated it like a ritual instead of a task.

Heart pounding, I tried not to notice the way his cologne tangled with the garlic in the air—or how my body buzzed at his nearness.

Tried being the operative word.

Even as I stirred the pot, I felt like I was unraveling.

He stepped away, giving me a brief reprieve, only to return with two silver spoons—handing me one before lifting his own and dragging it slowly between his lips like he had a vendetta against my self-control.

I tried. Truly. But I couldn't look away.

Never in my life had I wanted to be a piece of silverware so badly.

Did that make me an objectophile? Probably. I decided I didn't actually care.

"Give it another few minutes," he said, licking his lips before pursing them thoughtfully. "It'll be perfect."

I peeled away from him, forcing my attention to the fridge, yanking out the toppings I'd prepped earlier. Lord have mercy—I had to get myself under control.

Keeping my eyes—and body—as far away from Ollie as humanly possible, I lined the toppings up across the breakfast table in front of the dough I'd rolled out with the kids earlier. But I could feel him. Watching. Thinking.

Based on the wolfish spark in his eyes when I finally stopped playing chicken and met his gaze, he was scheming up ways to make *me* his next meal.

Determined not to squirm, I bit out, "What?"

"Nothing," he said, shaking his head as he rounded the enormous island.

So that's what Brexley meant when she wrote that an MMC "prowled," because holy *Hawkeye*, I felt like prey. Worse yet, the heat between my thighs and the butterflies in my belly said I liked it.

"Then stop staring at me. It's freaking me out."

He chuckled—low and sexy—and I hated how badly I wanted to feel it under my fingertips or reverberating through my ribs. This? This was why I didn't stay for dinner. Or show up for breakfast. Or willingly interact with this man unless we had buffers. And *Matilda Hart, so help me, if you don't get your head out of academics and come save me—*

"Just… thinking I could get used to coming home to this."

"A make-shift pizza kitchen?"

A huffed laugh. "To you."

"*Oh.*" It was a whisper. A broken exhale that sounded more like a plea than a realization. But it was the most ladylike alternative to the full-on "Are you trying to make me shit a brick?" screaming through my brain. Every muscle in my body locked up as he held my gaze. "That's kind of a dangerous thing to say to a woman who is… already way too attached to your kids."

"I just mean… I like you here, Trouble. In my house." A butterfly-inducing step forward. "Making Nona's sauce. Barefoot in my kitchen. Singing the music our parents grew up on."

"Okay," I hedged, dropping my eyes to the toppings and sliding the bowls around like the order of olives to pepperoni was a matter of national security. The soft creak of the floor beneath his feet told me he was closing the distance, even as my heart skipped a beat. A quick glance toward the dining room confirmed Tillie was still hyper-focused on her homework. As Ollie neared, my stomach folded like the first pancake that inevitably flops when you try to flip it too soon. Blowing out a slow breath, I asked, "But like… do you mean 'get used to' in a 'it's convenient having me look after your kids' kind of way, or… a 'we should pick out curtains' kind of way?"

"What would you say if I said it was the latter?"

"I'd say nothing's changed in the last six weeks, and we were pretty clear about no weirdness."

"And what if I said that was the mistake?"

"The *no weirdness* policy?"

He snorted. "The walking away."

The gold tongs I'd been fiddling with clattered onto the veggie plate as I jerked my face up to his. "Ollie, I have a heart condition, for fuck's sake." His chuckle did nothing to soothe the rapid-fire rhythm of my pulse. "You can't just go around saying shit like that," I snapped, glancing toward Tillie again, even as the hair on my arms stood up at his proximity.

"Why not?"

"We have a good thing going here."

"We do. But I gotta be honest, beautiful," he said, tucking a piece of hair behind my ear—like he didn't know that gesture was lethal—"I haven't stopped thinking about that night, Leigh. About what a colossal mistake walking away was."

"We were kinda interrupted," I pointed out, relieved I didn't sound like a breathless idiot, even as my stomach free-fell.

"And I should've walked out and said good morning."

"And gone toe-to-toe with my brother?"

"Worth it."

"*Stupid*. The word you're looking for is stupid. Pax is unbearably protective."

"And in the last six weeks, I've realized fighting with him would've been better than carrying this weight."

"What weight?"

"Regret, Trouble."

"Regret is for the birds."

"Agreed. Which is why we should've just said something."

"Maybe," I admitted, trying to slow my breathing. He wasn't the only one who'd rehashed that morning ten ways from Sunday. "But walking into family breakfast with a new scandal still sounds like a terrible idea."

"So, what?"

"What do you mean, 'so what'?"

"We're both adults. Let them think whatever the hell they want. Unless… unless that's all you wanted. Unless *you* don't want more."

Blinking, I let the weight of his words settle. This man…

"You…" I glanced at a still-focused Tillie, then back to those soulful brown eyes. "You don't regret me?"

"Jesus," he said, his voice tight with emotion. "Never. Just… how I handled it. How I let Grey get in my head and paint something beautiful in a light of shame. You make me happy, Leighton. I felt like I was on top of the world until I walked into my office and Grey called me out."

"What?!"

"That's not the point," he muttered, glancing over his shoulder. "And I'm not making excuses. The point is—it shouldn't matter. What *he* thinks. What *they* think. Who cares?"

"Literally everyone."

"So?" He shrugged. "I'm not ashamed of this." He motioned between us. "Never was. It just took a minute to realize that's what we were battling."

"Because of the family." Because… that's what it was for me. I didn't want to make Pax's last years in the league uncomfortable. Alice and Greyson's disapproval shouldn't matter, but somehow the idea of disappointing her did. Maverick and Axel would never stop cracking jokes about keeping it in the family. Jameson would inevitably disapprove. Elora and Broderick would mean well—but they'd analyze the whole thing six ways from Sunday until everyone was crying.

"Right."

"Because *we're* family."

"On paper, maybe. But watching you walk Mattie through that panic attack—putting her needs ahead of your own. Going toe-to-toe with Carly and watching her run off with her tail between her legs… You're killing me, Leighton."

"She's a special kid," I stammered. "And Cruella is a waste of space."

"Yeah," he agreed. "But seeing you with them—God, it's like a knife to the gut every time I walk through that door. Like getting a glimpse of the life I want. One you're already a part of. So I'll ask again. Why shouldn't I say anything?"

I set down the bowl of olives—now appropriately arranged beside the other veggies—as my mouth popped open.

Was he… *was he serious?*

Why would he do this to me?

Things were going so well. And could he possibly know how badly I still wanted him?

This man was standing in front of me, declaring his intentions so boldly that my brain couldn't buffer fast enough to convert emotion into words.

A lapse in control and a stolen kiss? Sure. I could tackle that. But this?

Hello, this is the Leighton Express, and we're radioing to inform you that the plan has officially gone off the rails.

"Ollie…"

"I mean it. I can't get you out of my mind."

"Well, me either. But you can't just say shit like that."

"Why not?"

Forcing my gaze up to his, I was caught by the turmoil in those bottomless browns. My voice came out a whisper, terrified and soft.

"Because I might just believe you."

13

Another One Bites The Dust

OLIVER

A quick glance over my shoulder showed Mattie still hyper-focused on her homework, but I wasn't about to back Leighton into a hypothetical corner. Not when a physical one was readily available.

She had to want this—*me.*

Snatching her hand in mine, I jerked my chin over my shoulder, watching as her eyes flicked to the dining room and back.

"What are you doing?" she whispered, but to my eternal surprise, she didn't resist, rushing along beside me until we ducked into the butler's pantry and closed the door. "Ollie…"

I rounded on her, cutting her off as I backed her into the door, a breathy gasp whooshing out of her as her eyes went wide. Planting an arm above her head, I caged her in, relishing the way her gaze darkened. Her cheek was impossibly soft beneath my palm as I cradled her face with my other hand. Leaning in, I brushed my lips over her forehead—just to keep myself from devouring her mouth.

"One night," I breathed. "Give me one night, Leigh."

"I did that already," she shot back, chin tipping up as she groaned when I retreated—denying her more than I was ready to give.

"Not to fuck you, Trouble. Not to worship your gorgeous fucking body."

"Marginally less interested in this conversation," she muttered, even as her hands found their way over my arms, my chest, my back —eyelids growing heavy. If desire had a face, it was this fucking woman, peering up at me through those dangerously long lashes.

Chuckling, I murmured, "I want to take you out, baby. I want to buy you a dress that fits like a glove and book a reservation at a restaurant you'll love. I want to show up ten minutes early because I can't stand waiting one more second to see you—even though I see you every damn day."

"*Ollie,*" she whispered, running her nose along mine before making a desperate lunge for my mouth. Laughing, I stayed just out of reach, thumbing her cheekbone and savoring the desperation in her voice.

"I want to bring you flowers. Help you into the car. Eat and drink and dance with you until you're nothing but putty in my hands. I want to call Arthur to drive us so we can blast your beloved oldies the whole way home—and I can spend the ride memorizing how you like to be kissed. I want to walk you to the door and tell you exactly how much I *love* being with you."

I pinched her chin gently, tugging her face to the side and kissing down the line of her jaw.

Chuckled again when she arched off the door. *Good.* She was just as desperate as I was.

"Then I want to beg you for another night, because one is never going to be enough."

Her hands fisted in my shirt, roamed down my back to my ass—and fuck me, I nearly lost it when she cupped it. My cock jerked against my zipper, aching for her touch, for her scent, for the feel of her skin against mine.

"Ollie," she panted, her fingers scraping down my sides.

"Say yes, Leigh." I smiled against her skin and dove for the curve of her chest, pressing a kiss into the base of that scar—savoring the memory of the last time I'd worshipped it. Any blood left in my brain headed south. Some day, she'd tell me her story—how she got those marks, who I should have killed for causing them. She'd feel safe enough and seen enough to tell me what happened. But I wouldn't push. Not now.

Right now, I only had one mission. And it wasn't talking.

"Say yes, beautiful. I'm begging you."

"*Yes,*" she gasped, yanking my hair until it stung.

I wasn't sure if she was trying to hold me there or pull me to her mouth, but either way, I sucked in a breath of sheer, relieved want.

"Yes, Ollie!"

I swallowed the plea with a kiss so raw, so claiming, I forgot all the reasons this was supposed to be complicated. Nothing this right could be wrong. She tasted like marshmallow lip gloss and heat and laughter. Electricity shot down my spine when she moaned into my mouth, and I realized she'd stripped me bare—left me exposed like a live wire.

She fit. She'd always fit.

From the moment she'd stomped into Greyson's house, Leighton

Rhodes had been *mine*. And I was going to make damn sure she knew it.

"Please, Ollie," she mewled, her breath hot against my lips. "Please."

"Please what, beautiful?"

"More. I need more of you."

Fuck, I wanted to give her the world. "Same."

"Then give me what I want. It's been six weeks of lady blue balls."

I huffed a laugh and shook my head. "The next time I fuck you, Leighton Rhodes, it won't be in a closet."

"Psh. This is the size of my old bedroom."

Grinning, I rubbed my nose over hers like the lovesick bastard I was. "Next time I fuck you, I won't do it just because it happened. I'll do it because I earned it. Because I showed you that what *we* have is real—and worth keeping."

"You say that with a great deal of confidence."

"I don't hear you arguing."

"No," she admitted, breathing hard. "No, you don't."

"I can't do this anymore. Can't pretend you don't mean the fucking world to me. Can't look at you like I'm not dying to touch you. I'm done hiding—from your family, from Grey, from my kids. Being with you would be the proudest accomplishment of my life, Leigh."

"I think you kissed me stupid. My mouth isn't doing the sentence-making."

When she bit her lower lip, I reached up and hooked it free with my thumb. "When do you leave for Christmas?"

"Monday."

"So... Saturday?"

"Dinner?"

"Yeah." I brushed my mouth over hers, smiling when she lurched forward like she couldn't stand one more inch of space. "I'll have Emmaline take the kids for the night. They'll love it. Then, it's just me and you."

"Deal."

"Good." I took a step back, sliding my hands to her shoulders to hold her in place. Her groan was music, and I wondered how many more sounds I could pull from her when I took my time. Her lips were kiss-swollen, her cheeks flushed, and those wide eyes locked on my face like she didn't want to miss a second. I reached out to smooth her hair—but she caught my hand and pressed it to her chest, right over her heart.

"You mean it? This. Me. You want *this*."

"More desperately than you could possibly comprehend."

A soft smile bloomed on her lips. "I think I can relate."

"*Daddy?*"

We both froze at Beau's voice—quiet, uncertain.

Shit.

We straightened ourselves in record time and rushed out of the pantry. I was still tucking my shirt back in when we rounded the corner and saw him stumble out of the living room.

"What's up, buddy?"

"There are crabs pinching inside my belly." His face was pale as paper. "*Daddy?*"

We both sprang into action—me diving for the trash can, Leigh swooping him up in her arms just as I shoved the can forward.

Poor kid exploded like a geyser.

Leighton winced. I wrinkled my nose. But when our eyes met, we both broke into tired smiles and shook our heads.

Well. That took a turn.

"You sure you're up for a life this glamorous?" I asked as she rubbed his back, trying to soothe him mid-heave. "Kinda a package deal."

Her answering smile could've thawed an iceberg. "So much for pizza night."

TUESDAY MORNING, a suspiciously peaky-looking Leighton showed up, insisting she felt fine. Mattie was down for the count by lunchtime.

As I strategically avoided my boisterous Uncle Reggie by ducking out of my office early, my phone buzzed—and I grimaced.

LEIGHTON

Another one bites the dust.

OLLIE

Nooooo.

Not you too.

LEIGHTON

Yep. The horrors persist.

OLLIE

I'm so sorry.

LEIGHTON

Been a few years since I acquainted myself so
thoroughly with a toilet bowl.

It'll humble me a little.

OLLIE

Oh man, I feel terrible.

LEIGHTON

It's fine, Ollie. I just hope Tillie feels better before
Friday.

MATTIE HAD THREE MORE PERFORMANCES–FRIDAY evening,
Saturday morning, and Sunday night—and missing them would be
a brutal hit to her self-image, so for all of our sakes, I hoped so too. I
told Leigh as much, then asked if she needed anything. Her
response had me chuckling.

LEIGHTON

Just for you to not change your mind when you see me
looking like I got hit by a bus.

OLLIE

Not a chance, Trouble.

LEIGHTON

You so sure? I have an octagon imprinted on my
cheek.

OLLIE

What?

LEIGHTON

Tillie decided laying on the floor was a proper coping
mechanism, and I have to say she's on to something.

OLLIE

I've never been more grateful for the fact that we have
a maid, because the sanitization on that tile would
otherwise be questionable.

LEIGHTON

My apartment would've dealt much stickier results.

OLLIE

Do I want to understand that?

LEIGHTON

Hairspray, you weirdo.

OLLIE

Laughing emojis

See you soon, beautiful.

LEIGHTON

I dare you to say that to octagon face.

OLLIE

Bet.

FORTY MINUTES LATER, I rolled into the driveway with a passenger seat full of crackers, white bread, ginger ale, and applesauce.

A nearly naked Beau was asleep on the couch—Batman underwear-clad ass in the air, face smashed into the cushion like he was trying to break his neck—with *Bluey* running on the television. There was a trash can lined up in front of him, and a half-drunk sippy cup had tipped over beside his feet, steadily dripping onto our blanket.

I dropped the groceries on the kitchen counter, set the water upright on the table, then coaxed Beau into a more conducive sleeping position and covered him up.

The house was silent until I got upstairs, where the softest voice filtered back to me—serrated at the edges, but no less sweet—and made my heart swell.

Leigh was singing about having a son who was "free as a dove," and I narrowed my eyes, straining my ears to catch more of the lyrics. Was she seriously singing "Danny's Song"? God, now *that* was a throwback. What, did she come from Alaska or through a time machine?

And did she have any idea that my children had never known this kind of maternal affection?

Carly hadn't sung to them. Hell, I was convinced she hadn't even *held* them much when they were babies.

A twinge of guilt threatened my resolve. Because what if I was wrong about this? What if she wasn't it—and I lost her because I couldn't get her out of my damn mind?

Gingerly pushing open the cracked bathroom door, I found them right where I'd imagined. Mattie was sprawled on her side across the tile, pale and small, her head resting on her arm.

Leighton was slumped against the wall like her legs had given out, eyes closed, a lazy hand circling over Mattie's back.

"Hey, beautiful," I whispered as I stepped inside.

Her lips quirked. She finished the verse before shaking her head. "Get out of the danger zone before it's too late."

"I'll be fine."

"Just in the mood to regurgitate your intestines?"

Snorting, I crouched in front of her. "I've got an iron stomach. Was never sure how I got it."

"Don't risk it," she said, turning away as I reached for her. When I laid the back of my wrist across her forehead, she sighed, "Oh, man, you've got a death wish."

"No fever. At least that's something." I checked Mattie next. A little warm, but not bad.

"I'm alright. Mattie seems to be the hardest hit."

"She doesn't get sick easily, but when she goes down, she goes *down*."

Leighton smirked. Her glossy eyes shimmered with something dangerous. "I relate to that sentiment on so many levels."

"Yeah?"

"Yeah."

"When was the last time she ralphed?"

"About an hour ago."

"And Beau?"

"Not since last night."

"Good. We should be through the worst of it then."

"My thoughts exactly."

"Think I can move her?"

"*Mmmmmmm*," Mattie groaned, cracking one eye open like a sea creature surfacing from the deep.

"Anywhere has to be more comfortable than here," I pointed out.

"I bet you'll sleep in bed," Leighton predicted.

"Uhhhhhhg. Fine."

I looked down at my little girl's grimace. "Sure. When Leigh says it, you listen."

"Sorry. I'm just that cool," Leighton said, fumbling to stand— then pausing. "Oop. Maybe not," she muttered, eyes scrunching closed as her face went ghost-white. She wobbled, hand reaching out for the counter—and coming up short. I lunged, grabbing her before she could hit the floor.

"Easy, Trouble."

"'M alright."

"Very convincing."

"I mean it. I'm okay." Still, she lowered herself to the ground and tucked her head between her knees.

"I'm gonna get Mattie to bed. I'll be right back, okay?"

"Mm-hmm," she mumbled, not lifting her head.

By the time I came back, Leighton had gone horizontal, cheeks slightly pinker than before. I knelt beside her and brushed the damp curls off her forehead, smiling as her lashes fluttered open.

"I'm sorry you're sick, beautiful."

"I'll get out of your hair," she said, "as soon as I can stand."

"Don't you dare." I stroked through her tangled bun, watching her melt a little. "I'm glad you're here."

She cracked one eye open to glare at me.

"I mean... if you have to be sick, I'm glad you're here so I can take care of you." Not helping, based on how her one eye narrowed. I grabbed a pink washcloth from Mattie's vanity and dampened it with cold water.

"You have a weird definition of 'nanny,'" she murmured.

Smirking, I pressed the cloth gently to her forehead. "You stopped being the nanny the moment I parked out front."

"Mmm." Her eyes drifted shut again. "Missed the memo. You have two sick kids. You don't need to worry about me too."

"Just let me take care of you, baby."

"I should hate that you just called me that," she mumbled, but tilted her face up anyway, letting me tend to her like it was instinct. "*But...*"

"It sounds good when *you* say it." Her lips curved, eyes fluttering open and shut like she couldn't decide whether to fight or surrender.

Well, fuck if that didn't make me preen.

"Hmmm. That's good," I murmured, brushing a knuckle along her jaw. "Take it easy, baby. I've got you."

LEIGHTON

I WOKE up on a plush bed the following morning, soaking up the drool-worthy scent of *him* on the sheets. When I peeled my eyes open, I blinked into the cozy warmth of his bedroom. A vague memory of me cradled to his chest as he carried me to bed had me blushing. Nope. Not gonna think about that too hard. I'd probably leave it out of my daily phone call with Mom. No need to plant that idea in her head. Not yet, anyways.

Mouth full of cotton, I reached for the water on the bedside table, grateful to wash away the lingering acid as I steadied myself.

Mercifully, my guts gave no hint of ejecting, so I did my business and washed up before tiptoeing through the doorway.

Laughter had me padding downstairs before creeping into the kitchen, where I found Ollie and the kids all huddled around the breakfast table, munching on sourdough toast and sipping ginger ale. Everyone had returned to their healthy complexions and—oh my god—that man's smile was like a shot to the chest.

Ollie's sparkling eyes landed on me, and his grin sloped up to the right. "Morning, Trouble."

The image of him in my bed, inked skin kissed by the sun, flashed through my mind, and my ribs constricted.

One night. It wasn't supposed to change anything. But as my hand settled on my palpitating heart and he slid out of the booth and closed the distance between us, I realized just how delusional I'd been, thinking I could taste this man and walk away.

Just sex. Lord, I was gonna have to eat so much crow when Alice found out.

The weight of that thought hit me before my focus scraped over the two kids lifting their heads to grin up at me.

Being with Ollie was an all-or-nothing scenario. And as he approached, looking at me like I gave the sun a reason to shine, I realized maybe that was exactly what I needed. His warm palms grazed over my cheeks, like he really wanted to cradle my face, but opted to brush my hair behind my ears instead.

"Morning, Ollie," I said, beaming up at him as my face heated.

"Feeling better?"

"Much," I assured him with a nod.

"Good. I don't like seeing you like that."

"The feeling's mutual."

"I figured I'd work remotely today. Make sure you three are back on your feet."

"That's okay. I've got it."

"I know," he said, that full mouth I should probably stop staring at hooking left. "But I like feeling useful. I'll whip up something light to ease you all back into the swing of things."

"You're too sweet, Ollie."

"I know," he sighed dramatically. "It's always been my problem."

BY FRIDAY, we were all back in our routines, and Tillie was thrilled she wasn't going to miss her final weekend of performances. I couldn't blame her—she'd worked her little ass off, and it showed in every beautiful motion of her performance.

Despite the warning that we'd all been sick, Emmaline was stoked for a night with the kids, and how on earth that woman was the progeny of Reginald Hart, I would never understand. The fact that his travels had kept him out of family affairs these last few months was a gift to all. His sunshine-fueled daughter was a very different story, and the kids seemed just as thrilled about the pairing.

Which left me, standing in front of my bathroom mirror, dressed in a fabric so far above my pay grade I didn't even have a name for it. Because—in true Oliver fashion—he'd kept his word, and a sexy sapphire-blue dress had been delivered by Freckles Thursday evening.

Normally, I would've sent him a middle finger emoji and worn jeans out of spite, but my breath hitched as the silky material spilled out of the bag and I decided I'd humor him. Not only was it precisely my size, but the sweetheart neckline dipped just low enough to reveal my scar before cresting over my boobs like they belonged on display.

I'd dated a few guys in college—all duds, obviously—and two of them had been embarrassed by the puckered line of skin, like my survival wasn't worth the price of my souvenir. Needless to say, they hadn't made it through the appetizer course before I moved the hell on.

But not Ollie.

The phantom sensation of his lips over my chest had my breath hitching again, just before a knock at the door sent both my lungs and heart sprinting into overdrive. With one last glance at my reflection, I marched out of the bathroom—grateful Kaia had taken the bait and gone to yoga with Alice—and made my way to the front door.

True to his vow in that pantry, Ollie stood there in his usual navy suit, holding a fistful of flowers so stunning my mouth dropped open.

"For the love of all things blush, what the fuck are those? When you said flowers, I'm not gonna lie—I thought roses or daisies or something normal."

He grinned. "Any idiot can get roses."

"And what are these?" I accepted the bouquet, all but burying my face in the giant pink blossoms.

"Ranunculus—"

"Gesundheit."

"Thank you."

"You're welcome."

"Sweet pea," he continued without missing a beat, "and, of course—"

"Morning glory," I finished on a ditsy-sounding exhale, fingers caressing the familiar vine. "Ollie, they're *stunning*."

"One more thing."

"What?" I balked, looking down at the ornate dress painted onto my body, then back at what might as well have been a bridal bouquet.

He laughed and reached into his coat pocket, pulling out—

"Is that a stuffed avocado?" I blinked, accepting the goofy little smiling plushie, shaking my head.

"In case at any point I make you feel *guacward*."

That did it. I lost it, laughing in the most unladylike way humanly possible, which only made his grin widen.

"*So cheesy*," I finally squeaked.

"You love it," he countered, and it was rude how good he looked.

"So, this is why your reputation precedes you."

"Nobody else got an emotional support avocado," he promised, arching a brow.

"You're like melty Chicago-style pizza kinda cheesy," I cackled, rushing to put the flowers in a vase and proudly setting my guacward avocado on the counter beside them.

"And *you're* breathtaking," he said, pressing a hand against the small of my back. When I turned to face him, he'd already closed the distance, fingers raking through my hair as his lips found mine. "Come on, Trouble."

14

Somebody to Love
LEIGHTON

"Oliver Hart, so help me, if you don't give me some kind of explanation, you will have to drag my carcass out of this car, because there is no good reason on God's green earth for us to be in a fucking alleyway right now and—"

"*Inhale.* Good girl." He smirked as I sucked down an obligatory breath, having just expelled the longest sentence known to man in one go. And why did that phrase make my toes curl? Ollie was leaning in the open door of the nondescript black SUV. A man named Arthur had driven us the long way into the city before parking between two buildings that were far too close together to be code compliant. The Harts used these cars when they didn't want to be easily recognized—I knew that. But why were we sneaking through a dank alley? Was he *trying* to get mugged?

"Stop analyzing and just let me have some fun."

My eyes narrowed to slits, which only earned a full-belly laugh and a more insistently extended hand.

Shaking my head—and failing to fully suppress my smile—I slid my palm into his. He helped me out and gave me a twirl, like he needed to see me in motion. The move made something in my chest swell with pride I didn't know I needed. There was something ridiculously wonderful about being this man's prize. His answering smile was blinding, a beat before he pressed a chaste kiss to my forehead.

Frankly, chaste was not my current vibe.

The man was delectable, and the fact that he'd clearly put effort into this when pizza on the couch would've thrilled me gave me the absurd urge to climb him like a koala right here in the alley. *Sorry, Arthur.*

132

Instead, I had to pretend to be civilized as Ollie directed me forward down the grimy asphalt, his hand warm at the small of my back. Arthur swept open a metal door with a groan, motioning us inside, and I nodded slowly, curiosity eating me alive.

"This is a slasher film," I muttered as I stepped into nothing but darkness. "My siblings have me on a tracking app," I called out. "You'll never get away with it."

"Shut up, Trouble," he teased.

God, the things I would do to hear the smile in this man's voice.

"There's always a slip-up. DNA under the fingernails. You'll miss something."

"I said shut up. Just let it happen."

"Ollie, it's black as pitch."

"Almost like that's the point or something."

"Can you just tell me what we're doing?" I demanded as he pushed me forward step by step. Okay, "pushed" might've been an exaggeration, but I did not care for the total lack of visibility. Only the faint light from a distant streetlamp cut the gloom. Another dozen paces in, he halted me with a gentle grip on my shoulders. He cleared his throat, turned me to face him—and then clapped his hands loudly twice.

I yelped, then burst into laughter.

That laughter died the moment blinding lights flicked on and revealed the *theater*.

But not just any theater.

This space was magnificent. My head tilted back on instinct as I gaped up at the elaborate burgundy, blue, and gold ceiling—intricate little details carved into every inch. Crystal chandeliers glowed warmly, twinkling as they caught the light. Whirling, I took in the art deco archways, swathed in draped maroon fabric, and the intricately framed stage at the far end. Art adorned every corner—down to the gold swirls etched into the bases of the plush velvet seats. It was old Hollywood personified. I could practically see the who's-who of the 1950s drifting through in tuxedos and gowns. He'd taken me back in time.

"Ollie," I breathed.

Empty. The place was completely empty—except for four smiling employees standing at the top of the red carpeted aisle.

"I don't understand."

"You deserve to be courted properly, Leigh," he said softly, "and while I fully intend to show you off like the proudest man on the planet, I won't do that to your life until you're all in. The last thing I want is the press in your business while you're still deciding what you want from this. Tonight is just for you, baby. Everyone here has signed an NDA."

Oh holy hell, my face tried to light on fire. My stomach flipped like it had just dismounted from a trapeze.

"But what are we doing?" I asked, my voice hushed, eyes still on the four employees—who seemed to spring into action the moment the words left my mouth. Had Ollie given them a signal?

Two in tailored red uniforms with vintage gold piping stepped to the sides while the other two, dressed in white button-ups, bow ties, and suspenders, approached us wearing retro snack trays slung around their necks.

"Ms. Rhodes, Mr. Hart, welcome," said the first man, offering me a popcorn container striped in red and white. "We're so pleased to have you for a private screening this evening."

I didn't even want to know what Ollie paid to pull this off.

"Please sit wherever you'd like," the second added, gesturing to the center row. Ollie guided me forward, hand still warm against my back.

Once we were seated—dead center—the attendants placed glass Coke bottles in our cupholders and filled the space between us with snacks: Milk Duds, Clark Bars, and some chewy-looking candy I'd never seen before.

"Enjoy the show," the first said, bowing slightly before both attendants slipped away.

"Say something, Trouble."

I turned to find him looking...*nervous?* That was cute as hell. With tears stinging the bridge of my nose, I croaked, "You're insane."

"Well aware. That's why God made me beautiful, to compensate."

"And humble too."

"Not a word the Harts are taught."

"How did you do this?"

"Just a few phone calls," he said, shrugging like this was no big deal—but the way he squeezed my hand said otherwise. His heart was in his throat, too. "But am I on the money?"

"That depends on what happens next."

He grinned, jerking his chin toward the screen just as the lights dimmed. Upbeat '50s music crackled to life. The projector hummed. Then the Paramount logo filled the space.

My breath caught as the opening sequence of *Funny Face* began.

"Ollie!" I barked, eyes already blurring.

"Good pick?"

I nodded, blinking fast. "You're insane."

"The good kind, not the rocking-in-the-corner kind, I hope."

"You're *incredible*."

"No, *you're* incredible," he corrected, just as Kay Thompson marched through the magazine office on screen.

"How did you know I love Audrey Hepburn?"

"You're into the classics," he said simply. Like it was obvious. Like he hadn't just arranged the most perfect date in the history of the world.

"You are *so* getting lucky," I whispered, prompting a full-hearted laugh as he wrapped an arm around my shoulders and tucked me in close.

"We'll see."

"We'll see? *Psh.* The things I want to do to you right now."

Chuckling, he shook his head, kissed my temple, and whispered, "Watch the movie, Trouble."

AS THE FILM CREDITS ROLLED, our uniformed ushers returned and the magnificent lights came back to life.

"Did you enjoy the show?" the first asked as they collected our empty snack boxes, motioning toward the aisle.

"It was perfect," I said, beaming over my shoulder at a smug-looking Oliver.

"Wonderful. Ready for the next phase of your evening?"

"Next phase?" I balked, turning to see him smirking at his shiny fucking shoes.

Ollie shrugged. "You didn't think that was it, did you?"

"Kinda," I squeaked. "*Yeah.*"

"Follow the gentleman in pinstriped pants, Leigh."

"You're bossy tonight."

"And you like it."

"How would you know?"

"Because your skin flushes every time I tell you what to do."

"Oh, it *does not*," I argued, even as I followed the ushers—limbs buzzing with what was definitely not excitement. (It was totally excitement. Maybe also the second bottle of Coke I'd chugged like a lifeline.)

"Whatever helps you sleep at night."

"Preferably an orgasm or two."

"Jesus, Leigh." Grinning, I rushed to keep up with the men in red jackets. They led us through the stunning space to a brass elevator with an old-school control panel. When the doors opened again, we stepped onto the roof.

String lights illuminated a concrete terrace bordered by potted greenery and the building's brick façade. Beyond that—twinkling city skyline. All to the gentle serenade of a live string quartet playing *Moondance.*

"Ollie," I whispered, shaking my head. "This is way too much."

"Do you know me at all?" he asked in mock offense. "I'm *just* getting started."

"Don't say that—I might keel over."

"You look just fine to me," he said with a smirk that could melt concrete.

The ushers led us to a sleek bistro table. One of them helped Ollie out of his jacket while the other pulled out my chair and scooted me in like I was royalty. White gloves. Gold name tags. I'd grown up on an island without traffic lights—this was *not* my normal.

He'd gone all out. No wonder he was so cocky about needing only one night. Some deeply masochistic part of me wanted to know what the hell Carly had been thinking, letting a man like this slip through her fingers. Real men didn't do this. This was fiction shit.

Maybe that was why she was so bitter. She'd lost a man who made Disney princes look like underachievers and was now making it everybody's problem.

Before I could ask for a menu, two silver trays were delivered—each topped with a domed lid that was lifted with theatrical precision to reveal... *street tacos.*

An artfully arranged pile of them. With ramekins full of lime wedges and what had to be hot sauce.

I burst out laughing as Ollie leaned back in his chair, looking far too pleased with himself. The music shifted again, the opening notes striking a familiar chord, and my spine straightened as my mouth dropped open.

"Are they playing Queen?" I gasped, recognizing *Somebody to Love.*

"They'll play whatever you ask them to," he said, rolling up his sleeves.

One of the musicians chuckled, clearly not a stranger to Oliver Hart.

"Michael Jackson?" I challenged.

Without missing a beat, they slipped into *Thriller.*

"*Sweet Child of Mine?*" They paused, conferred briefly, then launched into the melody so seamlessly I thought I might cry.

My mouth fell open so wide my jaw popped, and Ollie lost it.

"You like it?"

"You're perfect. Flamboyantly over the top for a woman content in yesterday's pajamas and reruns—but perfect nonetheless."

"You deserve over the top."

"There's nothing closeted about your romantic, is there?" I muttered, chewing on my lip.

"Aww, thanks." His flat tone made me laugh again as he nodded toward my tacos. "Eat while they're hot."

"*Bossy.*"

"You like it."

I did. I really, *really* did.

Many songs, five tacos, two pictures, and several dances later, Ollie finally ushered me back into the SUV, strung as taut as one of the quartet's bowstrings. By the time Arthur dropped us at my building and Ollie walked me up, I was positive the man could brush a feather over my skin and I'd go nuclear.

So when we reached my doorway and turned to face each other, my heart was thundering like a war drum in my chest.

There was so much fondness—bottomless certainty—in his eyes that I forgot how to breathe.

"I had a great time tonight. I hope you enjoyed yourself."

The memory of him whispering those words after making me fall apart in his arms ghosted over my skin. *One night,* he'd said. Hell, one night and I was already ruined.

"Ollie, that was insane."

"My first thought was a Vegas show, but I figured if I flew you somewhere, you'd punch me in the arm."

"Accurate."

"So this was what I landed on that didn't require stitches."

"Well," I purred, stepping in close and nearly groaning when his hands found my face and waist, "it pains me to admit it, but you were right on the money."

He chuckled, one hand easing to the back of my neck while the other tugged me against him. His kiss was slow this time. Intentional. Luxuriously indulgent.

My hands slid up his chest and around his back, holding him there.

This—this felt so right. It didn't feel like desperation or performance. It just... *was.*

Warm and pliant, and planting the steady flap of butterfly wings in my belly. Delicious and unhurried, as though we had all the time in the world.

A perfect exhale after a perfect night.

Which is why my heart stuttered because there was goodbye in his eyes.

"Goodnight, Trouble."

Then he turned and walked away.

"Are you serious!?"

His only reply was a low, bemused chuckle as he disappeared down the hall.

And my damn heels? Absolutely glued to the floor.

. . .

OLIVER

PERFECT. She was so goddamn perfect I could feel my pulse in every inch of my skin. The marrow of my bones sang with it. My cock had been at half-mast for most of the evening, and the look of stunned horror on her face as I walked away hadn't been enough to convince it to calm down.

But I had a plan. A strategy. One I intended to follow if I wanted to win her over—really win her over. Because this woman wasn't a fling. She was it. The answer to a prayer I didn't realize I'd made. The universe's defibrillator for my heart. Just as jarring. Just as brutally necessary. Probably twice as exhilarating.

One night. That's what I'd asked for, so I could beg for another. And that's exactly what I planned to do—right after I jacked off in the fucking shower. Because no amount of strategic restraint could convince my body to chill out after having her hands on me, her voice in my ear, and those gray-blue eyes looking at me like that.

All very noble in theory, promptly destroyed by the chirp of my alarm system and the sharp voice of the man Jackson called "Viper" over the comms: "Ms. Rhodes, is everything alright?"

Leighton?

Her sharp, "It's fine. Now at ease, or whatever it is you say that means 'go away,' please," had me laughing as I wrapped a towel around my waist and jogged into the hallway.

I met the steely eyes of Captain Reynolds' latest addition—dark hair, darker glare—who clearly didn't love finding me half-naked. He scowled, but dipped his chin and disappeared down the stairs.

Then she turned that fire on me.

"What the hell was that?"

"What?" I asked, amused—and more than a little distracted by her bare legs and wet hair. She'd changed into an oversized charcoal T-shirt and unlaced Docs. Her long hair hung in damp waves to either side of her face, and she looked like she'd just stepped off the cover of every punk-rock daydream I'd ever had. And she was pissed.

I wasn't sure if I should laugh, run, or drop to my knees and beg for forgiveness.

"*You* pursued *me*," she said, stomping forward. "*You* asked *me* out. Then you proceed to plan the world's most romantic evening in history, and you just leave me there with panties so wet they would've dissolved if they were edible?!"

"Jesus Christ, Trouble."

"That's one." She held up her finger like she was keeping score.

To his credit, Viper didn't crack a smile, but he did speed up his retreat. My parents would've rolled in their graves—again—if they knew how often I got scolded in my own damn house.

She stormed into my space before her eyes finally dropped to my bare chest, and widened like she hadn't realized I was wearing nothing but a towel until she could smell the body wash.

"I already told you."

"Told me what?"

"I want to do this right this time."

"By edging me out?"

"I mean…" I smirked when her eyes narrowed. "Edging can be pretty beneficial. You don't know what you're missing."

"You didn't even come in for coffee."

"You didn't ask."

"It was implied."

"Was it? I missed that."

"The kids are with Emma."

"Hence, the quiet house."

"Then why are they staying over if you didn't intend to use our freedom to its fullest?"

"I did, Trouble."

She blinked, her throat working in a way that was going to cause me problems sooner rather than later. This towel was *thin*.

"Hence the tacos?"

"Why? Do you not want—"

"Unless you want a pink outline of my hand on your ass, you will *not* finish that sentence."

She straightened. Pupils blown wide. "What if that's exactly what I want?"

"Then you're going to have to wait."

"This is what you meant by 'maybe' earlier? You knew you were going to wind me up like a top and let me spin out all by myself."

Grinning, I closed the distance. Her hands landed on my chest, but her scowl remained.

"You're not being punished, Leighton."

"My lady blue balls beg to differ. You're the one who went all caveman in the pantry. I didn't ask you to turn me on and leave me hanging. Is this a milk and the cow for free thing?"

"That's not quite how that saying—"

"Explain yourself, Hart."

I cupped her face and kissed her hard enough to shut her up. Her fists curled against my chest. She didn't push me away, but when she pulled back, there was something in her eyes that hit like a punch to the sternum.

"Do you not want me? Why go to all that effort if—"

"*Leighton*," I warned, noses brushing.

"Don't 'Leighton' me. Make it make sense, Oliver. If you feel half of what I do, there's no way you'd go to all that effort just to... *oh.*"

Her voice faltered as I grabbed her hand and guided it to the problem she was very much responsible for—still hard, still pulsing. Her eyes flew to mine.

"I've already gotten off with your name on my fucking lips tonight. I want you, baby. More than you know."

"Then why, prey tell, are we torturing ourselves?"

"Because I fucked up, Leighton. I made you feel like a cheap hookup, when you've been my world for the better part of a year." Her mouth parted, and I traced her bottom lip with my thumb. "I've been in love with you since long before I knew how good you taste. And it has *nothing* to do with how badly I want to ravage your body."

I brushed my lips over hers, savoring her, torturing myself. Her palm still pressed against my growing erection as I whispered, "For months, I've looked for ways to pull you closer. Irritate you. Befriend you. Take whatever scraps I could get—because any part of you was better than nothing. You deserve a man who worships at your feet without asking for anything back. Who makes you feel like the only woman in the world. And I'm telling you right now, I have no intentions of standing by and watching someone else be that man."

"You... you *love me*?" Her voice was small, eyes wide and glassy. But her hands were roaming over my chest again, so I held on to hope.

"I was a goner the moment you showed up in my life. Watching you with my kids. Watching you pull Mattie from the water and hold her like she was your own—I was fucking gone."

Her fingers traced slow patterns through my chest hair, eyes down. When the silence dragged too long, I leaned in.

"Say something."

"I don't deserve you."

"Motion denied. *Next?*"

"You could have anyone."

"I'm standing here with you, aren't I?"

"There are things I haven't told you."

"Then tell me when you're ready."

"You really mean all that?" she whispered.

"I've got all the time in the world to convince you."

"And... what if I already believe you?" She flushed as she said it.

"I promised to beg for another night, didn't I?"

"You can have all my nights, Ollie."

Fuck. If I wasn't a grown-ass man, I might have thumped my chest like *Tarzan*. "Good. Because I've been trying to think of how to steal them."

She laughed, rising onto her toes to kiss me again. I pulled her into me, spinning with equal parts joy and disbelief. She was here. She was mine. No screaming or anger, or veiled threats. But then Leighton was letting go, my heart sinking and then bolting forward as her fingers trailed down my abs, to the knot of the towel.

She looked up, eyes hungry. My cock jerked in response.

"What would you say," she asked, voice sultry, "if I wanted to thank you for the most perfect night out?"

15

Impossibly Possible
LEIGHTON

"I'd tell you there's not a fucking chance. We do this my way this time."

Before I could reply, he surged forward, scooped me into his arms, and pivoted toward his bedroom.

"Ollie!" I squeaked—right before his mouth crashed into mine, urgent and ravenous, licking deep until every painstaking hour of education melted into a slick puddle of brain-goop.

All sense? Gone.

Independence? Haven't seen her.

I was waist-deep in a rush of heat, thighs squeezing together as he carried us somewhere—who cared where? Oliver Hart was kissing me.

And he kissed like I'd starved him of oxygen, like the world began and ended right here beneath the sure command of his mouth and the possessive grip of his hands. I looped my arms around his neck, tugging him closer, shuddering when he bit my lower lip in invitation. My fingers buried in his hair.

"What are you doing?" I breathed.

"Taking my time." His words brushed my lips before he dove back in. "I was going to do this the right way, Leighton. I was going to *date you.*"

"You're my best friend in this city, and I've already sucked your dick, so that's wildly unnecessary."

"Jesus Christ, Trouble."

"That's two."

He clamped his teeth down on my lip and growled, "So bull-headed."

"Since when do men complain about women *wanting* sex?"

"Since I wanted to be a gentleman and show you the goddamn world first."

"That was adorably optimistic." I scattered kisses across his chest as he kicked the bedroom door shut.

"Stubborn woman—won't even let me woo her properly."

"Consider me thoroughly wooed."

"Persistent little thing, aren't you?"

"You've got no idea."

"I'm beginning to." He tossed me onto the bed, and I landed with a bounce, squeaking as he followed and—oh my God—his towel was gone. Every bronzed inch of him draped over me. I couldn't decide whether to ogle the tattoos or the delicious muscles running down his back.

His Monday confession slammed into me, short-circuiting logic while his lips and teeth found my neck. The man didn't need a Hollywood spectacle—he already had me. But damn, it felt incredible to be wanted like this, by a man confident enough to take the shot.

To kiss, taste, and touch like his life depended on it. And maybe it did, because every glide of his hands and bruising press of his lips said he needed this as desperately as I did.

But I needed more.

Needed him everywhere.

I hooked my legs around his waist and yanked him flush against me. He rocked his hips, grinding against me like I drove him just as wild. He did it again, sliding a knee between my thighs; his thick cock pressed against my center, separated only by the tiniest scrap of lace I owned.

"*Fuuuck.*" He scraped his palms up my ribs, stripping me of my tee the instant I arched for him. It hit the floor as his gaze dropped to my bare breasts; he pinched a hard nipple, and pleasure detonated, arching me off the mattress as he rutted again. "You came over wearing just *that?*"

My God, the sting of pleasure and pain was so fucking delicious. When he abandoned my breast I whimpered, but his hand slid down my torso, cupping my pussy through the damp fabric; a groan lodged in his chest as he pressed our foreheads together.

"Dammit, Leigh."

"Never met a man who complains ab—" The words died in a gasp when he shoved the thong aside and sank a finger deep into my center. He curled it, finding a spot no toy could reach.

"I love how responsive you are," he growled, "but you're gonna make me blow way before I'm ready."

"You say that like I'm not already planning round two."

"That so?" That smile could incinerate me. Heat flooded my

chest as my slick walls clenched around his finger. Some primal part of me begged him to take what he wanted, to come inside me—

"Whatever's running through that mind, *don't stop*," he breathed, licking down my neck, sucking a nipple into his mouth until it ached. I didn't remember them feeling bruised like that last time, but I didn't have long to think about it; the sight of him worshipping me shoved me over the edge. He withdrew and returned with two fingers, popping off my breast.

"So fucking stunning. So damn wet for me. You're the most beautiful woman I've ever seen."

A generous exaggeration, considering his supermodel track record, but the thought evaporated when he caged my head with his arms, eyes burning.

"I'm all in, Leigh. This isn't just physical for me. I need you to know that."

I nodded. *Good. I could still move.* That was something. Now if I could just find words…

"Show me," I whispered. "*Here.* Now."

His grin turned wolfish. "Oh, you're not ready for that, baby."

"Don't tell me what I'm ready for—*show me.*"

He captured my mouth, hand slipping between us to notch his cock at my slick entrance. He dragged his crown through my wetness, swiping over my clit, and I bucked, desperate for more.

His head dropped as pre-cum gleamed on his tip, and he ran a thumb over the pearl of liquid. Lust hooded brown eyes lifted to my mouth as he palmed his thick crown. "Open, beautiful."

I parted my lips, heat blooming as he cupped my cheek and slid that thumb between my lips. I sucked the salty trace of him, filthy and delicious.

"Good fucking girl." He pressed a kiss to my forehead, then stretched over me for the bedside drawer. Ink shifted on his chest—a pocket watch cradled in laurel leaves, frozen at 7:03—before he pressed a condom into my hand and shoved my thong down my legs like its existence offended him.

"Lift."

I obeyed, and the torn lace vanished.

Tearing open the foil with my teeth, I slipped out the slick rubber and smiled up at him as he straightened above me, his hand grazing over my face with so much adoration it nearly sent a chill down my spine. He stroked himself, and another drop pearled, my pulse spiking.

"Put it on me." His voice was pure command, and the throb between my legs answered *yes, sir.* He knew it, too.

Holding his gaze, I nudged his hand aside and fisted that glorious, veiny length. He moaned, head tipping back. I slid the condom down, cupping his balls; his eyes snapped open, ravenous.

He was going to devour me.

"Turn over, Leigh." He eased back. "All fours." I scrambled into position—anything but graceful, yet his grin said it was perfect.

Rough palms closed over my hips.

"My little Aphrodite is quite eager to please."

I nodded. What was a mortal supposed to say to *that?* The goddess of love? Holy shit.

"I fucking knew it." He folded his body over mine, one hand clamping my hip while the other skimmed up my side, raising goose-bumps until his fingers curled at my neck. Ollie turned my face, stealing a kiss so primal it bordered on worship. "Remind me— didn't you beg for my handprint on this pretty ass?"

I nodded—desperate.

The crack rang out a beat before the sting bloomed. A gasp tore free, my pussy clenching as my mouth fell open.

Polite, respectful Oliver was gone. This version—feral and commanding—lit me up.

Another nod, another slap, another quiver of anticipation rippled through my core as I arched back into him.

"You like that," he rasped.

I nodded again. A third smack sent a helpless moan spiraling from my throat; I braced on my forearms, pressing my ass into his palm.

"Good." He soothed the sting with a slow rub, then lined his cock at my entrance, sliding the swollen tip through my slick folds. "I need you, Leighton—more than you can imagine."

"Then take me."

He did—no warning, no preamble, no hesitation. One brutal, beautiful thrust filled me to the hilt. The stretch bordered on pain, pleasure spiking so sharp my legs trembled.

So.

Fucking.

Full.

Holy hell, the man *just* got inside me and my body was shud-dering around him.

"Good girl," he murmured. "You've got all of me, baby."

I sucked in a breath and arched, drawing him somehow deeper. He chuckled.

"Feeling needy?"

"Seven weeks," I panted into the crook of my arm. "You ruined Obi, asshole."

He laughed, gave my backside a playful clap. "Be mine and you'll never be left wanting again. I'm at your disposal."

"*Ten out of ten*," I shot back, breathless.

His husky laughter was wickedly *erotic*, especially as his hands raked along my sides. "What were you thinking earlier—when my fingers were buried in that pretty pussy?"

I hummed—or maybe squeaked—but couldn't put words to the filthy images in my brain, my neck flushing hot as he chuckled knowingly.

"Tell me, Leighton. What had you clenching around me?"

"You?"

"What about me?"

Heat flooded my cheeks. "You. Filling me with cum."

"Fuuuck." The growl rolled through him—and me. "Leaking down your thighs after?"

"That's the idea."

"Jesus Christ, Trouble."

"That's three," I taunted.

He exhaled a ragged breath. "Hang on, baby. I'm going to ruin you tonight."

"I dare you to try."

His grip tightened; he pulled almost free, then slammed home. My world detonated.

"Yes!" I cried.

Ollie settled into a punishing rhythm—harder, deeper—hands roaming as if he couldn't touch enough. Fingers fisted in my hair; he shoved my head down, looped an arm under my hips, angling impossibly deeper.

"Oh, my fucking—*Ollie*—oh god—fuck, fuck, *fuck*—"

"You're doing so good, Leigh." *Thrust.* "Take my cock like such a good girl." *Thrust.* Each guttural word arrowed straight to my core. He pounded into me like he meant to split me in two, and I devoured every ecstatic second, surrendering to the mattress, ass up, body his to command.

"Your pretty pink pussy looks gorgeous wrapped around me." My walls fluttered; sweat beaded over my skin as he drove me to the brink. "Who's going to make you come?"

"You are."

"Damn straight. Who owns your pleasure, Leighton?"

"You do." No contest. Not even a question.

"Good. Say my name."

"*Ollie!*"

"Fuck, yes. Now give me what I want—come for me, beautiful."

"I—*need*—"

"I know. Be my good girl and come all over my cock."

Praise and demand. Apparently that was the recipe for mind-blowing, earth-shattering, leg shaking orgasms. I came so hard my abs cramped. I convulsed around him, crying out as the orgasm shattered every nerve.

He rode me through it, then pressed a hand between my shoulder blades, grinding deep once, twice, before freezing with a guttural, "Fuuuuck."

We collapsed in a sweaty heap, his face buried in my neck.

"So," I panted, "*that's* what it's like to get fucked by Oliver Hart." No spanking the first time; he'd promised gentle, and I'd had no idea what the alternative was. *Holy hell.*

His laugh was ragged, satisfied, and impossibly bright. A woman could live off that sound.

"Yeah, baby."

"You held out on me the first time."

"Because you weren't *mine* on Halloween."

Jiminy. Fucking. Cricket.

I was toast—and I couldn't even pretend to be mad about it.

GOLDEN SUNLIGHT CREPT across the bed, and every muscle ached as I rolled over, reaching for Ollie—only empty sheets greeted my fingertips. I blinked into the warmth, stomach pitching as I propped myself on one elbow.

Before I could sit up, cheerful whistling floated in. The door swung open, and Ollie danced inside to Van Morrison's *Days Like This.*

His carefree grin made me beam almost as wide as last night's rose-oil bath had. As if half a dozen orgasms weren't enough to liquefy a woman, he'd pampered me with an Epsom-salt soak and a slow, oil-slick massage. What dumb bitch died and made me queen of Emerald Bay?

Still grooving, he balanced a huge breakfast tray on one palm.

"Hungry, Trouble?"

"Starving." I tried to stifle the ear-to-ear grin threatening to split my face. "We must've burned a million calories, because I'm nauseously hungry."

"Well, you've come to the right place."

"Have I?" I scooted against the headboard, dragging the comforter with me. "Don't hold out on me."

"Eggs benny and turkey bacon—you're gonna love it." He edged closer, tray held high while he moon-walked around the foot of the bed.

"Asshole," I laughed, cheeks aching as he broke into some head-bob-Egyptian strut. "Ollie!" I complained, stretching grabby hands toward him.

"Okay, okay."

"Someone is looking outrageously smug," I observed.

"Yes, well—Leighton Rhodes came on my cock last night. Forgive the swagger."

I snorted, biting my lip as he presented the tray with a flourish. Thick hollandaise glossed two poached eggs, dusted with cayenne and tucked against a juicy tomato slice and two asparagus spears. Turkey bacon lined the side; orange wedges rimmed the plate. Two glasses of juice wore matching citrus crescents, and coffee steamed beside a silver creamer and a tiny bowl of sweeteners—topped with a single pink blossom.

But the *smell*—was that butter in his hollandaise off?

Hot saliva flooded my mouth. Panic crawled up my throat. "Not good." I bolted.

"Leigh?!" Glasses clinked behind me as I sprinted to the bathroom.

Knees cracked against tile right as my stomach heaved—nothing but bile. I barely caught a breath before another wave forced me over the mercifully polished porcelain throne. Ollie's bare feet bracketed mine; he gathered my hair off my shoulders.

Fully naked.

Dry-heaving.

With Oliver Hart holding my hair. Perfect.

Fuck. My life.

When the spasms eased, I collapsed back on my heels, trembling. "Oh my God, I'm so sorry."

"Why are you apologizing?" He flushed for me, then helped me lean against the wall.

"I just—you made breakfast—what the fuck?"

"You good for a second?"

I nodded, mortified. He returned with water, crouching as I swished and spit.

"You okay?"

"I think so. Must be the tail end of that bug. Have you heard from Emma—are the kids alright?"

"They're at the zoo," he said, some unreadable warmth in his eyes. "Nobody's sick, baby."

He cocked his head, studying me. "Leigh, it's almost Christmas."

"Hey, left field called—they want their ball back."

He chuckled, then sat, peeling off his T-shirt in one smooth move before tugging it over my head. The humiliation eased the second the cotton fell to mid-thigh.

But my brain buzzed through worst-case scenarios.

Fatigue. Light-headedness. Now puking and shaking? The old fear of my heart condition slithered free. *Not again.* My pulse felt steady, but dread wound up my spine. *God, not again.*

"Leigh, did you hear me?"

I blinked up at him; the crease between his brows had deepened.

"It's late December. You haven't been down for the count once. You've never called in sick for cramps. When was your last cycle, baby?"

"What?"

"You said your cycles vary but never go longer than ninety days. When was your last period?"

October. The beginning of October. The answer crashed through me, silent and horrifying.

"Impossible," I whispered.

"Condoms break. We went through, what, six?"

"I can't get pregnant, Ollie."

Terror iced his features. "What do you mean, Trouble? Unsafe for your heart?" He glanced at the scars he'd worshipped but never questioned. "I know the best doctors in the city—say the word."

"Ollie, they told me I was sterile. PCOS, no ovulation, 'inhospitable environment.'"

Agony flickered across his face, but his hand cupped my arm. "Just to be safe, let me order a test."

I shook my head, finding my feet as the bridge of my nose burned. Terror turned my breaths shallow, and I fought to control them as every shaking muscle in my body begged me to *run*—to go anywhere but here. *Anywhere* I could actually let the tears roll without the world's most amazing man watching me crumble like a poorly-constructed house of cards.

Fuck, I needed my mom. *Great.* Twenty-three, and I needed my fucking mommy. *Pathetic.*

But as the echo of monitors rang in my skull, I realized I didn't care if that made me pitiful.

"Shit—I have yoga with the girls. What time is it?"

"Just after nine."

"Okay. I'm late." Literally and figuratively.

"Don't go—tell them you're sick."

"It's fine. I need to clear my head. I'll come back after, and we'll talk. I don't want them to be worried."

"Leighton, *I'm* worried."

"I'll take a test after class, and call my doctor either way."

"I'll drive—"

"You've got the kids waiting." My voice miraculously stayed level while I shattered inside. "I'm okay. Promise."

He didn't buy it, shadowed eyes following me while I gathered clothes, but he let me go. Tears hit the moment I slid into California traffic.

Two hours, one unfocused yoga class, and three pregnancy tests later, I sat on a different bathroom floor, staring at three sets of unmistakable double pink lines.

A knock at the door had me jumping out of my skin.

Kaia. "Leigh? You okay?"

16

Pineapple Does Belong On Pizza
LEIGHTON

<u>The Little Women Chat:</u>

KAIA

Emergency sister call in 10.

ALICE

You okay?

KAIA

Everyone is in one piece. Just need ears. All hands on deck.

I'm looking at you @Jeanne.

HADLEE

Can we make it 20? I'm right in the middle of something.

KAIA

Fine. Don't be late.

HADLEE

Rude.

ELORA

Like she's wrong, Hads?

ELORA

@Jeanne

Can I at least get an agenda?

ALICE

What am I preparing for? Are we destroying someone, or planning a yoga retreat?

ELORA

Two very different hats to wear.

JEANNE

Still pregnant, sissy?

HADLEE

Oh look, it breathes.

JEANNE

Do you have any idea what time it is here?

KAIA

Where is here?

JEANNE

Tokyo.

HADLEE

Makes sense.

JEANNE

What's going on?

ELORA

Yes. Still incubating the little man. Brex had Emma, but I am, evidently, enduring an elephant's gestation.

HADLEE

Maybe he's just his daddy's duplicate, and he's too busy overthinking the proper birth strategy to come out.

ELORA

Middle finger emojis

ALICE

Anybody else notice that mating season was rather fruitful this year?

JEANNE

Jesus, this family.

KAIA

Anybody with mom?

ALICE

What? Who's going early? Dammit, I thought Pax was first down tonight, and Leigh flies out tomorrow. Did somebody add Brex on the chat?

JEANNE

thinking emoji This is our only sacred bio-sister space.

ALICE

Why do we need mom on the call?

Wait a damn second.

Narrow chicken eyes gif

Is somebody pregnant?

HADLEE

Yeah, Elora.

ALICE

HahahahaHA. What ELSE would we have an emergency girls-only call for?

If somebody got promoted, we'd be bragging on the main chat.

Rubbing the guys' noses in it.

Jeanne was clueless, so she's obviously not coming home or something.

JEANNE

Hey, also rude.

ALICE

No. This screams women problems.

ELORA

Where the fuck is Leighton?

OLLIE'S CHAT

LEIGHTON

I need you.

"SISSY, you're going to be fine. We'll all tackle this together."

I was vaguely aware that I nodded, but my eyes were trained somewhere very, very far away. Through the floor of my bathroom and about three thousand miles north, in a hospital room that smelled like alcohol, panic attacks, and death.

"We'll find the best high-risk OB in the city," Kaia vowed, squeezing my fingers where they hung limply off my knees. "If, of course, you want to keep it."

"I'm keeping it—*them*," I snapped, that concept finally yanking me out of my stupor. "I'm keeping them. Him. *Her*." I scowled. I was not boy mom material.

"Okay. So do we need to call OBs or cardiologists first?"

"Both?" I guessed, still feeling beyond dazed. "I don't know, I've never thought about this. OB, I guess. Make sure she's okay in there before I worry about potential cardiac complications."

There was something unspeakably staggering about finding out something "impossible" might have, indeed, been possible. I guess Audrey Hepburn was right, after all. Part of me wanted to fly back to Alaska just to punch that stone-faced knob goblin of a doctor square in the nose for speaking with such authority when, clearly, he might've been wrong. But the rest of me was terrified that the jackass had been right, and this wouldn't be sustainable. That I'd lose her, just like the rest of my dreams—because that seemed to be how things went for me.

That Ollie would hate me when it happened. That I wouldn't be able to keep our baby safe.

I wasn't one for internalized misogyny, but for fuck's sake, living with the idea that my body couldn't do the one thing females of every species—well, except for seahorses, the adorable backwards weirdos—managed to accomplish had been a devastating blow.

Hell, I'd never even had a man, and I'd still carried that weight like a curse. Not because I wanted to please a man someday, or provide an heir like some Regency-era queen, but because I loved our packed house growing up.

When Rhyett, Jameson, and Broderick won their championship game, the entire football team lifted us girls onto their shoulders and carried us around like town royalty.

I loved that my brother's geeky best friend once hoisted some asshole up by the scruff of his collar and dumped him in a trash can to defend me. The sound of forty people reuniting over pumpkin pie and coffee every holiday.

I'd wanted that.

Terrified or not, if this pregnancy was viable, it was a gift I never thought I'd get.

"Reviews are mixed on this one, but his cesarean rates are the lowest in the city," Kaia murmured, swiping through her phone.

"Allegedly terrible bedside manner, but his complications are basically non-existent due to his willingness to trust mom's body and baby. Oh—this reviewer says he's autistic. That explains the bedside manner-to-competency ratio. I like him. Personally, I don't care if he's nice to talk to. I care about how quickly he can get baby out if you need him to. Let's schedule a consult." She scrolled again. "This lady has fantastic bedside manner and her stats are pretty solid, although she's more prone to interventions. Do you even care about that at this point? I mean, we already know there'll be extra precautions either way."

My nose stung as I blinked away the fog in my vision, trying to focus on my sister's glowing face. Kaia had always been the gentler, more polished of the two of us—but there, in my fancy bathroom lighting, she looked luminous. Her eyeshadow made our gray-blue eyes pop. It was the tight pinch of focus between her brows that had my throat thickening.

It would be okay.

If the doctors said we were safe, I would figure this out. Land on my feet. And this baby would be so fucking loved, she'd have no idea what to do with all the excess.

"Well?" Kaia demanded, her eyes snapping to mine.

"What?" I breathed.

"Honestly, Leigh, I love you, but take a cold shower or something, because we need to focus. You're probably what—nine-ish weeks?"

Halloween was almost eight weeks ago. I nodded.

"And the father? Do you want him involved? I will take this to my grave if he was some rando in a bar bathroom or something. Not all of us can be Rhyett with his one-in-a-million fucking luck."

A little giggle bubbled out of me as something like hope bloomed in my chest. "He wasn't a rando in a bar bathroom."

"Oh. Okay... and... do we *like* this not-a-rando?"

"So much," I admitted, my lip wobbling.

"Oh." The word was perky, but the pitch was not. It was the same one we both got when we were lying through our teeth. That was hurt, masked in enthusiasm. "I didn't even know you were seeing someone." *There it was.* "Hell, I had no idea you'd even popped your cherry."

"It's new," I said lamely, earning a deadpan fit for *The Office*. "And I'm pretty sure I popped that thing on a tampon in college."

"Two—don't be technical. You know what I meant. And *one*— obviously not that new. *Nine weeks, sissy?* You've been keeping this from me for nine weeks? Oh my god, the Turkey Trot. No wonder you were such a bitch."

"*Hey!*"

"What? You about snapped my neck when I asked where the tent was. *And you were dizzy!* Oh my god, Pax put us all on Leighton Watch because he thought you were hiding cardiac symptoms."

I mean… same.

"I wasn't keeping anything from anyone. There wasn't anything to tell. Our situation is complicated. I don't ask for a play-by-play of the dicks you're riding."

She beamed. "Your loss. I've had some spectacular hookups. If you ever need to get railed, the *Bomber* roster is ripe for the picking."

"Oh my god, Kaia."

"*What?* Look at their asses in those pants and tell me I'm wrong."

"No interest in baller ass, thanks."

"Again. Your loss. But this isn't about me. *My* eggo isn't preggo. Tell me how the hell this happened."

"We hooked up on Halloween," I admitted.

"That tracks. But why haven't I met him? Or heard an inkling? Since when do we keep secrets?"

"We didn't actually start dating until… well… last night was our first *official* date."

"And who is this mystery man?" she asked, narrowing her eyes.

"Don't you think I should tell the father before I go spreading the news all over?"

"Sure. Yes. Very good," she said solemnly. "But *I'm* not *all over.* I'm your other half. We are a package deal. Two-for-one special. Two musketeers."

"About to be three." I smiled weakly.

"Ha—good one. My point is, this turd burglar better get real comfy with me being all up in your business, because I'm not going anywhere."

"What does that mean?"

"That I'll stay," she said with a shrug. "You'll be due what, in July-ish?"

"That sounds about right," I muttered, discreetly counting it out on my fingers.

"So I'll stay after snowbird season ends."

"Kaia, what about work?"

"I can find clientele anywhere. That's the magic of social media."

"You're serious?"

"Bitch, like you wouldn't do the same if the roles were reversed, and—*ohmygod.*" Her eyes rounded comically.

"What?"

"You went home with Oliver Hart on Halloween."

"What?"

"Alice said he drove you home because you'd been drinking. Pax said you seemed fine. *Ohmygod*, you didn't let him drive you home because you were drunk. It was because you wanted to climb that man like a tree and—*apparently*—you did just that, and *now* you're carrying a Hart heir or heiress and—"

"Lord have mercy, *breathe*, Kai." No wonder Ollie always cut me off. Did I sound this unhinged when I connected dots?

"Oh my god, *I'm right*. Alice has said for months there was something going on there."

"Alice doesn't know what she's talking about."

"She said that *little* suit-daddy has had a thing for you ever since you told off *big* suit-daddy."

Apparently, Alice had a much bigger mouth than she let on.

"There is nothing small about Ollie," I muttered, rolling my eyes.

"Oh my god!" She slapped my shoulder, ignoring my pointed *ow* as she cackled and kicked her feet in the air.

"You look like a circus seal." My words only made her laugh harder. "Or a creepy-ass fucking clown."

"Well done, sissy. I never thought two of us would bag a Hart."

"I haven't bagged anything. He's just... Ollie." My face flushed at the memory of what 'just Ollie' had done to me last night. There was no coming back from *that*. Not ever. "God, I hope he doesn't hate me."

"Hate you!? I don't think he'd be parking his stallion in your barn if he hated you."

"Hate sex is hot."

"In books and movies, sure. But you two? No way. That man is so smitten, it's ridiculous."

"How would you know?"

"He looks at you like lunch."

Welp. She had me there. I buried my face in my hands. "You're the fucking worst."

"You love me."

"Debatable."

"But seriously. How could he hate you whilst churning your butter?"

"Ew. Stop with the food analogies, please."

"Fine. Just trying to lighten the mood," she said, rolling her eyes as she stood and reached down to haul me up by the wrists. "Answer the question."

But I wouldn't get the chance.

It sounded like someone rammed into the wall—and then a fist slammed on our front door three times in rapid succession.

My hand flew to my chest, heart hammering, as Kaia scowled and marched toward the noise.

I was five paces behind her when she flung open the door to find an uncharacteristically rude Oliver Hart.

"Where is she?"

"Well, hello to you too, suit daddy."

"*Leighton*, Kaia. *Where is Leighton?*"

Kaia gestured in my direction with a dramatic flourish, but Ollie was already moving, his eyes locking on mine before he collided with me, wrapping me up in his arms and crushing me to his chest. His face tucked into my neck like he couldn't get close enough, his breath ragged.

I barely had time to register the disheveled state of him—his shirt half-buttoned, his hair tousled—before guilt sank sharp teeth into my stomach. I'd left. Just... left him.

I'd always been a solitary processor, but I hadn't stopped to think about what that would do to him.

"You answer your phone after a text like that, Leigh. Are you trying to kill me?"

"Sorry," I whispered into his chest, my body melting into the safety of him.

"Don't be sorry. Be *safe*." His voice cracked. "What's going on?"

"Wait. How the hell did you know I wasn't her?" Kaia barked from behind us.

"Please," he muttered into my hair, still holding me like he had no plans of letting go. "You look nothing alike."

Snorting, I mumbled, "We're literally clones, Ollie."

"Bullshit. You might share DNA, but you hold yourselves differently, and she doesn't have the scar over her brow. Your skin is marginally darker, and your eyes are way brighter."

"Rude," Kaia muttered.

Then, so only I could hear, Ollie whispered, "And she's not *mine*."

Le swoon.

God, I hoped he didn't hate me for this—because this man might very well be it for me.

Finally steadying, he pulled back just enough to look me in the eyes, gently adjusting my loose tee back over my shoulder.

"I was right this morning, wasn't I?"

Studying the fear in his eyes, I searched for any trace of betrayal. Was that what was hiding under the panic? I hoped not.

Unable to find my voice, I nodded.

Silver flickered in his eyes just before he cupped my face again and kissed me—fierce, claiming, achingly tender.

"Are you safe?" he murmured, pressing a hand over my chest, right above my scar.

"I haven't seen a doctor yet, so I don't know if the pregnancy will stick or not."

"That's not what I asked, Leighton. Are you okay to do this? Do you *want* to do this?"

Tears burned my eyes, and my voice cracked. "Yeah. I do."

He nodded, like he was trying to commit the moment to memory.

"And it can't hurt you?"

"I mean… the squeezing a human through my vag probably won't feel great." His scowl told me he didn't find me very funny right this moment. I just told him I was carrying his child, and it was my heart he covered with his palm like he could keep me safe. Like what mattered in this equation was standing right in front of him. *Jesus.*

I lifted my hand to cover his. "Are you ever going to ask me what happened?"

"Are you ever going to feel safe enough to tell me on your own?"

A watery laugh slipped out, but the sob that followed startled both of us.

We turned to Kaia, where she stood crying into her hand, her other arm wrapped tight across her ribs. She waved us off, shaking her head as tears overflowed from her eyes.

"You said you hooked up on Halloween—I didn't realize you guys were in *love*," she sniffled.

"Irrevocably," Ollie said simply, and I nearly lost it again.

Kaia sniffed hard. "Listen, after that display, I'm team Ollie. When the guys give you shit, tell them to fuck off—I'll handle it."

"Kaia," I warned, narrowing my eyes.

She threw her hands up. "Sorry! I'll see—see—myself out."

"Thank yooooou. And please, can we keep this between us until I know what's going on? I don't need everyone henning me to death."

"Of course. Totally." She gathered her things, sniffed again, then grinned. "For what it's worth, I think this is great—you're both great. Together? My god."

"*Kaia!*"

"Sorry! Bye!" The door clicked shut behind her.

We both exhaled.

Ollie kissed my forehead, then drew back slightly. "Okay. So. The test is positive."

"Tests," I corrected. "Plural. Three, to be exact."

"Okay," he repeated, the tone suddenly businesslike, like I'd snuck into one of his conference rooms. Steady. Like he was bracing for impact. His hands slid down my arms to lace with mine. "Tell me what you need."

My lip wobbled. I was so tired of crying, and yet here we were again. "I need you to know I didn't do this on purpose."

"Leighton," he said, his jaw tightening.

"I swear, Ollie, I would never—"

His lips crashed into mine, rough and possessive, and when he pulled back, his voice was firm.

"So help me, if you ever put you and Carly in the same category again, there will be hell to pay."

"I just know what she did to you. And I don't want you to feel trapped. I swear, I will never—"

"Jesus Christ, Trouble."

"That's one," I whispered.

He chuckled against my lips, brushing his thumb over my cheek. "First of all, you're acting like you're in this alone."

"I just don't want to be another obligation."

He kissed me again—slower this time. "Breathe, baby. Good girl." Then he tilted my chin up, holding my gaze. "I told you last night I'm in love with you. And while part of what I love is that you're the anti-Carly, that is not why I fell."

"No?"

"No, baby. The only thing the two of you have in common is that apparently I have fire-breathing sperm that dissolves latex."

A watery laugh burst from me. "*Ow.*"

"I believe you, Leigh."

"You do?"

He nodded. "The idea that you'd do something like that would never have even crossed my mind."

"I didn't stab the condom box."

"What?"

"That girl at the bar said she would."

His eyes narrowed. "Jesus, Leighton. No. I don't think you orchestrated this."

"But—"

"That kiss was too sloppy to be planned."

"Hey!"

"It was the hottest moment of my life," he said, completely unapologetic, "but entirely... well, *you. Us.* Unplanned. Con-artists are usually more subtle."

"But Carly..."

"Taught me some very hard lessons," he said, voice low and steady. "This is why I've paid a small fortune to my therapist, Leigh. My ex is a textbook narcissist. Luckily for me, money can buy the best shrink in the city—and I never loved her. She was a necessity.

Nothing more." He took a breath, then added, "Which brings me to my next question. Who do I need to call?"

"Ollie—"

"And don't tell me you'll handle it alone. That phase of your life is over. We do this together."

"It can take months to get into a cardiologist," I hedged, the weight of reality settling on my shoulders.

"*For…?*"

I cleared my throat. "I had a mitral valve prolapse. Collapsed on the soccer field junior year. It was… a whole thing. Surgery, lots of flights to Anchorage and Seattle, specialists—zero out of ten, do not recommend."

"But you're okay now?" His voice softened, but the tension in his jaw told me he was cataloging every word.

"I should be. I've been asymptomatic since the surgery six years ago. My annuals have looked great. But with the pregnancy—and the hormone issues—they'll probably want to keep a close eye on things. I think."

"Okay," he said immediately, no hesitation. "I'll get you the best people."

"Kai already started digging."

"I'm sure she did."

"She found a few she liked."

"I'll take her research into consideration while we do our own."

We. Our.

He said it so easily. Like we were already a team.

"The family is going to riot," I murmured, finally admitting the fear that had me wringing my hands raw.

"Then they'll have to deal with me," he said flatly. "Because no one—no one—is doing or saying anything that stresses out my baby's mama."

"You're insane, you know that?"

"And you love it."

"Yeah," I admitted with a watery smile. "I do."

I love *you.*

I love you.

I love you.

It sat right there on the tip of my tongue. But saying it now—after this week, this morning, that test—it might feel like I was saying it *because* of the baby. Because he showed up. Like he'd earned it by swooping in wearing his Oliver Hart super suit, or because I was pregnant and scared.

And that kind of love needed the right moment. Something big. Something mine.

"I'm gonna make some calls," he said, stepping away with a kiss to my forehead. "Between Grey and me, we've got a few favors to cash in. I'll find someone."

"Okay," I whispered, voice trembling as he disappeared toward the converted guest office.

But then he turned, glancing over his shoulder—right at my wringing hands. "Oh, and Leighton?"

"Yeah?"

"You're going to be the most incredible mother." His voice cracked a little. "That's all I ever wanted for my kids."

THE LITTLE WOMEN CHAT:

KAIA

Waving white flag gif Abort Call. I got her to relent.

ELORA

Wait. What?

KAIA

Pineapple DOES in fact belong on pizza.

JEANNE

I hate you. I'm going to bed.

JEANNE

And blocking this number.

KAIA

It was very heated!

17

A Swift Dismissal
OLIVER

Not again.

That was the mantra on loop the moment she walked out this morning.

It wasn't that I wouldn't love mine and Leighton's baby. Of course I would. A tiny Leighton toddling around, running the show the second she found her feet? The idea was enough to bring tears to my eyes. My kids were the purest form of love I'd ever known. Unconditional. Fiercely loyal. The anchor in every storm.

It was just…the timing was shit.

But now that we were here? All I wanted was for them both to be safe.

Somehow, history was repeating itself. Only this time, it was with a woman I loved—who I was pretty damn sure loved me too, even if she wasn't ready to say it yet. But confirmation that I'd—*yet again*—completely thrown the plan out the window had my stomach turning.

Grey was going to have at least a dozen ways to say I told you so. And I wouldn't even be able to argue with him.

Someday, I wouldn't be the Hart family's personal PR crisis.

I stared down at the open notebook between us as we sat at my favorite cafe. Leighton cradled her latte. I cradled my guilt.

> *Mtg. cardio after New Year.*
> *Assess for meds. Heart stabilizers if needed?*
> *Regular EKGs. BP checks.*
> *NSTs after viability. (24 weeks.)*

Labor controlled. Induction ideal. Pulse ox. Possible epidural.

MY HANDWRITING HAD STARTED neat and professional. Now it looked like I'd written it on a moving bus.

Because this was real.

This wasn't a hypothetical. Wasn't a theory or a dream or even a plan. This was happening. My girls—

Okay, I didn't know for sure if it was a girl, but Leighton had been referring to the baby that way so casually that my brain had already accepted it.

She'd been self-conscious about taking a Sunday appointment, but Dr. Swift had assured us it was no problem—he was already in for a delivery. And in reality, there weren't many people who would risk the wrath of my brother or uncle, framed degrees or not.

Safe. That was the word that wouldn't leave me.

I had one job—keep my family safe.

Now Leighton was in danger *because* of me. Yeah, the doctor said she looked great. But fuck if I believed that until we were holding our baby and she was upright and laughing and telling me I was dramatic.

We'd be working with his team, possibly with Maternal Fetal Medicine too. Cardiology would be monitoring her heart closely. The valve repair should hold. We'd know more after her next round of tests.

We'd left with a two-foot long sonogram that she quickly tucked in her purse, after Dr. Swift—the very confident, very quirky, very *not*-swift doctor—assured us that everything looked great.

The man moved like a personified tortoise. He had too much neck— even on a rather tall body—was fifteen minutes late to the appointment, and crept in through a slow, creaky opening of the door. His steps were methodical, like he aimed not to startle a cornered animal, and he had a handshake that looked forced and a little painful. But for what he lacked in expediency, he made up for in confidence and pragmatism, something we both appreciated immensely.

And thank God for the Hart name. Because the best cardiologist west of Manhattan found a time for Leighton to come in when she got home from Florida.

But the only thing that still had me holding my breath?

Leighton.

Leighton wasn't *quiet*. Leighton was chaos in lipstick.

But right now, she was silent.

Still.

A latte—half-caff, because she was already thinking of the baby—cradled in both hands, her eyes distant as she stared out the window.

She looked beautiful. Radiant. She'd always been gorgeous, but this was something else. The calm, the composure, the way she'd peppered Dr. Swift with every smart, grounded question—it left me stunned.

This wasn't Carly. This wasn't twenty-one-year-old me flailing to hold it all together.

I didn't need to hover. I didn't need to worry she'd disappear for hours or forget to feed the baby because she was too wrapped up in a phone call. I wouldn't come home to chaos. To crying kids in a locked car under the August sun because 'she was just running a quick errand'.

Leighton would never opt out.

This was different. It had to be. The hand she'd set protectively over her still-flat belly said so.

It felt almost criminal to interrupt her peace, but after half an hour of peeling my cuticles bloody, I couldn't hold it in anymore.

"What'cha thinking, Trouble?"

She blinked, pulling herself back into the moment. "Hmm?"

"You okay?"

She took a breath. "Yeah," she said dreamily. "I think I am."

"Think?"

She faced me fully then, setting down the mug. "There's just been...a lot of change in the last twenty-four hours. It's a lot to process."

"Beyond baby?"

Her eyes narrowed. That was more like it.

"First, you take me on the most romantic date of all time."

"You're welcome."

"Don't get cocky."

"*Duly noted.*"

"*Then* you leave me with a high-strung hoo-ha."

"Which I remedied, thank you very much."

"*After* telling me you love me."

"That did happen."

"And basically admitted you've been pining."

"Also not inaccurate."

"And then—bam—*we're having a baby.* Something that—until this morning—I thought would never happen for me."

Yikes.

"Yep. That...sums it up."

"So, yeah." She bobbed her head. "Processing."

"Understandable."

"Isn't it?" she squeaked. Then she slid me her still-full latte like it was an offering. I accepted without hesitation.

"Wanna blow this popsicle stand?"

"If that's what you want."

"I'm craving pajamas."

"Fair."

We stood and headed for the door, and just like that, a new fear took root.

What if she left?

What if she woke up tomorrow, decided this life—me, my name, my family—was too much, and disappeared? Back to Mistyvale. Or to Florida. Or anywhere this wouldn't be front-page news.

Anywhere our baby would grow up safe from the shadow of the Hart legacy.

Anywhere but here.

Fuck, it might kill me.

I hustled to sidestep her, rushing ahead to open the door, and slipped my hand into hers. Relief rippled through me when her fingers threaded into mine without hesitation. We walked the three blocks in a simmering silence, unspoken thoughts bubbling just beneath the surface.

I needed to hit the gym. Or go for a drive. Or call my therapist. Preferably all three.

After helping Leighton into the car, I rounded the hood and slid behind the wheel of the Bentley, the purr of the engine offering a small sliver of comfort. Maybe the road under rubber would help clear my head.

But SoCal traffic had other plans. Within minutes, we were locked in bumper-to-bumper hell, and every inch of me itched to move.

I was drumming out a beat on the steering wheel when she cleared her throat. "Say something."

"Just... thinking."

"What are you thinking about?" Her voice was soft, cautious. The hesitation in her tone only deepened my self-loathing. I forced a smile and glanced her way as the sun glared off the back of a chrome-painted Tesla in front of us.

God, who the hell thought mirrored paint jobs were a good idea?

"*Ollie?*"

I exhaled slowly. "Just processing," I echoed back.

"Are we okay? You believe me, right?"

I was such an asshole.

"Yeah, baby," I breathed, shoulders deflating as I finally met her eyes. "We're okay."

"You seem... angry."

"Just frustrated with traffic, Trouble."

"Okay." But the way she said it made it clear she didn't buy a word of it. I flipped through the radio stations, but everything grated on my nerves, so I shut it off altogether. Which, in hindsight, was a mistake—now we were alone with nothing but engine hum and tension.

"Can I do anything?" she asked gently.

"I'm fine." A lie. I was a goddamn mess. The family fuck-up. The guy Grey would, yet again, have to clean up after. But saying all that out loud sounded like too many words for my brain to relay, so I just forced another smile and kept driving.

"You look like you sat in something unpleasant," she muttered.

The unexpected laugh burst out of me before I could stop it.

"There's my man."

That landed like a balm straight to my chest. "Your man, huh?"

"I mean... unless you've changed your mind."

"I haven't," I said quickly. Because if there was anything I was sure of, it was her. This woman beside me? She wrecked me. In the best possible way.

"Okay, well, that's good." Another silence. Heavier this time. "Tuning each other out doesn't exactly bode well for this whole relationship slash co-parenting thing, though. Can we talk about whatever's got your face pinched like you bit into a lemon?"

"There's just... a lot to think through."

"Okay," she said, and the disappointment was barely hidden. "But can we think *together*? Please?"

"About what?"

"Anything. Start with whatever's got you white-knuckling the poor Bentley. It's not his fault."

I huffed a small laugh and loosened my grip. "I don't know, Leigh. We'll meet the cardiologist when you're back and go from there, right?"

"Right."

"So there's not a lot to hash out before then."

"*I mean...*"

"Just whether or not you want me at your appointments—"

"*Of course* I do." Her eyes widened, like that was never in question.

"—and at the birth. Carly *hated* having me there for Mattie."

"Ollie, you're her father. *Of course* you can be there. Not like you haven't seen everything already."

"Right. But what if you change your mind?" Because that's what happened, right? People changed. Said they'd do things one way, then bailed when it got hard. I'd lived that story already. I knew how it ended.

"I won't," she said firmly, but I couldn't stop the next one.

"Will she be a Hart or a Rhodes?"

"Both?" Her brows furrowed. "Ollie, where is this coming from?"

"I'm just—what about school, Leigh? Didn't your family home-school? I don't think I could homeschool. Tutors, maybe? But if the kids are at Emerald Prep, why make the third the odd one out?"

"For a few years, but that's not—why are we thinking about all of this right now? Can't we cross those bridges when we get to them?"

"Carly said that," I muttered. "Then she left before we crossed any of them."

"*Ollie.*"

"I'm sorry," I said, closing my eyes and gripping the wheel again. "I'm just—"

"Panicking?" she guessed.

"A little."

"Okay. That's normal. But we're a team now, remember?"

"Yeah," I sighed, squeezing her hand. The Tesla finally turned right on red, and I crept up to the line, my heart still pounding in my chest. "I'm sorry. I really am. You're the one going through this —growing a whole person—and I'm spiraling about where baby comes home to."

"With me," she said with a crooked smile, trying to joke. But it didn't quite land. "Obviously."

"To your apartment?"

"No, *to a cardboard box downtown.* Yes, to my apartment. It's way too big for one person, anyway."

"What about my place?" I asked before I could stop myself. "We're already set up for everything, and you're over every day."

"Like... to live with you?"

"Yeah. That way I can be there—for both of you. For the late nights, the bottles, the sleep regressions. I'm practically a veteran."

"I know," she said, soft and sad. "It's not that, Ollie, it's just... isn't all of this moving a little fast?"

I swallowed hard and merged onto the freeway, my grip tightening again.

"I don't want to miss it," I admitted. "God, please don't make me miss it. At least with Carly, I got the kids."

"Ollie, I don't want you to miss *anything.*"

"But if you're *there*, and I'm here... I'll miss everything. First roll, first laugh, first step. How will I even know?"

"I mean, like you said, I'm at your house all the time anyway, and my place is only fifteen minutes away."

"Forty during rush hour. An hour from the office. What if something happens? You have a heart condition, Leigh. What if something happens and no one's there?"

"Kaia's staying until I'm on my feet."

"Right."

"What's *that* supposed to mean?"

"That it's supposed to be *me*."

"Ollie, I'm not saying never. I'm just asking for time to process everything before we flip my entire life upside down."

"Yeah," I said, nodding like it was completely logical. Because it was. But I still couldn't breathe. "That makes sense."

"Thank you. And I promise, I hear you. I'll think about it."

"Yeah?"

"Yeah."

"Good."

"It's just... it's a lot. Twenty-four hours ago, we were on our first date. And now, we're talking about babies and moving in."

"Why, though?"

When silence was my answer, I glanced sidelong—and sure enough, Leighton's eyes were wide, her jaw tight, every line of her face screaming *don't push me*. That sharp twist of dread in my gut was like watching a car wreck happen in slow motion. I couldn't stop it. And I couldn't stop my mouth, either.

"Ollie, be serious."

"I am." The words snapped out before I could stop them. "I told you I love you, Leigh, and you didn't say it back."

"I..." She faltered. Her voice caught like gravel in her throat.

I nodded once, sharp and resigned. "*Yeah.*"

"Ollie, I—it's not that simple."

"Of course it is. I love you. *Simple.*" I swallowed, hard. "You need time. That's okay. It wouldn't even bug me if—"

"We weren't having a baby together?" Her voice was flat.

"When everything feels this unfinished? Yeah."

"I get it. But I think you're projecting a whole lot of your past onto me right now, and I gotta be real with you—I don't appreciate it. I'm not Carly, and I would never put you through the shit she has. So let's just take a breath. One thing at a time. Okay?"

"I think we should get married," I blurted.

A record scratch couldn't have cut harder.

She sat up straighter in her leather seat, jaw dropped, eyes blown wide. Her hands splayed in front of her like she was checking for incoming debris. Her head tilted to the side like she couldn't believe what she'd just heard.

And neither could I.

If I could physically grab the words and shove them back down my throat, I would. It wasn't that I didn't want to marry her. *God, I did.* But it wasn't supposed to come out like that. Not now. Not like this. It was supposed to be after she loved me back. After we'd built something stable and solid. After we'd earned the smooth part.

"*Wow.* Nothing says swoony like fucking damage control."

"Leigh, it's not like that—"

"I'm not a PR fire for you to hand off to Alice, Oliver Hart," she snapped, voice trembling. And somehow, that was worse. The softness, the hurt. *I'd* hurt *her.* "This baby will not be papered over with a shotgun wedding."

"Leigh, I—"

"So much for not feeling shame about that night, huh?"

"No—Leigh, I swear I didn't mean it like that, I just—I meant it."

"You meant it?" she echoed, laughing without a hint of humor. "Is that your default reaction *to a positive pregnancy test*?"

"I didn't mean to say it like that—"

"But you *did* mean to *say it*," she cut in. "Ollie, it's not 1919. You don't have to marry a woman just because you knocked her up—"

"*I know that.*"

"Then what? You think I should feel *grateful* you're offering me a ring?"

I shook my head, hating every fucking second of this.

"And for the record?" Her voice dropped, firm and low. "A proposal should be something special. A botanical garden. A rooftop. A heartfelt speech because you can't imagine your life *without me*. It should be a memory, not a bandage."

"Leigh, I…" My throat burned. The words crashed around like a demolition site in my skull, but nothing that came out would fix this. I'd blown it. Again. I was supposed to do it right this time. Be the man she chose, not the man she was trapped with. Instead, I'd let every fear and insecurity fly out of my mouth like shrapnel.

She went quiet, her jaw clenched tight as she stared out her window while we wound up the ramp of her parking garage.

"Look, Ollie," she sighed, her voice barely above a whisper. "I fucking love you. And I'm trying really hard not to lose my shit right now. Because I have done nothing to make you think I would screw you over. But the last twenty-four hours has been *a lot*—too much, honestly—and I'm *not* in the headspace for some life-planning summit. Neither are you."

I pulled into the spot beside her building entrance and put the car in park. She still didn't look at me. The red glow of the exit sign painted her profile like a warning.

"Maybe this trip will do us some good," she added, almost to herself. "Some time to breathe. Process."

My head screamed *no*. This wasn't the time to pull back. But I nodded anyway. Because I didn't know how to say what I needed to say without hurting her again.

I got out and rounded the car, opening her door. She let me. Took my hand without hesitation. I reached up to thread my fingers through her hair, cradling the back of her head as I kissed the crown of it.

"I'm sorry," I murmured. "Everything's coming out wrong."

"I can see that."

"I know you're not Carly."

"Damn straight, Skippy."

I huffed a laugh I didn't feel and held her tighter, breathing her in, resisting the urge to drop to my knees and beg her not to go.

"Ollie," she warned gently.

I opened my eyes and found her looking up at me, stormy and sad and utterly beautiful.

"We'll talk, okay?" she whispered. "When I get back, we'll figure it out."

"Yeah," I said softly, brushing my lips over her forehead before I stepped back and shut the door behind her.

She turned to walk toward the elevator, but paused with her hand on the railing.

"Tell the kids Merry Christmas for me."

My throat burned. "Yeah," I said again. Slumped. *Wrong.* This whole thing was wrong. "Have a Merry Christmas, Trouble."

18

Well That's a Hail Mary of A Different Color
LEIGHTON

LEIGHTON

Congrats on the win today.

PAXTON

Thanks, Sis. Excited for some r&r.

LEIGHTON

How much do you love me?

PAXTON

Enough that I'm a little nervous we're about to bury a body. These tickets were first class, dammit.

LEIGHTON

You know you're my favorite brother, right?

PAXTON

Fuck me, we are burying a body, aren't we?

LEIGHTON

Not tonight. Are there open seats on your flight?

PAXTON

Um...

LEIGHTON

You board in ninety minutes, right?

PAXTON

Yeah, I'm already through security.

You okay?

You want me to check?

LEIGHTON

Please.

You've got that fancy VIP thing, right?

PAXTON

Saluting emoji I assume I'll get an explanation later?

LEIGHTON

Fine. Just get me the fuck out of here before I do something stupid.

PAXTON

Punky, pick up your phone.

LEIGHTON

I'm in an Uber, five minutes out.

PAXTON

Pick.

Up.

Your.

Phone.

At least tell me you're okay.

LEIGHTON

Physically? Never better.

Please tell me I've got a seat locked in, Pax Man.

I wouldn't ask if I wasn't desperate.

PAXTON

I know. Why else would I be worried?

Can you even make it in time?

I think they cut off bags two hours out.

LEIGHTON

I've just got me, myself, and a backpack.

I will sprint barefoot through TSA if I have to. I've got pre-check, and no luggage.

Kaia can bring my shit with her Monday.

I just need to be home right now.

I'm sorry, I swear I'll explain later.

PAXTON

Leighton, wtf?

LEIGHTON

We're pulling off the freeway, Pax.

I'll pay you when I get there. Promise.

PAXTON

Jesus Christ. Please hold.

I don't need your fucking money.

Who the fuck am I putting out a hit on?

LEIGHTON

Oh, please. *Middle finger emoji, kissing emoji* Just Venmo'd you.

I would not cry in front of a stranger.

That was the only sentence I let run on a loop in my head the entire drive to the airport. In all my time in Emerald Bay, I had *never* been more grateful to live in a major city—because never, in a million years, would I have been able to get a same-day flight out of Mistyvale. Much less one within two hours.

But the thought of Kaia's inevitable interrogation… of climbing into that too-big, too-cold bed alone after the longest fucking day in recorded history… made my stomach pitch.

This was so fucked.

And all I wanted—all I *needed*—was to be home. To curl up in the thick arms of my teddy bear brothers. To bury my face in my mama's neck. To snuggle my beautiful nieces and let the world be quiet for five damn minutes.

Fuck this city.

Fuck adulting.

Fuck whatever demon spawn crawled up Oliver Hart's ass and laid crazy eggs in his gorgeous, stress-wrinkled brain because—*what the actual fuck was that?!*

We should get married?!

We'd boned twice. Been on one legendary date. Yes, I loved the lunatic. Yes, he was my best fucking friend—even if he was, *apparently*, certifiable. But marriage?

I wasn't ready for that.

Hell, after the way my hands shook putting on socks this morning, I wasn't even sure I was ready to be a mother. This was a cataclysm-level math problem I wasn't equipped to solve. I needed someone with the patience of a saint and the calm of a Buddhist monk.

I needed Juniper Rhodes. Because if anyone could talk me off this ledge before my brain melted down into nuclear sludge, it was my mother.

My phone buzzed.

PAXTON

First class, locked in. Boarding pass in your email.
Where are you?

LEIGHTON

Pulling into the parking lot now, and headed for departures. Email received, just checked in. Thank you big brother.

PAXTON

Grabbing coffees. Double or quad?

LEIGHTON

I'm okay, thank you though.

PAXTON

Who the fuck am I talking to right now? Rhyett?

LEIGHTON

Long day. Probably will buy a neck pillow and sleep.

PAXTON

You're freaking me out.

LEIGHTON

Seems to be a theme today.

PAXTON

...

I SLIPPED my phone into my bag as the car pulled to the curb, thanked my driver, and bolted before he could get around to open the door. Eye contact was a *hard* no. One look of sympathy, and I'd melt into a useless puddle of emotional goo—and goo couldn't sprint through TSA.

And sprinting was the only thing on today's agenda.

Blessedly, the pre-check line was short: a middle-aged Black couple whispering sweet nothings to each other, and a thirty-something corporate type in a suit that looked like it came with a boarding pass for the Oliver Hart trauma express. I ignored the once-over he gave me as I stepped in behind him.

Sorry, Bucko. Currently carrying more baggage than you checked downstairs.

Was dropping a stupid amount of money to fly out eighteen hours earlier impulsive?

Probably.

But was it more impulsive than marrying a man I'd technically only agreed to date last week?

Absolutely fucking not.

By the time I reached the gate where Paxton stood waiting, the dam had cracked. Tears had been threatening since Ollie started unraveling in the Bentley, and now they spilled freely. I didn't even try to stop them. Pax dropped what was presumably a very expensive duffle bag off his shoulder and opened his arms for me.

"Hey, kiddo. What the hell is going on?"

All I could do was cry into his chest.

He didn't press. He just wrapped me tighter, resting his chin on top of my head like a security blanket with biceps.

"You know I'll kill him."

"You will not," I sniffled, though I appreciated the sentiment. Yeah, he was driving me absolutely insane. But Ollie was mine. I just needed time to figure out what that *meant.*

"You're right," Pax sighed. "I'll hire out the dirty work. My hands are far too valuable to risk in a physical altercation. But the sentiment stands."

A watery laugh broke loose against his shirt. My shoulders sagged with the kind of exhale that only came from being wrapped in unconditional love. They called something over the speakers, but I barely registered the words. I just breathed, held together by my brother's presence long enough to keep from unraveling.

Eventually, I peeled myself out of his boa constrictor hug, and without missing a beat, he slung his arm around my shoulder and led me toward the stiff plastic airport chairs.

"So," he said, watching me carefully. "What the hell has you running out of the city?"

I wiped my hand over my mouth, cringing when I realized I hadn't washed up post-security. "You ever just need to be anywhere but here, bubba?"

He studied me for a beat, the same stormy-gray-blue eyes as mine narrowing slightly before he gave a slow nod. "Yeah, kiddo. But, generally, I still pack a bag."

A choked laugh cracked in my throat. "*Spontaneously restless,*" I mumbled, giving a weak shrug. "Figured I'd raid mom's closet when we get there."

He snorted and ruffled my hair like we were ten. It made me smile. Somehow, it always did.

"I hate when you cry," he muttered. "So I'm going to pretend I believe that story, punky."

"Appreciate it."

"*Oh, hey—look.*" He pulled out his phone, the corner of his mouth tipping up as he flipped it around to show me the family thread.

There, in high-def glory, was a picture of a brand-new, rosy-cheeked baby with a full head of dark curls and a pout that would put any Instagram influencer to shame.

Tears pricked my eyes all over again.

Elora and Broderick were *parents*. Holy shit.

THE FAM DAMILY:

BRODERICK

Meet Robert Milo Allen. 8:39 pm, 7lbs, 7oz, 20 inches long. Elora and baby are both perfect.

RHYETT

Congratulations, brother! Kiss my sister on the noggin for me.

JAMESON

Man. That's surreal. Congrats El and Brod. Rest up sis.

BREXLEY

Welcome, baby Milo!! El, you did amazing!

BRODERICK

She's a fucking warrior.

MAVERICK

Language, teach.

HADLEE

laughing emojis

Amazing news!! Congrats, you guys.

AXEL

Damn, you beat me to it.

JEANNE

???

Congratulations Brod. Love you guys!

ALICE

Wow. I'm at a loss for words.

KAIA

Something you need to tell us, Axe?

AXEL

Meet my son, Gimli. 7lbs, 12 inches long. 12 weeks old.

THE PHOTO my idiot brother sent through next was the cutest damn Frenchie I'd ever seen—a beautiful gray coat with a white spot over his chest, and round blue eyes set in his squished little face. Pax and I burst out laughing at the same time.

MAVERICK

PUPPY!!!

JAMESON

Who the fuck let you have a dog?

RHYETT

Jesus, Axel. Let El have her moment.

ELORA

PUPPY!!!

PAX SHOOK his head as he tucked his phone back in his pocket, but his crooked smirk had me wiping the tears off my cheeks. "Family will cure just about any ailment."

"Yeah," I breathed, my chest constricting. But as I pulled out my own cell to admire my new nephew, and moment-stealing fur-nephew, I couldn't help feeling like I was leaving mine behind.

OLIVER

"GREY!"

Perhaps shouting for the master of the manor—especially when both he and his head of security are retired SEALs—wasn't my

178

brightest idea. But then again, bright ideas hadn't been my forte today.

Em had been gracious enough to keep the kids for another hour so I could handle something with Greyson. I needed to get my act together.

"Grey?"

Viper, the ever-stoic security guy, didn't flinch from his post, but his eyes tracked me as I moved through the Hart House foyer.

"Everything okay, Mr. Hart?" he asked.

"Just peachy," I muttered, making a beeline for the study when Greyson didn't respond. "Greyson!"

Rounding the corner into his office, I found my brother's gaze flicking to me, unbothered as ever. He motioned to his earbuds.

I paced in front of his massive desk like a caged animal, resisting the urge to run my hands through my hair—a tell he'd chastised since we were kids.

"I understand, Griff. We'll address it promptly... Yes... That's fine. Listen, an urgent matter just came up. Let's resume this conversation on Monday... Thank you." Greyson ended his call, removed his earbuds, and stood from his chair in one fluid motion, eyes locked on my face.

"Oliver, what are you doing here?" he asked. That wouldn't have been a question four months ago. Why did that tighten my chest? "Mattie and Beau..."

"They're fine. Everyone's fine."

"You don't look fine," he noted dryly.

Pain tore through my chest as I met his eyes, nearly choking on the confession. "I fucked up."

Casually tucking his hands into his slack pockets, Greyson rounded the desk and leaned against its edge, observing my pacing with a furrow between his brows.

"Should Captain Reynolds be privy to this conversation?"

"What?" I scowled, realizing he might call in Jackson if I'd created a security threat or needed a cover-up. "No. Not like that."

"Color me intrigued."

Alright, Oliver, quick, like ripping off a band-aid. "Leighton's pregnant."

Greyson's poker face was legendary, but his hazel eyes hardened, the muscles in his forearms flexing as he likely clenched his fists inside his pockets.

"Please tell me this is an episode of jealousy and not how I find out about a new niece or nephew."

The imploring glare I shot him as I raked my hands through my hair was answer enough. He sighed, eyes closing briefly, arms crossing as he ran his tongue over his teeth.

"What did I tell you, Ollie? When have I ever warned you off a woman, except this *one* time?"

"You told me not to date Carly."

"Different reasoning. You just had to go after her after I—"

"It was Halloween, Grey."

"He shoots, and he scores," he muttered, pinching the bridge of his nose. "Is she keeping it?"

My growl was all the answer he needed.

"Of course, she is." A dark chuckle. "Jameson is going to beat you to a pulp."

"Given the meltdown I just had with her, yeah, probably. I'd be grateful if you'd do me the mercy and just put a bullet between my eyes now."

A slight twitch of his lips. "Come on, it won't be that bad. Jameson's a beast; he'll make it quick."

"And Axel?"

A humorless chuckle. "Now that kid is a little unhinged. Best of luck."

"This your idea of a pep talk?" I bit out, chest heaving as I fought to steady my breathing.

"You didn't come here for a pep talk."

"No," I admitted, collapsing into the stiff leather armchair in the corner of his study.

"You came here for advice."

"You're the last person qualified to dole out romantic tips."

He held up his left hand, the gold band gleaming. One dark brow arched pointedly.

"Don't act like hot shit—you coerced Alice into marrying you, jackass."

"Semantics."

"Besides, I already tried your tactic."

He scowled before narrowing his eyes at me. "Ollie, tell me you didn't." When I just grimaced, he blew out a haggard breath, unceremoniously standing from the desk and heading to the gold and crystal drink cart in the corner.

When media allegations targeted Grey over the summer, he'd *correctly* deduced that publicly confirming years of speculation about him and Alice would divert attention. Miraculously—and due to Alice's self-destructive sense of justice—she agreed. Somewhere along the way, her brand of crazy matched his enough to make it real.

But his initial proposal likely hadn't been any smoother than mine.

Grey grabbed two glasses in one hand and a bottle of Macallan with the other. "You're an idiot," he muttered, returning to set down the glasses before pouring a healthy finger of scotch into each.

"Tell me something I don't know," I growled, accepting the offering.

"You're in love with that woman, so tell me why in the hell you'd do something so stupid?"

I blinked. "What?"

"Please, Ollie. You couldn't hide the way you feel about Leigh if I paid you to do it. You've been smitten since she first opened that ridiculous mouth."

"*Watch it,*" I snarled. The asshole just smirked, brow flicking up again.

"Way to prove my point. Which brings me back to my question—why, on God's green earth, would you scare her off by going and doing something as impulsive as *proposing?*"

I knocked back my glass, welcoming the smooth heat with a heavy swallow before blowing out an agonized breath, my shoulders slumping. "I panicked."

"*You think?*"

"It was bad, man."

"The woman is embodied wildfire, and you tried to lock her to a ball and chain. When did she find out about the baby?"

I grimaced, rubbing at the back of my neck. "This morning."

"*Fuck you, man.*" He palmed his face. "What the fuck?"

"That sums it up."

"That's why she was so spacey at yoga?"

"You do sunrise yoga with the girls?" I asked skeptically.

"Not a chance," he snorted. "Alice was worried about her."

"I thought I was going to have a heart attack waiting to hear back from her, and when she said she needed me, I was terrified something was wrong."

"Because of the mitral valve thing?"

I jerked my gaze to his, scowling. "Alice told you?"

"*Please,* the woman is a vault. She'll give me a run for my money by the time we're done training her."

"Then how…"

"Ollie. It's my business to know things."

"Fucking psycho."

"Plus, there are only so many procedures that leave a scar like that."

"Why the fuck are you looking at her tits, man?"

Greyson didn't flinch. "Like you don't notice a woman in a bikini. It's not exactly subtle."

"Keep your eyes to yourself."

He rolled his. "Go on."

"I got us in with a high-risk OB this afternoon."

"Dr. Swift?"

I leveled a glare at him, but the asshole just chuckled and turned to swipe the scotch bottle again. Perks of him being in charge of security—his guys reported to him, not me.

"Yeah."

"And?"

"Everything looks perfect," I said, the tension in my chest loosening when Grey's shoulders sagged in relief.

"Then what happened?"

"I just... I panicked, man."

"Because of *Cruella*?"

"That's a bullshit excuse."

"Maybe. But narcissistic abuse leaves wreckage, Ollie—and you tolerated hers for years under the banner of 'keeping the peace.'"

"Maybe."

"Keep going. Fill me in so we can sort out your mess."

On a groan, I buried my face in my palms, then collapsed back into the chair, grateful when he handed me a second pour. So I told him everything. From the high of seeing the first ultrasound and realizing one of my kids would finally have an incredible mother—to the spiral that followed. The gut punch of hearing about her valve repair. The freefall of trying to get it right and reaching for control in all the wrong places. The coffee shop tension. The Bentley meltdown. The accidental proposal.

"Alright," he said, nodding slowly. "Give her time."

"*What?*" My stomach lurched at the thought. "No. I need to fix this now."

"You go after her now, you'll just piss her off more. Let her breathe. Try again tomorrow—or better yet, Monday."

"She's flying to Florida tomorrow."

"Right. Well. Sucks to suck."

"Fuck you."

He just laughed, dragging a palm across the back of his neck. "Ollie. You'll figure this out—but you're gonna have to grovel."

"You think?"

"Probably for months. She's fucking feral."

"I hate when you say that."

"And I love that about her. So get the fuck over it. There are few people I'd want with me in a dogfight, and Leighton Rhodes is one of them."

That caught me off guard. My eyes must've gone wide, because he just grinned.

"She's young, yeah. But she's sharp. Protective. Loyal as hell.

Bigger balls than most men I know. She'll make you work for it, but she's worth every step."

"What do I do?"

"Own it," he said simply. "Own the panic. Own the mess. That whole proposal thing? That was a grasp for control if I've ever seen one."

"I don't want to control Leighton."

"Bullshit. You were trying to anchor yourself to something—anything—you could actually hold onto. I get it. Kid on the way before you had a chance to properly lock it down. Her heart history. Your unresolved trauma from Carly. That's a lot of shit. But proposing was a tactical error."

"I just wanted her to know I was serious."

"Then say that. Without the ring next time." His eyes narrowed, spotting the telltale box as I tugged it from my pocket. "Oh, fuck. You *have* thought this through."

"She's it for me, man. I saw her slipping through my fingers, and I just…panicked."

"Christ, Ollie." He downed his drink—and then, evidently thinking better of handing me mine, swallowed that too. "Okay. Here's what you're gonna do. Tomorrow, you bring her one of those ridiculous bakery treats she likes, and *ask* for the chance to drive her to the airport. Apologize. Profusely. Then tell her you'll go at her pace."

"What if I can't?"

He tilted his head. "Then you'll lose her."

I stiffened.

"Look, you don't bullshit your way through a relationship with a woman like Leighton. She's not some executive assistant waiting for you to take the lead. She's going to need a life she *chooses*. One you build with her, not around her. You want compromise? You earn it."

"How?"

"You shut the fuck up and let her lead. If she wants to stay in her apartment, let her. If she wants to keep her name on the baby's birth certificate first, let her. You don't get to negotiate before you prove you're worth being in the room."

"What if I already lost her?"

He shook his head. "Nah. Leigh might be quick to swing first and ask questions later, but the woman's all heart. She doesn't give up on people she loves."

"And you think I fall in that category?"

"Don't be dense. She's been on call for you and your kids since the day you met. She practically lives at your house. You've seen her grocery list. She buys snacks based on *Mattie's* cravings."

I sucked in a breath, my throat tight.

"You've got a shot. But only if you slow the fuck down, apologize like you *mean it*, and stop trying to solve everything before she's even asked you to."

I nodded slowly, turning the ring box in my hand as I tried to picture what she'd say if I showed up with it tomorrow.

Grey snorted. "Not that. Save that move for next year. Maybe longer."

Nodding, I palmed my jaw before pushing out of the armchair. "Okay. I'll beg her for the chance to explain tomorrow."

"Practice groveling," Grey said dryly. "We're not exactly hard-wired for apologies."

"No," I agreed, my voice low. "We're not."

"Hey, Belle," he called, his tone softening instantly. I turned to find Alice beaming in the doorway, radiating sunshine like always—and fuck, that smile. So much like her sister's it made my chest ache.

"El had her baby! Also, my idiot big brother got a French bulldog and named him Gimli, and now I need one."

"No more dogs," Grey muttered, but Alice didn't even flinch. I just shook my head. If Alessandra Hart wanted a Frenchie, Greyson would have her flying to Paris tomorrow to hand-pick the most genetically superior one on earth.

"Oh!" she added brightly, completely oblivious to the way the air had gone still. "And Leighton hopped on Paxton's flight tonight—the shithead. Guess the Florida sun was calling her name."

The words slammed into me like a truck.

My chest seized. My ears rang.

The room tilted.

I turned to Greyson, searching his face for denial—an eye-roll, a smirk, *something* that said this was a joke. But his lips curled tight against his teeth, his gaze dropping to the floor like he couldn't bring himself to meet mine.

"Grey?" One word. Just one. And I hated how much it sounded like that six-year-old version of me, the one who'd screamed his name when the rattlesnake coiled next to my ankle. I was just as helpless now.

Fuck. I'd done it again.

Pushed too hard. Reached for control when all I had to do was trust her.

Grey sighed, crossing his arms over his chest. "Well... shit. You've done it now, kid."

"What—?" Alice stepped forward, frowning between us. "What did I just walk in on?"

19

There's No Such Thing As Ready

LEIGHTON

OLLIVER HART

I'm so sorry, Trouble. I'm an idiot.

If I were in your shoes, I'd feel the same way, and I'm so sorry. My anxiety got the best of me. Please forgive my lapse in sanity. I didn't mean to put you on the spot like that, or ever make you feel like anything other than the love of my fucking life.

This baby is a blessing, Leigh. Not something to cover up. You deserve the world, and so does she.

Call me when you're ready, please. I promise not to freak out on you twice in twenty-four hours.

I woke up to the sound of my niece giggling maniacally—no doubt under attack from a pair of merciless tickle monsters disguised as my brothers—and for a blissful second, that sound was a balm to my bruised heart. Warm, familiar, safe.

But reality came crashing back the second I rolled over and checked my phone.

Ollie's name lit up the screen like a siren.

Texts. Plural.

Had the man even slept?

Judging by the timestamps… I was going with a firm no.

My chest squeezed. *Big*, dumb, beautiful idiot. Somehow, I was equally annoyed and concerned, which made no goddamn sense. Why was it that I could be so *mad* at someone, and still want to hug them until my arms gave out?

If that's what love felt like, maybe I didn't want it after all. It was way too confusing. Way too much.

Still scowling, I tapped out a response.

I'm safe at my parents' place. We're okay, Ollie. Breathe. Just…give me some time to process, please.

EIGHT-THIRTY IN THE MORNING.

So…I counted on my fingers, palming at my face as I sat up in bed, already aware my stomach felt precarious at best. Five-thirty my time. *Yikes.*

I sipped my water and blinked into the cute, decked-out guest room, smiling at *all* the seashells and starfish and other nautical nonsense my mother had painstakingly curated for her little Florida farmhouse. There was color coming out the yin-yang, and lord knew Juniper Rhodes thrived in all this blue and yellow and coral. Each shade would make her smile for a different reason.

The sun catcher in the window was beaded out of sea glass from Mistyvale—the familiar teals making me inhale deeply, like I could feel the chilled mist on my face.

That was the thing, though.

I might've grown up on the black shores of the Alaskan archipelago, but in a family this size—one that roamed as freely as ours did—*home* was never a place. It was our people. Their voices now filtered up from the stairwell beside this bedroom, and a familiar warmth bloomed in my chest.

The squeal of laughter and slap of tiny feet had me opening the door with caution, just in time to see a tubby, curly-haired blonde toddler go sprinting past with her little fists raised triumphantly above her head—Paxton hot on her heels.

"Mornin', punky," he said, grinning as he 'chased' our niece down the hallway.

"Mornin'!" I chirped back, shaking my head, cheeks already aching when Pax scooped the tiny little-girl version of Rhyett into his arms. Quinn shrieked with laughter as he blew raspberries on her round belly, then tossed her over his shoulder like a sack of grain —still squealing as he tickled her legs.

"Breakfast is on the griddle," he called.

"Nice." I yawned, stretching my arms as I followed him down the stairs. "Morning, Quinny!"

"Hep, Kai!!!"

"I'm *Leighton!*" I said in mock outrage, loving the way her little eyes rounded like I'd just announced I was Santa Claus.

"Hep, Auntie!!"

"Safe bet, kid—but you're on your own."

My feet had barely hit the last stair when the Mom Radar activated. Juniper Rhodes turned from the stove, radiant in a flowy, sapphire-blue tie-dye sundress. Her wavy mane of blonde hair was pinned up in a claw clip, and her eyes landed on me like a heat-seeking missile.

"Mornin', Mama."

"Oh, sweet girl," she cooed, like I was six instead of twenty-three. But fuck, if those open arms didn't make my knees wobble. Okay, my chin too. Knowing settled in the crinkles around her eyes as she crossed the kitchen and wrapped me up.

"God, it's like hugging myself," she teased, tightening her grip. I forced a chuckle. That wasn't the first—or the five hundredth—time she'd made that joke. We were pretty much the same height, and it was no question where I'd gotten my figure from. "I love you so much, sweet pea. Glad to have you here early."

"Just couldn't wait to see us, beautiful?" Rhyett's voice floated over from the griddle where he manned the pancakes. I took two steps back. The smell of bacon on deck was not gonna settle well with my current stomach.

"Obviously," I drawled, earning a dimpled grin. He looked exactly how he sounded these days—sun-kissed, blond, and sunshiney, with a worn baseball tee and beach dad energy.

"Hey, Leigh!" Brexley chirped from the sectional near the window, her long tan legs folded under her. She had their two-week-old baby girl cradled in her arms, happily nursing like a champ. Her bleach-blonde hair was in a top knot that definitely wasn't from today, but her smile? Brighter than I'd ever seen it.

"Hey, Brex," I returned with a watery smile. "How you feeling?"

"A hell of a lot better than after Quinn. Second babies are a breeze, comparatively."

"Glad to hear it." I smiled, but my eyes snapped to Mom's the second she loosened her hold on me, her too-knowing gaze locking onto mine. She peeled herself from our hug and cupped my shoulders.

"Come with me. I want to show you the garden."

"She's *seen* the garden, Juniper," Rhyett said with a knowing smile.

"But she hasn't seen the new nasturtiums," she argued breezily, rolling her eyes in that way that reminded me exactly where I got my sass.

"She's gotta see Nostradamus," Rhyett muttered under his breath.

Fuck. That actually would be helpful right now. I didn't say that though—just laughed as Mom gave him a smacking kiss on the cheek and passed me a mug of tea she'd already prepared. Before I knew it, she was swiping a blanket from the ladder and jerking her head toward the back door.

"Come along, sweet pea."

I followed her out into the morning sun, the Florida humidity already sticking to my skin as we padded barefoot across the grass. Juniper Rhodes in her sundress with tea in hand was a full-blown Earth goddess, and she led me right into the sanctuary of her garden, settling me into one of the hanging egg chairs like I was one of her babies again.

The second she tucked the blanket around my lap, my throat threatened mutiny.

"So," she said brightly, tucking her own legs up into the chair beside me, "what is it you need to tell me?"

"How do you do that?" I sipped my tea just to stall.

"All mothers know when their babies are carrying something too heavy."

God, I hoped that was true. Hoped I'd be even half the mother she was. Because at this rate, I was gonna need backup.

I looked around the yard—our family's oasis. The garden over-flowing with blooms. The string lights over the movie screen my brother had built. Everything about this place screamed love. It was sacred ground.

I wanted this. Every piece of it. A partner I'd still dance with, barefoot in the grass at sixty. Kids who came home because they felt safe with us. Because *we* were home.

Mama let the silence stretch, unafraid of it. She'd waited out far more stubborn kids than me.

"I still say Christmas in eighty-degree weather is sacrilege."

"And yet you're here a day early," she pointed out helpfully, all false innocence.

"Yep." I nodded, my lips twitching. Okay. I could do this. Just… go for it. Right into the deep end. Three, two, one. "Mama… I'm pregnant."

She blinked. Twice. Then her mouth fell open, tears immediately springing to her eyes.

"Oh, Leigh. No wonder you look like you've seen a ghost."

"Gee, *thanks*, Mama."

"Well, you do! You're not exactly known for uncertainty, darling."

She had me there.

"So. How far along?"

"Nine and a half weeks."

"How are you feeling?"

"Queasy," I admitted.

"And your heart?"

"OB says everything looks good, but I'll see cardio after the holidays."

"Good. That's good." Her smile was tender. "And your mind?"

I broke.

Lip wobbling, I didn't even get the words out before she poured out of her chair and landed on her knees in front of mine, wrapping up my hands in hers. "Oh, honey," she breathed as the tears poured down my cheeks.

"I'm petrified," I whispered.

"I know, baby. But you are not alone. Pax, Alice, and Kaia will be there in Emerald Bay. And you know you always, *always* have a room here."

I sniffled and nodded, throat tight.

"But Leigh? I believe in you. It was always criminal to me that they spoke that kind of finality over you. You—of all my daughters —were born to be a mother."

I didn't expect the images that flickered through my mind. Tillie and Beau, Ollie's smile, his warmth curling around me in bed.

"So. The father?"

I guess that's where I got my blunt delivery, too.

"What about him?"

"Tell me it's that handsome Hart boy."

"Mama!"

"*What?* I saw the way he looked at you. And honey, you turned into a goddamn lioness after the accident. I thought they might have to sedate you when the nurses tried to take his daughter from your arms. That wasn't neutrality. That was instinct. And don't get me started on those Halloween pictures. Now *that* is America's ass."

"Mother!" I nearly dumped my tea into my lap.

"I'm old, not blind."

"You're not old. But you *are* married."

"Happily so, might I add. But window shopping never hurt anyone. And let me tell you—your daddy may have a flat ass, but he makes up for it with—"

"STOP." I buried my face in my palms. "Oh, god. So *not* something I need to think about." I glared at her as she snickered. Little shit. She would finish that sentence just to see me squirm. "Also, back to less horrific concepts—me loving *Tillie* does *not* equate to me loving Oliver."

"No, but you rearranging your life to look after the three of them just might. Him being the star in every story you tell me might."

"*Mom*," I groaned.

She just laughed, rising to dust off her dress before spooling herself back into her swing. The chair rocked slowly in the morning breeze, like the conversation wasn't about to gut me alive.

"Mothers know these things. I was just waiting for you to come to grips with it yourself."

"Come to grips," I muttered under my breath.

"What did he say? How'd he react?"

"He was amazing at first," I admitted, trying not to melt at the memory of his arms wrapped tight around me. "Focused on me. Making sure I was okay. But after the doctor's appointment?" I hesitated. "I dunno… he just…"

"Panicked?" she offered gently.

"Yeah. You could say that. He *proposed*, Mom." I said it pointedly, like it was the punchline to a joke she hadn't asked for.

Her lips twitched. "Oh, Ollie," she sighed. "Sweet boy."

"He's *thirty-two*, Mom."

"*Like I said.*"

I snorted, shaking my head as I stared at the giant pink flowers climbing her fence—thick green vines crawling up and around each slat like they were holding everything together.

"I think I broke him," I admitted quietly before walking her through the day. "He said he loved me and I couldn't say it back. I mean, not at first."

"And why is that? Do you not love him?"

"Isn't this all moving awfully fast?" My eyes burned. "I wanted to say it back. So badly. But he makes my head spin. All I could think was: *Dear* god, things are moving too quickly."

"Oh, honey, that's part of falling in love—that out-of-control feeling." She smiled sympathetically. "I'd say the nausea is part of it too, but yours has a…different root cause."

"*Funny.*"

"I'm serious."

"How do you do it?" I asked, voice cracking. "You've always been the best mom. I don't know if I'm ready."

"Can I let you in on a little secret?" When I nodded, she leaned closer. "Nobody's ready."

"What?"

"Nope." She shook her head like it was the easiest truth in the world, then sipped her tea. "We're all out here bullshitting our way through life."

"*Mom*," I chastised, half laughing, half scandalized. "You're *swearing* during a soul-searching chat?"

"What? It's true." She nudged the silt with her toes, keeping her swing moving lazily. "So. Do you? Love him?"

I nodded, my throat thick. "But I wanted something better than a panic proposal, you know? I want the whole thing. The fireworks. A kiss he can't wait to give me. A ring picked just for us. Not some band-aid slapped over a meltdown."

"You always were a romantic."

"And is that a bad thing?"

"No. Look who you're talking to." Her smile softened. "You don't get married and knocked up at nineteen without being a hopeless romantic."

"But it worked out for you and Dad."

"It did." Her eyes misted a little. "But the road wasn't smooth, baby girl. You think I was ready for Jeanne? Let alone Rhyett a year later? I was twenty, married to a man who spent most of his time at sea, with two babies under one year old."

"Jesus."

"Is precisely what your father said when I took the second test."

I burst out laughing, the sound cracking through my chest like sunlight.

When the humor faded, I sniffled pathetically. "How did you do it?"

"Do what—life with someone else?" When I nodded, she gave a knowing smile. "Marriage can be beautiful. And it can make you contemplate the merits of felony charges for attempted—but never completed—strangulation. Both are acceptable stages."

"Oh my god, Mom. Be serious."

"I am, honey. I love your daddy, but he's not always an easy man to like. He can be stubborn as a mule. The same generosity that made me fall in love with him bites me in the ass just as quickly."

"I don't get it."

"The man would donate us out of house and home if I didn't hover over the budget. Once, we were down to twenty dollars in our account—and half that in cash—and he gave his away to a man on the street. Along with the coat off his back."

"Sounds like Daddy," I muttered, smiling despite myself.

"He always had this faith. That God—or the universe—would provide. And it always did," she added like an afterthought. "Didn't stop me from wanting to throttle him a time or two. And if you wanna talk *impulsive*, your father still holds the crown. You know he proposed to me with a Ring Pop?"

"Yeah," I said with a laugh. "I just... I wanted to get married because I found *that*—you know? Not because we're panicking about an unplanned baby."

She leaned in, voice soft. "Sweetheart, it sounds like Ollie flayed his heart open and flipped it upside down. And now he doesn't know how to sew it back together. Doesn't sound to me like he loves you less than you deserve. Sounds like he fell too hard, too fast—and he's terrified."

A watery laugh slipped out. "Then why doesn't he trust me?"

She shook her head. "I don't think it's you he doesn't trust. If I had to guess—and I've raised six good men—I'd say he doesn't trust *himself.*"

After Carly... yeah, maybe that tracked. A little. A teeny, tiny bit.

"But now I'm sitting here, drinking your weird stinky-sock tea, wondering if I'm about to raise a baby *and* babysit a billionaire man-child prone to emotional whiplash. How does a morning start with him begging me to be okay—and *end* with him proposing? *And* telling me to move in?"

"They usually go hand in hand."

"Hardy-har-har. *Focus*, Mom."

"I am focused, honey."

"I always wanted to wait. To hold out for the kind of love you and Daddy have. Or Rhy and Brex. Even Jameson found Noel when no one expected it."

"And none of those stories came tied up in a perfect little bow, did they? What love story have you ever read, or watched, or heard, where the path was an easy road? Life's messy. So love is messy. The stories that matter are the ones where people choose each other. Over and over. Especially when it's hard. *Especially* when they're scared. They *stay.*" She gave me a look I felt in my gut. "Sounds to me like you're not the only one who's scared."

"He's not the one about to grow a human, or be poked and prodded like a science experiment."

"No. But he is the one about to watch the woman he loves risk her life and body to bring his baby into the world. You said he panicked? I think he looked at you, saw all the ways he could lose you, and jumped before he could stop himself."

I nodded slowly. The lump in my throat made it hard to do much else.

"Only you can listen to your instincts on something this big," she said. "But I know you'll figure it out."

"*How* do you know?"

"Because you've never needed the world to make sense before charging in, Leighton."

"I'm reckless."

"Maybe. Or maybe you're just brave. You've always known what you wanted, baby. Don't stop now just because the stakes are higher."

"What if I wasn't supposed to conceive because I won't be a

good mom?" The words cracked free before I could stop them. "What if Ollie realized I was a mistake?"

Her face softened—but her voice turned steel. "Leighton Alexandra," she said firmly. "You—and this baby—are not a mistake. I believe every baby comes exactly when they're meant to. Jeanne gave me purpose when your dad was just a grunt on the boat. When I was alone in that terrible little apartment by the marina with no money to go anywhere. Rhyett balanced her out. Jameson made me laugh when I needed it most. And you and Kaia? You brought your siblings together. They all rallied around you."

She squeezed my hand. "Maybe you and Ollie would've stayed too stubborn. Too loyal to Alice, to the family, to everyone else. Maybe this little miracle decided to give you a push toward the love story you didn't even know you needed."

I shifted, fidgeting with my phone before deciding against it and reaching for my tea instead.

Mama just smiled and stood, brushing her hands off on her dress.

"I'm all for letting men sweat when they put their feet in their mouths, but don't make him suffer too long, okay? If you're in— make sure he knows it."

"How do I know what to say?"

"You'll figure it out." She winked. "And when all else fails... fight naked."

BY THE TIME Christmas Eve arrived on Thursday, my parents' house was full to the brim. All of my siblings—except Elora (for obvious reasons) and Jeanne—had crammed into every nook and cranny. Brex and Rhyett even put a couple of them up, so we weren't literally spilling off the furniture. Not that that would be new to any of us. Not that any of us would mind.

To my surprise, Ollie hadn't called since Monday, and I wasn't sure if that should make me panicked or grateful. We'd texted a few times to check in, to say we missed each other, but the metaphorical elephant? Alive and well.

I still didn't know what I'd say if he called.

But God, I missed him. From the moment I woke up to the second I closed my eyes, I missed him. His laugh. His smile. The way he looked at his kids. The feel of his hand in mine. All of it. And the more time I had to process his steady descent into "we should get married," the more my mother's words began to coat his panic in soft edges instead of sharp ones.

I woke to baby Quinn's giggles—only now amplified by the roar of chatter that meant the Rhodes house was at full capacity.

Paxton, Jameson, Rhyett, and Axel were playing some kind of cutthroat card game at the kitchen table.

Brex and Noel—Jameson's fiancée—were curled up on the couch with coffees, a sleeping Emma, and a dog pile of Kaia and Hadlee.

Finn and Mav were chasing Quinn around the house, their faces lit up brighter than Mom's elaborately decorated tree.

We were just waiting for Alice and Greyson to show up in time for dinner.

My chest swelled at the contented glow of it all, and I made a beeline for my parents, who were already manning the stove.

This kitchen—quaint in design, but heavy on function—boasted double ovens and two massive islands, one of which was completely covered in pies. We did not play small in this family, and the desserts were no exception. I was pretty sure we were outnumbered four to one.

"Hey, Daddy," I chirped, sliding in beside him for coffee.

"Morning, punky. Merry Christmas Eve!" he greeted, pressing a kiss to the top of my head.

"Merry Christmas Eve!" I echoed before sliding my arm around his waist in a squeeze. He was a little softer around the middle these days, but still Milo Rhodes through and through—firm, steady, and with that same heart-eyed grin aimed solely at Mom.

That. I wanted *that.*

I stepped away just in time for Mom to wrap me in her own hug, her tie-dye sundress flowing around her like water. But as soon as Dad threw the first batch of bacon on, a terrible smell hit my nose— and my stomach lurched in betrayal.

The mug slammed onto the counter, and I bolted for the trash can.

"Oh, shit," I heard Mom mutter before she was behind me, scooping my hair out of the path of destruction the same way Ollie had a few days earlier.

I barely registered the clang of chairs or the echo of twelve collective gasps before I was upright again, wiping my mouth and grimacing at the queasiness still rolling through me.

"Jesus, Leigh," Axel called across the kitchen. "You hungover or something?"

"No," I groaned. "Not exactly."

"Oh my God," Hadlee gasped, eyes going huge. "No way!"

"Dammit," Paxton muttered. He reached into his wallet and handed a bill to Jameson, who smirked like the smug bastard he was and tucked it into a stack of cash in front of him.

They'd made bets?!

"Seriously?!" I barked, flipping them both off. Jameson just raised his coffee in a toast.

Axel appeared with a cup of water, brows drawn. "Come on, Leigh. What's going on?"

"I'm pregnant, okay?" I snapped, snatching the water and taking a long sip.

"What the fuck?" Axel barked just as Gimli the dog came skittering into the kitchen, nipping at his ankles.

"It's a Christmas miracle!" Maverick declared, grinning like a lunatic. "Thy virgin Leighton hath conceived!"

Kaia and Hadlee lost it, bursting into giggles, while Finn socked Mav in the arm and muttered, "What the fuck, dude?"

But it was Paxton, Jameson, and Rhyett—crossing their arms and bearing down on me like a judgmental Greek chorus that had me bracing.

"I didn't even know you were seeing anyone," Rhyett said, concern thick in his voice.

"Because she hasn't said shit about it," Jameson pointed out, eyes narrowing. "Are you safe? Can your heart handle this?"

"Yes, I'm okay," I said, setting a hand on my chest like it could will the queasiness away.

"Do we know this asshole?" Axel asked, cradling Gimli like a football.

"More pressing question," Pax cut in. "Do we *like* this asshole?"

"Does he treat you well?"

"Why isn't he here for Christmas?"

I held up my hands. "It's new. And I never said he was an asshole."

"But you've been hiding him," Axel observed, his intimidation factor greatly diminished by the furry thing lapping at his face. "Which means either he's embarrassing or a prick, so which is it?"

"Be nice, boys," Mom warned, resting her hand on my back.

"Yeah, lay off," Kaia added, pushing to my side.

"We just wanna make sure she's taken care of," Rhyett said again, softly this time.

"I'm perfectly capable of taking care of myself," I grumbled, even as Axel looked at me like I was a puzzle missing half its pieces.

"Come on, Leigh. Who the hell is the father?"

A throat cleared behind us, and everything stopped.

There in the archway, stood Oliver Hart, in slacks and a charcoal sweater.

Fuck me, he was beautiful, my heart stuttering in agreement. God, a smile that breathtaking should be illegal. It was blinding.

Even as he sheepishly waved a hand at the room packed full of inquiring Rhodes.

"*Uh…* that'd be me."

20

The Naughty List
OLIVER

Axel, Leighton's middle-brother with the long hair, cleared his throat pointedly, his hand frozen on top of what I assumed was the infamous French bulldog. "Well. That's certainly one way to keep it in the family."

Kaia stripped the puppy out of his arms, handed it off to Leighton, and landed a punch to his gut in one quick motion.

"*What?*" He grinned as the rest of them burst out laughing. "We were all thinking it."

"Facts," Maverick muttered, but the big idiot beamed and wrapped a lanky arm around my shoulders, pulling me in for a bro-hug and slapping my back. "Congratulations, boss man. I guess we know why you're on the naughty list this year."

"Gonna be one good-looking kid," a curly-haired guy with freckles said with a smile, pulling me in for a quick hug before I could counter Maverick. I think I recognized him from the first game of the season, but everything from that day was a bit of a blur. It was in the eyes though—that telltale blue-gray.

Reaching out my hand, I said, "Oliver Hart. I think we've met?"

"The day of the accident," he filled in. "No worries, man. I'm Finn—number nine."

"Oh, damn, that's right. It's really nice to see you."

He laughed good-naturedly before patting my back. "Good luck, today."

He seemed to mean it.

Leighton and I were individually passed from sibling to sibling, although it seemed the grilling was mostly directed toward her, while I was given hellos and congratulations. Nobody threatened my life, but Jameson did grip my hand tight enough to make his feelings known.

Those solemn eyes locked on mine as he growled, "You take care of our girl, understand?"

I'd gone head to head with CEOs that didn't make me feel like I was going to shit myself half as much as this fisherman did. No wonder Greyson liked him. I had the distinct impression he could make me disappear, and sleep like a baby afterward.

I nodded. "With everything I have," I vowed.

Like my brother, the idea of a smile seemed to offend the towering tank of a man. But I was almost certain his mouth tipped up, albeit incrementally.

"I'll hold you to that."

"Counting on it," I chuckled, before finding my girl in the kitchen, where her sisters were all cooing and peppering her in questions.

"Excuse me, ladies, but I'd love to steal a moment with Leighton, if she'll humor me?" *Please say yes.*

Luckily for me, she nodded, a sheepish smile on her face as she snatched my hand and led me out into the yard and over to a raised deck. To my immense relief, she turned to face me, wrapping my hands in hers.

"*I'm so sorry*," we breathed in unison.

"What the hell do you have to be sorry for?" I scoffed, reaching up to cup her cheeks in my hands. Her palms found their way to my chest, her thumb brushing just beneath my jaw.

"Leaving. I should've stayed with you—"

I ghosted my lips over hers, relief sluicing through me when she raised on her tiptoes to capture the teasing touch with a kiss that sent that addictive electricity flaring between us.

"Baby, this one is on me." I shook my head. "I *lost it.*"

"Of all the times not to have Guacward the emotional support avocado."

"Honestly." I snorted.

"After everything you went through with Carly, I should've tried to be more empathetic."

"You're growing a person. You're doing enough."

She gave a watery little laugh, and I captured the sound with my mouth. "You came after me," she breathed.

"Of course I came." My fingers slipped under the hem of her shirt, palm pressing to her side—just to feel her.

"Thank you. I missed you so much."

"You have no idea."

"I think I might. Wait. Where are the kids?"

"With Grey and Alice at the hotel. They had no complaints

about Christmas in Florida. I thought I'd take them to Orlando before we head home."

"Beau will love that."

"Believe it or not, Mattie loves Disney."

"With the crowds?"

"She wears headphones a lot, but she loves all the magic of it enough to deal. She just needs a little extra sleep afterward."

"I love that for her," she said, tears welling in her eyes. My god, pregnancy made my girl a crier. How hadn't I seen it sooner? Her next question sent them spilling over the rim. "You're not done with me?"

"*What?*" I would've staggered if I wasn't holding onto her. My hand found her waist, slipping under the hem just to feel her smooth skin. The other dropped to squeeze her ribs, my thumb grazing under the edge of her breast, body humming with the need to memorize every inch of this woman.

"You're not done with me? After I left like that? I can't imagine it brought up any good memories for you. I swear, I never considered what that would feel like for you. I just wanted to be home and talk to Mom."

I shut her up with another kiss, shaking my head, our noses brushing against each other a beat before I lifted my chin to kiss her forehead. "I wasn't sure you'd even talk to me again. Much less still want anything to do with me. I'd understand if you wanted child support and to put as much distance between us as physically possible."

Her breath caught, and her eyes shimmered. "Don't say shit like that," she whispered fiercely.

"I came here to beg for your forgiveness, Trouble. To ask you to please give me a chance. I was in shock, that was all."

"That makes two of us."

"I said some stupid shit."

"*That makes two of us.*"

I chuckled and shook my head, brushing a kiss to her temple.

"I really, really want to be a family with you," Leighton confessed, and my ribs constricted. "I'm just... I'm not there yet." A long silence stretched between us, until she added, softer, "Not the way you mean."

I nodded slowly. "Leighton. We don't need a baby to be a family. You're already mine—and I'll wait way longer than nine months if that's what it takes for you to believe it. I don't need you to wear my ring, or to live in my house, or carry my name for that to be true. Those things are just bonuses, baby."

Her eyes glistened. "Really?"

"Really." I drew her into my arms again. "And I promise, if you give me a chance, we do this at your pace. You want to stay in your place? I'll figure it out."

Leighton narrowed her eyes, mouth curving slowly before she bit her bottom lip. "Okay."

"Yeah?"

"Know when to stop while you're ahead, Hart."

I burst out laughing, tugging her flush against my side as we turned back toward the house.

From inside, we heard Kaia yell, "If you don't propose for real, I will!"

"Don't tempt her," Leighton muttered.

"Oh, I've learned," I said with a grin.

LEIGHTON

EVERY CHRISTMAS EVE AFTER DINNER, we gathered around the tree with classic music playing and exchanged jammies. Some years they were silly, others sweet—entirely dependent on the collective mood of the family.

And this year? Peak chaos.

To my surprise, everyone had been… well, frankly, awesome about the whole Ollie thing. They'd laid the jokes on thick throughout dinner, but he handled it even better than I did— laughing along and letting the jabs roll off his shoulders.

Now he was trying to squirrel his way out the door, mumbling something about not wanting to intrude on "family traditions." But saint that she was, Alice had already wrapped pajamas for him and the kids.

Beau was following Quinny around with literal hearts in his eyes, Ollie in his wake—but when I scanned the packed living room, I couldn't find our little lady anywhere.

Couldn't blame her. This was the best kind of chaos, but it was still chaos. If you weren't born into it, it could be sixteen kinds of overwhelming.

Greyson was chatting with my dad but still reached out to squeeze my shoulder as I passed. Alice's glittering eyes caught mine from across the room.

I checked under the breakfast table, lifting the palm tree-print tablecloth just in case. Just a snoring Gimli and some discarded pie crust. With Axel and Mav now trying to out-sing Sinatra, I wandered toward the hallway.

"Tillie," I hissed, trying not to announce the hunt to the entire house. "Tillie?"

"In here," a small voice called back.

I rounded into the formal dining room and burst out laughing. An arm was tenting up the red tablecloth from underneath.

Groaning, I dropped to my knees and crawled under the table, flopping onto my back beside her.

"You okay?" she asked, skeptical.

"I ate too much."

"Oh." She nodded like that explained everything.

"*You* okay? Just needed a moment of peace?"

She looked up at the table. "Your family is very big."

"Yes it is."

"They all talk at once."

"Sure do."

"And two of them are singing louder than the music."

"That would be Maverick and Axel. They're goobers, but harmless."

"I remember Uncle Mav. He plays football. Daddy says he wants him."

I snorted and slapped a hand over my mouth.

"What?" she asked, frowning like I'd offended her.

"Nothing, babygirl. You're right. He's a damn good receiver."

"Why can you say 'damn' and I can't?"

Shit. "Because adults make dumb rules. There are 'adult words' and 'kid words,' and apparently that's one of them."

"Feels like bullshit."

"That's… fair." I tried not to laugh. "Just maybe don't say that at school, okay?"

She shrugged. "Uncle Grey lets me sometimes."

Of course he did.

We lay in companionable silence, listening to off-key crooning and the clatter of laughter from the other room.

"Aunt Alice got you guys pajamas so you can wear them with us."

"I have pajamas."

"I know. But these are tradition pajamas."

"Traditions are illogical."

"Sure, but they make people happy."

"Why?"

"Because it's fun."

"Why?"

"Because…we like to have routines. They make us feel safe. Also, watching my six-foot-three brothers wear onesies is hilarious."

She giggled and turned to me. "They wear *onesies*?"

"Some years. We were unicorns last year."

"Are there unicorns this year?"

"I don't know. Only one way to find out."

"Okay. But maybe in a minute."

"You two okay down here?" Ollie ducked into our makeshift fort. God help me, my stomach flipped just looking at him.

"We're fine," I said, smiling up at him. "Discussing the Cuban Missile Crisis."

"Ah. As one does." He glanced between us. "Is this a no-boys-allowed club, or can I join?"

"You can only come in if you play with us," Tillie said primly.

"Cuban Missile Crisis?"

"No." I laughed. "Would You Rather."

He crawled inside and laid down opposite me, looking absurdly large under the table. Tillie scooted into my side, and I tucked her close as Frank crooned *Have Yourself a Merry Little Christmas* overhead.

"Alright, Tillie. Your turn."

She sighed, like she was entertaining children. "Would you rather build a fort or bake cookies?"

Ollie groaned and clutched his chest. "I *have to* choose?"

"Yep."

"It can't be both?"

"Nope. That defeats the whole point," Tillie chirped.

"If I *have* to pick, I'm going with cookies. Because then we get to eat them."

"Leighton?"

"I'm with your daddy," I said without hesitation. And maybe it was my imagination, but then the cheeky bastard had to smile at me like I'd said something a hell of a lot bigger than an answer to the game. I smiled back and gave him a little nod. *Yeah, big guy. I'm with you.*

"I'm going with cookies too," Tillie decided.

"Really?" I tickled her side. "I'm surprised."

"You do like your forts," Ollie pointed out.

"But if you two are doing cookies together, I want to bake too."

Cue lump in throat. "Yeah?"

"Yeah. You work well together. You're... glowy."

"Glowy?" Ollie asked.

"Like Christmas lights. Not loud. Just... happy." She wrinkled her nose. "That sounds dumb."

"No," Ollie scoffed, the grin stretching his face permeating his sexy voice. "That's not dumb. My turn?"

"Yep."

With his eyes on me, Ollie asked, "Candlelit dinner or breakfast in bed?"

"Why would I eat dinner with candles?" Tillie wrinkled her nose. "That seems unsafe."

Fuck me, my cheeks hurt. I loved this kid. This man. All of them.

"It's for ambiance," I explained.

"Ambiance?"

"Like… the vibes," I said with a shrug. "Personally, I hate mornings, so waking up to food and coffee already made for me is pretty special."

"Hmm. Yeah. I like when Daddy makes cinnamon rolls. But they're too sticky to eat in bed. That would get messy, and just—no fucking thank you."

To my relief, Ollie laughed at the same time I did, both of us shaking our heads. But his eyes stayed on me when he said, "Very good to know."

"Whatcha doin'?" Beau's little voice cut through the tablecloth seconds before his head popped underneath it, knocking a few plates across the top in the process. Ollie and I both scrambled to lift the fabric from his forehead.

"We've been discovered," I whispered to Tillie, who scowled at her brother.

"Having family time," she snapped, completely unaware that her words hit me square in the sternum.

"Welp. I'm family. Why 'm I not in here?"

"Cause you're a boy," she pointed out.

"So is Daddy."

"Yeah, but that's *Daddy*."

I gave her a warning pinch on the arm, shooting her a look. She huffed. "*Fine*. Come in."

I opened an arm, and Beau grinned before dramatically crawling over me to nestle in tight. Somewhere beyond our little haven, Noel and Brexley were laughing, my sisters were arguing over Santa's cookie-to-carrot ratio, and Kaia was calling my name. But when Ollie slipped his hand into mine where Tillie couldn't see, I didn't care enough to holler back.

With a lion-sized yawn, Beau declared, "We have a very good family."

"The best," Tillie agreed.

Ollie just squeezed my fingers—like he knew. Like he knew those tiny voices saying those words had my chest clenching. Like he knew how badly I'd needed to hear them to believe it.

"Yeah, buddy," he said softly. "We sure do."

A FEW HOURS LATER, I had a cookie-drunk Beau passed out on my shoulder while Ollie carried his unicorn-clad daughter to the car. A little drool spot on his red sweatshirt told me she was truly zonked. By the time I'd gotten Beau transferred into his seat and buckled, I turned to find Ollie leaning against the car beside me.

"Merry Christmas, Ollie."

"Merry Christmas, Trouble."

Fuck me, that man could kill me with a smile like that. His fingers grazed the lowest stretch of my belly, eyes dipping to where new life quietly stirred.

"Merry Christmas, little one."

"It's like you're trying to see how many times you can make me cry today."

He chuckled, then leaned in—closing my door and pressing me back against it. "I promise I'll do everything I can to make sure you never cry again, Leigh."

"Tall order, sir. These hormones are brutal."

"Then let's say this—no tears because of me. Unless they're happy. Or naughty. Those are allowed."

"*Naughty tears*, huh?" I tried to sound flippant, but nerves prickled in my chest. Not when I kissed him at a party. Not when we slept together. But now—here—I was nervous.

Because for the first time in years, I cared what someone outside of my family thought of me. And I'd sworn never to give that kind of power away again.

But Ollie?

Ollie mattered.

And that was terrifying.

"Those are my personal preference," he breathed, and then he brushed his lips over mine. The touch was so gentle, so tender that my heart sang. I dug my fingers into his waist, holding him against me and fighting the urge to grind against the thigh he wedged between my knees.

Like one of those pretty bikini bitches had waved a checkered flag, my libido flew off the starting line, determined to finish first.

Dammit, hormones. I could blame those for everything, right? Like the heat igniting in my skin, and the way my hands wandered of their own accord? Like the bone-deep need to taste this man in the back of my throat?

Ollie's tongue skillfully slipped between my lips, his flavor bursting over my tastebuds sending me sucking down a breath a beat before those strong hands I loved slipped under the cropped t-shirt I'd gotten for pajamas this year. Warm and rough, he was apparently just as desperate as I was. I moaned when he slid his palm up my ribs until he could tease my nipple and send a jolt of energy down my spine.

"Leigh," he warned, but I just swallowed the word. I'd never been a tremendous fan of my name, but God, when *this* man growled it…I could hear *that* forever. I slid a hand down between us to cup his cock through his new red sweatpants. He groaned into my mouth when I stroked my thumb down the length of him. "Trouble," he growled again.

I didn't stop.

"What's it say about me that I want to feel you between my legs tomorrow," I whispered. "So I know this is real."

"That you're mine?" he asked.

I nodded, slipping my fingers into his hair, clutching tight.

Mine. The word reverberated through me like a bell. Terrifying and intoxicating all at once.

"*Yours*," I breathed, loving the way that word dripped off my tongue for him to devour with each decadent kiss.

Then he broke away just enough to murmur, "Come with me."

"To the hotel?"

He nodded.

"Aren't Grey and Alice staying with you?"

"We booked the top floor. Two separate suites. Two bedrooms each." He searched my face. "Let me make it up to you tonight."

"You don't need to make up for anything—"

His fingers settled over my lips.

"Let me show you how good I can make you feel."

"Our predicament would indicate I'm already familiar with your pleasure stick."

He smirked, lips twitching. "Just getting started."

"That sounds like a challenge."

"You *like* challenges."

"I do," I whispered, grinding against his thigh.

"Then come with me." He winked. "We'll see who can get the other off faster."

My smirk crept up my cheeks until it was a full on grin, and I shook my head. "And you call *me* trouble."

21

Mended Hearts
LEIGHTON

Everything about Ollie's suite felt decadent. From the thick drapes to the secluded rooms and plush bedding, no expense had been spared. It was beautiful—but it had nothing on the view. About thirty minutes later, I pushed the curtains back, revealing a straight shot to Tampa Bay, glittering under the moonlight. I was standing in nothing but Ollie's shirt, which I'd swiped from his meticulously organized drawers while he tucked the kids in.

There was something deeply soothing about watching the water while waiting for him. And I wondered if it was possible to drown in the smell of him, because just the scent clinging to this shirt had me salivating and desperate.

"Stunning," I muttered, only for the door to creak behind me. I turned to find Ollie leaning against it, clicking the lock into place as his eyes scraped over my bare legs. When his bottom lip rolled between his teeth, I swore my vagina purred in anticipation. That was one of the things I loved about this man—his intent was always written all over his face.

"Yes, you are," he said simply, and my soul sang at the sincerity in his voice. He shrugged out of his hoodie, dropping it at the end of the bed as he prowled toward me—nothing but lean lines, defined muscles, and modest hints of ink. When he stopped just short of touching me, I pressed my palms to his chest as his hands melted onto my face.

"Missed you, Trouble. Desperately."

"Same."

"Let's agree to never do that again."

"I like that plan."

He dipped down to steal a kiss, hands sliding down my neck,

over the curve of my breasts, my waist, my hips—until they slipped beneath the hem of the shirt. Goosebumps erupted as his fingers found my bare ass and Ollie exhaled like it pained him.

"Your skin is so soft."

"And your hands feel incredible."

"Yeah?"

"Yeah."

"Well, that's very good for me."

"Indeed."

My gaze snagged on the tiny red nick beneath his jaw, just below the bob of his Adam's apple. I ghosted a finger over the mark, smiling as he offered, "Shaving."

"You mean you weren't held at knifepoint?"

Something flickered behind his eyes before he smirked, brushing a loose wave off my forehead.

"Not recently, no."

"*Recently?*" I squeaked, eyes going wide.

A low rumble of laughter shook his chest. "Relax, baby. Nobody's ransomed me in ages."

"That's not funny," I bit out, only to lose my breath when he spun me in his arms, aligning my back to his chest and guiding us both to face the window.

"Would you get 'em for me, killer?" he murmured at my ear, his fingers sliding over my chest and neck.

"Maybe?" It came out as more of a puff than a word, and I melted when he slipped one hand beneath the neckline of his shirt. His warmth skimmed over my clavicle, down to cup one breast. I gasped, my head tipping back onto his shoulder as he began to sway gently with the music he must've queued up earlier.

And as I let my weight rest against him, something clicked. Official title or not, I wanted all my dances to belong to Oliver Hart.

A whimper escaped when he pulled his hand away, but it didn't last. He scraped both palms over my ass, then lifted the shirt up and over my head, leaving me completely bare in the dark.

"I prefer you this way," he said, husky and low, as he tossed the shirt aside. "You should never wear panties again."

I laughed, breathless, my stomach flipping as I stared down at the marina. We were high enough up that the scattered few people below looked like ants. High enough that no one could see us—not really. Still, the idea sent a thrill racing up my spine as Ollie trailed his fingers across every inch of skin with a feather-light touch.

Chest tight. Throat thick. Goosebumps everywhere.

He leaned in, breath warming my neck—but he didn't touch. Like he was just breathing me in. Maybe it was the scent of my tropical shampoo or my vanilla body wash. Maybe it was me. Some wild chemical thing he needed the way I needed him.

His fingers skimmed my sides and I swore my nipples could cut glass.

"I fucking love how responsive you are, Leigh," he rasped, still not touching me where I wanted. The anticipation made my thighs clench—something he clearly noticed. He slipped one palm over my belly and nudged a knee between my legs. "Look at you. So fucking beautiful, baby."

I did. I let my focus drift from the world outside to our reflection in the window—two silhouettes bathed in moonlight, pale skin glowing like ghosts against the glass. His hand greedily covered my belly, like he needed to claim it. The other trailed up to my throat, wrapping around it like the most erotic necklace I'd ever worn.

"I love you, Leighton Alexandra." His hand slipped up to cover my mouth. "I don't need you to say it back. Don't need you to rush. I just need you to know it." He traded his hold for a fist in my hair. "We do everything at your pace, okay?"

I nodded, heart hammering, molten heat pooling low in my belly as he pinned me tighter to his chest.

"I was terrified I'd lost you after our argument Sunday."

"Not really an argument," I whispered.

"Bickering match?"

"Spat?"

"Spat," he agreed with a smirk—and then his hand slid lower, cupping my mound. Even in the blurry glass, I saw his eyes darken.

"I've only been more terrified once. And both times, I thought I lost you."

He didn't need to say more. That accident haunted both of us.

"I just don't want to be one more obligation you regret."

"Leighton." He sighed, like my words physically hurt. "You're the only decision I'm absolutely sure of. My name, the company, all of it—that was expected. But you? You're just for me. Mine. I get to be selfish, just this once. And baby, I want to be right here."

And then his fingers slid between my folds. I shuddered as he growled, "You're *soaked*. Tell me that's mine. Tell me this is *for me*."

"It's not for me, handsome."

He chuckled, a devilish smile blooming. "Honestly? I couldn't blame you if you wanted to fuck yourself. *Look at you*."

"Little preoccupied with the god behind me."

"A *god*, huh? That's one hell of an upgrade."

I gasped as he slipped one blunt finger inside me, the sudden intrusion somehow amplified by watching him in the glass. "*Hmmna*."

"I don't think that was English, baby."

I laughed—barely—before it caught on a gasp. His fingers sank into me and the sudden stretch sent a jolt through my core. The reflection made it worse. Better. All-consuming. And when he curled those fingers just right, pressing deeper, my knees nearly gave out. Ollie held me steady, circling my clit, then slipping in a second finger, dragging pleasure through every nerve ending like it was an art form.

"Can…can they see us?" I panted.

"Would you like that?" he whispered. "Would you like the whole city to watch me pleasure you until you soak my hand?"

"I…um." My panted attempt at forming words turned into a hard swallow as an unexpected rush of need mixed with adrenaline.

Did I…did I like that idea?

"Would you like it…" he whispered, sliding his sticky fingers over my ass before slipping them between my cheeks, thumb pressed against my asshole as his fingers plunged even deeper into my pussy. "I think you *would*. I think you're so fucking wet because you like the idea of them watching me ruin you. Watching as I make you shake until your cum is dripping down your legs. Watching as I slide my cock into that sweet cunt and fuck you until you shatter for me all over again."

Those filthy words ignited me from within. Before it should've been humanly possible, my knees buckled. Ollie wrapped his free hand around my waist to keep me from crumpling as tremors of pleasure ripped through me, my legs shaking with each wave he coaxed from me. But he didn't stop. He fucked me with his fingers through each wave, dragging it out until all I could do was lean against his chest. Instead of easing, he fucked me harder. His free hand slid down my stomach until he reached my clit, circling it in rapid motions. My eyes rolled back in my head as my mouth dropped open.

"Quiet, Leighton," he rasped, and I swallowed the scream building in my throat. "Good girl."

By the time I could breathe again, I shoved at his hand. Every inch of me was vibrating like one exposed nerve ending.

"You're so fucking sexy," he murmured, kissing down my neck, easing his fingers out. He brought them to my mouth. I opened, no hesitation, and the look on his face when I sucked my release from his skin nearly undid me again.

"I need to see you," he said, turning me in his arms. When my back hit the glass, I hissed at the chill, but he was already moving— reaching for his pants, then turning to the luggage.

"Where are you going?"

"Condom."

I grabbed his wrist. "You can't get me more pregnant, Oliver."

His eyes flared. "Are you serious?"

"I trust you."

"I'm clean. I always play it safe, but——"

"I believe you. Now come fuck me."

He showered me in a smile that took my breath away, then closed the distance. Without another word, he hooked one of my legs over his hip. The fat, dark head of his cock sent my body shaking as he rolled it over my clit—once, twice—then pushed inside with one deep, steady thrust that had me slamming back into the window.

He clamped a hand over my mouth. His other cupped my ass as he pressed kisses down my jaw and throat, his cock twitching inside me. For all his filthy words, when Ollie looked into my eyes, his rhythm turned reverent. Every stroke was a reluctant turn of a page in a book he didn't want to finish.

Ollie slowed his motions to press a kiss to my mouth, each movement delicate, a forbidden prayer whispered against my skin. Steady, intentional, methodical strokes pulled against my innermost walls as he searched my eyes. For what, I wasn't sure, but his intensity had the bridge of my nose burning. My nails scored over his shoulders as I wrapped my leg around his hips, pulling him closer.

He growled as he pumped into me. Literally *growled*—the sound deep and carnal—his fingers tightening where he gripped my waist and threaded into my hair. Then he fucked me harder. Rougher. His mouth found mine as he pulsed inside me, holding me tight, like the release ripped something from his chest.

When Ollie opened his eyes, they seemed to search me for an answer to a question I didn't hear. My mother's advice played in my mind—if you're in, make sure he knows it.

Holding his intense gaze, both of our chests heaving, I nodded. The man smiled, softly, tentatively, like I'd given him what he needed even though he didn't know how to ask for it.

"I love you too, Oliver Hart."

Oliver

January

LEIGHTON and I spent New Year's Eve locked in a towering Orlando hotel *Hart Investments* held shares in, watching fireworks explode over the city.

By nine a.m. on the first, we were wheels up and headed back to

Emerald Bay on our jet, with Matilda running up and down the aisle snapping photos of us with the Polaroid camera Leigh gave her for Christmas. Apparently, they were taking up scrapbooking together—and the absurd array of glitter, specialty paper, something called washi tape, and ribbons in every color known to man currently charged to my card was all in preparation for "proper scrapbooking adventures."

Based on the gleam in Leighton's eye, I had a feeling that was just the beginning.

On Monday, we met with the new cardiologist who'd be monitoring her for the foreseeable future. Thankfully, the doctor was fully confident that Leighton could carry the baby to term safely. She recommended an induction to avoid the unpredictability of spontaneous labor, but aside from that—and a few follow-ups—there was no need for daily medication or constant visits unless symptoms appeared. Leighton was elated.

Week two of the new year brought a note taped to my front door. A QR code and a scribbled message in Mattie's handwriting: *Scan me.*

I sighed, humoring her, and scanned it.

A video clip from *Taken* played—Liam Neeson growling *Good luck* —and nothing else.

"What the fuck?" I muttered.

Inside the door, I found a fully loaded Nerf gun and a pair of safety goggles waiting like an offering. Grinning, I grabbed both, kicked off my shoes, and shouted, "You're all toast!"

A screech rang out from Mattie. A war cry from Beau. And absolutely no sound from Leighton, which worried me more.

I rounded the staircase into the living room just in time to see Mattie's ponytail disappear into the kitchen. Beau barreled at me, firing wildly. Once we were both out of ammo, I hoisted him over my shoulder and crept forward—only to be ambushed by the girls with what had to be a foam-dart bazooka.

The entire kitchen was littered with little blue and orange darts by the end of it. Mattie and Leighton were limp with laughter on the breakfast bench, my girls shrieking as I tickled them to pieces.

But it was week three that locked itself in my heart forever.

The kids were staying with Grey and Alice for the weekend, and I picked Leighton up at the crack of dawn from her apartment. Two cups of coffee—one half-caf—and breakfast burritos waited on the console. She climbed into the passenger seat looking murderous.

"Worth it, I promise," I vowed, handing over the goods.

By the time we made it to the first stop, a scenic overlook three hours north, she'd fully commandeered the radio. The second she stepped out and took in the coastline, her face lit with awe.

"Jesus, the view is insane," she breathed, taking it in.

"Right?" I breathed, watching the sun glint off her tan skin and play in those slate eyes.

"It doesn't matter how many times I see it, the ocean is always stunning."

"Oh," I chuckled, still locked on her profile. "I was talking about you, Trouble."

She rolled her eyes, fished out her camera, and motioned for me to turn around. A second later, she jumped on my back, legs locked around my waist. I held her steady while she kissed my cheek and snapped a Polaroid over my shoulder, presumably of us and the view. The film would take a few minutes to develop, so we wouldn't know what we got until we hit the road again.

I didn't set her down until we were back beside the car, where I stole a kiss before ushering her inside and glancing nervously at my watch.

Three hours later, we were on the outskirts of Pacific Grove when I made her blindfold herself.

"Kinky," she said, tying the fabric around her head.

"You're giving me ideas," I muttered as I turned onto the road that led to the sanctuary.

"Good," she replied. "We've got the hotel to ourselves. We'd better have ideas."

Chuckling, I led her out of the car, through the eucalyptus grove, swatting her hands away every time she tried to cheat. "Just another damn second."

At last, I swiped her camera from her bag and backed up a few paces. "Stay," I said. She danced in place but didn't peek.

Only when I had her perfectly framed did I whisper, "Now, Trouble."

She tugged the blindfold down—and froze.

Even with the sun blazing through the trees, it wasn't the light making her squint. It was the sight before her. Monarch butterflies, hundreds of them, drifting like orange and gold confetti through the trees behind her in the stillness of the grove. I snapped my photo. The hum of the camera printing the picture drew her shrink-wrapped eyes to me, just for a heartbeat. I smiled, jerking my chin up, redirecting her to the view above us.

They clung to the eucalyptus branches above and fluttered through the air like notes in a song only they could hear. The air was thick with that vaguely spa-like scent of the grove that tugged on memories of my childhood, standing right here with my mother.

I could see it the moment it hit her—the awe, the overwhelm—it looked like she'd taken a hit to the chest, staggering back a step as her hand came to hover over her lips. One word cracked out like a prayer.

"*Ollie.*"

Everything we hadn't said since Christmas was wrapped in that one breath. It wasn't just the butterflies. It was us. It was the fear, the healing, the hope. It was her saying yes—without saying a single word.

Tears glinted in her eyes as she turned in a gentle circle, looking up like the whole world had shifted beneath her feet.

I stepped behind her, wrapped my arms around her waist, and rested my hand on her belly. My chin settled on her shoulder.

The view was breathtaking—but nothing compared to holding Leighton in that moment.

There was something sacred in these trees. Something I hadn't felt since I was a boy, holding my mother's hand in this exact spot. I never thought I'd feel that kind of magic again.

And then Leighton bulldozed into my life, and proved me wrong.

Nothing about this woman embodied these tiny creatures, and yet I saw them in the light she created everywhere she went.

She was bold in her love. In her joy. In her sense of adventure. She made the world more beautiful just by being in it.

"Worth it?" I whispered.

Yeah, I meant the trip. But beyond that, I meant the detour—hell, all of it. The hard conversations we hadn't finished. The tangle of emotions I still had no fucking clue how to voice.

When she turned in my arms and looked up at me, it was like she could see it all written across my face. Like she thought I'd carved this place for her with my bare hands.

I would've, if I could.

"Absolutely," she whispered.

Forgiveness. That's what that word tasted like. Like I hadn't imagined the bliss of the last few weeks. Like she was in this—for real—as much as I was.

"Leigh," I breathed, voice thick, raw. "You're perfect."

She huffed a soft laugh, her lips twitching with the beginnings of a smile, but she didn't argue—just dropped her gaze to her feet. More butterflies floated lazily around us, flitting from blossoms to shrubs like they hadn't a care in the world.

"Far from it," she murmured after a beat, swallowing audibly.

"We'll just have to agree to disagree."

She shot me that look—dry and sweet all at once, a sarcastic challenge wrapped in affection. "Well, aren't you generous."

"Maybe," I said with a small smile, lifting her camera and giving the printed photo a gentle shake—old habit, I guessed. "But I think you're exactly what we needed."

Her brows pinched, just slightly. "We?"

"Me and the kids," I said quietly, barely above a whisper. "You mended our hearts without even trying. Just... by being you, Trouble. I don't think you realize it, but you're the first thing to make me feel whole in years. Maybe *ever*."

The truth snagged in my throat. I didn't talk about my parents. Or the way Greyson had *always* stood between me and the worst of it. Or the fact that it still haunted me how little warmth had existed in the elaborately decorated shell of a house we grew up in.

But she didn't need the words. She didn't need me to voice the fears telling me I was doomed to repeat it.

She just stepped closer, laid her hand gently over my heart, and offered the softest smile.

"I think you did that all on your own, handsome."

"Of course, you do." I laughed, cradling her chin between my fingers and tilting her face up. God, I loved her mouth. Her sharp tongue. That relentless, resilient heart. I tucked a loose strand of hair behind her ear and just... soaked her in.

Right here. In the one place I'd ever believed in magic.

"My kids are happy. You're glowing. I couldn't ask for anything more."

Luckiest damn man alive. That's what I was.

Especially when she blinked, like she was fighting tears.

"Mom used to bring us here, you know?" I added.

"Yeah?" she asked, her smile still resting soft on her face.

"She said magic lived in the eucalyptus grove."

It was one of the only times she ever loaded the three of us into the car on her own. She'd have the chef pack us snacks, and we'd drive six hours up the coast—stopping at every lookout and bathroom she could find. We'd blast music, pick up donuts and fries we weren't usually allowed to have. And for a few fleeting hours, away from the cameras and our father's shadow, she'd laugh with her whole chest.

Those were the only days I remember her being truly happy.

Leighton's eyes softened like the memories tucked into her own chest were folding open. "That's exactly what I was thinking."

"I think the magic lives in *you*, Trouble."

I lifted her camera and stretched my arm out, tilting it up to catch the sky and the grove behind us—and caught her with a kiss.

If she ever glued anything into a scrapbook we'd want to remember forever, I hoped it was this.

When we pulled apart, she swayed her hips, biting her bottom lip before a wide grin broke free like she'd lost the battle to contain it.

I wanted all of her smiles.

"Thank you," she whispered.

I nodded and slipped her camera into the side pocket of her bag, tucking the two Polaroids in beside it before lacing my fingers through hers.

We wandered the grove together in silence, the hush broken only by the occasional gasp from another visitor.

After a few minutes, Leighton's voice soft, she asked, "What are you hoping for?"

I turned toward her. "Today?"

"For the baby," she clarified, her eyes trained on the trees. "Boy or girl?"

"Oh." I smirked. "I thought that was obvious."

"Well, apparently not, because I'm asking."

I laughed. "A girl. Just like her mama."

She tried—and failed—to hide her smile.

"And if it's a boy?"

"Then he'll love his mama just as much as Beau does."

Because that boy of mine… he was a goner. Leighton held his little heart in her hand. Just like she held mine.

We slowed as a kaleidoscope of monarchs drifted down around us, spiraling in slow, mesmerizing arcs. One landed on her shoulder. She froze. Another touched down on her head.

Then another.

And another.

Leighton's breath caught, her lips parted in silent awe. She didn't move, like her body didn't know what to do with that much joy all at once. And I—God, I just stood there and watched. Watched the woman I loved be cloaked in living magic.

My mom once said butterflies were hellos from beyond. From the people we'd lost.

I couldn't help but wonder if she was somewhere in this silent parade, fluttering down to say hello to the woman I was determined to make my wife.

"I told you," I murmured, barely above a whisper as I stepped closer. "You're magic."

22

It's Not a Party Until Someone Gets Evicted
LEIGHTON

February

<u>The Nanny Diaries: Oliver Hart Falls For The Help</u>
<u>Double Trouble: It Looks Like Oliver Hart Is Off The</u>
<u>Market</u>—and <u>His Brother's Sister-In-Law Is The</u>
<u>Lucky Lady</u>
<u>Rich, Hot, and in Love: Heir to Hart Dynasty Seen With</u>
<u>Brunette Bombshell</u>

"Are we out of yogurt?"

"*We?*" I didn't bother glancing up from my laptop.

Ollie and I had decided to 'soft launch' our relationship after we told the kids we were dating at the beginning of February. We picked the restaurant, showed up looking like fire, and Ollie obliterated any questions when he kissed the life out of me in our booth in the back. Unfortunately, a soft launch was not what the tabloids had in mind. They were having way too much fun with it, in my opinion. A bunch of parasitic dumpster ferrets.

"You. I meant are *you* out of yogurt?" Paxton clarified as he popped out from behind my fridge like an oversized jack-in-the-box. The man was anything but subtle. He'd been hovering constantly for weeks. If Kaia was out, Pax was miraculously around. I wasn't sure if they thought I'd spontaneously keel over—entirely disregarding the board-certified physicians monitoring me like overpaid hawks—or if he really was just sick of his roommates, like he claimed.

"Yeah, I need to go shopping."

"Dammit."

"You have your own house, you know?" I shut my laptop with a sigh. "And I'd bet your bumbling band of meatheads has an abundance of Greek yogurt and chicken breasts for you to pillage."

"And go without your sparkling personality? How *ever* would I survive?"

"Peacefully, I imagine."

He snorted. "Give me a list. I'll tackle groceries."

"And risk being spotted in public?" Being a star quarterback came with paparazzi, but dragging a once-downtrodden team back into playoff contention before falling short had put a neon bullseye on his back. On second thought, maybe he *was* hiding out here—for both the peace and the yogurt.

"I said I'd tackle them, not that I'd go myself."

"You don't need to order me groceries, bubba."

"And you don't need to feed me five-thousand calories a day, punky. So shut up and make a list."

"You're crabby."

"Look who's talking."

I scowled at him, but he wasn't wrong. I was exhausted. Eighteen weeks pregnant and still waiting for that miraculous second-trimester energy boost everyone promised. It had yet to appear. "I have an excuse."

"Juniper sang her way through her pregnancy with you and Kaia, so cling to that loosely."

I deadpanned. "Mom is a freak of nature."

"Valid. But hey, you're keeping food down again."

"That part is nice."

"And your obsession with Indian curry has only grown."

"Christ, you have been here a lot lately." I raised an eyebrow. "Everything okay at home, darling?"

Paxton flopped onto the couch, the frame groaning under his weight. He poked at the takeout container he'd just retrieved, kicking his feet onto the coffee table like he paid rent.

"They're gross," he grumbled.

I laughed, tucking my computer into its bag. "The vast majority of the female population can attest to that."

"Why's everything gotta smell like sweaty socks? And for the love of God, we're grown men. Wipe the seat if you make a mess."

"Ew." I wrinkled my nose. "Any luck finding a new place? You've got more money than God—I find it hard to believe there's *nothing* in your budget."

He sighed. "My agent's shown me a few spots, but nothing says *home*, you know?"

"I'd be more concerned if inanimate objects started speaking to you."

"Hardy-har-har."

"You'll find the right one." I smiled at him—a smile that narrowed immediately when he opened his big mouth again, dimple flashing like a warning light.

"About that…"

"*Paxton.*"

"What if I proposed a deal?" He balanced his takeout on his knee.

"Holy guacamole, just spit it out."

"What if I crash here for a while? Two birds, one stone."

"If by 'crash' you mean 'move in,' you better butter that biscuit and present it properly."

"You are preg-a-nante."

"Very observant."

"I am mis-rob-lay."

I laughed. I didn't mean to, but the big sap was looking at me with those damn puppy eyes. Six-foot-four, 240 pounds, and America's sweetheart was *pouting*.

"That sounds like a *you* problem."

"You're gonna need—" He caught the look I gave him and popped his lips, eyes lifting skyward like he was praying for divine guidance. "—what I *meant* to say is, I would like to be here to help. Make sure you get enough rest, help with the baby, etcetera."

"Kaia will be here for that." Although, the idea of raising this baby in a proper village of people who loved them already had my heart melting.

"Well, then. To replenish the Greek yogurt. That kind of thing."

"Mm-hmm."

"Plus, living alone in Chicago was brutal. The *quiet* drove me nuts."

"The worst," I said, doing my best to keep a straight face.

"And we have fun together."

"We do."

"*And* you don't smell like a jockstrap."

"Thank you for noticing."

"So, temporarily, I could rent the spare bedroom. Just until I find or renovate something perfect."

"I still don't see the perk for me."

"Apart from my dazzling presence?"

"Yes."

"That's it. That's all I got. Also, I'll cover rent."

"Greyson paid off the mortgage."

"Well, fuck." His shoulders drooped.

"God, you're such a baby."

"I hate being single," he muttered. "I need someone to talk to. Someone to make coffee and cook with. Solitude is for the birds."

"Luckily, you have the merry men of Emerald Bay."

"That might be worse." He perked up again. "Come on, punky. It'll be fun. Like old times."

There was something stupidly endearing about a man with more zeros in his bank account than I cared to count, begging to voluntarily subject himself to the chaos of his twin little sisters.

"Yeah," I sighed dramatically. "Alright."

His grin stretched full Cheshire. "I promise I'll make it worth it." He stood and opened his absurd arms for a hug.

"Try that again," I muttered into his chest, arms wrapping around his waist.

"I promise you will not have to clean the bathrooms ever again."

"*Now that's* what I'm talking about."

March

ARMS LOADED with party store supplies in a color scheme better suited for a funeral, I kicked open the door to *Sip Happens*. Nestled in the heart of Emerald Bay, my favorite coffee shop was an eclectic little hipster-approved haven—walls plastered in thrifted finds, obscure collector's records, and even a few comic books I recognized.

The last few weeks of February flew by in a flurry of Santa Ana winds, sister-led party planning, and nailing down final details for our trip to Florida for Jameson's wedding at the end of March.

Our little ballerina was turning eleven this weekend, and the three of us may have gotten a wee bit carried away with the party prep. But a black card with no limit will do that to even the most reasonable of us—especially for a kid like Tillie.

"Okay, all that's left is the cake delivery and we're good to go," Alice said, tapping away at her phone with one hand, iced coffee in the other. She was always working—even weekends—and I didn't envy how tightly the Hart family business seemed to cling to its people. She, Grey, and Ollie might as well have their phones surgically implanted.

"Caterers?" I asked, dumping my bags at a table and scanning through our mental checklist.

"Confirmed this morning," Kaia chirped, making her three-inch heel shuffle look effortless while I felt like a sweaty cow. "Planetary cupcakes too."

"Floral?"

"Delivered," Alice confirmed, slipping her phone into her purse just as Jax lumbered inside behind us, clearly less than thrilled to be here. Greyson had only intensified Alice's security after the accident. If he couldn't be at her side, Jackson was. Though honestly, they were together most of the time anyway. Poor guy was permanently third-wheeling.

"Okay," I sighed, nodding more to myself than to them. Everything was checked off. The event would be as close to perfect as humanly possible, and Mattie would know—without question—just how loved she was.

"Relax, sissy! We've got everything," Kaia reassured, that radiant smile of hers blooming with ease.

"Right, yeah, okay. It's great—it's gonna be great."

"Breathe."

"Yep!" I sucked in a dramatic inhale through my nose and, to my surprise, some actual relief settled into my chest on the exhale. "Okay. Coffee, then we decorate."

"Aye-aye, captain!" Kaia gave a mock salute. As if summoned, Jackson's eyes flicked our way. She snickered into her palm. "Easy, *Old Yeller*. We're just grabbing drinks."

He harrumphed, arms folded like a mountain in a polo, but didn't move from his post. He did, however, glare at Alice like all of this was her fault.

I led the way to the counter, grinning at Jasper—the barista? baristo? I never knew which—and asked for my regular. I motioned the girls up to order behind me, then glared pointedly at our security shadow.

His response? A slow smile.

Rolling my eyes, I added a black coffee to the order and handed Jasper my card.

"Thank you very much! Sure nice to see you ladies!" he said cheerfully, handing it back.

"Same, thank you!" I turned to go, but the shop manager zipped over, curls bouncing.

"Hey, girl! Someone was looking for you earlier!"

My brows lifted. "Really? Who?"

She shrugged, brown eyes narrowing thoughtfully. "Not sure. He wasn't a regular or anything. Big beard, tall—six-three? Six-four?"

I scowled at Alice, who froze mid-scroll. "James in town?"

"Not that I'm aware of." Greyson made it a point to know where all of us were, as if he was avoiding a family ambush. If Alice didn't think our brother was here, he very likely wasn't.

"Weird." That familiar icy crawl snaked down my spine.

Alice shot a look at Jax, who was already moving, scowl deepening as he lumbered through the shop to stand beside us.

"Well… thanks anyway," I said, accepting the cups from Jasper as my brain tried to pin down who the hell would be looking for me. Paparazzi, maybe? They'd been having a field day with our relationship, so it wouldn't be the first time.

Fucking creeps.

"NOT TO TOOT my own horn or anything, but I think this was a huge success," I whispered to Kaia, who was grinning ear-to-ear. Our little super genius asked for a galaxy-themed birthday party, and Ollie had suggested a star-gazing night in the backyard, but Tillie—who *insisted* on inviting her classmates, as to avoid 'social suicide'—didn't seem particularly keen on having so many people in her safe space.

I'd gingerly suggested the planetarium.

Naturally, Ollie booked the whole damn venue.

The lights were dimmed to a dusky glow. Fairy lights sparkled. The color palette was navy, black, violet, and gold. A Lofi *Lord of the Rings* playlist drifted softly through the air as guests moved through "Tillie's Universe." Yeah, the nickname was sticking.

After a few moments of wide-eyed overwhelm at the number of people who'd come to celebrate, our girl lit up once the kids were broken into smaller, more digestible groups.

Kaia ran a "star jar" station where each kid made their own glittery constellation in a mason jar. Alice helped man the constellation card table, where they punched holes in black cardstock and got to name their own stars.

Tillie's idea for a "star swap" instead of gifts had been a hit—each kid brought a token they loved, something small but meaningful, and swapped with someone else.

But it was the stargazing show that stole the evening. A grandfatherly host named Howard narrated a custom sky presentation in dulcet fairytale tones instead of the usual thundering drama.

When it ended, he revealed Ollie had purchased her a *real* constellation. There was officially a cluster of twinkling balls of gas up in the universe named 'Matilda Hart', and, better yet, it had been visible the night she was born—she burst into tears and threw her arms around his waist.

I nearly joined her.

The staff swept in with galaxy-themed cupcakes while we regrouped at the front of the venue.

"Brilliant, sissy," Kaia said.

"The sensory modifications were such a win," Alice added,

blinking rapidly. "Seriously, Leigh… you're already such an amazing mom."

I blinked at her. "Why are you looking at me like that?"

She shrugged one elegant shoulder, clearly fighting emotion. "I'm just… grateful. That's all."

"Aww, sissy," I cooed, wrapping her up as she held me tightly in return.

"You deserve the world, Leigh."

"Back at you."

"And the way you've stepped up for these kids this year…" She shook her head. "They needed you so desperately."

"It's nothing," I mumbled, uncomfortable with the praise.

"It's not nothing," Kaia argued. "You didn't have to do all this."

"It's easy," I said with a shrug. "You love somebody, you show up for them." You love their daddy… and you'll do anything to see him smile.

Alice's voice was thick. "You're showing them something they've never had—outside of Ollie."

My throat tightened. Across the room, I spotted Beau racing toward his sister with a cupcake held high like a trophy. He presented it with a dramatic flourish, and the three of us burst out laughing. My gaze flicked to Ollie. He was already watching me, and when we smiled at each other, something deep passed between us— silent, certain.

Then…

A voice cut through the soft lull like a scalpel. "Well, isn't this *just precious!*"

Beau swerved. "*Mommy!*"

Tillie, however, froze.

My stomach sank with the speed of an asteroid.

"Oh, fuck," Alice breathed as we all turned to see Carly standing at the entrance in a beautiful violet dress and silky gold heels, gift bag in hand, face painted to perfection. She looked ready to walk a red carpet.

Ollie was already moving toward her, jaw tight, expression set.

I was already moving too—straight for our birthday girl.

"I thought this was a party!" Carly crowed. "Where's the music? Let's turn up the volume, shall we?" She shot a sharp look at Howard, who wisely ignored her. "Happy birthday, baby girl!"

Tillie's eyes were wide with panic. Her body locked up.

Cruella hadn't seen her kids after the fiasco at the theater before *The Nutcracker.*

She hadn't even bothered to send them Christmas presents, much less speak to them through the holidays.

The tension in the room could be carved with a damn ice pick.

Even the staff and fellow parents were going still, like they knew something about this picture didn't fit.

I reached Tillie just as her lip began to wobble. I knelt beside her and opened my arms without a word.

She flew into them.

And behind us, Carly kept smiling.

Fake. Cold.

Unwelcome.

As Carly scooped Beau into her arms, she announced, "I found you those glitter pens you love so much, and a brand new notebook!"

"You're supposed to let her *open* her gift," Kaia growled beside me. The moment we flanked Tillie, her small hands landed in ours.

"I'm so sorry I'm late. I know I messed up, sweetie," Carly said —loud enough for every parent, nanny, and bystander to hear. She descended the aisle with Beau on her hip and all the poise of royalty. I wasn't sure I'd ever hated anyone more than I did this woman as she came to a stop in front of our birthday girl. Ollie was right behind her. Carly set Beau down and tapped Mattie's nose with one perfectly manicured finger. "So, I grabbed something extra special to make it up to you."

She scowled at a staffer. "I said, *let's get the party started*. Turn up. The *music*." The poor girl bolted like she'd spotted a bear.

"*Wait*," Ollie warned, and I caught Greyson trailing the girl toward the exit.

People around us awkwardly resumed their conversations, doing their best not to openly stare. Carly extended the pink and purple gift bag toward Mattie. Her eyes sharpened when Tillie shied back, moving a step behind me. She crouched to eye level.

"I've gone through a lot to get here, baby. I worked so hard to pick the perfect present. Take it, Matilda."

"We didn't do presents this year," I said, arching a brow. "She doesn't like being the center of attention. It was in the e-vite. Or can't you read?"

"Go make yourself useful, Leighton," she snapped, just as Ollie stepped up, his arm settling around my waist.

"Leighton planned the entire event," Ollie said, voice low and biting. "How did you contribute?"

"Party planning too? Some people really can't help inserting themselves where they don't belong." Her gaze dropped to Ollie's hand on my waist. "Planning a wedding next, Leighton?"

"Maybe," I said, tone flat, smiling when her eyes narrowed.

Dismissed, but not deterred, Carly turned back to Tillie. "After everything I've gone through to be here, you're really going to embarrass me like this? Take the bag."

"I'm just amazed you can see her when your bar's in hell," I muttered, yanking the bag from her hands to stop her from shoving it at the birthday girl. "Refreshments are in the corner. I'm sure you'll make the rounds."

She straightened like she'd just been slapped. The music switched to something peppy and poppy, the volume rising, and I cursed under my breath.

"Matilda Hart. I *made* you. *I* gave birth to you. You will treat me with the respect I deserve as your *mother*." Her voice dropped into a hiss. "You can't humiliate me just because your nanny likes to play pretend. She only cares about you because your daddy signs her paycheck."

Tillie stiffened, eyes flicking to me, her face crumpling. I tightened my grip on her hand as Ollie barked, "*Enough*, Carly. For fuck's sake."

"You use that language in front of *my* kids?" she gasped, offended. "Well, then I'm even happier to share my second present, baby." She yanked the bag from my hands and pulled out an envelope, shoving it at Ollie. "I've filed a petition to modify our custody order."

"What!?" Ollie thundered.

"This is *not* the time or place," I snapped, nausea coiling in my gut.

"Oh, it's all right there. I think it's past time my children got to know their mother. Don't you?" Then, to Tillie: "We're going to have such fun once you come live with me."

"You won't get away with this," I growled—but Tillie suddenly launched forward, slamming both hands into Carly's ribs.

"Go away!" she screamed, her voice shrill and broken. "I don't want you!"

Carly flinched, then tried to recover, placing a hand on Tillie's shoulder. "Matilda, darling, I'm trying. *I miss you*—"

"I *hate* you!" *Shove.* "You *left me!*"

"Baby," she cooed, a convincing edge of hurt in her lowered voice. "I'm trying to be better."

"Then *leave!*" she shrieked, her little voice breaking and tears pouring down her face. Beau started crying, but Alice scooped him up, taking calm steps away and toward the cupcake tower. "Just like you always do!"

"Matilda Hart," Carly snapped, her veneer cracking.

"*No!*" Tillie screamed. "I don't *want* to see you! Life would be better if you were *dead!*"

Carly stumbled back like she'd been struck. Tillie didn't wait— she turned and ran, sprinting up the aisle. Ollie hesitated, eyes flicking between Carly and our daughter.

"Go," I told him, already stepping between Carly and the rest of the room.

"It's time for you to leave," I added, voice like steel.

Jackson was suddenly there, motioning toward the exit.

"I will *not* be ushered out of *my daughter's* party by *the nanny*."

"Let's go, Carly," Jax rumbled, low and unflinching.

"This is ridiculous." She scoffed, but shrank back when he took one deliberate step forward.

"You think you're so clever," she sneered, gaze narrowing on me around Jax's shoulder. "Following in my footsteps. It won't last."

"Let's *go*, Carly," Jax repeated.

"You can pretend you're different all you want. But he'll get bored. Just like the rest of us. You'll be yesterday's news the second that baby's off your tit."

My eyes widened. Jax didn't blink. Instead, he took her arm and steered her toward the exit. Kaia and I were left standing alone in the heavy silence that followed, thirty pairs of eyes pretending not to look.

Greyson's voice came over the speakers. "The party is officially over. Please enjoy the refreshments and take a favor on your way out."

Beside me, Kaia hissed the only question I'd been asking since Carly showed up.

"How the hell did she know?"

Plus One, Always
OLIVER

"Baby girl, I'm so sorry," I breathed, holding my daughter's shaking hands in mine, right where I'd caught her in the lobby.

"I don't want her here!"

"She's leaving, I promise. Leighton and Captain Reynolds are making her leave."

"She ruins everything!" she squeaked, trying so hard to suck in a breath, to blink back her tears.

Furious didn't even begin to cover it. This had gone on too fucking long. And now, I was done playing nice. It was time to let Greyson and Alice off the leash—to let them dismantle whatever pathetic custody attempt Carly thought she had a shot at.

"I'm so sorry, baby. That should not have happened." This would be the last time I hosted anything in a public venue. I tipped her chin up until her eyes met mine. "Not today. Not *ever*. You deserve so much better, princess."

"You said she wasn't coming," she croaked, wiping at her face. "You promised!"

"She wasn't supposed to, baby. I know that rattled you, and it's not okay for her to blindside you like that, Mattie."

"I hate that name," she snapped, still swiping angrily at her cheeks. "I hate *her*. And *she* gave me that stupid name."

"Then we don't have to use it anymore, okay? If you don't love it, I'll call you Tillie, or Sunflower, or anything that makes you smile."

She looked up at me then, those glassy blue eyes lit with the smallest flicker of hope. "Really?"

"Really." I shifted where I was crouched beside her, squeezing her hands in mine. She gave a wobbly nod, wiping her nose, then straightened the black tulle skirt we'd picked out together.

"Why didn't you stop her sooner?" she whispered, her voice tight and trembling. Her fingers slipped from mine to twist in the fabric of her dress.

"I should've," I admitted. "I should've walked her right back out. I was trying to avoid a scene."

"But she made one anyway. She always does."

"I know, champ. And I'm so, so sorry."

Carly's voice echoed through the lobby—yelling something at Jax as he walked her out—and Tillie flinched, her eyes darting toward the sound before swinging back to mine. Then a scowl carved across her face, rage spilling out in hot tears.

"I hate her," she cried. "I really, *really* hate her." A sob cracked through her chest. "And I hate her stupid gifts. She brought that so *she* could feel better—not for *me*."

Jesus, she was too smart for her own good.

"Does that—" another sob "—make m-me a bad k-kid?"

"Tillie. Look at me." When her eyes flitted to my chest instead, I gently palmed her head, brushing the long strands back. "You are not —and have *never* been—a bad kid. You are *allowed* to be angry. You're allowed to stand up for yourself, just like you did. And I am so proud of you. You shouldn't have to be, but you were so strong back there."

I cradled the back of her neck, pulling her little forehead to mine as she fidgeted and fought to hold it all in.

"You don't have to be okay right now. You don't even have to pretend to be. But I need you to hear something. You listening?"

She gave a small nod, her gaze still dropped to the floor, shoulders hunched.

"What she said isn't true. None of this is your fault. You are a spectacular kid. The sweetest little girl. And you are so damn loved. No ifs, ands, or buts. Look at all these people who came today—just for you."

Her watery eyes lifted to mine. "Is Leigh my friend because you pay her to be?"

Oh, *fuck*.

"Oh, baby girl, *no*." I shook my head, my heart cracking open. "Think back. She was our friend before she ever worked for me. I hired her *because* of how much she already loved you—not the other way around."

"Okay." Her throat bobbed. "I yelled at her… in front of everyone. That was cruel."

She looked up through those wet lashes, guilt spilling from her expression.

"What if I grow up to be just as mean and terrible as she is?"

"No." I shook my head. "Sometimes we say mean things when we're hurting. That doesn't make us mean. And sometimes people need to hear how they've hurt us. I know it probably didn't come out like you wanted it to, but it took guts to stand up to her."

"Yeah?" she asked, her voice soft.

"Yeah."

"What if…" her chin trembled, and I had to resist the urge to lift her face again. "What if she makes you guys love me less?"

"Impossible."

"But—"

"I'm gonna stop you right there." I brushed my thumb over her cheek. "There is *nothing* you could ever say or do that would make me go anywhere. You know that, right?"

She nodded, this time with more certainty. Her spine straightened just a bit. "Leighton either?"

"Leighton either."

"I don't want to live with her, Daddy. She can't make me live with her, right?"

"No, baby." My voice was steel. "That is *not* happening. I won't let it."

She gave a final little nod and one last sniffle.

"Can we just go home?"

I COLLAPSED onto the couch after tucking both kids in that night. Face buried in my palms, I blew out a breath that carried the full weight of the day. When I finally looked up, Leighton climbed over my lap, straddling me, her hand settling against my face. I dropped a kiss into her palm, my hands finding her waist as she sank onto my legs. Wordless, my girl pressed her forehead to mine, our noses brushing as we both dragged in a much-needed breath.

"We do not have to go to Jameson's wedding," she announced, brushing her nose over mine before straightening to look me in the eye.

"What?"

"We need to focus on fending off *Cruella*, not taking another family trip to Florida."

I smiled softly, affection blooming in my chest as I tucked a curl behind her ear. "I promised to be your plus one."

"It's not important right now." She shook her head, those blue-gray eyes torn. "Jameson will understand. Our babies. That's all that matters."

Our babies. Goddamn, I loved this woman. Her words wrapped around me so completely, I nearly missed the shift in her tone.

"Speaking of which…"

"That doesn't sound good."

She blinked, irritation pinching between her brows—an expression I always wanted to smooth away with my thumb. "How did she know about the baby, Ollie?"

"What?" I snapped, sitting up, only for her to press a calming hand to my chest, guiding me gently back down.

"When Jax was escorting her out, she said something—at first I thought she was just being a bitch, implying I was following in her footsteps—but then she said you'd be done with me by the time the baby was off my tit."

Rage reignited like dry brush in my chest. My fingers tightened reflexively on her hips and belly.

"Leighton, don't believe a fucking word she says."

"I don't." She brushed her lips over mine, nuzzling my nose. "But we haven't told the kids or anything, right?"

"I've said nothing," I promised.

"Well… we're going to have to now. *Everybody* heard her. Pretty sure Beau heard her, although Alice had him in hand by then."

"I'm *so* sorry," I breathed, eyes closing. "That had to be so uncomfortable."

"It wasn't my favorite," she muttered with a grimace. Then, sighing, "But I still don't understand how she found out. My family wouldn't say shit. Neither would Grey or Alice."

"I'll look into it," I promised, dragging soothing circles over her back. Realistically, Greyson's people would handle it better than I ever could, and they'd find the leak. "Everyone signs NDAs. When we find them, I'll ruin them."

She nodded slowly, clearly weighing her thoughts as she slunk inward. I palmed the side of her neck, grounding her, thumb tracing her rapid pulse.

"*Together*, right, baby? We do this as a team."

Another nod, this one a little steadier. She exhaled and whispered, "Yeah."

"Good."

"Good. Now. About the wedding—"

"We're not missing your brother's big day."

Her scowl reappeared. "Making sure the kids stay where they belong—that that raging cuntosaurus can't sink her claws in and fuck them up more than she already has—that's all I care about."

Chuckling, I ran my hands along her sides. "There's not really anything we can do here that we can't do from Tampa right now. She delivered her *custody* demands at our daughter's birthday party

—I don't think the court is going to love that. Besides, Greyson had our legal team on the phone before I even got the kids buckled in."

She muttered, "Gotta love the grump."

"He has his moments."

"I still can't *believe* her. *She's such a bitch.*"

"No arguments here."

"She has no grounds, right?" Fury darkened her eyes. God, I loved how hard she fought for my kids. How naturally she'd become their shield.

"I mean… she never legally terminated her rights. That's what we were pushing for. I guess this is her idea of retaliation."

"She's pathetic. I've eaten gas station sushi I trusted more."

I chuckled and tilted my head, beckoning her closer. Her lips met mine, and I hummed, sliding my hands up her sides until I could cradle that beautiful face.

"I fucking love you."

"I fucking love you, too. Obviously."

"*Obviously?*" I smirked against her lips.

She leaned back, arching a brow. "Contrary to Greyson's assumptions, I don't think about disemboweling people regularly."

"No?" I huffed a surprised laugh. She made it impossible not to smile. Made it hard to be sad. Whatever I'd done to earn this woman, I'd spend the rest of my life making it up to the universe.

"Not generally," she said. "But holy fuck, I want to end her."

"Easy, killer," I murmured with a grin.

"I mean it," she growled. "Who does that? Who delivers a custody petition at a kid's birthday party? If it wouldn't impact the case, I'd have throat-punched her. Seize her fucking heels for restitution. For *existing.* I've met *cacti* with better maternal instincts."

I smiled softly, shaking my head. She barreled on.

"And the way she talked to Tillie? Calling herself a mother? *Please.* Merriam and Webster are rolling in their graves."

I slid my hands to her waist, pulling her forward over my dick where it laid thick in my sweats.

"You're cute when you're angry, you know that?"

"Oh, piss off." Her eyes narrowed playfully. "I am not."

"You're *always* cute."

"You have to say that. I'm growing your child."

"Remind me how that baby got in your belly."

She beamed, glowing with amusement—and something hotter. It lit her from the inside. She rocked forward, slow and deliberate, and my cock twitched.

"I thought that was just a superhero fetish."

"Mmm-hmm," I murmured, pressing kisses up her jawline, my

fingers tugging the off-shoulder tee down to reveal the swell of her tits—fuller, rounder. Perfect. I kissed the scar between her breasts.

"Ollie," she gasped, grinding over my lap again.

"You're cute when you're angry. When you do your little coffee wiggle in the morning. When you sleep. When you look up at me with my cock in your mouth—"

She smirked. "Ah, I see where this is going. Continue."

Chuckling, I scooped my hands under her pert ass and stood, her legs wrapping around my waist.

"You're especially cute when your face is all screwed up with pleasure while you come on my fingers."

She groaned into my neck, lips brushing my skin. "If I pretend to believe you, will you give me a demonstration?"

"I'll give you anything you ask for, baby."

ONE WEEK–AND many calls with my attorney—later, we danced beneath the twinkling string lights of her brother's wedding tent.

Noel looked stunning as she ruled the dance floor like the queen of chaos, dragging nearly every single woman into the fray. Meanwhile, Jameson watched her with a quiet, satisfied smile—perfectly content to remain on the sidelines so long as his new wife was happy.

Opposites really did attract, I guessed.

As for me? My nerves were in my throat as I danced with my daughter, who kept glaring up at me with impatience, clearly irritated that I hadn't given Leighton her gifts yet.

Leighton—whose tan skin shimmered with a dusting of gold beneath the twinkle lights. Leighton—who was letting my son dance on her bare feet so she could spin him in a slow, steady circle. My heart did a full three-sixty every time they moved.

"Daddy," Tillie hissed, squeezing my fingers as hard as she could. "The sun's down."

"I know, love bug."

"It's almost bedtime. *Hurry*," she bit out.

Right about then, Maverick sidled up, bowing gallantly at the waist to offer her his hand like something out of a fairy tale.

"Princess Tillie, may I have the honor of this dance?"

"I am *not* a princess," she replied, stone-faced.

Mav grinned, rubbing his dejected hand over his bearded jaw. "Well, good thing. Or I'd be beating off the competition with a stick."

"I think that's a bit of an exaggeration."

He shot me a pleading glance, then turned back to her with a dramatic sigh. "You're killing me, kid. Come dance on my shoes so your daddy can ask my sister to join him."

Laughing, I passed her hand to his mammoth one as Kaia swept Beau from Leighton's arms. My eyes met Leigh's across the floor, and we both smiled as Maverick spun Tillie into a circle so wild it earned a trill of laughter. Nobody did chaos quite like the Rhodes family.

By the time I crossed the distance between us, my kids were both grinning—Tillie spinning between Mav and Axel like a ballerina yo-yo, Beau blushing under the adoration of five giggling aunts. Kid was loving every second of it.

Like father, like son.

"The kids and I have a little surprise for you," I said, watching Leigh arch a skeptical brow.

"Don't look at me like that," I laughed. "They picked it themselves when we were waiting for you at the mall."

"Okay…" she said warily, letting me take her hand and lead her to our table.

I fished the first box out of my pocket and slid it toward her. That sly smile of hers deepened as she slowly peeled apart the ribbon and popped the lid.

Her breath hitched. "Ollie…"

The bracelet inside was silver and chunky, exactly the kind Tillie said would match Leighton's favorite outfits. It was weighed down with hand-picked charms—each of our birthstones, including baby's —and a handful of tiny Marvel characters they swore she'd love.

"You win," she said with something suspiciously close to a sniffle. "That's amazing, Ollie. What the hell is this for?"

"Turns out I'm not the only one in love with you."

"God, I love you," she whispered, leaning over to kiss me before straightening with a misty grin. *All of you.*"

She held out her wrist. "Would you help me put it on?"

Nodding, I lifted the clasp and fastened it gently, my hand trailing up her forearm as she twisted it to examine the charms.

"You like it?"

"*Love it,*" she corrected, her eyes already drifting back to the dance floor. She lit up when she spotted Tillie giving her a big thumbs up from between two very amused uncles.

"Dance with me, beautiful?"

Her throat worked as she nodded, slipping her hand into mine.

We stepped onto the floor just as the music slowed. My hands settled on her lower back as she wrapped her arms around my neck. Her eyes were heavier now—like something unsaid had taken root there. We spun slowly among the other couples, her body warm and close, my heart hammering with something more than nerves.

She must've felt it too, because she pulled back, narrowed her eyes, and asked, "You okay?"

"Yeah," I said—but it came out strangled.

"*Very* convincing."

I chuckled and dropped a kiss to her crown. "Just thinking about how much I love you, Trouble."

"Ahh. So it's a fun heart race?"

"You could say that." I pulled her closer. "Listen, Leigh. There's something I need to tell you."

"You're pregnant?"

"What?"

"Oh. Never mind."

"Jesus, Trouble."

"That's *one*."

I kissed the tip of her nose. "Will you just let me say this?"

"Yes, *fine*. My bad. I just like to see you smile."

"I'll smile a lot more if you let me get this off my chest."

"Well *that's* terrifying. *Carry on.*"

"I'm in love with you, Leighton Rhodes."

She blinked, smirking like she was waiting for a punchline. "Yes. Well established. Feeling's mutual."

"I already told you you're it for me. That I knew before I even realized I'd knocked you up."

Her eyes widened as she glanced around at the nearby couples. I grinned.

"We're about to tell the world anyway, Trouble. I'm not worried. Are you?"

"I guess not," she said, though a pretty flush colored her cheeks.

I pinched her chin lightly, coaxing her gaze back to mine. "Like I said. You're it. I'm all in. Three months ago, I blurted out a question that deserved a million lights under the stars."

"Ollie…" she breathed—but I kissed her before she could say another word.

"Shhh, baby. Let me finish."

"You better make it quick, big guy, because my heart's about to claw its way out of my chest."

"Well, that would be unfortunate. Because I'm halfway to a decent speech." I reached into my pocket and pulled out a small velvet box. Her breath caught. "Now wait," I said. "It's not what you think it is."

In the back of my mind, I could practically hear a goddamn chicken squawking at me in mockery.

"Leighton Alexandra Rhodes—you're the woman I'm going to

marry. Someday. *Somehow.* I will earn the right to be your husband. I'll convince you to let me be your plus one, for always. I've been in love with you since you first marched into my life, and I've only fallen deeper with every layer of you I peel apart." When she waggled her brows, I just grinned. "Yes, that way, too. *Focus.*"

"I'm focused," she whispered, eyes shining.

"Really?"

"No, I'm actually freaking out on the inside."

"Brownie points for still dancing."

"Thank you. Glad you noticed."

"Of course I did. I'm freaking out too."

That earned a broad smile, and she rose onto her tiptoes to steal a kiss. "You don't look it."

"An arduously acquired deceptive calm."

"Well done."

"Thank you. *Focus.*"

"*Right.*"

She wiggled nervously, and I had to fight the urge to laugh.

"I told you we're doing this at your pace. That hasn't changed, baby. Because I had this ring in my pocket the day you told me you were pregnant."

Eyes watering, she grinned mischievously. "You're insane."

"It wasn't for *that exact moment,* for fuck's sake."

"Right. Carry on."

"Right." I gave her a pointed look. "It was for when we were ready."

"Which was not during an existential crisis."

"Correct. But now we're here."

"Now we're here," she echoed, glancing up at the twinkle lights with a soft smile.

"And I'm just a man, standing in front of his woman, begging her... *to think about it.*"

"What?" She laughed, a rapid strobe of emotion flashing across her face.

"Yep. That's it. Just... think about it, Leigh. Because I've already made up my mind, and I'll wait as long as you need."

"Ten years."

"Fine."

"*Thirty.*"

"I hope I'm a sexy silver fox, or you're out of luck."

"Oh, you will be," she said with a wink.

"I appreciate the vote of confidence."

"But... Ollie, I'm lost. What are you saying? Because I *have* been thinking about it. A lot, actually."

"Good. That's good." I pressed a kiss to her forehead, slowing our circle as I popped open the box with my thumb. Inside was the engagement ring I'd picked just for her—stunning, simple, sapphire—clipped into a delicate gold chain.

She arched a disbelieving brow as I held it out, fingers curled around the chain as our steps slowed to a crawl.

"Wear it for me?" I asked quietly. "No rush. No pressure. No expectations. Just the promise that whenever you're ready, I'll be here. Waiting."

My voice went lower as I added, "But make no mistake—the moment you slide that sapphire onto your finger—be it tonight or ten years from now—we're either hopping a flight to Vegas or setting a date. Because I cannot wait to give you my last name."

She straightened abruptly, her hand flying to her lower stomach, eyes wide and lips parted.

"Woah."

"Leigh?" I dipped my chin, concern gripping my chest. "Baby, you okay?"

"I… I think so," she breathed. "What do baby kicks feel like?"

"What?" My hands dropped to the small swell of her belly.

"I thought I was having heart palpitations from your proposal, but then it happened again—lower this time. Like butterfly wings flapping."

Grinning, I pressed both palms to her stomach and leaned in, our foreheads touching again.

"Yeah, Trouble. I think our baby has an opinion."

"Oh, she does," Leighton said confidently, stealing a kiss that turned my bones to dust. "She says *of course* Mommy will wear your necklace… until she's ready to be a Hart."

24

Pakoras, Proposals, Panic Parties

LEIGHTON

"Well. There's no denying *that*," Ollie said with a chuckle, grinning down at our sonogram.

"I don't know how to be a *boy* mom," I squeaked, staring at what was blatantly a twig and berries between my *not*-a-baby-girl's legs. I hadn't believed the doctor when he said it—partly because I'd been calling this peanut *she* since I found out about her—*his*—existence. But mostly because there was a dull roaring in my ears that didn't go away until the doctor ran all the tests and told us we had a very healthy baby growing inside my belly.

Which, frankly, still looked like I'd just eaten one too many burritos.

"What the hell do I do with a boy?!"

Ollie just laughed and pressed a kiss to my temple as he guided me out of Dr. Swift's office into the sterile-smelling hallway.

"The same things you do with Beau every day, baby."

"But every day? Forever? This poor guy is going to come to me after riding his bike off a hill, and I'll be expected to know how to patch him up. He'll need me for the *talk*. And *oh my god*—he'll hide his sheets and sneak 'em into the laundry and I'll have to keep a straight face like I just think he's becoming more responsible or some shit."

"*Puberty*. You're panicking over something more than a decade away. There are, like, a million terrifying moments between now and then."

"Gee, thanks. That's very helpful. *Oh my god*, we have to get rid of your knives."

"My *what?*"

"All those scary-looking cleavers you lob through lamb bones!"

"Um. Why?"

"What if baby finds one and chops off a finger? Severs an artery?! Oh my god, Beau's *Legos*. It's like a landmine of choking hazards."

"Oh, lord. Welcome to intrusive thoughts. They never stop."

"And fuck those staircases. I used to think they were beautiful, you know? Swoopy. Dramatic. Great for photos. But we're absolutely looking for a single-story house."

"Honey, Tillie and Beau toddled just fine in our house."

"But what if this baby isn't that coordinated? What if he goes tumbling down and breaks something?"

"I think I still have the baby gates in the garage."

"But what if he hurts himself?"

"Kids break bones, Leigh. They spend the first decade perpetually bruised and use their disproportionate skulls like battering rams. We'll take all the precautions."

"You think I don't know that? Six brothers, Ollie. Do you know how many casts I saw in my house? Fucking Axel cracked his skull open once."

"Ouch."

"Jameson and Rhyett were hell on wheels."

"I believe it. But girls aren't always easier—don't look at me like that," he added as I scowled. "I saw your home videos while we stuffed bags of almonds before the wedding. As much as I love a good slide tackle, they are against the rules in rec leagues."

"They are *not*."

"If you're going for *the ball*, Leighton."

"Who says I wasn't going for the ball, *Ollie*?"

"Well, the ref, for starters. Secondly, my eyeballs—she'd just passed the damn thing."

"I was already mid-slide! You can't just change momentum!"

"*Please*. You saw a window for revenge and took it."

"I *might've* been sick and fucking tired of her fouling me all game and the ref doing monkey shit about it."

Ollie threw his head back, laughing, and I grinned down at my lap, muttering bitterly, "Buncha pussies."

"And the dickhead in co-ed that kept fouling Kaia?"

"He got what he deserved."

"For sure. But don't pretend you were some demure little angel."

I just grinned, waggling my brows.

"See? Right there. You're so full of shit. Axel said you weren't even allowed to get your license until you were eighteen because Milo thought you needed to leash your temper first."

"Oh my god, we have to teach them all how to drive! Ollie, *you* have to tackle that. Boys are crazy. They hood surf. They do parkour. They think they're in *The Dukes of Hazzard*."

"Not a lot of ramps in Emerald Bay, baby."

"Still," I squeaked as the elevator dinged.

"Yes, Leigh. I'll teach our son how to drive."

"Good," I croaked, palming at my face as I stared at that little black-and-white picture. A wave of joy finally overrode the panic. *Our son.* Ollie and I were going to have a son.

Another mini Oliver, running around.

"*A boy*," I whispered.

I pulled out my phone, snapped a photo of the sonogram, and fired it off to the family group chat. Internally, I apologized to my battery for the incoming deluge.

"Hey," Ollie said cheerily when we stepped outside.

"What?"

"We just discussed many years worth of plans without either of us forgetting how to inhale."

"A monumental occasion."

"*Indeed.*"

"We shall rename today a holy day."

Snorting, he said, "I'll mark it on the calendar," and pulled me into a kiss on the forehead.

"I'll do one better," I promised, flipping my phone to selfie mode and snapping a photo just as he sneak-attacked me with a kiss on the cheek.

"You're fucking adorable," he declared, tucking me into his side.

"The feeling is mutual."

"Excellent. Want to grab lunch on the way home? Pickup, so you don't have to cook?"

"Indian?"

Smirking, he nodded. "Of course."

"Sounds great."

"Your brother home? Should we grab him some?"

I stopped dead on the sidewalk, a hand flying to his chest. "Oh my god, I meant to tell you!"

"Pax found a place?"

"No," I grinned. "I caught him with *a girl*."

"Finally."

"Harsh," I laughed.

"What? He's been holed up all winter."

"Fair."

"Was she pretty?"

I nodded. "The back of her head was."

"Excellent frame of reference."

"It's my personal favorite."

"*So?*"

"She was petite. Maybe five-foot-three. Prettiest curly black hair."

"I meant, what did Pax say?"

"Oh! He kinda glared like I wasn't supposed to come out of my room, then gave me the 'you didn't see anything' eyebrow arch."

"Like the penguins."

"*What?*"

"Never mind."

He handed me his wallet and his phone—already queued to our favorite Indian restaurant—as he opened my door. I watched with a totally appropriate level of admiration hitherto unachieved, as I tracked that perfect ass as he rounded the car. That man walked sexy.

"*Madagascar,*" I muttered.

He beamed. "There she is."

"Oh. Very nice."

"Beau loves the zebra."

"Naturally."

One absurdly large order later, we were carrying back bags of food when one split open—aluminum, cardboard, and spiced sauce hitting the pavement in a glorious mess.

"Fuck," I barked, scooting back as pakoras and curry rained down.

"Dammit, I'm sorry," I muttered, squatting down to clean it up —only to be ambushed by tears. *Fucking tears.* What the hell?

"Leigh, are you okay?" Ollie asked gently, already kneeling beside me, gingerly setting down his own bags and rolling up his sleeves. For the first time, the sight of his beautiful forearms wasn't enough to make me salivate because my throat was tight and my eyes were stinging, and—

Oh my god what is wrong with me?

"Fine," I squeaked. Liar. Then I saw the pakoras. And I was *not* fine.

"I just really wanted veggie pakoras," I whimpered as he scooped me up.

"Baby," he cooed, wiping my cheeks with kisses. "Do you want me to go get another order?"

"Mm-mm." I shook my head, lip wobbling. "Stupid fucking hormones."

He chuckled, pulling me against his chest. "If my girl wants pakoras, I'm getting her pakoras."

"Stupid," I mumbled into his shirt. "Wasteful."

"You didn't design the bags, Trouble."

"So much food," I complained against his firm chest. Honestly, I was surprised he could understand my petulant words where I suffocated them in his shirt. But he just laughed, dropped a kiss to my crown, tucked me into the Bentley, piled my lap with the survivors of the Great Curry Massacre, and then closed me inside. I watched in the mirror as the love of my life knelt in his ridiculously expensive pants to gather the remaining mess, dumped it into the trash, and then vanished into the restaurant for exactly twelve and a half minutes.

While I waited, sniffling pitifully, I turned on the radio. Declan J Donovan's "More Than A Feeling" filled the car.

Ollie was… Ollie was everything… more than I ever could've asked for. Patient. Steady. Loving. He never made me feel like a burden—not once. Even when I unraveled in the middle of a sidewalk over dropped pakoras.

With the workload on his shoulders, he couldn't be at every appointment, but he FaceTimed for a few minutes during ultrasounds whenever he could manage it.

The prickle of being watched pulled my attention up the street to a black sedan, where I locked eyes on a man about Ollie's age—dark hair, scruffy, broad-shouldered. Handsome, in a very *not-Ollie* way. He smiled and dipped his chin when I caught him staring, and then stepped out onto the sidewalk and loped away.

A year ago, that smile would've made my stomach flip. But not now. Not with Ollie. I reached for the necklace around my neck, unclasped it, and slid the sapphire ring onto my finger.

Bold. *Mine.*

Tears welled in my eyes again, but for a completely different reason.

The glamorous cushion cut sapphire surrounded in sparkling white diamonds was precisely my size. Because, of course, Oliver Hart would never accidentally get me the wrong size ring—God forbid. Hell, it even complimented my fingers.

I sat there, staring at the sparkling gems and wondering what on earth had compelled this man to fall for me in the first place. If chaos had ever had a vessel, I was it. Chaos was the last thing this man needed more of, yet, here we were.

Movement had me glancing in the mirror, where I spotted the man in question. Arms full of warm food, pretty Indian hostess beaming behind him. My wonderful, too-understanding man. The one on a mission to make sure his pregnant, emotionally unhinged girlfriend got her deep fried snacks.

I slipped the ring back onto the chain, re-clasped it, and smiled.

Mine.

Forever.

. . .

CHAOS GOBLINS:

MAVERICK

FINALLY.

MOM

Awe, sweetheart, congratulations. Look at his little pout! He has your full lips.

KAIA

And Ollie's nose!

AXEL

Finger gun GIF He ain't shy. Definitely a Rhodes man.

KAIA

Barfing emoji Gross, Axe.

MOM

Don't mind your brother, he's been spectacularly proud of his genitals since birth. Used to come bursting into the sun room and play it like a banjo when I had the girls over for tea.

HADLEE

Spitting water out laughing GIF

JEANNE

OMG, I forgot about that. *crying laughing emojis*

Congrats, sissy!

BRODERICK

Look at the size of his noggin, though. Gonna be a smart kid.

AXEL

Christ, Mom, seriously?

MOM

You walked right into that one, darling.

ELORA

Wtf do you mean 'finally'?

MAVERICK

A boy!

ELORA

Photo of smiling three month old What the hell is Robert?

MAVERICK

A boy on the EAST COAST. I get to squish this one more often. Make sure he's holding a football the first time he walks.

KAIA

How the fuck are you gonna do that from Washington?

MAVERICK

I have my ways.

PAXTON

I mean, sure, at least until you get drafted.

DAD

Axel, mind how you speak to my wife.

Congratulations, punky. He's gonna be beautiful.

MAVERICK

A blessing from the GOAT?! I'll take it. But that's years away.

PAXTON

IDK kid, with all these NIL changes and the chaos with the trade portals, the sport is changing. We saw way more juniors in this year's draft.

MAVERICK

I'd only have two years of playtime. Seems a bit ambitious, don't you think?

PAXTON

Two years plus your redshirt year. It was smart, Mav. Less chance of getting hurt, still got the training. Better physical development. Just saying. I'm hearing good things.

CHARLIE

Same, kid. Your name popped up on a youtube podcast the other day.

Leigh, congrats!

MAVERICK

Crying llama GIF

Thanks, guys.

HADLEE

Welp. Not any denying that, sissy. Can I start buying all things blue or is this one of those new age green situations?

JAMESON

Gonna name him after me?

JAKE

Clearly, she's going to name him after me. I did save her from that feral raccoon that one time.

RHYETT

I am the favorite brother. If she's naming him after any of us, it's gonna be me.

PAXTON

That's cute.

FINN

Psh. I shared half of all my popsicles.

LEIGHTON

Food is the fastest way to my heart.

KAIA

Um. We share a genome, and 'Kai' is totally gender neutral.

LEIGHTON

Actually, we were thinking Stetson, Ledger, or Beckham.

AXEL

Literally none of those have a namesake.

HADLEE

Yes, and?

JAMESON

As in a cowboy hat?

RHYETT

As in Heath?

FINN

As in 'Bend It Like'?

LEIGHTON

Precisely. *Laughing emojis*

ALICE

I am in a MEETING. What is on fire?

MAVERICK

This is more important. Leighton is having an alien.
Buy green.

ALICE

Awee *heart eye emojis*

25

No such Thing As Coincidence
LEIGHTON

June

Spring flew by in a blur—May's gray days filled with doctor appointments, end-of-school programs, and Beau's first tot soccer season, which may go down as the most chaotic games in the history of organized sports. June gloom had rolled in by the time school let out, but once the warm coastal breeze shoved the clouds inland in the late afternoons, I was always desperate to get outside and soak up the sun.

Which led us here.

Second week of summer break, recovering from the most decadent baby shower anyone on any planet had ever seen, with "A Summer Song" by Chad & Jeremy playing over Ollie's Bluetooth speaker. Tillie and I layered picnic blankets over the backyard's manicured grass, scrapbook supplies now scattered like confetti across the quilts.

"This is what magic powers look like," Beau observed, sprawled on his back like the tiny king he was. I looked up just in time to catch him trying to shake glitter glue off his fingers. When that failed, he wiped them directly on the lawn before I could stop him.

The perk of third trimester pregnancy? No one mistook me for someone hoarding calories for winter anymore. The disservice? I now moved like the sloth from *Zootopia*—Beau's words, not mine.

"Totally, dude," I said, fishing out a wet wipe and maneuvering my swollen self over to him to clean his fingers before the inevitable meltdown hit.

Scowling at the dried flecks, he muttered, "Sunshine makes glue faster. Which means it's a wizard."

"*Gandalf* the Yellow," Mattie muttered, tongue poking out between her lips as she carefully cut out construction paper hearts. My snort earned dual glares, so I raised my hands in surrender and let them go back to work.

Beau nearly dislodged my grip as he dove forward to snatch up a sheet of stickers, still sticky-fingered as I wrestled the last of the glitter from his palms. He cocked his head. "Do you think unicorns eat pizza?"

Fuck, my face hurt from smiling. How anyone could walk away from these two was beyond me—it was nauseating. If Carly wasn't such an irredeemable monster, I might've felt bad for how expertly the Harts' legal team kept delaying her custody petition.

But we were out of moves.

And in just a few too-short weeks, Ollie would be in front of a judge who would decide everything. Our future. Theirs. The weight of that made my smile falter.

I cleared my throat, turning over Beau's little hand.

"Pizza?" I echoed.

"Yeah. 'Cause I got a rainbow sticker already. But I think unicorns would like pizza."

"I don't know anyone who doesn't like pizza," I pointed out as he stared intently at his glittering sheet.

"What if they eat rainbows?" Tillie offered from her spot, now focused on gluing a Polaroid onto her page.

We'd all agreed a scrapbook just for Ollie was the best possible Father's Day gift for a man who had everything. Each photo had a note from one—or all—of us, listing the reasons we loved him. Because really, how the hell else do you impress a billionaire? A cute-ass scrapbook of him and his kids was my best bet.

"Like Skittles?" Beau asked, eyes narrowed in focus as I wiped his other hand.

The instant I let go, he scrambled for the pile of unclaimed Polaroids, flipping through them one by one before a giggle burst out of him, his grin spreading wide.

"What'd you find?" I asked.

"This one looks like Daddy hasn't had coffee yet," he declared with an affectionate smile. Tillie glanced over, smirking as she nodded in agreement. Beau scrambled to hand it to me once he'd looked his fill, returning to the stack as he muttered, "Very brave for Mommy to love him anyways."

My heart...froze. A brick lodged in my chest, creeping up my throat as I looked down to see a sleepy-looking Ollie, with rumpled hair, and me pressing a kiss to his cheek. Both of us were entirely washed out by the flash, and his squint looked part amused, part exhausted.

"Did you mean to say 'Leighton'?" I chirped, trying not to let the quake in my chest make it into my voice.

He frowned. "I didn't *say* Leighton," he declared indignantly, his tongue sticking out just like his sister as he flipped through the prints. ."

"Did you just call me Mommy?" I asked, the word breaking in my throat.

Tillie's eyes snapped to me. And—unless I was dreaming—there was hope there. Hope and something else. Something fragile.

"I mean," Beau said, brow furrowed in concentration, "you're my brother's Mommy, and you do all the things a Mommy does. And you love Daddy. And Mommies and Daddies are people that love each other and love their babies. And *you* love *us*."

"Daddy says he thinks you'll marry him someday," Tillie added quietly, like it was a wish she didn't dare say too loudly. "Will you? Marry Daddy?"

I swallowed hard, curling a hand around the chain at my neck—his ring resting just over my scar.

"Can you guys keep a secret?" I asked.

They nodded in tandem. Terrible liars, both of them.

"Look at the last page," I said, voice low.

Tillie lunged for the scrapbook like a mountain cat, flipping through our work in progress with an energy that sent Beau into a half-hearted whine as he tried to swipe it back.

"Hey! I wanna see!"

"Me first!"

"What do whiners get?" I asked sternly, arching my brows.

"Nothing," Beau grumbled.

"Good man." I pulled him into my lap as Tillie kept flipping. "Both of you can see. No need to squabble like raccoons."

"We're not raccoons," he muttered as Tillie grinned.

Finally, she reached the last page—a Polaroid I'd taken in my favorite Bomber's hoodie. Ollie's hoodie. I was grinning, holding up my hand, the ring clearly visible.

"I knew it," Tillie declared triumphantly.

Beau blinked between the book and Tillie before craning his neck up at me. By way of explanation, she added, "Leigh is gonna marry Daddy!"

"*Yes!*" he whisper-cheered, fist punching the air so enthusiastically I had to dodge it. Then he turned in my lap and grabbed both sides of my face to plant a kiss directly on my mouth.

I burst out laughing. Probably not the right reaction to such a heartfelt moment, but I couldn't help it. I scooped him up and blew raspberries on his belly while he squealed.

"Okay, okay, *okay!*" he screeched, writhing in my arms. "You win!"

Smiling so wide my cheeks hurt, I kissed his cheek and looked over at Tillie. Her expression had turned serious again—soft and tentative.

"What's on your mind, sweet girl?"

"I want Daddy to be happy," she said. "And... I'd like you to be my Mom."

Tears burned behind my eyes. I nodded, brushing a strand of hair behind her ear.

"Soon, sweetheart. I'll be your stepmom, but still." My voice wobbled. "Is that okay?"

Tears welled in her hazel-blue eyes, and then she was nodding, her chin trembling as the strongest little girl I'd ever known threw her arms around me. Something in my chest clicked. I could never have been her mother—biologically speaking, the age gap between me and my oldest siblings was larger than the one between me and Tillie—but she still felt like she'd always been mine. Like I was always supposed to raise this girl, be the one cheering from every auditorium, the one curling her hair in the mornings.

Yes, I loved Ollie—with every ounce of my soul and every scrap of my patchwork heart. But I fell for Matilda Hart first.

With a sniffle, I pulled her in tight, holding both of them against my chest as tears spilled down my cheeks—harder, the tighter they held me. My waterworks turned into a laugh when their little brother decided he didn't like being crammed in his womb condo and used my belly like a punching bag.

"Woah!!" Beau shouted, maximum enthusiasm and volume engaged, as his little hands rushed to the swell of my stomach—right as Tillie did the same.

"He's like a little gymnast," Tillie said, dead serious.

"Or a fighter!" Beau crowed, wide-eyed. "You see how fast 'dere hands move!"

"He can be whatever he wants to be," I told them, smiling. "Just like both of you."

"Hmm. I wonder if he'll like me."

"You're his big brother," I reassured. "You'll bicker like you do with Tillie, but he'll love you more than anybody. Just be ready for him to think everything you own is his. And everything Sissy or Daddy or I own too."

"Hmm," he huffed. "We'll jus' have'ta teach him."

"Exactly," I said, dropping a kiss to Tillie's head as she disentangled herself—clearly at her limit for affection. Blinking more than usual, both kids returned to their pages as the music shifted, little hands gluing and sticking with renewed focus.

Curiosity got the better of me as I set down the book and peered over Beau's shoulder. "Can I see?"

"Yeah!" he blurted, turning proudly to hold up his work. Equal parts monster trucks and dirt, glitter rainbows and unicorns—and Ollie never batted an eye.

"I love your photos!" I said, sneaking a kiss onto his squishy little cheek.

"Mine too?" Tillie asked, handing her page over.

I looked down, grinning at their little faces, until a prickle of awareness spider-walked up my spine. My throat tightened.

The photo of Tillie and Beau at the park had a black sedan parked in the background. Feeling borderline crazy, I flipped back to Beau's page—this one outside the art museum, both kids covered in paint, their smiles squinty from the sun—and there it was again. Same style car, parked at the curb.

A memory struck. The day of the anatomy scan—when preggo-brain had me crying over spilled pakoras—and a man standing beside a black sedan. A bearded man. Towering. Smiling.

My chest flushed with warmth, and my bones felt too tight, like my skin couldn't hold the pressure.

Coincidence. It had to be coincidence.

But...the "funny guy" at the park had a "fuzzier face than Maverick," Beau said. Dread—thick and oily—settled in my stomach as I flipped through the rest of our pages.

Disney World. Siesta Key. Our own backyard. Me and Ollie at the butterfly migration. Tillie in full recital costume. And in the background—blurred but unmistakable—was that same black sedan. Always just far enough away to miss.

My heart galloped as my mind jumped.

The bridge.

Royce.

"They were going to shoot at us! What the fuck is going on!?" I shouted, cupping my hands over Mattie's ears.

"They're trying to kill us—or capture us," Jax said. Like that helped.

"I fucking see that, but why?!"

The engine roared as Jax floored it.

Royce's voice cracked. "Because your sister stuck her nose where it didn't belong."

My concussion-muddled brain clicked disjointed pieces together. All of it—the fuzziness, the holes—roared back into clarity.

The tension between Ollie and Greyson after the accident. The weird distance between Alice and the truth. Detective Riviera blowing off my questions. The official report calling it random. Alice's sudden memory loss.

But Royce had turned a gun on Jackson. He wasn't sick to his stomach—he was a traitor.

It wasn't random gang violence. It was connected. And I'd been too shaken to see it.

"Hands on the wheel, Reynolds," Royce ordered.

Jax froze, glancing at Alice in the rearview.

"Royce," Alice pleaded. "Don't do this. You don't have to do this."

"Didn't want to," he said, voice strangled. The gun stayed on Alice, but his eyes were locked on Jax.

Alice glanced down at Mattie's untied boots, then looked at me. Her fingers twitched.

Garrote.

I reached down, pretending to adjust Tillie's laces, pulling gently at the ends.

"Slow down!" Royce barked.

"You're going to kill us either way," Jax said. "I'll take you with us."

The car surged forward. Tillie sobbed. I kept working the laces.

Alice tried to reason with him.

"I don't have a choice—they took them."

"Who?" my sister asked.

"All of them, Alice."

"The kids?" Her voice trembled.

"When we didn't turn you over, they—they took Miranda today."

His wife.

"Who?" Alice demanded.

"I—it wasn't supposed to go this way," Royce choked out. "I let them in, Alice. I let her in. It's my fault. If something happens to them, it's my—"

My hand flew to cover my mouth.

Oh my god.

What the fuck had Alice gotten herself into?

What kind of fallout were we standing in now?

Why did her sudden loyalty to Greyson suddenly make perfect sense?

With a shaking hand, I grabbed my phone, dialed Ollie on muscle memory, and stepped away from the kids just far enough to breathe. I collapsed into the teak furniture on the back patio, unwilling to let them out of my sight—even from behind glass.

Hart family security didn't lurk. They didn't sit in parked sedans like creeps in a low-budget thriller. They stood at inconspicuous distances, dressed like off-duty dads, hovering close enough to act but far enough that Ollie didn't feel suffocated.

This? This wasn't that.

"Hey, beautiful," Ollie answered, his voice warm and easy. "How are you?"

"I've been better."

"Leigh?" His tone snapped from afternoon delight to panicked in a heartbeat.

"Ollie, what happened on the bridge?"

"What do you mean, baby?"

"*The bridge.* Royce. That wasn't a fucking coincidence, was it?"

"Leighton, I—"

"Don't bullshit me, Oliver."

"Are you okay?"

"Yes. Kind of. No."

"What's going on?" he demanded, voice shifting, breath heavier now. Walking. Moving fast.

"I'm scrapbooking with the kids," I managed, watching them— so perfectly unaware, surrounded by glitter glue and construction paper and sunshine.

"Okay…"

"And the photos, Ollie. There's a car. A black sedan. I think a Toyota. I've seen it before."

"Okay? There are a lot of black Toyotas, Leigh."

"No," I said firmly. "I'm telling you—it's in at least three photos. And I saw a guy. A bearded guy. He smiled at me that day at the Indian place, and I thought it was nothing. But a while back…" I sucked in a breath, trying to steady the quake in my voice. "*A while back*, Beau and I were at the park. He said the kid he was playing with didn't like 'the funny guy.' When I asked about it, he told me it was a big guy. Fuzzy face. And he asked questions about his uncle."

"What?" Ollie snapped, temper flashing in his tone. It wasn't aimed at me, but it still sent my walls flying up. "Why didn't you tell me about that?"

"I—" I shook my head, even though he couldn't see it. "It felt paranoid. I didn't think my unsubstantiated anxiety was worth mentioning."

"Anybody talking to our kids that we don't know is important. Anything that ever makes *you* uncomfortable is important, Leigh. Where the hell was security?"

"Giving me distance," I bit out. "I thought it was a coincidence. Maybe they recognized him. But the guy downtown matched Beau's description, Ollie. And now I'm sitting here looking at these photos *and…*" My voice cracked, a sob clawing its way up my throat. "Someone is watching the kids. Somebody's been following us. And I can't shake this sinking feeling that it's all—"

"Go to Greyson's," he cut in. "Now, baby. I'm on my way home, but get to Hart House. They'll keep you safe."

"Ollie—"

"*Now*, Leighton. Grab Viper at the gate and have him walk you over. I'll meet you there."

"Ollie, just—tell me what's going on."

"I will," he promised, the words tight and raw. "I swear, I will. Just get inside. Get to Captain Reynolds. I love you."

"I love you too." The fear bled into my voice, no matter how hard I tried to keep it from the kids. I stood from the patio chair, smoothing my face, swallowing my panic, and heading back toward them with measured steps.

"Wait for me there, Trouble."

"Kay."

26

Fight Naked

OLIVER

"Let me get this fucking straight," Leighton said, about an hour later. Her tone was deceptively calm—terrifyingly so. But her eyes gave it away, flashing with uncontained rage. "*You*"—she jabbed a finger at my brother, where he sat braced behind his desk—"fund and oversee a covert, *illegal* mercenary ring with a name that sounds like some dumbass teenage boy's street hockey team."

"*Thunderstrike*," Greyson muttered against his clasped fists, elbows braced on the desk's polished wood.

"Essentially, you're the dollar store equivalent of Bruce fucking Wayne—only with a whole motherfucking team. And you're fighting some equally bullshit covert group of psychopaths who use their secret powers for evil instead of good."

"*Obsidian*," he added, not catching the fucking hint.

Leighton's fists clenched at her sides. Her knuckles blanched white as her body started to shake.

"And *you*," she snapped, eyes cutting toward her sister, nostrils flaring, "fucking lied to me. For *months*, sissy." Her furious blue-grays hesitated on Alice's bowed head, then lifted to mine.

I hadn't moved. Just stood there, statue-still, one arm folded under the other, propping up my chin with a clenched fist like it was the only thing holding me together.

"You *too*," she breathed. "You've all been fucking lying to me."

"Trouble, I—"

"Save it." She sliced me off without looking, then turned her fury back to Alice. "It was *me* in that car with you. *Me* that almost died. Me that scrambled through that goddamn SUV as it fucking sank in that frozen fucking water to save that idiot—" she flung an arm toward Captain Reynolds, who smirked incrementally from where he leaned against the study door.

"Thanks for that," he muttered.

"You're fucking welcome. You'd be even more welcome if any of you had been honest with me. Like I couldn't handle it or something? You three paint a target on our entire family and think I'm better off in the goddamn dark?!"

"Leighton," Greyson started.

She slammed her hands on his desk. The sound cracked through the room, sharp and final. Death burned in her eyes as they locked on his face.

"You, of all people, Greyson Hart, disappoint me the most. You're the one who kept me in the dark, are you not?"

"It's classified."

"Bullshit," she snarled. "*You* classified it. You should've unclassified it when I hauled Tillie out of that fucking car and to shore. You should've unclassified it when the twelve of us were huddled in that goddamn waiting room, not knowing if Alice would come back through those double doors."

My throat tightened. My eyes flicked to Alice as she wet her lips. She had almost died—because she refused to let them treat her until she was sure Jackson, Tillie, and Leighton were safe.

Greyson had almost lost the only person who'd ever cracked him open.

He sucked in a long breath, shoulders back as he leaned into the chair and laced his fingers over his stomach. Calm, precise—until you noticed the twitch in his jaw. Then he stared straight into the eyes of the very pregnant, very pissed-off woman across from him.

"You're right."

Two words. That's all it took. Her spine straightened. Hands dropped to her sides. Her mouth parted, stunned.

"What?" she whispered.

Greyson gave a humorless huff. "You're right, Leighton."

"Somebody better have that on fucking record," she muttered.

"Please. Sit down." He gestured to the chair in front of the desk, then to the sofa beside me.

"Can't. Need to break something."

"I'll let you destroy the office afterward if it helps. Just let me get this out."

"Fine."

"I should've told you."

"Damn straight. All of you are fucking assholes."

"That's a valid emotion to be feeling," he said evenly.

"Please. *You* don't fucking feel anything, you fucking *cyborg*." Her words hit hard—harder than she realized. Greyson's brow pinched, just slightly. His jaw flexed.

He looked like he did the night I got high and drove home in his truck—seconds from losing control.

"Trouble," I warned softly, but she shot me a look so sharp I nearly swallowed my tongue.

"Don't you fucking *'trouble'* me, Oliver. Or should I say *Mr. Hart?*"

"Leighton," I said, my tone dipping into a quiet plea.

"*Well?*" Her voice broke like a whip. "Do I even know you? How could you keep something like this from me, Ollie? I thought we were a team. All that bullshit about doing this *together*, and the entire time you've been *lying to me?* About what happened on that bridge? About the fact that we were safe with security hovering? Meanwhile, I've been walking around oblivious—letting the kids run off to fountains and playgrounds, free like normal children, with no idea there were fucking *targets* on their backs?" She scoffed, half bitter laugh, half growl. "Like I wouldn't handle it?"

She tilted her head in that lethal way—a cat about to pounce.

"For fuck's sake, I would've reported that guy at the park *months ago* if I'd known there was a bounty out for our entire family. All thanks to knockoff *Iron Man* and his broken fucking parts over here." She waved a hand at Greyson without looking at him. "And I'm the idiot for not asking more questions about the armed fucking guards posted outside your house. I thought that was just some entitled billionaire shit."

"I'm sorry," I whispered.

"If you could lie about something this crucial, how the hell am I supposed to trust anything you've said in the last ten fucking months?"

"Baby, just let me explain—"

She didn't walk away, didn't scream—just stood there, trembling, one hand pressing protectively to her belly. Feeling our son move, maybe. Grounding herself. It scared the shit out of me more than if she'd screamed. Leighton only went quiet when she was done. Or when I was dead to her.

"He wanted to tell you," Greyson said, gaze steady on the woman he had clearly labeled the biggest threat in the room. "I didn't let him."

"*Let him?*" Her voice went flat. "Is there something you should tell me? Got his balls in a duffel bag, Greyson? Last time I checked, Ollie's a grown-ass man who can speak for himself."

"You're right," I said quietly, shaking my head. Every muscle in my body screamed to go to her, to close the fucking distance. "Leigh, baby, I should've told you. I chose you months ago, and somewhere along the way, I should've trusted you with this."

"So why didn't you?"

"For me," Greyson said. "I put Ollie in a terrible position. His loyalty should never have been tested between his wife and his brother."

"I'm not his fucking wife."

"But you will be," he said like it was already carved in stone. "Won't you?"

What the fuck was he doing? Trying to scare her?

But Leighton wasn't scared. She was *furious*. *Beautiful* in her righteous anger.

"That's none of your business," she said, cold and clipped. The same tone that my brother used to clear a boardroom in thirty seconds.

"Listen to me," Greyson said, more urgently now. "I thought you were safer——"

"Oh, go fuck yourself."

"*I thought you were safer* not knowing. I thought you'd go digging and get yourself in deeper."

"Is that what you did?" Her attention snapped to Alice.

"This information is dangerous," Alice said, voice low. "Knowing puts you at risk. And if anything fell through before the op was legitimized, you could've been forced to testify. Against Greyson. Against *me*."

Leighton blinked. "That's why you married him," she said, voice hollow. "Last summer. That's why you married him when you hated his fucking guts—no offense."

"None taken. I earned it," Greyson said evenly.

"Yes," Alice said quickly, like she wanted the blame redirected onto herself. "Yes, sissy. I found out when I was digging for proof he'd been embezzling."

"And you married him for spousal immunity," she said flatly.

"So I wouldn't have to testify against him. Or take Ollie—and the kids—down with the ship."

Leighton turned her scowl on Greyson. "What the fuck is wrong with you?"

"I love her," Greyson said, and for once, the words weren't sterile. "I've been in love with your sister—her infuriating mouth, her spine of steel—from the moment she stepped into my office."

"Please," Leighton muttered. "You were a total prick for years."

"To push her away," he growled. "To keep her out of reach. Safe. From HR violations and my extracurriculars."

"Yeah. That worked *great*, didn't it?"

"Leighton," Alice said gently. "What he's doing—it's *good* work. They're saving lives."

"It's not the mission I'm pissed about."

"It's that we kept it from you," I said.

Her eyes found mine, glassy and betrayed, chin trembling like she was holding herself together by will alone.

She sucked in a shaky breath, then looked back at Greyson. "Are the kids safe?"

"I've done everything I can to keep them out of it."

"Like you kept Alice out of it?"

"I'm trying. But bringing you in? That should've happened the moment you were in their lives daily. That's on me." Greyson sat forward, voice lower now. "The information we started with was classified. Just me and the team. But the op's grown. So have the risks. And you're right—you deserved to know. Ollie worked with the information I gave him. I've kept him at a wide berth, too."

"So what now?" she asked, shaking her head. "What about this car? The one in the photos. *With our kids?*"

"Jax submitted the images for processing. We'll find them."

Leighton exhaled hard and cleared her throat, palming the scar beneath her tee. "Then do it fucking fast, or I swear to God, I'll feed you your testicles on a spoon."

"Valid stipulation," Greyson said without blinking.

"And I'm stealing Captain Reynolds."

"Pardon?" Jax asked from the door.

"You're the best, right?" she snapped. "That's why you and Viper are here."

"He is," Greyson confirmed.

"Then he better be within arm's reach of Tillie and Beau every waking fucking *second* until this is under control."

Greyson's gaze flicked to Alice. She nodded. Then he turned to Jax, who dipped his chin.

Leighton tracked the entire exchange with a predator's focus.

"Good. We have an understanding. I'm going to tuck the kids in and make sure they're safe. And if I see *one more* black fucking sedan on this goddamn street, I will not be held liable for my actions."

And with that, she glared the mountain of a man away from the door and marched through it like she was going to war.

"Well," Jax sighed, flicking his eyes toward Greyson, who was rubbing at his temples like he could massage the migraine out of existence. "That went well."

"You're lucky she didn't clock you," I muttered, dragging in a breath as I gathered the courage to follow her.

"I said *every waking moment*," she barked from the hallway. "That means *now*, Reynolds. Ollie, let's blow this popsicle stand."

"You weren't kidding," Jax grumbled, amusement glinting in his eyes as he glanced sidelong at my brother. "She's feral."

"And all fucking mine," I said with a terrified, relieved chuckle, before following the warpath she left behind.

LEIGHTON

IT TOOK every ounce of my composure to hold it together long enough for our nightly routine. Teeth brushed, hair combed, stories read, songs sung—all while I bit back tears at the unfathomable truth: they'd been in danger this whole time, and no one had bothered to tell me.

I grew up in Alaska, for fuck's sake. I had *five* older brothers and more cousins than I could count—one of whom was the town sheriff—all of whom made damn sure I could load and fire a .45 with bear-dropping accuracy. Everyone in Mistyvale was versed in firearms and bear spray. Hiking without them was a suicide mission. I had a mean swing with a metal bat and nothing—*nothing*—on this earth would stop me from protecting these precious little people.

Precious little people who'd healed my entire soul when they asked me to be their Mommy.

Mine.

That's all I could think as I brushed Beau's curls off his forehead while his eyes drifted closed. They were mine. And someone had gotten close enough to study them—photograph them. Talk *to Beau.*

That knowledge made my bones rattle and my brain buzz inside my skull, even as his breathing evened into sleep.

By the time I slipped out, Ollie was waiting in the hallway, still in his work clothes. His tie hung loose, hair disheveled in the way only the worst days left it. I marched past without a word, into our bedroom, sensing him trailing close behind. The latch clicked closed. I yanked my shirt over my head and launched it at him, whirling around with a scowl carved into my face.

"So. Turns out you and I have very different definitions of what being on a team means, Oliver Hart."

"Baby, I'm so sorry."

"You should be." I unclasped my bra in one practiced motion, freeing my heavy breasts—and watching his mouth part, and eyes flare.

"Wha—what... what are you doing?"

"Fighting naked. Care to join me?"

"...What?"

"Welp. Mom said when all else fails and I wanna scram like the Kool-Aid man, her best advice is to fight naked."

"Um." He swallowed hard, eyes locked on my hands as I slid my leggings over my belly and kicked them aside. After a long pause—probably brought on by tit-induced paralysis—he dropped my shirt, which *had* to physically hurt him, and stripped.

Goddamn. Mom was onto something.

Hard to stay mad when you're both standing bare, stripped to your full, vulnerable selves.

In nothing but our underwear, chest to chest, my hands found his back on instinct. Lifting my chin, my voice came out soft, like melted butter. "You should've told me."

"I know," he breathed, cupping my face with those big palms, close enough to taste my air but not quite kiss me. "And I'm so sorry. Greyson said it was classified and he could face serious consequences just for telling me."

"About *Thunderstrike?*"

"About why *Thunderstrike* exists."

"Hmm." So it started when he was still in the Navy. What the fuck had our big grump gotten himself into?

When I didn't say anything, Ollie hesitated. "*Hmm?*"

"What do you want me to say to that?"

His hands slid from my neck to my shoulders, down my arms. "I guess I expected you to rail a little, I don't know."

I turned to look out at the starry sky for a beat, then brought my gaze back to him. "It was an impossible scenario."

"What?" he asked, disbelieving.

"You honor me and betray him. Or you protect him and lie to me."

"Yes, but that doesn't mean you're not the most important part of my fucking life, it's just—"

"Ollie," I breathed, the chaos in my head finally quieting. "I have eleven siblings. I get it."

"Really?" he chuckled, warm breath brushing my cheek.

"I still say you guys should've looped me in. I still say *you* should've told me. But I was thinking about it—about James or Pax or Axel. And yeah, trouble. I get it."

He cracked a crooked smile—the kind that made my knees feel weak. "Oh, now *I'm* trouble?"

"Obviously."

"Please forgive me, baby. I'm so fucking glad you know now. I hated keeping it from you."

"I believe you," I said softly, soaking in the warmth of his eyes.

"But do you forgive me?"

"Got any more skeletons in your closet I should know about?"

"No, baby."

"Then yes," I said, curt and sure. "I forgive you, Ollie."

"Thank fuck," he panted, diving into my hair to kiss me breathless. When he finally came up for air, he vowed, "We'll keep them safe. You and the kids. That's all that matters."

"We don't have another choice," I whispered, rising on my toes as his hands curved protectively over my belly. I stole another kiss, tugging gently on his lower lip.

Ollie made a low, contented rumble in his chest, then pulled back just enough to rest his forehead to mine.

"Gotta say—I like this fighting naked theory."

27

If You Put Lipstick on a Pig...
OLIVER

July...

I ran the pad of my thumb over the diamond-studded ring on Leighton's finger in slow, steady strokes—reassuring myself this was real. She stood beside me, looking like the perfect aristocratic mother in her navy dress and structured black blazer, her basketball belly front and center. Twenty-three, and already elegant enough to dominate any gala she stepped into.

Instead, she was here—humming quietly, worrying her bottom lip as the elevator carried us toward the second floor of the courthouse.

"Still surreal seeing you wear it," I murmured to break the silence, though my voice came out tight. Strangled. A fitting match to the knot in my chest.

How could I feel so much joy—just knowing my best friend would be my wife before next summer—and still be weighed down by what we were walking into?

"If showers weren't mandatory, I'd never take it off," she said lightly, though her voice was tight, her teeth returning to her lip almost instantly.

It was also surreal knowing for the first time it wasn't just me whose life would be impacted today. This woman had fallen in love with my kids as deeply as she had with me. She would do anything —*anything*—to keep them where they belonged.

But it wasn't up to us anymore.

The elevator chimed a cheerful little ping, like lives didn't get wrecked in these walls on the regular, and we stepped into the hallway.

Greyson was already there, leaning against the hideous wallpaper, his hands tucked into his pockets and his expression sharper than usual. He looked less like a diplomat and more like a man heading into war.

And really, that's what it was.

My screwups as a college kid had put us all here. Grey. Leigh. The kids. All of us haunted by my poor decisions.

"Hell raiser," he said with a smirk, stepping forward to tuck Leighton into a quick hug. "You look beautiful today."

They'd found some sort of truce in the weeks since the *Thunderstrike* reveal. Captain Reynolds' permanent post at our side probably helped—he hadn't let the kids out of his sight since.

"Groucho," she purred, reaching up to dust an invisible speck off his shoulder. "This suit looks spectacularly suity."

Grey chuckled, but his gaze flicked to mine. "You ready for this?"

"Is anyone ever ready for this?"

"Valid point."

"Is Alanzo ready?"

"She's waiting for you."

We said nothing more as the three of us made that slow march down the corridor. Okay, so maybe it wasn't the gallows, but my nerves sure as hell thought so.

Sure enough, outside room 208, Katie Alanzo—best damn family lawyer in the state—was hammering out a message on her phone at such breakneck speed I wasn't sure my fingers could've kept up even if I was just mashing keys. She popped a pink bubble between her lips and casually tucked her stick-straight black hair behind one ear.

"Ollie, breathe," she said by way of greeting, extending her hand. I obeyed the order as I shook it. She turned to Leigh next. "Nice to see you again, Miss Rhodes. You clean up well."

"Really? You sure it's not too politician-pandering-to-the-populace in an uninspired polyester pantsuit?"

Greyson made a strangled noise as he pinched the bridge of his nose. "Dare you to say that ten times fast."

Katie's lips twitched. "The dress is just professional enough."

"Phew. I was afraid it was giving Hillary Clinton, circa early 2000s."

Katie snorted, eyes flicking to me before returning to Leigh. "Relax, Miss Rhodes. If anything, it's more Kate Middleton at a casual Saturday brunch."

"Wow," Leighton gasped, pressing a hand to her chest with a blinding smile. And damn if she didn't look royal—dark chocolate hair curled to her ribs, makeup subtle and perfect, shoulders back, my ring gleaming on her finger as her hand cradled her belly.

"Imagine what I could do with taller heels and an iota of motivation to spend a day not bathing in glitter."

Katie raised a brow at me. "Keep this one, Ollie. I like her. She'll lighten you up."

"That's the plan," I said, the lump in my throat turning that into more of a croak.

Katie laughed, slapped my back, and dumped her gum in a hallway trash can. "Come on, slugger. Let's get this over with."

"Please," I muttered, guiding Leighton forward with a hand on her back. I'd rather be anywhere else. The feeling only worsened when I saw the empty faux-oak tables flanking the judge's bench. Leighton followed Greyson into our usual row, but hesitated and turned back toward me.

Katie paused, pulling out her phone. "I'll give you a second. You remember the rules?"

"Yes, ma'am."

"Good. I'll see you up there."

As she moved toward the front, I stepped into Leighton's space and pressed a kiss to her forehead. "It's just five feet, love."

"I know," she whispered, voice barely audible. "I just wish I could be up there with you."

"I know, baby."

She forced a smile. It almost worked—if I hadn't known the ache behind it.

She was about to say something else when the hinges groaned. We both looked up as Carly walked in with her lawyer, Niko Volkov. He made a beeline for the table, but Carly paused long enough to level a slow, smug glare at Leighton.

"Still playing house?" she drawled, just as the bailiff cleared his throat. "*Cute.* One way or another, someday our kids will know you stole them from me, Oliver. They'll come home. To their real mother."

Leighton didn't so much as flinch. She ran her tongue across her teeth, lifted her chin, and turned back to me with icy poise.

Me, though? My hands started to shake. Goosebumps crawled up my neck. All the months of prep felt suddenly, completely inadequate.

But before I could react, Leighton grabbed both of my hands in hers and curled my fingers over the backs. She brought them to her lips and kissed each knuckle, then pressed her forehead to mine.

"Hey," she whispered. "This is going to go our way. Don't let her see you rattled."

I nodded.

But God—was it hot in here, or was it just the noose tightening around my throat?

"Ollie," she breathed, squeezing my fingers. When I forced my eyes to meet hers, she nodded incrementally. "We've got this. I'm right here."

The bailiff signaled for the beginning of our session, and I pressed a kiss to her forehead before moving around the divider in a rush, sitting just in time to be told to stand for the judge entering the chamber. As we all sat, I shot a glance backward, my chest constricting when I found my brother with my girl tucked under his arm—I wasn't sure if it was in comfort or to keep her from rocking in her seat like I wanted to. She offered a smile, which I returned quickly before forcing my game face on and looking up at the woman who would determine our future.

She looked bored—like she'd smoked one too many cigarettes on the roof, thinking dark thoughts about petty human drama. The judge rifled through the folder in front of her, letting out a deep sigh before announcing, "This hearing is regarding the motion filed by Ms. Carly Hart..."

My mind went blank—a dull buzzing in my ears as we went through the agonizingly familiar motions of introductions. It wasn't until Niko said the words, "Petitioning for full custody based on evidence that the change will be in the children's best interest," that my soul snapped back into my body. As he assured the judge they had evidence to present, I glanced at Katie, who sat with her hands folded together, elbows braced on the table, looking entirely unfazed.

My job—that was Carly's angle. That I was gone too much, that my career meant I was neglecting my kids.

Bull. Fucking. Shit.

My kids were my fucking world. My heart pounded, my head spinning with a million variations of the same question—how could she do this? How could someone so selfish pretend to want the kids she'd walked away from?

My shark in a pantsuit set her hand on my forearm, and I realized I was trembling. I quickly stuffed my fists beneath the table, settling them in my lap, flexing and balling them against my thighs as I listened to Katie counter through what felt like a hundred-foot tunnel.

"Your Honor, my client, Mr. Oliver Hart, has had full custody of both children for the entirety of their lives. He has provided a stable, loving environment for them, and we strongly oppose the motion to change custody."

The judge turned her attention to Niko, whose smug face looked spectacularly punchable.

"Your Honor, we are requesting full custody of Matilda and Beau Hart, as we believe Ms. Hart is the more capable parent and better equipped to meet their needs. She simply seeks the opportunity to care for them."

Or pocket child support, since she'd made a habit of blowing through her alimony like water.

"Noted," the judge said dryly, then glanced back at Katie. "Counsel for the respondent?"

All five feet of Katie Alanzo stood beside me, hands folded with military precision.

"Your Honor, my client, Mr. Hart, has been the children's primary caregiver since the initial custody hearing more than four years ago. His record of providing a safe and loving home is well documented, reinforced by updated testimonies submitted to the court, including letters from Matilda's principal and therapist.

"By contrast," she continued, "I'd like to draw your attention to existing documentation in our case. Most notably, the incident that led to the divorce: Ms. Hart's neglect and abusive behavior culminated when she left young Matilda and infant Beau in a hot car while shopping. The event was reported and properly documented by authorities, along with several others that ultimately led to Mr. Hart gaining full custody."

And paid the misdemeanor fine with my fucking money.

"These were not isolated lapses," Katie went on, her voice calm and clinical, "but part of a persistent pattern of neglect. Ms. Hart has not demonstrated meaningful improvement—in fact, she continues to display patterns of narcissistic abuse. In light of that, we maintain that preserving the current custody arrangement is unequivocally in the children's best interest."

"Thank you, Counsel," the judge said. Her attention shifted to Niko, who stood and shuffled his papers, tongue working at a back molar like he was chewing the world's most tasteless gum.

"Your Honor," he began, "while the petitioner's past may not be spotless, we must consider the significance of reuniting a biological mother with her children. That bond cannot be overstated or replaced. My client is taking steps toward rehabilitation. She is currently attending therapy, enrolled in a parenting course, and has secured full-time employment."

"I see," the judge replied flatly.

Not a good sign for them. I could feel it, the tiniest undercurrent in her tone—one of skepticism, not sympathy. Still, it took every ounce of discipline not to shift in my seat as the nerves gnawed through my insides like maggots.

The judge turned her gaze to Carly. "Anything you'd like to add, Ms. Hart?"

From behind me, I could practically feel Leighton and Greyson trying to glare her into a pile of ashes as Carly stood.

"Your Honor, I've done everything I can to land on my feet after our divorce," she began. "And frankly, I'm appalled I'm being treated like a mother who doesn't deserve her own babies. I'm not playing games," she said, flinging a glance Leighton's way with a smug smile. "Oliver is an absentee father at best, relying entirely on hired help to raise my children. He consistently demonstrates immaturity—" she gestured at Leighton "—as evidenced by knocking up his *much*-younger nanny out of wedlock. What kind of example is that for a young girl like Matilda?"

"Your Honor," Katie cut in crisply, not missing a beat. "Mr. Hart's fiancée and their unborn child have no bearing on his parenting capabilities."

"Agreed," the judge said with a curt nod, directing a glare at Carly that made my heart thump. A single raised brow, and I felt hope surge in my chest. Carly might torpedo her own case.

"This court is concerned with the well-being of *your children*, Ms. Hart. Your opinions about your ex-husband's fiancée are irrelevant."

Niko grabbed Carly's arm, trying to pull her down, but she wasn't done.

"Of course. My apologies," Carly said. "It's just so important that my kids know their real mother—"

"*Enough*, Ms. Hart."

The judge's voice cracked like a whip, and Carly flinched. Her cheeks flushed red, eyes going wide. What the fuck did she expect? Applause?

"We are here to determine where these children will be safest and most supported. I don't need additional time to review. Frankly, my decision is clear. Given the existing and extensive record of neglect and—bluntly—emotional and physical abuse, your efforts at rehabilitation fall drastically short. Court-mandated classes do not constitute initiative.

"Granting full custody to Ms. Hart would be a failure in judgment. In fact, granting any form of custody without concrete evidence of reform is out of the question."

"This is ridiculous—it's been years!" Carly snapped.

I couldn't even look at her—I'd laugh. She was imploding on her own, and we hadn't even pushed her.

The judge's expression hardened. "Given your continued outbursts, I'm also ordering supervised visitation, effective immediately."

"*What?*"

I turned my head just in time to see Niko trying—and failing—to drag her down into her seat. Carly's face was too busy turning various shades of mottled red to comply.

"Given the severity of evidence," the judge finished, "I would advise against further petitions without meaningful behavioral progress. Your current arrangement is more than *generous*. You will provide proof of therapy and parenting classes to maintain visitation. Court is adjourned."

The gavel cracked.

I sat frozen until Katie elbowed me and muttered, "That's your cue."

"Thank you, Your Honor," I stammered.

She dipped her chin in acknowledgment, waving us off as Carly erupted again—insults flying toward her attorney, who was now shoving his files into a case without even bothering to organize them.

Slowly, I stood. I turned first to Greyson—his face was calm, proud. Then my gaze slid to Leighton. Her hands were crossed in front of her chest, eyes shining with tears, lips trembling as she smiled through it.

I moved to her, offering my hand. She took it without hesitation. Greyson supported her other arm as she rose—more graceful than any woman carrying that much baby had a right to be.

The moment we stepped into the hallway, we whirled simultaneously, and she threw her arms around my neck. Mine found her hips. And then we kissed—chuckling softly when Carly's yelling filtered down the hall.

"Scariest thing ever," she whispered, her voice still shaking. "When he said full custody, I thought I'd keel over."

"We knew that's what she was going for," I murmured, unable to take my eyes off her.

"I know. But hearing it like *that?*" She shook her head. "I can't imagine not seeing them every day. Can't fathom them living in a house that doesn't feel like *home.*"

"I know," I said again, just as Katie stepped up beside us.

"Ollie, I'd like to talk through next steps with both of you," she said.

Relief swept over me, full and blinding—until it stopped cold.

Greyson's posture stiffened. His phone pressed to his ear. And his eyes—haunted and sharp, locked onto mine.

"Excuse me," I muttered, already moving toward him. He grabbed my bicep as soon as I was close enough, his breath coming faster, tugging me further down the hall.

"Leigh!" I called over my shoulder.

She turned. And I watched the color drain from her face as she saw Greyson's.

She said something to Katie, but I didn't hear it.

All I could hear was the roar in my ears.

All I could hear was Greyson's voice, raw and tight, as he repeated words no parent should ever hear.

"Slow down, Jax. What do you mean? *Where are the kids?*"

28

Chaos, Cradles, and Silver Spoons
LEIGHTON

Never in my life had a drive across this damn city felt so agonizing.

A home invasion.

One dead assailant.

Multiple intruders unaccounted for.

Guns.

Kids.

Jax.

They're okay.

Alice.

My brain kept throwing broken fragments of Greyson's words against the wall, letting them splatter like paint as I tried to make sense of them. A creeping nausea rolled through me as we followed Greyson—going at least twice the speed limit.

They'd broken in.

Someone—some group—had gotten through security and into *Hart House.*

Dead. Two of Greyson's men were dead.

My sister had killed one of the intruders.

My *sister.*

The girl who got straight A's and taught me how to braid my hair. Who'd been there for all of us. Always. Of all my siblings, Alice had always been the gentlest. Her rebellion was quiet—staying up all night reading, microdosing edibles to shut up her anxiety. She didn't cause problems. Was vehemently opposed to violence. She studied. She stayed small.

Until last summer.

Until Greyson. Until whatever-the-fuck she got dragged into.

And now... *now* she'd killed a man. In her house. To protect Ollie's beautiful kids.

My heart pounded, throat tightening, every inch of me stretched taut like a bowstring ready to snap. With every pulse, my back ached, and I realized I was clenching every muscle in my body, trying—failing—to make the vehicle move faster.

Jax had, allegedly, gotten Tillie and Beau out of harm's way before it escalated. But it never should've gotten that close.

They'd breached the study window. Which made... my soon-to-be brother-in-law the target.

They were okay. *They had to be okay.*

I must've said it aloud, because Ollie's eyes flicked to mine as he took a corner dangerously fast.

"Yeah, baby. Jax got them out."

I nodded, but my brain wouldn't accept that answer. Not until I saw them.

Tillie. *My* Tillie. My glitter-covered rocker in a leotard, the girl who'd school any grown man on *Lord of The Rings* trivia. The little girl who mended the pieces of my broken heart back together. Who showed me my purpose had never been a scholarship or a perfect transcript. It was them. These kids. This life.

Beau. Our sweet little tank. The boy who planted sloppy kisses right on my mouth and thought unicorns probably liked pizza.

Fuck, I loved them so damn much.

I pressed a hand to my belly just as the baby kicked, the movement grounding me. *Okay.* He's still in there. Still safe. My body kept tightening with those relentless Braxton Hicks, but I could breathe. Sort of.

We were all going to be okay. Captain Reynolds had done his job. He'd gotten them out before they could see anything too horrifying. But even so—this? This was going to leave a mark.

Tears streamed silently down my face as Ollie took the exit, following Greyson through a yellow light.

We just had to get there. Just had to hold them. See them.

My anxiety burrowed deeper into my body, my back aching like I'd wrapped a band around it and pulled it taut, tugging at my spine and around my ribs.

By the time we turned onto the driveway, a sob clawed its way up my throat.

The *Hart House* gate was mangled.

Flashing red and blue lights pulsed in every direction.

Two ambulances. A fire truck. Too many police cruisers to count. And more arriving by the second. First responders were swarming the grounds like ants on a hill.

A familiar black sedan sat in the drive, doors wide open.

Ice sliced down my spine, bile rising in my throat. Ollie and I jumped from the Bentley in unison—only for Greyson to bark, "Don't move!"

I froze. His eyes were on me, hand raised in that universal stop signal. My mouth parted. My instincts screamed at me to run—to bolt into that house and find Tillie and Beau and never let them go was so overwhelming that my body seized.

"They're okay," Ollie breathed. "They're okay, baby." His eyes flicked to his brother. "Listen to Grey."

"*Slowly*," Greyson ordered. "Move *slowly*," he demanded, his voice riddled with the authority of those years in the Navy as the three of us stepped in front of our vehicles, the doors still open. "Keep your hands visible."

He stepped in front of us, between us and the chaos, his palms up.

That's when I heard it—police radios blaring. A chopper overhead.

"Oh my god," I sobbed, following his instructions as Greyson stepped between us and the police. I mimicked him, glancing at Ollie, where tears poured down his beautiful face. Officers swarmed, shouting commands. Guns drawn—but thankfully, aimed at the ground.

"Step away from the vehicle! Hands where I can see them!"

My body trembled as I raised my arms. The second officer's hand hovered near his holster. His gaze fixed on me.

"Nobody move. Identify yourselves."

Greyson's voice was calm but firm. "Greyson *Hart*. That's my house. My *wife* is inside." His voice cracked, just barely, and the officers visibly relaxed in recognition. "That's my brother, Oliver Hart, and his fiancée, Leighton Rhodes. Their children were inside."

The first officer's face softened in sympathy and he lowered his gun another smidge. I'd never been more grateful for the reputation of Emerald Bay's Titans.

"Copy that, Mr. Hart. We need you to stay here until it's clear to escort you in."

The third officer reached for the radio clipped to his shoulder. "Confirming ID—Greyson Hart, homeowner."

"*Are our kids okay?*" I blurted, tears pouring down my cheeks. "Please, I—"

I clamped my mouth shut, throat burning, eyes flicking from the officers to Greyson, then to Ollie when his brother didn't look back. Another band of pressure wrapped around my back and belly. I forced myself to breathe.

The second officer answered, while the others peeled away in opposite directions, scanning the perimeter. "Ma'am, we need you to remain calm."

Calm!?

Tillie and Beau were inside that house, surrounded by cops, terrified out of their minds. But I bit my tongue and gave a trembling nod.

"We have units securing your family now," he added, voice softening. "I'll get you answers as soon as I can."

That was when a vaguely familiar man in plain clothes pushed through the cluster of officers—stocky, barrel-chested, wearing a black leather jacket like it wasn't eighty degrees. His walk was all intent, all irritation.

"Hart, you're good," he said, thick East Coast accent curling around the words as he waved the uniforms off. I watched tension drain from both Greyson and the officers as his hands slowly lowered to his sides. "We'll get this under control. Just stay right there, you hear me?"

"Yes, sir. Thank you, Detective."

Greyson's unshakable fucking calm had never been more welcome. Jesus, he was the only one of us keeping our shit together. I was shaking so hard I could barely stand. And Ollie—Ollie looked like he was trying to stare straight through the walls to see his babies.

"I can confirm ID," the man said, already tired of this shit. I recognized him now—*Detective Lucas Riviera.* The same one who'd been dodging my calls. He'd been at Alice and Greyson's engagement party. One of their inside guys.

His slicked-back hair glistened in the late sun, and his black shirt pulled too tight over his stocky frame as he stepped in front of Greyson. "You know the drill, Commander Hart. We've got to lock the scene."

Greyson gave a slow nod. "Do what you need to."

"Any weapons on your person?"

"No, sir," we all answered at once.

He nodded. "We think it was targeted. Looks clean on your end. Active manhunt for the last guy."

Then louder, to all of us: "Alessandra and the kids are safe. I'll take you to them—but we gotta follow protocol."

"Where are they?" Ollie asked, his tone teetering on begging.

"Ambulances by the garage."

A sob tore up my throat as Greyson and Ollie took off. I ran after them.

"Go slow!" Riviera shouted after us. "They're pretty rattled!"

We skidded to a stop between two white ambulances. Alice sat on the bumper of one. Our babies were inside the other.

Grey ran to Alice.

Ollie and I went for the kids.

Tillie flew into her dad's arms with a cry the same instant Beau leapt into mine. I cradled him, settling his legs across my belly as he wrapped his sweet monkey arms around my neck.

The tears came hard and fast as I buried myself in his shoulder, breathing him in. He curled into my hair, his tiny body trembling. I couldn't tell if it was his sobs or mine shaking us—but I wasn't letting go. Ever.

This. This is what they meant when they said parenthood was like having your heart walk around outside your body.

Would it be even worse with my biological baby?

Ollie reached out, one arm wrapping around us both. His other hand cupped the back of my head, and the four of us folded into each other, sobbing against his chest.

They were okay. They were really okay.

"Miss Rhodes? Mr. Hart?" an officer asked gently. "I have a few questions."

I turned toward him—stone-faced, trying not to let the scene get to him. We nodded in unison.

"Can we stay with the kids?" Ollie asked, not letting go.

"Of course. I just need to run through a few things."

But just then, that dull pressure in my back surged. It wrapped around my sides and settled deep in my belly, intensifying until it clenched hard and sharp.

I grimaced.

"Baby?" Ollie said, a second before a hot gush soaked my tights and splattered on the concrete.

I looked down. My mouth dropped open. "Oh no. No, no, no…"

The officer blinked. "You've got to be kidding me." He waved someone over, but when he looked at me again, his tone softened like I was a skittish horse. "Easy, Mama. We've got you, alright?"

Dread and embarrassment flushed hot up my chest.

I carefully set Beau down—which, unfortunately, gave him a direct line of sight to the evidence.

"Mommy, did you pee your pants?"

A wild, hysterical laugh burst from my chest. "No, sweetheart." My voice wobbled. "We're gonna have a baby."

I pressed both hands to my belly, heart pounding, searching for movement.

There. A flutter. He was okay.

An EMT hustled over. Ollie's voice cracked as he gestured to me. "She's in labor!"

"Well," the medic said, smiling easily at Beau before turning that same calm warmth on me, "this kid's already got a flair for the dramatic."

"Hell of a birthday party," the officer muttered as the EMT offered his arm and helped me into the ambulance.

Ollie stayed close, Tillie clinging to his leg as he climbed up behind me. I spotted Greyson holding Beau, Alice beside him, Riviera a few steps back.

"Hey, you're gonna be just fine," the EMT said. "Let's grab your vitals real quick, alright?"

I nodded, because what else could I do?

Ollie gently peeled Tillie off, passing her to Alice, then climbed in fully, grabbing my hand and pressing it to his lips, eyes shimmering.

"I'm so sorry, baby," he breathed. "This isn't how this was supposed to go."

I shook my head as tears fell, even as he swept my hair off my forehead and pressed a kiss to it.

"Breathe for me, Trouble." His eyes flicked up to the medic as I complied.

"She looks great," the EMT said, glancing at the monitor. "Heart rate's a little fast, blood pressure's elevated, but given what she's just been through? She's golden. I just want to track baby's movement for a few minutes."

I swallowed hard and nodded, the bridge of my nose stinging.

Ollie looked between me and the kids outside the door.

"Stay," I said softly.

"Leighton…"

"They need you. I'm a big girl. I'll be okay. Right, guys?" I asked, flicking my gaze up to Mr. Sunshine and his scary looking needle.

"We've got them," Greyson said from the open door, his voice steady. Alice gave a small, shaky nod behind him.

We had them. They were safe.

And I was…going into labor.

The officer still hovering beside the doors dipped his chin as Ollie looked between me and his babies, both of their chins trembling.

"Trust us to keep your kids safe, sir. We need to get her to a hospital."

"I… I'm…" Ollie stammered, the color draining from his face.

God. It was an impossible choice.

"I'll bring them after," Greyson vowed, stepping in. "*Go*, Ollie. She needs you right now."

I needed him.

I needed him with the kids—*and* with me. My heart tore in two. Everything about this felt wrong.

A female officer appeared beside the first, her voice gentle as she knelt next to Tillie. "You're both doing so good. Your Aunt and Uncle will bring you to meet the baby later, okay?"

Beau nodded, but tucked his face into Greyson's neck.

Tillie, though—Tillie's eyes locked on mine. Brimming with tears, she launched herself into the cramped ambulance, scrambling onto the bench before throwing her arms around my lap.

I stroked a steady hand down her hair.

"Shhh, brave girl. It's okay. I'm okay."

"I don't want you to leave," she whispered, pulling back enough to meet my eyes, her lower lip trembling.

"I know, baby," I breathed.

Ollie leaned over my legs and pressed a kiss to the crown of her head. "We just have to take Leighton to the hospital to have the baby, okay? Can you be strong for me just a little longer?"

She sniffled, nodding, then wiped at her tears with her fists before rounding the bench to hurl herself into his arms.

I glanced up at Mr. Sunshine—our EMT—who gave me a gentle smile and a quiet nod as Ollie whispered I love you's into our daughter's hair.

Then, before I could process it, they were gone. Our miraculous little humans were ushered gently from the vehicle, the doors pulled shut behind them.

The engine rumbled beneath us. A few seconds passed, and then the siren screamed to life.

When I looked back at Ollie, he was already focused—steadying himself, steadying *me*. Like everything started and ended right here.

"Okay," he breathed, setting his hands on either side of my legs. A calm intensity lit his face, sharpening those strong, steady features I knew better than my own reflection. "Let's do this."

"Mm-hmm," I squeaked.

"Leave all that back there," he said, his voice firm and sure. "We'll deal with it later. Right now, all that matters is you and our baby. Understand?"

I nodded, even if I didn't quite feel it.

"Leighton," he said again, and something in his tone snapped my eyes up to his. That beautiful, tanned, tear-streaked face. His voice softened as the smallest smile broke through.

"We're gonna have our baby."

29

Respect Your Elders
OLIVER

The only sound on the planet sweeter than our baby's first cry after a long, grueling labor was his mother humming to herself in my arms.

"You did incredible, love," I murmured, probably for the thirtieth time. I couldn't help it. I was in awe of her—of her strength, her grit, and her stubborn, unshakable trust in me through all of it.

Our son was bundled up and snoozing contentedly in Paxton's arms—who'd somehow managed to make one of those absurdly uncomfortable hospital chairs look like a recliner—and we'd jumped at the chance to finally get Leighton showered off.

"Mmm," she purred, resting her head on my shoulder, eyes closed as her face tilted into the spray. I slid a soapy palm over her collarbones and swollen breasts, washing away the gunk and silently thanking every higher power I could name that she was okay. That they both were.

In the past forty-eight hours, I'd stared down my worst fears. And by grace alone, I was here—holding her, counting blessings. The kids would be by soon to meet their brother, and my bride wanted to "wash the yuck off." Couldn't blame her. My own chest had taken on a sticky sheen of vernix and assorted birth fluids, and I was itching to do the same.

The stall was a tight fit for two, but after twenty-six hours of back labor—right around the time my forearms seized from applying counter-pressure and I had to start squeezing her hips with my thighs—Leigh had finally opted for the epidural. I'd be lying if I said it wasn't a relief to watch her doze through contractions instead of fighting her way through every last surge.

Still, she was on fall watch after a dizzy spell earlier, the first time they let her stand.

Enter me—the watcher. Because over my dead body was some nurse going to be the one washing her hair right now.

"I love you, Leighton Alexandra," I breathed against the shell of her ear, shifting her slightly to rinse out the conditioner she'd packed in her baby bag.

"I love you too."

"You're a fucking warrior."

"Nah," she sighed dreamily. "I'm just a mother."

I smiled, chuckling softly as I combed my fingers through the slick strands, gently working out the tangles. "Same thing."

"Maybe," she murmured, voice light.

Peaceful. After everything—after all the chaos—Leighton had come out the other side peaceful. Even as she rolled her eyes at me, I took my time. I cleaned her skin and her hair. I soaked in the privilege of being here—wanted, trusted, valued—as I helped her into those awkward, diaper-adjacent postpartum briefs, and then into the cozy floral pajamas she'd packed from home.

Paxton was still curled beside the window, letting sunlight soak into his skin while the baby snoozed in his arms. Leighton padded back to the bed, grimacing as she climbed up with my help. Once she was settled on the crinkly sheets, I grabbed her brush and the almond-scented oil she loved for her hair. I was still brushing the long strands when a gentle knock drew both our gazes to the door.

Kaia peeked in, smiling through tears as she stepped inside.

"Hey, lovebirds. How are we?"

"Sleepy," Leighton admitted with a yawn. "How are the kids?" God, I loved this woman.

"They're just fine, Mama Bear. Grey and Alice crashed at your place last night so they could sleep in their own beds." And not be inside a murder scene, no doubt.

"And Alice?"

"She's okay." Kaia's smile wobbled as she stepped inside, careful, like she didn't want to disturb anything. She held a drink tray with four coffees. "Reality will probably hit later, but you know Alice—obstinately pragmatic. It was him or her and the kids. She'd make the same call every time. Any of us would. They all just want an update on you, sissy."

"We're good," Leigh said, stifling another yawn. "Just exhausted."

"Well, squeezing an entire human out of your body will do that," Kaia quipped, setting the drinks down on the bedside tray. She peeked at the baby in Paxton's arms, then crossed to Leighton, gently shooing me aside. Kneeling behind her, she brandished a tool more weapon than comb and began parting Leigh's hair with swift expertise.

"How you doing there, Daddy?" she asked, glancing up at me. "You're awfully quiet."

Clearing my throat hurt. The sound felt jagged, like it didn't belong in the room. "Just... unspeakably grateful."

Her smile softened. "Good answer."

"Your sister is a champion."

"Just a victim of physiology," Leighton said airily, making Kaia snort as she tied off the first braid and started on the second.

"That really was terrible before the epidural. But then the *epidural* is terrible because you turn into a useless limp noodle. There's no winning in the labor department."

"But you finished," Kaia pointed out proudly. Paxton smiled down at our little man, his giant hand dwarfing my son's tiny face as he silently trailed a finger down his nose.

"And he's perfect," he declared.

"Agreed," Leighton murmured with a sleepy smile. "Just like his daddy."

Her heavy lids fluttered open long enough to find me, a blissful little grin tugging at her lips.

"Hardly," I scoffed.

"The man has all the money in the world and never bothered to buy a mirror," Kaia muttered in a stage whisper.

Her comment earned a sharp pinch to the leg, which sent her snickering as she finished the second braid. "Just looking, no touching."

"I'd hate to have to get rid of you."

Leighton scooted back automatically when Kaia slipped out from behind her. "I've grown rather fond over the years."

"For once in our lives, I actually have a chance at outrunning you."

"Shut up and respect your elders."

"*Elders*," Kaia snickered like she hadn't heard the same joke her entire life. "Lean back."

She fluffed a pillow into place, letting Leighton sink into it. And I just... watched. Really watched.

My bride tilted her face toward the morning sun pouring in through the window, her eyes closed, her features relaxed—like a tulip in bloom. Mom had loved tulips. She would've adored Leighton.

She'd always been beautiful, but there was something transcendent about witnessing her surrender to something so much bigger than us. About seeing her trust our medical team—trust me—when she couldn't even form words anymore. It magnified everything.

She was radiant. Magnificent.

And glowing with that exhausted, new-mommy bliss that stole the air from my lungs.

Her hands still rested over her swollen belly, my ring already back on her finger, glinting in the light.

The baby whimpered and squirmed in his uncle's arms.

Paxton smiled gently. Revered like a god on the football field, he was just an enormous teddy bear in person. Stiff from training, he stood and lumbered over, carefully settling on the edge of the bed with tears in his eyes.

"I think he's hungry," he said, grinning as he ran his knuckle over the baby's cheek. The little guy turned instinctively toward him.

"Two hours on the dot," I observed.

"Your child would eat on a schedule," Leighton teased as she nervously accepted the bundle.

Pax stepped back toward the window as she worked to get him latched, her hands shaking slightly with focused, clumsy tenderness. I smiled, even as the bridge of my nose started to burn.

None of this was easy—not even close—but I was already convinced she'd take to it so naturally that in a few days we wouldn't even remember how scared we'd been.

"There you go, little prince," she cooed.

All I could do was watch.

She rolled her bottom lip between her teeth, uncertain if she was doing it right, and I was floored.

"You're perfect," I promised.

"Yeah?"

She looked up from our son's sweet face and dark, thick hair, gifting me a watery smile.

"Yeah, Trouble."

Months ago, I'd been terrified I was walking into a repeat of the past. That I'd stumbled into another train wreck, destined to go up in flames.

But sitting here with two of her infinite siblings, with my girl completely at peace—watching our son at her breast—I knew how wrong I'd been.

This woman was everything.

My best friend. The lover I'd spent years dreaming of.

She was where my life both began and ended.

The space between breaths where the world fell away and I could just exist.

And somehow, somewhere along the way, she'd become mine.

A knock on the door pulled me from my thoughts. I turned, breath catching, just as Tillie collided with my chest, burying her face in my hoodie.

"Hey, babygirl."

"Hey, Daddy. Is Leigh okay?"

"She's doing great. So is your brother. You alright?"

"I'm okay," she insisted.

I opened one arm, and Beau wriggled free from Alice's hold, sprinting to me and wrapping his little arms around my leg.

"Hey, big guy. You okay?"

"Yeah. I jus' miss you."

"I missed you too, bud. You wanna meet your brother?"

They both nodded emphatically. I glanced up at Grey, who smiled softly and pulled Alice closer as the room suddenly felt even smaller.

"Quiet now—he's pretty sleepy."

Another round of nods.

Beau scrambled onto the bed, clambering over Leighton's legs and giggling when she snagged him under the arms and hauled him up with a kiss to the cheek.

"Easy, Leigh. You just had a baby," Pax scolded gently.

"And I needed to smooch my other one," she chirped, completely unfazed as she tucked Beau against her side.

Pax shot me a look, all smirk and silent warning—*good luck*—and he wasn't wrong.

Matilda stepped carefully to Leighton's side, peering over the swaddle like she was afraid she'd detonate a bomb if she moved too quickly.

"What's his name?" she asked softly, peeling the blanket back just enough to see. Her nail polish—Leighton's handiwork from earlier this week—was already chipping.

The room held its breath.

Every gaze shifted to me.

I looked at Leigh, who gave me an encouraging nod.

"Guys," I said, voice tight with emotion, "meet Beckham Rhodey Hart."

Epilogue

LEIGHTON

Ten months later…

"Daddy's gonna shit his pants."

"Tillie!" I barked, clasping my hand over her mouth—just for her to lick it, as everyone burst out laughing.

"What? You look *amazing*."

"Lead with *that*, you punk."

Giggling, she grabbed my slimed hand and wiped it across her shirt. "He's pacing in his room, just so you're aware."

"Aww," I swooned, one hand fluttering to my heart. "Like I could ever walk away."

"Nobody said love was logical."

I thought about that for a long moment, because... "You're not wrong."

Love came in a million shades of every color on the spectrum, each story painted in its own unique light. We grew, laughed, danced, played, and made love through the marvelous monotony of everyday tasks—blessed to do it together. Love was found in the little things. The way he'd set the coffee maker before leaving in the morning so I wouldn't have to make it myself. It hid in the two-item delivery consisting of a bouquet of flowers and my favorite soda— because he'd swiped the last one on his way to work and knew my shoulders would slump when I found the shelf empty at lunch. In the way he adjusted our meal service to make sure I got the calories I needed to nurse and get back in the gym.

And, occasionally, in momentous moments I'd never forget.

In the paperwork Katie drafted that would officially start the adoption process after today.

Or… if you were my brother-in-law, apparently in mysteriously unearthing enough scandal that Carly hit the road and got the fuck out of town. I mean, we *assumed* Grey and Alice had something to do with her dirty secrets coming to light in an anonymous delivery of a one-inch-thick manila envelope.

In a fucked-up way, that's what family did, wasn't it? Protected each other from the threats in the world, no matter what that entailed.

A knock at the door had me turning from the mirror just as Kaia pinned the last embellishment in place.

"Hey, punky," Pax said from the doorway, and my eyes welled with tears. My big brother was a walking miracle these days. After everything that happened this winter, I'd never take a single chance to hug him for granted. "You make a beautiful bride."

I was already halfway across the room when Kaia cried out, "*Are you serious?* God, you've always been the worst at sitting still."

I would've waved her away, but I was too busy hugging Paxton like my life depended on it, still nervous I could squeeze him too hard. His smile was blinding as he grabbed my hand and held me out for inspection.

"Ollie is a lucky man, sis."

"Thanks, bubba. Daddy ready?"

"Just about. The boys were taking shots."

"That tracks," Kaia smirked, sidling up next to us and snaking her arm around his waist.

"Alcohol seems like an irrational risk for limited payout," Tillie declared, earning a laugh from all three of us as my bridal party buzzed through the room.

"Good. Keep it that way."

I was getting married today.

The love of my life was down the hall in Greyson's other guest suite, probably sitting asses to elbows around a poker table much too small to accommodate my brothers and his. A squeal of laughter had us both turning in time to see Robert—his dark, spring-loaded curls bouncing—as he toddled into the room with maximum enthusiasm and minimal experience fleeing his older cousins, who were tight on his heels. I bent down and pressed a kiss to Quinn's head as she wrapped her arms around his little belly with a victory screech, and I couldn't help but laugh. Their mothers came in right behind them.

"Aww, Leigh, you look so beautiful," Elora crooned, her eyes already misting.

"Seriously stunning," Brex said—right before grunting, "Ouch!" as Noel collided with her backside. They all but tumbled into the room, Brex smirking and Noel beaming.

"He's gonna plotz."

"Skittles!" We all looked up when James entered the room with a huff, scowling at the hem of his sleeve. He glanced at me long enough to say, "Looking good, punky," then immediately turned to his wife. "You insist on me wearing these things, so the least you can do is help me out."

Noel grinned. "I watched you pull apart and reassemble an entire 1957 Chevy pickup, but you expect me to believe you can't fasten cufflinks?"

I snickered, roping an arm around Tillie's neck as she wandered by and pulling her against my belly. My brother said some smartass thing back, and the two of them bickered like they'd been married for a few decades instead of just one calendar year.

I dropped a kiss to the crown of my daughter's head, then whispered, "Go get your dress on, beautiful."

"I didn't wanna dirty it."

"Which is why I've let you wait until the last possible moment, darling. Now hurry up before Kaia slips into hers and then won't touch a makeup brush."

"I'm already done."

"And let's hope you still feel that way once you wrestle out of that," I said, motioning to her skin-tight tank top. Because that phase had started, to my and her daddy's chagrin.

By the time the chaos had been wrangled and I was walking arm-in-arm with my dad toward the beach aisle in Grey and Alice's backyard, my nerves had finally caught up to me. Something about laying eyes on two hundred people here to witness this exact moment.

"Don't let me fall," I breathed, trying to steady myself.

"Never," Dad assured, though when I looked up at him, I found misty eyes and a wobbling chin.

"Daddy," I scolded.

"Shut up," he blubbered, blinking skyward and wiping at his eyes.

"If you cry, I'm gonna cry. And then Kaia will kill us both."

He gave a watery laugh and nodded. "Can't have that."

"No," I agreed. The music changed when Tillie reached the end of the aisle, throwing her arms around her daddy's waist where he stood facing the ocean.

"I don't think I could do this if he was anyone less worthy,

Leighton. Ollie is a blessing to this family, and still… it's agonizing to officially let you go."

"I'm not going anywhere. Promise."

"I'll hold you to that."

"Counting on it." We reached the end of the aisle, and everyone stood as Ollie's favorite string quartet began playing *Somebody to Love*, just like that night on the rooftop.

Hundreds of eyes landed on me, faces capturing every emotion on the spectrum. But it was Greyson tapping my groom on the shoulder that held my attention. The man had an evil smile on his face that made my stomach turn—but it was Ollie who finally sent it plummeting.

Because the man took one look at me and his face crumpled, his hand rising to cover his jaw as tears poured down his cheeks.

Aaaand there went my makeup.

The moment I locked on Ollie's teary gaze, my own tears spilled over, and I fought to suck them back in.

Getting here wasn't easy. I was fully aware that the road ahead wouldn't be smooth either—how could it be? We were only human. But what I knew, with no doubt at all, was that it was worth it. Every bump in the road. Every scar. Every moment.

Trying pitifully to suck the snot back into my face—along with the emotions—I looked to the flowers in my other hand.

A stunning arrangement of asters, morning glories, and ranunculus blossoms wrapped in a soft blue ribbon, cute little butterfly clips tucked among the branches. Tillie and I had found them in a darling antique store, and she'd insisted they were a part of the day.

Our girl had great taste—what could I say?

By the time my dad presented me to Ollie, I'd gotten the tears mostly under control. My man tried to do the same, dabbing at his eyes with his silky blue pocket square. He accepted my hand and bowed low at the waist, pressing a kiss to my fingers without dropping his glassy gaze from mine, drawing a sob from my chest before I could stop it. When he straightened, Ollie pressed a kiss to my cheek, then turned to face the minister, sliding his hand into mine.

And my god, this bouquet was heavy as shit. And not just because I'd hidden something extra inside it.

As the officiant led us through the ceremony and we exchanged rings and vows, my eyes kept flicking between the ocean and Ollie's face—where he brimmed with unfiltered joy.

When we were finally pronounced *The Harts*, he stepped into my space, robbing the breath from my lungs like he always did. He dipped me low enough to earn whoops and cheers, kissing me so passionately I was pretty sure I traveled through galaxies before landing back in my body.

But as we straightened, his expression faltered.

Because Jax was approaching the platform, scowl in place.

It took everything I had not to burst out laughing when I spotted Beau and Tillie in the front row, now wearing aviator-style sunglasses. Hell, Mama had somehow managed to wrestle a pair onto Beckham in his tiny baby suit and bow tie.

"Mr. Hart, a call for you," Jax said with an impressively stony façade.

"Right *now*? Are you kidding me?" Ollie growled, earning a disapproving nod from the mountain of a man I'd grown rather fond of.

Captain Reynolds handed him a phone, already on speaker, and my husband—*holy shit, my husband*—cocked his head to the side as the line crackled, audible to at least the first few rows of spectators.

"Good luck," rasped Maverick with an impressive growl.

Ollie's brow furrowed for a beat before Beau and Tillie popped up from the front row. I fished the tiny Nerf gun from my bouquet and, together, we all opened fire. The crowd erupted with laughter just as Ollie did—right before lunging.

I shrieked, sprinting barefoot down the hot sand, cackling. I didn't even make it to the end of the rows of chairs before the man hooked an arm around my waist.

"Get her, Ollie!" one of my brothers shouted, while Beau and Tillie chased after us, giggling and firing foam darts like mini mercenaries.

The moment we were nose to nose, he swallowed my laughter with a kiss, threading his hand through my loose curls as cheers broke out behind us—naturally, the guys were the loudest.

Then Ollie bent low and threw me over his shoulder, landing a solid smack on my ass as I howled with laughter.

"That's a wrap, folks!" he called, carrying me down the beach to more laughter and applause.

"Ollie!" I squeaked, cheeks aching from smiling so hard.

"You started it," he pointed out, marching us inside—but bypassing the staging area where the photographer was supposed to meet us. "It's only right I finish it."

"*Ollie*," I gasped as he rounded the corner into Greyson's study, closed the door, and backed me against it with no ceremony at all. His mouth descended on mine in a kiss so bruising my head spun, heat blooming low in my belly as his hands swept over every inch of lace and ribbon painted onto my curves.

When he finally pulled back, breathless, he growled, "I fucking love you, *Mrs*. Hart."

Smiling softly, I said, "I fucking love you too, Mr. Hart."

"'Til death do us part, huh?"

"I demand to go first."

"You're *nine years* younger than me." He spun us, laughter bubbling in my throat as he pressed me against Grey's floor-to-ceiling bookshelf.

"Then we'll get struck by lightning or hit by a bus or something. I'm not picky, as long as we're old."

"That would be epic," he muttered, barely holding onto composure before chuckling against my lips and stealing them again. His hand slipped through the slit in my dress, hiking my leg around his hip. A satisfied rumble vibrated in his chest as his hand slid up my thigh, then under the barely-there scrap of lace I called underwear. He groaned, head tipping back like it physically pained him when he found how wet I was. "That *for me,* trouble?"

"Always."

"Where does my wife want to get fucked the first time as a Hart? In bed at the honeymoon suite at two a.m., or right here against the bookshelf?" One blunt finger slipped inside me, making my back arch.

"*Ollie,*" I gasped, his hand clamping over my mouth as a wicked grin curled his lips.

"Which is it, trouble?" he asked, curling his finger just right—he'd long ago mastered the art of detonating my orgasms on command. His thumb pressed against my clit, sending my eyes rolling back in my head.

"You own me," I breathed, fighting to suck down enough air to think logically.

"Damn straight," he murmured against my neck as he buried himself there.

Before I could think better of it, I was already unfastening his belt, then his suit pants, pushing his boxers down just enough for his cock to spring free.

"That's my good fucking girl." He smiled against my lips as he crowded in closer, tugging aside the lace and lining himself up, spreading my arousal over my folds. "Can my good girl be quiet?"

The instant I nodded, he thrust inside me with one claiming snap of his hips, his hand tightening on my thigh where he kept me pinned. My hands flew to his back, clawing at the muscles beneath his suit jacket as he fucked me like it was a soul-deep need.

Oh fuck, oh fuck, oh fuck.

I must've muttered it against his palm, desperation clawing up my chest as his hold tightened.

"Eyes on me, Mrs. Hart."

I peeled them open, locking on deep brown eyes so full of adoration they could've welded my broken pieces together—if I'd had any left to fix. A soft smile spread over his breathtaking face, and I slid a hand to his jaw as he drove into me with that relentless, ruinous rhythm he'd perfected.

This man had a gift for waking me up in the sexiest ways possible on his days off, so I should've known we wouldn't make it to the hotel before he wrecked me again.

Books rattled on their shelves, our chests heaving in sync as pleasure ignited through our bodies on the best damn day of my life.

When my body clenched around him, Ollie growled, "Yes, baby, come with me."

I did. *We* did. Our releases hit in perfect tandem—one surreal, electric moment. Like even our orgasms knew we'd just sealed something sacred.

I chuckled softly as he pulled his hand from my mouth and replaced it with kisses. Sweet. Adoring. Unending.

But he wasn't done.

He squeezed my thigh and sank to his knees, throwing my leg over his shoulder. He pressed kisses along my inner thighs, shoving my dress up to trace the stretch-marked skin of my belly, then lower.

Much lower.

Burying himself between my pussy, Ollie ran the flat of his tongue straight up my center, like he'd just lap up our releases.

Holy filthy hotness.

"Ollie," I gasped as he did it again, then circled my clit with practiced precision. My legs buckled, but he pinned me effortlessly, holding me open for him with one hand and a shoulder.

By the time he was satisfied, and my limbs were liquid, Ollie grabbed tissues from Greyson's desk and cleaned me up with gentle, thorough care.

"You look like the cat that ate the canary," I murmured, still panting as he straightened my dress.

"Is that what we're calling it now?" he asked, pressing a kiss to the scar between my breasts. My fingers found the silky strands of his hair before I remembered we still had photos to take.

"An excellent code word."

"Agreed. Canary time—should I say that when I want to bury myself in you until I know my seed is spilling down your thighs? Until I know you'll feel me with every step you take?"

Grinning, I couldn't help myself. "Funny you'd say it like that."

"Oh yeah?" he asked, brow lifting. "Why's that?"

I pressed my lips to his throat, up the strong line of his neck to his ear, and whispered, "Because you and your 'seed' already planted our next adventure."

Ollie leaned back, his palms dropping to my waist, eyes wide with awe. "Leighton, are you saying what I think you're saying?"

With watery eyes and a smile that ached, I nodded. "How's another little Ollie sound?"

He kissed me hard, his tongue tasting like us and salt and insatiable need.

"Like I'm the luckiest man alive. But I gotta be honest."

"That sounds terrifying."

"It might be."

"And why's that?"

"Because I'm praying for a pint-sized version of you."

"Oh," I sighed. "Oh, *wow*."

He brushed his lips over mine, then laced our fingers together.

"Come on, Mrs. Hart. Your court awaits."

And with one last glance down the length of me, my husband opened the study door and led me out into the beginning of our forever.

Acknowledgments

My readers: First and foremost, I will always thank you guys! Thank you for reading, for reviewing, for popping into my DMs to squeal or giggle or kick your feet with me. There's nothing better than seeing someone fall in love with these fictional people that are so dear to my heart.

The dream team: Sam, Heather, Jess, and Mercedes! Thank you for reading the hot mess manuscripts so that we can create a polished story to send into the world. Mostly, thank you for keeping me from doing the stupid things, or throwing in the towel over the frustrating parts of this journey. I couldn't do this without you!

Megan, Jess, Joe, Hannah, Brittany, and Marie: Thank you for helping me do my due diligence and handle sensitive subjects as carefully as possible. Appreciate y'all big time.

My hubby: Baby, thank you for being the kind of man that shows me a patient love. A second order of pakoras kind of love. For cherishing me in my pregnancy-scrambled state and all,

Shannon— Thank you for creating a gorgeous line of covers for THOEB!

About the Author

Sydne Barnett is a lover of spunky, badass heroines, and heroes that embrace their wild. She's an avid reader, never turns down a good cup of coffee, loves hiking with her hubby, and lives for finding their next adventure.

If she's not writing, you can probably find her behind her camera, swimming, or curled up with a homemade pastry, watching Friends, HIMYM, or Gilmore Girls.

Let's connect!

Reader's Group: https://www.facebook.com/groups/grayshell babes

Tiktok: https://www.tiktok.com/@barnettbooktalk

Instagram: https://www.instagram.com/barnettbooktalk/

Newsletter: https://shorturl.at/acJSZ

Also by Sydne Barnett

Nomadic Rhodes

South of The Skyway (book 1)
Brewing Temptation (book 2)
Finding A Way Back Home (book 3)

The Hearts of Emerald Bay

(Rhodes universe continued, billionaire edition)
Salvaged Hearts
Mended Hearts <—you are here.
Winning Hearts, release date TBD
Catching Hearts, release date TBD

Romantic High Fantasy as S.J. Barnett

Commanding Flame And Shield (Grayshell Rising, book one)
Commanding Earth And Shadow (Grayshell Rising, book two)
Commanding Blood and Bonds (Grayshell Rising, book three), coming September 16, 2025